House

———◆———

Julian Gloag

PUBLISHED BY POCKET BOOKS NEW YORK

OUR MOTHER'S HOUSE

Simon and Schuster edition published May, 1963
A *Pocket Book* edition

1st printing.........August, 1964
2nd printing.......February, 1968

. . . I found him whom my soul loveth: I held him, and would not let him go, until I had brought him into my mother's house, and into the chamber of her that conceived me.

Song of Solomon 3:4

CONTENTS

SPRING

1

Mother died at five fifty-eight. Her last act was to reach out for the gold fob watch that lay on the bedside table. Unsurely grasped in the thin fingers the watch fell and its soft rhythm ceased, marking the precise minute as if in evidence of some crime.

It is possible that Mother lived a few moments longer. But there was no way in which she could signal her children. For weeks she had been able to speak in no more than a whisper, and the embroidered bell rope that hung above her bed had long been disconnected from its clapper in the kitchen. "Can't abide bells," Mother had said when, years ago, she had taken the lease of 38 Ipswich Terrace. "Have quite enough of *them* on Sundays and at funerals." But even if the bells had functioned, she was too feeble to tug the bell pull. Her once inexhaustible energy had lately withered to where she could not lift a spoon without Elsa's aid.

And Elsa, who had looked in as soon as she got back from school, to find Mother asleep, would not disturb Mother's quiet hour.

Yet Elsa's anxiety, which being the eldest she bore for the others, forced her continually to come to the bedroom door to listen. She heard nothing. There were plenty of noises in the house: the sound of clashing crockery from the kitchen where Diana and Jiminee were washing up; the gurgle of Willy's laughter in the playroom and Gerty's "It's my turn now, Willy"; Dunstan's perpetual cough as he sat with the leather-bound volumes of sermons in the "library"; a sudden burst of hammering from Hubert in his workroom. Elsa was aware of them all unconsciously—if any had stopped for too long, she would have gone to investigate—but she did not listen.

When the downstairs clock began to strike half-past six, the waiting was done. She opened the door and stepped inside. The room smelled exactly the same, of old curtains and night lights, of lavender soap, of the dust that rose up between the polished floor boards, and of the polish itself that came in red and gold tins from the lady who called three times a year.

Mother smelled the same too. Mothersmell—the white calm scent that came from the big bottle on the dresser.

Mother's head was turned towards Elsa, her eyes only half closed. Her left arm was outstretched, supported just above the elbow by the edge of the bed, hand open to receive. Touched by the evening breeze from the open window the ends of the knot that tied the turban about her head fluttered like desultory pennons.

Elsa crossed the room and stood on the burlap mat close to the bed. Briefly she laid her hand on the cold wrist. Then she bent down and picked up the watch. It too was cold. She warmed it in her hand, turning it rhythmically over and over. The night light rippled, then straightened. It needed snuffing.

Outside the starlings were in their evening twitter before settling down. From the gloom of the high-walled garden came the perfume of the lilies of the valley that grew thick below the window. It was a warm May, almost summery. The lilies had begun early and they were almost over now.

Elsa lifted her head a little. Outside she heard the murmurings of the children waiting to be called in. Alone of them, she knew of Mother's death; just as only she had realised that Mother was dying all these last weeks. Mother had known too of course, but it had been a secret unshared between them. Mother did not believe in dwelling upon unpleasant things.

Suddenly Elsa said aloud, "I'm thirteen." She repeated it, "I'm thirteen," as if to rebut the growing shadowiness of the room—a shadowiness only increased by the small flame of the night light. She looked down at the watch in her hand. Five fifty-eight, it said. She knew that was not the right time. She put it back on the night table where it belonged.

She turned away from the bed and went across to the dresser and took the wigstand and Mother's wig and put them on the table in the centre of the room. She fetched the tortoise-shell comb from the top drawer where it lay among the faintly scented men's handkerchiefs that Mother always used. Then she sat down on the edge of the wicker chair and began to comb the wig.

She pressed the comb firmly down into the auburn curls, pulled them almost straight and let them fall back into place. Ever since Mother had become too weak to move, this had been Elsa's nightly duty. She had always known that Mother wore a wig, and all the other children knew too —she had explained about it as soon as they were old enough to know. Even Willy, the very youngest, knew now. Yet the subject had only been referred to twice in Mother's presence: most recently, when Mother had said, "I'm tired tonight, Elsa dear, comb my hair for me like a good girl." The other time had been two years ago, when Jiminee was five. It had been at teatime and Jiminee had suddenly looked up at Mother and said, "Hello, Wiggy." There had been a hushed sigh of silence as Mother gazed at the blushing Jiminee over the tea table. Then all at once Mother had burst out laughing. She didn't say a word, she just laughed. And all of them began to laugh and rock back against their chairs and shake the table until the teacups rattled. Only Jiminee remained untouched; he sat there, blushing and flickering his eyelids, his smile flashing on and off like a Christmas tree light. And when the laughing was finished, they had gone back to eating their tea and nothing was ever mentioned about it afterwards, except that Jiminee was looked at with a new respect for a few days.

As Elsa combed, she remembered that warm laughter in her stomach and she wanted to cry. She let her hands stay still and bent her head. "Elsa never cries." She struggled with the thick feeling in her throat and screwed up her eyes tightly. And at last two tears came and trickled down her nose. They dried almost immediately.

The room was dark now and the figure on the bed was only a vague whiteness. The motion of combing soothed Elsa.

Suddenly the night light flickered bright and then almost went out. Stilled with alarm, Elsa looked up. Someone stood just inside the half-open door. "Who is it?" she whispered, "Dun?"

"No. It's me—Hubert."

She relaxed slightly. "What is it, Hu?"

"It's struck seven, Else."

The candle flame wobbled precariously. "Come in, and shut the door."

As the light grew brighter and Hubert came closer, Elsa turned her face so that he would not see she had been crying.

"Is Mother asleep then?" said the boy, still whispering.

Elsa reached forward to put the comb on the table. In the silence the creaking of the basket chair at her movement startled them both and the comb fell to the floor with a sharp snap. Hubert got down on his knees and picked it up and handed it to the girl. She let her head turn to him as she took it; she didn't really mind if Hubert saw.

"You been—"

"Yes!" she said.

"What's the matter, Else?" Already he had stood up and was looking towards the bed.

"No, Hu, stay here."

"It's Mother, isn't it?"

"Yes," she said. "She's—it's all over now."

"But she can't—"

"It's all over, Hu. I know, I . . . it isn't any good hoping."

For an instant in the half-light Hubert's frown made him look so like Dunstan that Elsa caught her breath. Then he put up his hand and brushed away the hair from his forehead. On the distant main road a bus accelerated, and the noise of the traffic grew momentarily loud and then diminished like the pulsing of a tired heart.

"What are we going to do, Else?"

"I don't know. I mean, I've got to think. I've got to plan."

"We've got to think of something."

"Don't I always think of something?"

Hubert didn't reply. In the passage outside the door came a burst of coughing.

Elsa stiffened. "Dunstan."

"All of them," said Hubert. "You got to tell all of them."

"Not tonight. I'll tell them tomorrow."

"You got to tell all of them. It's no good putting it off, Else." Hubert spoke slowly.

"Don't go telling me what to do. I'm the eldest, remember!"

The nine-year-old boy looked at her and nodded. Elsa drew a deep breath and rose. The basket chair creaked. "All right. I'll just wash my face, and then you fetch them in."

She went over to the washstand and dabbled her fingers in the cool water of the jug.

"I better put the light on," Hubert said—and now they had stopped whispering.

"No, Hu, leave it off." She reached out for Mother's towel, but hesitated, glancing at Hubert. Then quickly she bent her head down and dried her face on her skirt. She went back to the chair and sat down again. She patted the back of her hair, smoothed the dampened skirt over her knees, and folded her hands in her lap. "All right then," she said, "I'm ready."

2

They were reluctant to enter. It was only when Elsa called out "Eldest first!" that Diana had ceased to hang back and led the way in. They waited, nervous in the face of Elsa's solemnity. Only the figure of Dunstan, leaning against the door, was impassive.

Elsa spoke, her voice hard to conceal its tremble. "Children . . . children . . ." She stopped.

In the silence four-year-old Willy left the group in the middle of the room and went to Mother's bedside. The children watched him. He touched the ends of Mother's scarf and patted her outstretched arm. He put his head on her shoulder and sniffed. Slowly he turned round. "She's very quiet," he announced.

As if Willy's words were a signal, the children gathered around the bed, Dunstan alone remaining still by the door. They stared down at Mother, head huddled upon shoulder in the attitude of final exhaustion, knees humped under the blanket. The light caught only her broad forehead and her cheekbones, so that her eyes were huge and black, staring down at the children's feet. From the Mother they loved she had become in the twinkling of an eye an object of silence and strangeness.

"Children," said Elsa, "Mother has passed on." They did not seem to hear her.

Diana leaned down and placed her hand in Mother's. "Mother," she called softly, "Mother. It's cold, Mother," she said and she tried to lift the arm to slip it back under the covers. The jarring movement caused Mother's head to roll to the left, and the shoulders slid a little, then stopped. Diana cried out and let go of the hand.

In a second Dunstan was beside the girl. "It's all right, Dinah, it's all right." He put his arms round her as she sobbed.

Although there was two years' difference between them, Diana was small for her twelve years and always sought protection from Dunstan, who defended her with an intensity that at one time or another had frightened all the children. Now she sobbed, her head with its gold hair cut like a cap lowered against his dark one. "It's all right, Dinah."

"But she's cold, she's so cold."

The children stared. Then Jiminee, his grin still coming and going, began to cry too.

Hubert took a step forward from his place beside Elsa. "Mother's dead," he said loud enough to cut off the sobs.

Elsa nodded. "That's right. Mother's dead."

There was a small sigh from the children. Willy lifted his chin, "What's *dead?*" he demanded.

"Dead?" Hubert murmured. "Dead is like—like Jesus."

"Crucified, *dead,* and buried," Dunstan said, "and on the third day he rose again and . . ." he faltered, "rose . . . and . . ."

"Mother won't rise again," said Elsa firmly.

Dunstan frowned. "She might, how do you—"

"No, she won't."

Diana lifted her head from Dunstan's shoulder, and the two of them stared at Elsa. Physically they were utterly disparate; his face was almost a caricature of the purse-lipped, thin-cheeked figures that pursued the narrow road to heaven in the big coloured chart that hung in the little downstairs lavatory. His dark eyes, magnified in froglike menace behind the thick glasses, and his spiky black hair contrasted exactly with Diana's smooth blondness and her blue eyes that seemed to belong to another world.

Dunstan could make even the most ordinary words sound vicious, but now he held his silence. Diana drew away from him and stood in the middle of the room, suddenly a stranger in the midst of all this familiarity, so that, Hubert thought, if you asked her her name she probably wouldn't remember.

The group by the bed began to split up. Little Gerty came over to Elsa and looked up into her face earnestly. "Can I play with the comb now, Elsa?" Elsa nodded. Gerty was only five, but it was an old privilege of hers to use the tortoise-shell comb. Before she could properly walk she used to crawl, a fat bundle, towards the table and reach up for the comb. And she would sit on the worn rug, as she sat now, playing with the comb and her hair, unaware of the other children or of Mother's Jesus voice reading from the book.

Hubert moved away from Elsa's side and drifted over to the washstand. The cake of soap lay in its china dish. He touched the still sticky surface and raised his hand to sniff the familiar lavender scent. It was as if this familiarity had to be examined, tested. At the rim of the white washbowl, patterned on the inside with sharp leaves and dark blue flowers, was a jagged triangle which had broken off months ago and which he had mended with waterproof glue. He pushed his finger against it. It yielded gently, like a tooth almost ready to come out. He'd have to try again, with stronger glue perhaps—and there would be time for it to dry properly this time.

"Mother's not dead!"

It was Diana. She stood, fists clenched, voice high-pitched, a guardian angel by the bedside. The children stared.

"She's cold, that's all she is—cold!"

The chair crackled uneasily as Elsa stood up.

"No, Elsa! She's cold. We must get blankets to warm her—and a hot water bottle."

Elsa glanced uncertainly round the dim room. She opened her mouth to speak, and then closed it so that all the blood left her lips. The children waited for her words, but she found none to deny Diana's vehemence.

"She's cold!" Diana said again.

Her answer was the sound of Hubert's feet running across the room and the click of the switch as he turned on the light. They winced at the sudden brightness that exposed the bleak white ceiling above and dropped hard-edged shadows where there had been none before. Diana cried out in pain, "Oh, no!"

But she, like the others, turned and looked. The soft

dusty lines of Mother's face were now hard cuts in the flesh
and the blue eyes were without expression. Her mouth was
half open in the loose wonder of death, which there was no
mistaking. Diana knelt down and put her head on the blanket.
She raised her hands and cupped them over her ears.

For a while no one spoke. And then, "You see, children,"
said Dunstan.

There was no reply. He moved over to the bedside table
and picked up the black Bible that lay beside the watch.

"Read to us, Elsa."

"Yes, read to us, read to us," the echoes ran around the
room.

Slowly Elsa sat down and reached out her hand for the
book. Dunstan hesitated for a moment and then walked
over and gave it to her. He stood over her looking down as
she held it clasped shut. "Open it," he said.

Elsa looked away from him. "What shall I read?" she
asked the children.

"Jesus," said Willy, but none of the others answered.

"Go on, open it," said Dunstan.

Elsa let the book fall open in her hands and it broke at
a much-read section. She looked down and started to turn
the page, but Dunstan held her hand. "Read what it says,"
he said. Elsa didn't answer. She read silently for a moment,
moving her lips to the words. She frowned. Then she
smoothed the page and drew in her breath. She began to
read:

> Whither is thy beloved gone, O thou fairest among
> women? Whither is thy beloved turned aside? that we
> may seek him with thee.
> My beloved is gone down into his garden, to the beds
> of spices, to feed in the gardens, and to gather lilies.
> I am my beloved's, and my beloved is . . .

Elsa stopped. "Jiminee," she said softly, "where are the
lilies?"

Jiminee blushed and then smiled. "I . . ."

"Where are they, Jiminee?"

Jiminee rubbed the tear stains on his face with his bony thumb. "I . . . I forgot." He grinned. "I didn't m-mean to . . ." He glanced quickly at the other children.

"It's your day, isn't it, Jiminee?"

He said nothing. He was quite white now.

Still kneeling by the bed, Diana said gently, "Oh, Jiminee, how could you?"

"Yes, how could you?" Dunstan spoke sharply.

"I didn't m-mean to, I d-didn't."

"It's your duty, isn't it?"

Jiminee's smile flashed and vanished. "Yes."

"You failed, didn't you?"

"I didn't m-mean to, Dun. Honestly I didn't. I just f-forgot."

"Forgot!" snapped Dunstan.

"I do forget, you know I forget. Mother knows I forget, doesn't she, Elsa? Mother doesn't m-mind me forgetting—I didn't m-mean to do anything b-bad." He began to cry. The children stared at him so and there was no place to hide.

"He must be punished," Dunstan said. "He can't go on forgetting. He must be taught a lesson. We must—"

"Shut up, Dun."

"What?"

"Don't say *what*, it's rude," piped five-year-old Gerty.

Hubert spoke again, "I said shut up."

Dunstan tensed himself and marched three steps towards Hubert. "You tell me to shut up?"

Hubert waited. At nine, he was a year younger than Dunstan and a good deal shorter, but he was sturdier and there was something about the way he held himself that gave an impression of imperturbability.

Dunstan darted out a finger and pointed menacingly at the other boy. "Titch!"

"You're a bully," said Hubert, "so just shut up." He raised his voice. "It's all right, Jiminee, you can pick them later."

"Don't you dare, don't you dare! It's not all right! He's got to be punished. He forgot the lilies for Mother and he's got to pay for it. He's a sinner, that's what he is! And he's got to pay!"

"Pipe down," replied Hubert.

"I won't pipe down. Don't you dare tell me to pipe down." He stepped closer, his voice high and hard. "You cheeky little twirp, don't you dare. Don't you understand? He *forgot*. He—forgot—the—lilies—for—Mother. See? And he's got to—"

Hubert shook his head. "Mother won't mind now, Dun. It doesn't matter."

Dunstan lowered his arm slowly. He began to turn away. Then suddenly he was quivering and shouting, "But *I* mind, *I* mind—I don't care—*I* mind!"

The screams darted round the room like blind arrows seeking to get out. "*I* mind, *I* mind!"

"Don't do that, Dun," Hubert said at last, "please don't."

But already Dunstan's rage was dwindling to grief. He sank to his knees and bent his head and wept. The words shivered in a meaningless litany between his tears. And among the children, Gerty and Willy had begun to cry too. Then, one by one, all except Hubert and Elsa.

And the sound of each particular grief joined in a soft and general lamentation that filled the brightly lit room and crept out into the dark beyond the window, where the garden shifted uneasily under the cool wind of the spring night.

"Read, Elsa, go on reading," urged Hubert.

The girl lowered her eyes to the page and found another place. She laboured with the archaic language.

O that thou wert as my brother, that sucked the breasts of my mother! when I should find thee without, I would kiss thee; yea, I should not be despised.

I would lead thee, and bring thee into my mother's house, who would instruct me: I would cause thee to drink of spiced wine of the juice of my pomegranate . . .

As she read, the sobbing of the children quietened. And when she spoke of Mother, a small sigh came from their lips.

. . . I raised thee up under the apple tree: there thy mother brought thee forth: there she brought thee forth that bare thee. . . .

Many waters cannot quench love, neither can the floods drown it: if a man would give all the substance of his house for love, it would utterly be contemned.

Elsa stopped reading and looked up. Her gaze took in the children in their various attitudes of listening and the still figure on the bed, but she seemed to be thinking of something else entirely. The children felt hushed and none disturbed Elsa until Hubert took the book from her knees and carried it over to the bedside table, where it belonged. As he laid the book on the embroidered cloth, he noticed the watch lying face down. He raised the dented case to his ear. He shook it and then turned it over and opened the back. Inside the initials *C.R.H.* were engraved in nearly indecipherable script. Hubert traced the letters with his thumbnail. He sighed. "Mother's watch is bust," he said.

The remark woke Elsa from her thoughts. "Yes, I know," she said and became suddenly brisk. She stood up and clapped her hands together. "Now come along, children, it's time for cocoa."

"Cocoa time!" said Gerty, getting to her feet. Somebody yawned and a general murmur began.

Gerty stood in front of Elsa and put her head to one side. She smiled winningly. "Elsa, can I keep the comb now?"

"Of course not."

But Gerty stood her ground. "Why can't I keep the comb?"

"Why?" said Elsa in astonished irritation. The children stopped to hear her reply. "Because—because I say so, that's why."

"But Mother won't need her comb now."

Elsa drew breath sharply.

"She won't, will she?" Gerty used the voice she put on to wheedle a second helping.

It seemed to Hubert that, only an hour ago, Gerty would not have dared persist like this to Elsa. No one, not even Dunstan, had ever challenged the eldest girl's authority. But already it was different, and Hubert knew instinctively that the children would be wolves to any weakness of Elsa's now.

"She won't, will she?" Gerty repeated, her plump face replete with a smile of triumph.

"Yes," Elsa said stiffly. "Yes, Mother does need her comb." Suddenly vehement, "Mother needs *everything!*"

"But—" began Gerty with a pout.

"Mother needs it!"

"But not now," Gerty clasped the comb to her chest.

"Now . . ." Elsa grappled with the word, "now's no different. Now's the same as it always was." She looked round at each of the children and her frown cleared. "It's just the same as it always was. Just because of—of what's happened, that doesn't mean . . . that doesn't *change* anything. You understand, children?—nothing has changed." She spoke with the power of special illumination. "Everything is going to be the same as it always was—*everything.*"

The children were silent. Elsa held out her hand for the comb. Gerty clutched it to herself for a second, then slowly relinquished it.

"Come on!" said Dunstan abruptly.

They began to move out of the room. Hubert stayed where he was, watching Elsa.

The thump and clatter of feet grew less as the children reached the hall and went through the big door, down the steps into the basement kitchen.

Upstairs all noise ceased. Hubert and Elsa looked at each other, not letting their eyes turn towards the bed.

Caught in the breeze between the open door and the window, the night light bowed and swayed in a drunken curtsy.

"We'd better be going," Elsa said.

"Yes." Hubert looked away from the candle and a multitude of yellow, flickering swords darted before his eyes. "I'll turn out the light."

"No, I'll turn it off. It's your turn for cocoa, isn't it?"

"Yes."

"You better be going then."

"What about you?" He shut his eyes as he asked the question, and the swords danced more wildly.

"I won't be a minute."

"All right." He opened his eyes again. "Elsa . . ."

"Yes?"

"Elsa, do you . . . do you . . ." He turned his head a little and stared up at the naked bulb in the centre of the ceiling.

"Do I what?"

The solitary bald image of the light glared.

"Nothing," he replied.

3

He stirred the water and the milk in the big saucepan. The silence of the children sitting at the table behind him was broken only by the grating of the spoon against the sides of the pan. Slowly the bubbles of cocoa powder dissolved in smearing trails. Hubert watched for the liquid to fizz at the edges.

They were quiet as they waited. No disgrace or guilt had ever silenced them like this. Even while Mother had been in bed, they had talked and laughed just the same. And Mother had managed to come down to Sunday dinner until . . . until— suddenly to Hubert it seemed an age impossible to remember since she had been there, calming them, teasing them, watching them. And laughing—how Mother laughed. And they would all eat, Mother too, until they were full up to dolly's wax. And then she would say, "Is there any more hunger?" And she'd say grace in her Jesus voice. Afterwards she'd stand up, wiping her hands on her apron; then, "Done!" she'd say.

The cocoa started to boil and Hubert took it off the light and began to pour into the first of the mugs lined up on the draining board. "Done!" Suddenly his hand began to tremble and a dribble of cocoa sprouted from the base of the saucepan. He took a deep breath and bit his lip hard. He glanced down at the scar on his right forefinger. "Be a man!" she had said when that scar had been a wound in which the white glimmer of bone had shown. "Be a man!" he said now between tight teeth. He had not paused in his pouring. Now he filled the last mug with a steady hand. He took the pan to the sink and filled it with cold water.

"It's ready," he said.

Elsa rose and came to his side. Together they passed round the mugs. The children murmured their thanks as they took the cocoa. "Thank you, Hu." "Thank you." "Thank you, Elsa." "Thank you." They kept their eyes downcast. Only Gerty had the temerity to take a sip.

"More sugar," she said as Hubert and Elsa sat down. Without answering they looked at her. A white moustache surrounded her lips. "Well," she said, "it isn't sweet enough."

"Hush, we haven't said grace yet."

"Yes, grace," said Elsa.

They pushed back their chairs and stood up with heads bent. Hubert looked down at the table. Already on the surface of his cocoa a skin was beginning to form. Gently he blew down on it and watched as it wrinkled.

"Oh, Lord," said Elsa, "we thank thee for these thy gifts—"

"Listen!" Jiminee broke in upon her.

"Jiminee, why—"

"What is—"

"Listen!"

"It's somebody knocking at the door."

They all listened, and the sound came again. Hubert went to the swing door of the kitchen and pushed it open.

The sound came sharp. It would stop for perhaps ten seconds and then begin again—*crack, crack-crack!*

"Who could it be?" murmured Gerty.

"Perhaps it's Mrs. Stork," said Diana.

"Mrs. Stork wouldn't make all that row," Elsa said. "Anyway, Friday isn't her day."

Jiminee grinned quickly. "I remember she c-came on Friday once, she c-came to—"

"Why don't you remember the important things for once?" asked Dunstan, suddenly fierce out of his own dark reverie.

"She doesn't *usually* come on Fridays, Jiminee. Besides," said Elsa, "what would Mrs. Stork be coming at this time of night for?"

"Perhaps it's the delivery boy."

"Perhaps," said Jiminee, "they'll just g-go away."

"Well, whoever it is," Hubert said, "we ought to go and see."

"Of course we must," said Dunstan.

They all turned to Elsa. "All right," she said, "I'll go."

"I think a *man* ought to go," said Gerty suddenly, smugly.

"Who cares what you think?" said Dunstan angrily. "You're just a silly baby."

No one answered him. In the silence came another burst of knocking—*crack-crack, crack*. From the door Hubert watched Dunstan whiten and his lip tremble with the awareness of his role as the eldest "man." Gradually the quiet force of the children's opinion pressed in upon him. "Who cares what you think?" he said again, almost tentatively this time.

Crack-crack, crack-crack! sounded the knocker.

"W-why don't you g-go, Dun?" asked Jiminee.

" 'Cause he's afraid," Gerty said. "That's what I think."

Dunstan clenched his fists on the scrubbed top of the table. He shook his lowered head tightly. "No I'm not," he whispered.

"Well, why don't—" began Gerty. Hubert interrupted her. "I'll go," he said. "I'm nearest anyway." And he stepped into the passage, letting the door swing to behind him. For a moment he stood still, listening to the shivering swish of the door. It steadied, and he began to walk along the passage and up the stairs into the front hall.

The man at the door was large; he wore a light-blue uniform with a cap set squarely on his head so the peak hid his eyes.

"Well," he said, "at last. You're about as nippy as a superannuated bleeding undertaker." He laughed.

"Not today thank you very much," said Hubert, beginning to close the door.

"Hold on, hold on," said the man. "You haven't even asked me what I came for."

"Well, what did you come for?"

"I came to see Vi."

"Vi?"

"Yes, Vi. The old lady." He stepped over the threshold. "I reckon that's your mum, laddie."

"I'm afraid she's not in."

"Ha! Not in, eh? This is number thirty-eight, isn't it?"

"Yes, but I'm sure this is not the house you want."

"Dead right—it's not the *house* I want." He laughed again. "You just tell Vi it's Flight-Sergeant Millard. She'll be in to Flight-Sergeant Millard."

"I don't—"

"Been away for a bit, see? Aden—cor blimey!" He glanced round the hall and smiled. "I remember it now. I'm not one to forget a good thing. My first leave for a year and I come straight here."

"I don't think we know anyone called Miller."

"Millard! Not Miller—*Millard*." Flight-Sergeant Millard stiffened, then relaxed. "Well, she may not remember my name—but tell her, tell her to cast her mind back to, let me see, to the night of January the eighteenth, last year." He chuckled. "Card index memory, that's what I got, laddie. Just press a button, flip the file and up I come with the answer. Bam—like that!" Flight-Sergeant Millard suddenly leapt a couple of feet into the hall and smashed his hand down on the table with a smart clap, "Like that!"

Hubert didn't move. "Mother is not in."

"Don't give me that, laddie," he said softly, "don't give me that. That's what they all say—'I don't want never to see you again.' But you don't want to pay no attention to that, see? There's one thing you got to learn about women, lad—I'm telling you out of the very kindness of my heart—and that is, what they mean is the exact opposite of what they say." He stared hard at Hubert. "So just nip along and fetch her, will you?"

"I'm very sorry, Mother isn't in."

"Now listen, laddie, I don't bear no malice. If your mum ain't in, she ain't in. But she wouldn't leave a little nipper like you all by yourself, would she now?"

"But she isn't in, really she isn't."

Flight-Sergeant Millard advanced on Hubert. "Don't give me that, son. I'm a patient man. Just go and tell her, will you?"

Hubert braced himself against the menace in the man's voice. "I think you'd better go, if you don't mind."

The Flight-Sergeant jerked his hand up. "Hop to it, you little—'ere, 'ere," the arm was lowered slightly, "you haven't got a dad, have you? Your dad isn't in, is he?"

"We haven't—I mean—"

The man grabbed him by the shoulders. "Is that it? Your dad's in?"

Hubert tried to step away, but the man held him tight and gave him a shake. Hubert smelled the beer on his breath. "Yes," he said, "that's it."

"You creepy little bastard, why didn't you say so?" He let the boy go abruptly. "Come all the way from Victoria, I did." He looked down the hall. "Bloody nuts," he murmured. The hall clock said nine-thirty.

"Well, they're still open, that's one thing." He went to the door and stood there for a moment, looking at Hubert. The light from the lamp above the door shone on the brightly polished floor at his feet, so that his heavy silhouetted figure seemed to stand at the edge of a sea of gold.

"Bloody nuts," Millard repeated slowly. "Here, I'll give

her something to remember me by." He stepped forward, lifted his heavy boot and stamped down with all his force on the floor boards.

Hubert heard his footsteps on the front path and the click of the gate and then there was silence. He went to the door and got down on his hands and knees. The nails in the boot had made deep indentations in the smooth wood. Hubert ran his fingers gently across the holes, like a tracker tracing the marks of an enemy who had been this way before. Suddenly he thought of the watch upstairs and the delicately inscribed initials *C.R.H.* As he touched the sharp impressions of the nail marks in the floor, it seemed to him that their regular pattern, like the convoluted initials on the watch case, was cast in a code, the secret of which only needed to be deciphered for all to be clear and clean again. He felt a strange comfort as he crouched over the damaged floor boards, a reassurance somehow over the emptiness within the house.

He stood up. It seemed a very long time since he had left the kitchen. He switched off the porch lamp and shut the door on the spring night outside. It was well past their bedtime now.

4

"Who was it, Hu?" Elsa asked.

Hubert took his place at the table before he answered. He touched his mug of cocoa. It was stone cold. All at once he was tired. "It was a man," he said. "I sent him away."

"What did he want?"

"I sent him away." He could hardly keep his eyes open, yet there was a question pressing against his mind. He forced his eyes wide open and looked round the table. They were all sleepy and quite uninterested in the man at the front door.

Even Elsa didn't bother to go into it. "Why don't you warm up your cocoa, Hu—it must be cold now."

He shook his head. "I don't mind. I don't want it anyway." Something had happened, and none of them seemed to realise it. *It's no good just sitting there*—the words seemed to come directly into his mind from Mother's lips. They had to do something, they had to decide, they had to— "We got to get Mother's watch mended."

The children gazed at him uncomprehendingly.

"I said we got to get Mother's watch mended." That was it. That's what they had to do. It was so clear that he spoke loudly. He challenged them.

"Why, Hubert?" said Elsa.

"Because we got to."

"Why?"

"I'm sleepy," murmured Gerty.

"Why don't you mend it, then?" said Dunstan.

Hubert frowned. "I don't know if I could. But we can take it to the watchmaker's—he'll do it."

"I don't see," said Dunstan, "why it needs to be mended at all."

"Tell us, Hu," Elsa said.

"Because—don't you see—because . . ." He thought of all the times he had put the watch to his ear and listened and the times he had held it, staring at it to try to catch the minute hand in motion. Sitting on Mother's bedside table, broken, always telling the same time—it would be like a lie. It wouldn't be right. "Because you said everything was the same, Else—yes you did. How can it be the same if Mother's watch is broke?"

"Don't be silly, Hu. I didn't mean that," answered Elsa.

"But, Else—we got to keep things going. Don't you see, we got to—"

Diana stood up to interrupt him. "It should stay as it is, Hubert," she said. She lifted her head so that the fair hair fell away from her face. "Mother wouldn't want it any other way." She didn't look at him, nor at anyone else, but her words were definitive in their very gentleness.

Hubert felt suddenly helpless. "But, Dinah . . ."

"And besides," Dunstan said, "if you want to know the time so much, there's always the clock in the hall and the kitchen clock."

"Come on, children, it's time for bed." Elsa rose and they all followed her example. Only Hubert remained seated. He glanced up at the clock on the wall above the sink. It was an electric one, with a slender red second hand that moved smoothly around the clock face—round and round so steadily that sometimes you wished it would speed up or slow down or just stop. No, thought Hubert, it wasn't the same as Mother's watch. That second hand, it didn't care— it just went on and on.

"Hubert!"

He looked down. "Yes?"

"I said, would you help Jiminee with the washing up? Dinah and me are going to tuck the little ones in."

"Not little," said Willy sleepily.

"All right," said Hubert. "All right, I will."

Already Jiminee was gathering the mugs. "B-bags I wash," he said.

Hubert scraped his chair back. "I'll dry them."

"Oh, and Hubert," said Elsa from the door, "don't forget to turn out the lights when you come up."

He nodded. "All right." He took the dish towel from its rack and stood by the sink watching the water spurt from the rubber nozzle on the tap. He thought, even Elsa doesn't understand really.

5

Jiminee followed him up the stairs. "What was the m-man like, Hu?" he asked.

Hubert paused on the little landing in front of the library and looked down into the hall. "Just a man," he said.

"What k-k-k- sort of a man?"

"Well," suddenly Hubert didn't want to go on up the stairs that led past Mother's room. "He was a big chap—with a moustache."

"Like the other man, was he?"

"What other man?" Hubert went over to the small bank of switches in the corner and turned off the hall light.

"The other man that came."

"What do you mean? When?"

Jiminee grinned, "I d-don't remember when. The other d-day. He came at night too and . . ."

"And what?" said Hubert.

"And—and Mother answered the d-door. And sent him away . . ."

"I don't remember any man. You're bats."

Jiminee's smile ebbed, then flowed more strongly. "But I heard her, Hu. She said, 'You g-go away and never c-c-come back.' I heard it."

Hubert didn't feel tired any more. "When?"

"I told you, I dunno, Hu."

"Try and remember, Jiminee."

"I c-can't—you know I c-can't." His voice quivered.

Hubert switched off the light on the little landing, so that only the light from the upper landing illuminated where they stood. "How could you have heard anything, Jiminee? You must have been in bed."

"I dunno, Hu. But I d-did."

"Were you walking in your sleep again?"

"I expect so."

The tick of the clock in the hall sounded very loud in the darkness. Hubert knew it was no use asking Jiminee any more questions—he would just get flustered and then he'd start to lie. It wasn't ever any good asking Jiminee questions.

"I'm sorry I said you were bats, Jiminee."

"That's all right."

Jiminee never bore any malice. Hubert sighed. "I suppose we better go up," he said. But he didn't want to move. He

wished he shared a bedroom with Jiminee—not Dunstan—
even if he did talk in his sleep and walk about the room.

"Hu?"

"Yes?"

"Aren't you afraid of the dark, Hu?"

"No, not much."

"N-no, I'm not either. I like it." It's true, thought Hubert.
Jiminee never switched on the lights if he had to go upstairs
to fetch something. He seemed almost to be able to see in
the dark too.

"Dinah is, though," Jiminee said. "She's always frightened
of the d-dark."

"I know, poor old Dinah."

"Yes, poor Dinah. It's a shame. There's such a lot of
d-dark, isn't there, Hu?"

Hubert reached out for the other boy's arm. "Come on,
we better go to bed."

The oak staircase was broad enough to take three abreast
and they went arm in arm. At the main landing it narrowed
and the steps became steeper up to the top floor, where
the children's rooms were. Off the main landing was Mother's
room and Hubert's workshop and a spare room with an
upright piano in it. Neither of the boys looked in the direction of Mother's room and, as they climbed to the upper
landing, Hubert found himself hurrying, as though it were
not Jiminee following him, but some ominous silent creature
from the darkness.

"What you run for, Hu?" said Jiminee as they reached
the top of the stairs.

Hubert stopped under the landing light and the presence
of the other children in their rooms filled him with a sense
of relief. "I wasn't running," he said. "We better get to bed
quickly. There's a lot to do tomorrow."

"G-good night then."

"Good night, Jiminee."

As Hubert went into the room he shared with Dunstan,
his hurried excuse for running to Jiminee—"there's a lot
to do tomorrow"—bore down on him with the return of

the oppression he'd felt in the kitchen. What were they going to do?

The moonlight struck full across the room and Hubert saw a piece of paper resting on his pillow. He opened it. The moon was strong enough to read by. The note said: "Meet me in Mother's room at 7—Elsa."

As he undressed and got into bed, he comforted himself by thinking that what they would do could be decided in the morning. Elsa was good at making decisions. He put his hand up to his face and just before he went to sleep smelled the lavender scent of Mother's soap on his fingers.

6

She had been up before him. She was standing by the window when he entered. They greeted each other quietly. She had tidied up. Mother lay flat on the bed now; her head was covered by the sheet and her arm no longer protruded. A lance of yellow sunlight touched the wall above the bed. Hubert looked away. The summery scent of early morning filled the room.

"Well?" he said at last.

"I was waiting till you came. I found the key of the desk." She displayed it in the palm of her hand.

"Where'd you find it?"

Elsa shook her head. "I'm going to open the desk."

"But Elsa—" he hesitated; no one had ever seen inside the desk.

"But what?"

"Hadn't we better wait . . . I mean, do you think we should?"

Elsa turned to the desk and fitted the key in the lock. "Why not? We've got to know, haven't we?"

"Yes, but . . . I think we should leave it for . . . for whoever . . ."

"Whoever what, Hu?"

"Whoever we tell—about Mother."

Elsa's lips were firm. "We're not going to tell anyone about Mother."

Hubert opened his mouth. He glanced round the room. None of the children ever dared argue with Elsa when she wore her tight face. Then he looked at the white form on the bed, and suddenly he gathered himself. "We must tell the doctor. That's what you're supposed to do when someone dies. We must tell the doctor."

"The *doctor*," said Elsa contemptuously—but still she did not turn the key. "*What* doctor?"

"I dunno." Hubert frowned. "Yes I do. The one down the road on the corner, with the brass sign. 'Joshua Meadows, M.D.' it says. That means he's a doctor, doesn't it? We'll tell him."

"Do you think Mother would want us to tell a *doctor*?"

"I—" No, he knew she wouldn't. Into his head came words he'd heard so often: *Doctors—if you can't keep alive without all that stuff and nonsense, you're better off dead.*

"We've got to tell someone, Elsa. What about the funeral?"

"There isn't going to be any funeral, Hubert."

"There must be a funeral. There must be."

Elsa took a deep breath. "There's not going to be any funeral an' we're not going to tell any old doctor. No one's going to know except us."

"We can't keep it a secret," Hubert whispered.

"Yes we can. I've thought it all out. All the time Mother was ill we managed, didn't we? We'll manage now. Don't you have any faith, Hu?"

Hubert lowered his eyes. Slowly he traced the faded pattern of the rug with the toe of his shoe. "Yes," he muttered, "of course I do." For a few moments, the ordered convolutions of the carpet absorbed him completely. Then he straightened up and gazed at his sister. "All right, open it then."

Elsa twisted the key and lowered the lid of the desk. They both stared at the array of drawers and pigeonholes.

"There's the savings book," said Hubert.

Elsa nodded; she reached into the pigeonhole and took it out. She turned the pages until she came to the last entry. "Balance," she read, "four hundred and thirty-three pounds, six shillings, and threepence."

"That's an awful lot of money," said Hubert.

"No it isn't," Elsa said. "That wouldn't last long. That's savings. It's money for a rainy day. I knew it was there. I saw it when Mother sent me to get the money from the post office."

"Is it—is it a rainy day now, Else?"

She made no answer but reached into the desk and drew out a bundle of papers. She slipped off the rubber band and took the top paper and spread it out on the desk so they could read it. "Mrs. Violet E. Hook, 38 Ipswich Terrace," Elsa read aloud. "Please find enclosed cheque for forty-one pounds, thirteen shillings and fourpence, representing the payment on your annuity held with us for the month of April."

"What's it mean?" asked Hubert.

"Well, it means every month Mother gets this money."

"What's a cheque?"

"It's a little piece of paper, only really it's money. You put your name on the back and you take it to the red bank in Marlowe Street and they give you money for it. Real money. Last month—and the month before—Mother let me do it. So I know."

"I see," said Hubert. But he didn't really. Forty-one pounds —that was an awful lot of money too. He'd never seen that much money. It was different from the sums they made you do at school. This was real. He thought of his weekly pocket money: he and Dunstan got a shilling, Elsa two shillings, Diana one and six, Jiminee ninepence, and Gerty and Willy sixpence each. If you added all that up, it wasn't even a pound—and here was forty-one pounds. "We're rich!" he burst out.

Elsa looked up from a bunch of letters tied with string that she'd just pulled out. "No we're not. We're not rich. We're poor—Mother said we were. That's why we go to the council school. Mother said we shouldn't have to go there really— her father wouldn't have liked it, that's what she said. Only we have to 'cause we're poor. We aren't rich—don't you go getting that idea, Hubert." She turned the bundle of letters over in her hand. "Look at these."

Hubert glanced over her shoulder. A portion of the top letter was visible. He spelled it out—" . . . going to knock them for a six. So we are all cheering loud and preparing to run. Forward, naturally. The girls here drape big brown blankets over themselves—even their clocks. You can't tell top from base. No wonder you never see any kids round here. It makes me glum, but you needn't worry about your ever-faithful . . ." The writing was large, but neat and easy to read. Elsa started to pull out the sheet from the bundle. Then she hesitated. "Perhaps we oughtn't to read any more."

"No," said Hubert, "it's private, isn't it?"

Elsa looked at the package. "Yes, it must be private. Anyway, it doesn't make much sense." With one finger she bent over the protruding letter so that they could see the other side. All that was visible was the right-hand head, which carried the notation: "89216 L/C Hook C. R."

"Hook?" said Hubert. "That must be a relation of Mother's."

Elsa slipped the letter back under the string without answering and put the bundle back in the pigeonhole.

"Wait a mo, Else," Hubert said. "Let's have another look."

"It's private, Hu, you said so yourself."

"But—but it might be important. Hook—L/C, I know what that is. It means lance-corporal, and C. R., that's initials. C. R. ‚Hook. *C.R.H.* Why," he said breathlessly, "that's what's on the watch, Else—that's what's on the watch!"

"What watch?"

"Mother's watch, of course. Don't say you never seen it." He ran to the bedside table and came back with the watch. "There." He displayed the inscription on the case to Elsa.

She looked at him in surprise. "How did you know it was there, Hu?"

"You don't notice things much, do you, Else?"

"I *do* notice things. How can you say that? I noticed the savings book, didn't I, and the letters and the cheque, all about that cheque—I noticed them, didn't I?" She challenged him, almost ready to be angry.

Hubert realised he wasn't afraid. Instead there was an odd feeling he had, a feeling which somehow he always connected with Jiminee. He hesitated in wonder, then he said, "Of course you did, Elsa. I didn't mean that . . . of course you notice things."

"Well then!" Elsa said, still mounted on her high horse.

"But don't you see? *C.R.H.*—it must be a relation of Mother's—of *ours*. It must be Mother's brother."

"Mother didn't have any brothers."

"Well then, an uncle—or a cousin. It means we got someone, Elsa—don't you see that?"

"Oh, don't make such a fuss, Hu," Elsa said in a voice tinged with superiority. "It isn't an uncle or a cousin or anything like that at all. If you really want to know who it is—it's Mother's husband!"

"Husband!" whispered Hubert. He stood very still, his head cocked slightly to one side. "Husband," he repeated. He looked up; out in the garden the tops of the apple trees were stirred by the faintest breeze. "But, Else—that means we got a *father!*" A great surge of excitement bubbled into his chest and rose and burst out. "A father! A father! We've got someone, Else. We got a father!"

Elsa spoke abruptly. "No, we ain't. We haven't."

Hubert was chilled. "You mean, he's—he's dead too?"

She pulled her lips together. "Better dead!"

"What do you mean?'"

"What I say. That's what Mother said. She told me when she was ill. Mother wouldn't have anything to do with him. He never came near her. He ran away. Mother said he was a bad lot. He wasn't a gentleman."

"But he's our dad—he must want to see us *now!* He must love us, doesn't he? Doesn't he, Else?"

"It's no good, Hubert. Mother said he never loved anyone but Charlie Hook. He's never even *seen* us—so how could he love us?"

"But he must, he *must!*"

"Hubert! You're building castles in the air. He doesn't love us and he doesn't want to see us. And that's that. I knew I shouldn't have told you. I thought you were supposed to be the practical one."

Hubert went slowly over to the basket chair by the table and sat down. He lowered his head and covered his face with his hands. After a while he felt Elsa's arms come round his shoulders and her cheek rest against the top of his head. "Don't cry, Hu," she said softly. He pressed his fists hard into his eyes. "I love you, Hu. Don't cry. We've got each other. We've all got each other."

Gradually it dwindled, the hard feeling in his throat—as if there were a lot of heavy diamonds wanting to choke him. He dropped his hands and opened his eyes, waiting for the flickering stars to diminish.

"I'm okay," he said at last.

He got up, Elsa's arm still on his shoulder. "Why don't we get on with it?"

They began to turn out scraps of paper, receipts mostly, haphazardly stuffed into drawers amidst bits of string and paper clips and old penny stamps. The only letters were from tradesmen. One package, tied as carefully as Charlie Hook's letters, was labelled "Father's Sermons" and contained yellowing half-sheets covered with handwriting so tiny as to be indecipherable. The centre pigeonhole was empty except for one long envelope, which Mother had inscribed simply "My Will." Elsa turned it over. It was not sealed.

"It's all right, isn't it?" she asked.

Hubert nodded. "Yes, I think so." In the garden a pigeon cooed.

She took a single sheet of paper out of the envelope and

started to read. "Listen," she said. "Last Will and Testament. I, Violet Edna Hook, of 38 Ipswich Terrace, being of sound mind, hereby bequeath: the lease on 38 Ipswich Terrace; all the furniture and contents of the house; the money in my post office savings bank; and all my personal effects to my dear children, Elsa Rosemary, Diana Amelia, Dunstan Charles, Hubert George, James McFee, Gertrude Harriet, and William John Winston, to be divided equally among them as they shall decide. I leave them also my blessing in confidence that all will cherish each other and in the hope that, having no other, they shall find continual solace and encouragement from the words and deeds of Our Heavenly Father. To my husband, Charles Robert Hook, I hope I can truly say I leave the forgiveness which one day I pray he will deserve and the love which he never used but as a sword to twist under my heart, yet which, despite all, I will always bear for him. Violet Edna Hook."

The curtains flapped gently and the breeze stirred the white sheet hanging from the bed. High on the wall the patch of early sunlight had shifted slightly. *Violet Edna Hook*, thought Hubert; it didn't sound like Mother. He walked over to the bed and looked down at the hidden form. Suddenly in his mind's eye he saw the long sharp sword twisting and twisting in Mother's flesh and splashes of darkred blood staining the white sheet. He turned his head away and, bending down, carefully tucked in the loose sheet.

"Else, how can love be a sword?"

Elsa smoothed the will in her hands. "I dunno." She frowned. "You're an odd one, Hu."

"I wonder why Mother never told us we had a father," he said.

"She did tell us—here," she tapped the will, "and anyway she told me. An' I told you—we don't really have a father. You mustn't mind, Hu. Mother said it doesn't make any difference. You don't mind, do you? I don't. I promised Mother I didn't mind."

Hubert said slowly, "He must have been a beast."

"Yes," she said eagerly, "that's right. He *is* a beast."

"You don't think—you don't think we ought to tell him about Mother?"

"Of course not!"

"Do any of the others know, Else? Does Dinah?"

"Just you and me."

From upstairs came a burst of shouts from one of the children. They'll all be up soon, thought Hubert.

"You won't tell, will you, Hu?" she enquired anxiously.

He shook his head. "Noooo," he said, sounding doubtful.

"Please, Hu. You're on my side, aren't you? Please don't tell—*please!*"

He saw her plain, rather pointed face, and the earnestness of her eyes and mouth. Elsa the strong one was begging him. The feeling he'd had all morning came up inside him, a great emptiness, as if something that had always been there— perhaps it was his heart—had fallen out and left a big hole. "No," he said, "I won't tell."

"Promise?"

"Cross my heart and hope to die." He raised his hand and made the sign of the cross over the emptiness in his chest.

Elsa nodded, satisfied. She slipped the will into the proper pigeonhole and closed the desk. "We're going to have a meeting after dinner—all of us."

"Why?"

"To decide things—we got a lot to decide."

"Well, why don't we have it after breakfast?"

Elsa looked at him, and she was strong and authoritative again now. "Because we got our chores to do. I got to do the shopping and get the money out of the post office and— oh—millions of things to do."

"And I got to clean the front room and the sitting room."

"That's right. So we'll have the meeting after dinner."

"We can't stop doing things just because . . . I mean we got to go on doing things, haven't we?"

"Yes. We got to go on."

As Elsa spoke, both of them heard a tiny sound from the door. It was the handle being turned from the outside.

Squeaking gently, it turned and slipped back and then began to turn again.

"Who could it be?" Hubert whispered.

Then suddenly it clicked and the door swung inwards. Willy tumbled into the room.

"Willy!" said Elsa.

The little boy smiled at her and then grew serious. "You must go away," he said, pointing at Elsa and then at Hubert. "Elsa and Hubert must go away. I want to talk to Muvver."

Hubert stepped forward. "You can't do that, Willy. It's nearly breakfast time—let's go and have breakfast." He tried to take Willy's hand.

Willy shifted towards the bed. "Muvver always talks to me before brea'fast. You go away."

"Willy, you can't." Hubert advanced quickly and caught the little boy in his arms.

"Let me go!" He struggled fiercely. "Muvver," he called, "Tell Hu to let me go!"

"Mother can't hear you, Willy." He lifted the boy in his arms. Willy hit out as hard as he could, banging his fists at Hubert's face.

"Muvver, Muvver!" he screamed. "They're taking me away. Muvver!"

Elsa ran forward and gripped his arms. "Stop it, Willy. Stop it at once!" And Hubert felt the little body become tight and still in his arms.

Willy stared up at Elsa. His face was white. He drew in his breath and held it as he stared and stared at her.

"That's better, now," she said, letting go of his arms. "Take him downstairs, Hu."

As Hubert began to move, Willy let all the air out of his lungs at once in a great wail. "Muvver," he wailed—and his cry filled the house so that upstairs the other children stopped what they were doing and the next moment were running down the stairs.

"Take him down, Hu," Elsa said.

"Muvver," came the wail again. Hubert gripped the child

more closely and carried him from the room. The children stood in the passage, looking with big eyes as he brushed past them.

"Muvver! Muvver!"

All down the stairs the cry was repeated and repeated. It echoed round inside him with a thousand voices. It was not just Willy's cry; it was his own, and Elsa's, and the cry of his brothers and sisters watching white-faced at the top of the stairs.

It seemed to Hubert that he would give anything in the whole world to stop the little boy's wail.

7

He caught the back of the swing, lifted it and sent it spinning down. Up it went till Willy's toes brushed the leaves of the apple tree. Then down and back again.

"Five," said Hubert as he sent it down again.

"Higher, higher!" screamed Willy.

"Six!"

Gerty tugged at his shirt. "It's my turn now, Hu." She bounced beside him.

Up and down. Ten times each, and then he had to go back indoors to his job.

Filtered through the leaves, the sun played dances on the shaggy lawn. The spring grass needed cutting, but that job didn't begin till the end of May. Yet already it felt more like summer. In the next-door garden Mr. Halbert was standing on his stepladder clipping the hedge. Every now and again he would stop and brush an imaginary leaf off his bald head. What a head it was—it gleamed, magnificent in the sun. Hubert wondered whether it was true that Mrs. Halbert polished it every night with Mansion polish. No wonder old Halby took such care of it. He bent forward

and clipped, and grunted, and paused, and patted his head.
Clip, grunt, pause, pat.

No one had ever heard old Halby speak—except just
to say good morning in a gruff way. But that was in the morning, when they were on their way to school, and Halby looked
quite different then, with his bald head protected by a bowler
hat. Don't talk to strangers, unless you've been introduced,
Mother always said. Perhaps Halby felt the same way.

"Now it's my turn, Hu," said Gerty anxiously.

"Eight!" said Hubert. "Two more to go, Gert."

The Halberts' garden was neat and dapper, not like their
own. It had pruned rose bushes and the lawn was cut in loops
and circles with a wooden arbour in one corner and lots of
neat little box hedges. Halby even had a sprinkler which
made a steady *whoosh-whoosh* as it went round and round.
Sometimes in the summer Hubert went up to his room in
the afternoon and looked down on the Halberts having tea
in their garden. Mr. Halbert read the paper and Mrs. Halbert sewed. They never said much. It was a waste really—
that lovely garden—when all they ever did in it was to read
and sew.

Read and sew. Sew and read. Up and down. "Ten,"
cried Hubert.

"It's me now, it's me!"

"All right, Gerty." As Willy dropped to the ground, Hubert
put his hands under Gerty's plump armpits and hoisted her
onto the seat. "I can go higher than Willy 'cause I'm older,
can't I, Hu?"

"We'll send you high as a kite, old Gert." He lifted her
back and let go. "Mind the bricks, Willy," he called.

The bricks were piled precariously at the edge of what
Mother had promised them was to be a proper sunken garden. Now it was just a big square ragged hole in the middle
of the lawn. Mr. Stork had come every Thursday and
spent all winter digging it. He'd seeded it at the beginning
of March and soon he was going to start lining the sides
with bricks—old yellow bricks that he'd got cheap some-

where. None of the children liked Mr. Stork—or Mrs. Stork, who came to do the cleaning, either. "The old Talk-Storks," they called them. Both Mrs. Stork and her husband—"my Tiger"—loved to chatter and, particularly, to ask lots of questions. The only good thing about them, Mother said, was that they were cheap. *I know more about flying aeroplanes than Stork knows about gardens.*

Stork and talk. Talk and Stork. Up and down. "Six," said Hubert, pushing hard down again.

He closed his eyes for a moment and felt the pre-summer warmth all around him. He caught the faintest scent of lilies of the valley. He opened his eyes and looked at the ordered ranks of the lilies as they lay in the dark shade of the house. Only the lilies would not have disgraced the Halberts' garden. Automatically Hubert glanced up to Mother's room and then up to the room he and Dunstan shared. He was just in time to see a white face disappear from the window. It must be Dunstan, he thought. And he felt suddenly chilled. It had happened before that he would be absorbed, usually making something in his workshop, and he would turn round and there would be Dunstan watching him. "Just watching," Dunstan would say when asked, or sometimes, "A cat may look at a king."

"Ten—that's all, Gert." He slowed the swing.

"Can't I go on by myself, Hu?"

"Oh, all right then, but don't fall off."

He looked up high in the sky and blinked away the dizziness of swinging. There were three or four fluffy white clouds coming up. He sighed. He didn't want to go indoors and leave the garden and the sun and the swinging. It would be chilly in the house. But there was a lot to do—and after dinner, the meeting.

Willy was making a little subsidiary pile of bricks. With great intentness he fetched and placed them, making sure first that they weren't cracked or broken. For a brief instant the wish that he could be like Willy crossed Hubert's mind. He dismissed it, but as he walked towards the back door, he wondered whether they would ever have a sunken garden now. The thought was like a little hand squeezing inside him.

Over in the next-door garden old Halby's clippers went *click-click*.

8

". . . no one—not even your best friend. Do you understand?"

"Can't I tell Miss Deke?" asked Gerty.

"No. Not Miss Deke, nor anyone." Elsa surveyed them all sitting round the table. "You know what they'll do if they find out? Do *you* know, Dun?"

Dunstan stared at her as though he had some secret knowledge, but all the same he just shook his head.

"Well, I know," said Elsa. "They'll take us away. They'll take us away and put us in a *home!*"

There was no sound in the kitchen and the children lowered their eyes as if they had been found out at last.

"What's a home?" Gerty asked timidly.

"It's a place that has bars on the window. Big iron bars, so you can't get out. And you're not allowed to go outside except when they say. And they whip you. They whip you with whips, even if you're the teeniest bit naughty. And they never give you enough to eat. They put the little girls in one place and the little boys in another place and you're not allowed to talk or they'll whip you."

"Is it like a loony b-bin?" Jiminee asked.

"Worse."

"Why'll they put us in a home?" asked Gerty.

"Because we're orphans, silly." She paused for a moment, and then said impressively, "It's called an *institution*."

"Institution," sibilantly the word was murmured.

"So we mustn't let anyone know—except for us. Not even the—funeral man."

"Undertaker," said Dunstan.

"Undertaker then. No one. If we do, they'll tell. Any grown-up will tell. We got to do everything ourselves." Her voice rose higher. "We got to look after Mother ourselves. We got to bury Mother ourselves."

They listened with pure attention. Elsa went on with a quick trembling rush of words: "We're going to bury her in the garden. We're going to do it tonight, when no one can see. Not old Halby, nor no one. We'll dig a grave and put her in the garden. That's where she'd like to be. In the garden where she can rest in peace and where—and where—"

"Where she can watch over us," Diana softly put in.

"Yes, where she can watch over us. That's right—isn't it, Hubert?"

"Yes," he answered reluctantly, "I suppose that's where she'd like to be."

"We'll bury her among the lilies," Diana said. Hubert gazed at her, surprised at her confidence—she who was always the least talkative of all. "Like it says in the Book—among the lilies. Then we'll know all the time she's there."

Jiminee shifted in his seat. "How can she be there if she's d-dead?"

"Her body," said Hubert.

Diana smiled. "No, not just her body. All of her. Mother is with us all the time. We must never forget that. She's in this room with us at this very moment. How could she leave us? We're her children. She's here." She closed her eyes and lifted her head a little so the gold hair fell back from her face. "You're here, aren't you, Mother?"

Willy banged his fist on the table. "Mother! Where's Mother?"

Diana opened her eyes. "She's here, little Willy."

"Where are you, Mother? I don't see Mother. Dinah, I don't see Mother."

"But she's here just the same, Willy. That's why you must be extra specially good."

"How long for?"

"Why, for always. Mother is always with us now."

Willy frowned. "Doesn't she ever go to sleep?"

"Not anymore, Willy."

Willy turned his head this way and that. "I don't believe you, Dinah. You're fibbing. Mother's not here."

"Yes, where is she, D-Dinah?" said Jiminee earnestly.
"How d-do you know she's here?"

"Because I feel it," Diana answered serenely. "Because I
have faith."

"I feel it too." Dunstan clenched his fist. "Willy and Gerty
are just too little to feel it, that's all."

"I do feel it, I do, I do," asserted Gerty.

"So do I," said Willy.

Dunstan gave a humourless grin and shrugged. "All right.
Everyone feels it. You do, don't you, Hubert?"

He didn't like it—Dunstan had no right to do this sort
of thing—but he was cornered. "Yes, I suppose so," he
said.

"You *suppose* so?" echoed Dunstan.

"Oh, all right. I do, then." If it hadn't been for Diana,
he wouldn't let himself be bullied like this.

"And Elsa, of course, Elsa—"

Diana smiled. "I'm sure Elsa knows just as well as we do
that Mother is with us. And Jiminee too." Her voice had
the same gently inexorable confidence as an autumn breeze
detaching leaves from the trees. "It's obvious, isn't it?"

Like the leaves, the children uneasily whispered their
assent.

"Well," said Elsa, "now let's be sensible."

"Sensible!" shouted Dunstan.

"Oh, Elsa," said Diana.

Hubert took a deep breath. "What Elsa means is that
we've got—got to get down to brass tacks. That's it,
isn't it, Elsa? Talk never baked a cake. We've got to have
a plan, and we've got—"

"That's right. There's a lot of things to do and it's no
use us just sitting here and chattering and—and things."
She gathered strength. "We'll start at midnight—that should
give us lots of time, an' we'll take turns. Gerty and Willy

are too young to do the digging, so they'll have to go
to bed. And there's another thing—we must all get plenty
of rest this afternoon, so we'll be strong for tonight."

"Midnight," Jiminee said, "g-gosh!"

Elsa stood up. "If there's anything we haven't thought of,
we can decide that tomorrow. Of course, from now on,
we'll be having meetings more often."

She had started to turn away when Dunstan said, "You
don't show much respect, do you, Elsa?"

"What do you mean?"

"You don't show much respect, that's what I mean. Who
gave you the right to settle everything? Who gave you the
right to decide? You're not Mother."

Hubert leaned forward. "Who *is* going to decide then—
you, bookworm?"

Dunstan whitened. For a moment he said nothing; when
he did speak it was with a dignity the children had not seen
before. "We're not going to get anywhere by calling each
other names, Hubert. I should think you ought to know
better."

"Well, you called *me* names," Elsa said.

"I didn't call you names. I just asked," Dunstan paused,
"I just asked who gave *you* the right to decide everything.
You don't even ask us anything, do you? Meetings never used
to be like this. We *all* decided—all of us. I'm right,
aren't I, Hu?"

"That was different, Dun, you know it was. Christmas
meetings and birthday meetings was just to choose Mother's
present—it wasn't anything like this. It was——" Hubert
tried for words to express the difference, "Well—now it's
changed, that's what I mean."

Diana rose, touched her hands to the table, and leaned forward to Hubert. "Oh, no, Hu, you're wrong. You really are
wrong. Why, Elsa herself said it—nothing has changed."

Elsa interrupted quickly, "That's not fair, Dinah, I did-
n't——"

Diana smiled. "I think," she said before Elsa could finish,
"I think we all ought to go and lie down."

Elsa remained silent. One by one the children got up and
followed Diana out of the kitchen. At last only Hubert
remained to keep Elsa company. They didn't look at one
another. Hubert found a little patch of grease by his hand
and began to rub it with the tip of his finger. It was so quiet
they could hear the burr of the electric clock. There was the
taste of salmon pie in his mouth. It made him feel a bit sick.

Elsa went to the sink and came back with a damp cloth.
She lifted Hubert's hand and carefully wiped away the
grease. They both stared at the clean wet patch.

"What did I do wrong, Hu?"

He shook his head and fingered the dampness on the
table. "You should of told me—you should of told me
about what we're going to do."

"You don't—you don't think I'm wrong, do you, Hu?"

He didn't look at her. "I dunno. It isn't a question of
right or wrong. It's just that . . ."

"Yes?"

"I dunno." He didn't want to speak anymore.

"Well," Elsa swung the dishrag in her hand. "I've never
seen Dinah like that before."

"Dinah's barmy," Hubert said sharply. The damp patch on
the table was dry now. He got up. What's done's done.
We're all barmy, come to that.

"Hu?"

He looked at her quickly and away again.

"Hu?"

He shook his head emphatically. "I'm going to lie down."
He pushed by her and went to the door. Then he looked
back. There she was, standing with the dishrag in her hand,
staring at him. She was small and it made him angry. "Do I
look like a freak or something?" She'd no right to look at
him like that—like a little kid. He knew she was going to
cry, and if he stayed he would cry too. *Crippen!*

Crippen. He left her standing there and slammed the door
behind him. "Crippen!" he said aloud. He ran down the
passage and into the front room that was so seldom used.

At once he smelled the wax polish and the everlasting dust from the thickly upholstered couch.

It was warm with the windows closed and the sun shining in most of the day. It was bright and white where the windows were, but dark inside with brown wallpaper and dark furniture and the dark carpet and the dark floor. It was like the darkness of a church—but nice and looked after. When he'd had measles and the room upstairs had been kept dark because the light was supposed to hurt his eyes, it had been like this almost. He didn't have to do his jobs then. It was peaceful. He didn't have to think.

He stood in the centre of the room. He felt tired and weak —as though he'd got the measles again. Slowly the sun went behind the clouds and the shimmering white veil in front of the windows became just net curtains again.

Hubert sighed.

He shouldn't be cross with Elsa. It wasn't her fault. But if only they'd rung someone up—even old Halby. They could have told him. It was all wrong to put a deader in the garden.

A deader—that was Mother!

Hubert went down on his knees. "Oh, God," he said, "don't let me forget Mother—*please* don't!"

9

There was no moon.

The soil under the wall of the house where the lilies grew was stony and hard. Perhaps only lilies of the valley could ever have thrived there.

The afternoon's drizzle had moistened the top layer of earth, so that the digging had been easy at first. But now, however hard he drove the spade, it didn't penetrate more than an inch or two. A rigid bar of iron bore down on Hubert's shoulders as he dug. He stood in the shallow trench and forced the spade down. He kicked at the blade to drive it deeper and lifted a meagre scoop of earth and dumped it on the side. Down, kick, up. Down, kick, up. He didn't bother to count anymore. Straight black stalks—his brothers' and sisters' legs—surrounded him as he worked, but he didn't notice them either.

Long ago he'd had a dream of standing on a high cliff with nothing but darkness below—not the sleepy darkness when the lights were turned out upstairs, but an icy darkness of falling. He'd been afraid. When he'd woken, there'd been a funny hard excited feeling between his legs. And now, as he thrust the spade in and prised it up, the feeling came again. Down, kick, up—gradually he and the spade seemed to become one moving thing drawing its power from the hard pulsating centre.

"Sssh!" said somebody as the blade grated on a stone.

He went on digging. They said if you dug deep enough you'd come out in Australia. Down, kick, up—Australia. The hair tickled his forehead and he smelled his own sweat. He'd get there—to Australia. When one of the sides fell in, he didn't join in the groans, but attacked the fresh heap of soil. The trembling in his arms and the hard arch of his hand were nothing beside the throb within him of Australia.

"How much have we done now? Let's have a look."

Hubert was on the upswing and the light of Jiminee's torch caught him full in the eyes. He blinked hard and the light shifted downward. Hubert stared at the shallow hole, ragged at the edges and unevenly dug.

"It must be at least two foot," a hopeful voice said.

Hubert shook his head to himself. The ground was pitted with smooth brown sockets where stones had come out. Like holey cheese, he thought. They must have been at it for hours and look what they'd done! The throb within him slackened slowly.

"It's my go now, Hu," Elsa said.

He handed the spade to her and climbed out. His legs ached so that he could hardly bend them. He straightened

up and stood a little away from the others. Jiminee switched
off the torch. It had begun to rain.

Hubert lifted his head so the rain could fall on his face.
It chilled the sweat below his hairline like a cool hand on
his brow. There was no wind and the rain was so fine it was
noiseless. The only sound was Elsa's breath and the scratch
of the spade and the new earth landing on the pile at the
side of the grave. He closed his fist and felt the tightness of
a rising blister under the caked dirt.

The garden was full of black heavy shapes that suddenly
swelled up and then shrunk as he looked. The denseness of
the trees hid the greenish neon light on the other side of the
wall, and only the leaves at the very top were touched with
the glow. He smelled the wet bark and tried to think of the
daytime. Long ago the Halberts had gone to bed and the
windows of the houses further down the terrace were light-
less. Everyone was asleep but them. The garden was an
enormous pit of night. The darkness concealed them, but it
did not comfort.

Elsa's whisper came up to him. "You four go in. You'll
catch your death out here. I'll come in when I've finished my
turn and the next one can go out."

He left the graveside and followed the others reluctantly.
When Dunstan turned the light on in the kitchen he blinked
again. No one had anything to say. They stood, hands hanging down as though they had done a crime.

Hubert looked at the clock and noticed with surprise it
was only half-past one. For a moment he thought perhaps the
kitchen clock had stopped too, but the circulating second
hand still moved confidently round. Maybe, he thought,
we'll do it after all.

"Why d-don't we have some cocoa?" Jiminee said tentatively.

No one answered him for a moment. Then Hubert said, "I
don't want any."

"I don't think," said Diana, "that it would be right to
have cocoa now."

Jiminee sniffed and slowly wiped his nose with the back of

his hand, leaving a thin streak of mud-free skin across his cheek. There was a warning intake of breath from Dunstan.

"Sorry, Dun," Jiminee said quickly.

It seemed much colder in the kitchen than outside. Hubert shivered. The pulsing warmth had completely left him. He could feel the coldness of his kneecaps and the backs of his hands. They could easily light the oven and warm the room up, but Hubert didn't suggest it. It seemed somehow right to be cold now.

"Keep still, Jiminee," Dunstan said in his high voice, breaking the silence and halting Jiminee's perpetual jiggling dance. Jiminee's grin flashed on and off as he tried to keep himself rigidly still. The only time Jiminee really ever stopped the constant flicker of his limbs was when he was absorbed in drawing. Hubert wanted to tell him it didn't matter; but the effort of speaking was too great.

He leaned against the kitchen table and stared down at the mud on his shoes. Sunday was shoe-cleaning day—but perhaps Mother would let them off tomorrow. *Mother!*—he glanced up hurriedly as if he had uttered a blasphemy. But the others didn't notice. Hubert looked at them. They weren't looking at him. They were by themselves. Dunstan frowning, always frowning in at himself, as though, thought Hubert, he saw a big fat ugly toad inside him. He smiled and pushed down a burst of giggles that suddenly rose from his chest. Diana—there was a bit in the Bible about her: beautiful is Diana of the Ephesians, only it wasn't "beautiful," it was some other word. He often thought of that when he looked at Diana. And Jiminee, poor old Jiminee—his tongue coming out guiltily to lick his lips and hopping in again. They were all so by themselves. Why don't we talk, thought Hubert—but he knew they were too far away. Why, even if he yelled, they wouldn't hear him perhaps.

It was so hot now. Why didn't Elsa come? She was so long and poor Mother was waiting for her cool bed among the lilies.

Suddenly there were five of them. Hubert blinked. It was Gerty. She stood in the doorway, her face smooth with sleep and her unbraided hair around her shoulders. The blue dressing gown, only last year handed on from Jiminee, was much too big for her and hung almost to the floor. Her hands were quite lost in the enormous sleeves.

"What do you want?" said Dunstan.

"Bicky," muttered Gerty. She walked determinedly to the cupboard.

"Biscuit," said Dunstan. "You can't have a biscuit every time you want one!"

Then Hubert laughed.

"What are you laughing at?" snapped Dunstan.

"You're always against everything, Dun, aren't you? Can't, can't, can't—that's what it is with you."

"Stop laughing at once!"

"Can't, can't, can't, stop, stop, stop!" chanted Hubert, caught in a whirlpool of laughing.

"Shut up!" Dunstan shouted, but Jiminee was bemusedly mouthing the words too now. And then Gerty, the biscuit tin secure in her plump hands, joined in as well.

"Stop, stop, stop—can't, can't, can't—stop, stop, stop!"

The singsong was overpoweringly delicious and witty and it need never end. Hubert felt weak with it so that he could hardly stand up. "Can't, can't, can't—stop, stop, stop!" They were oblivious of Dunstan's shouts of "Shut up!" The laughs bubbled out of Hubert's mouth so fast that the words only had time to be high-pitched whispers as he gasped for air.

Then something rose out of the top of Hubert's head and rose and rose so that it almost touched the ceiling. He found himself looking down upon the kitchen—and he could see Jiminee dancing and Gerty banging the biscuit tin and Dunstan standing frozen and still. And he could see himself laughing and holding onto his stomach. And he could see Diana, her big eyes open wide looking from one to another.

Then he saw the door open and Elsa enter. She had the spade in one hand and with the other was trying to push back a lock of hair that had escaped from a pigtail and hung down on her cheek. It took her a long time to get the piece of hair back and all the while she just looked at them.

The noise stopped—except for Hubert. He could· hear himself, his voice dwindling, still going on and on: "Stop, stop, stop—can't, can't, can't . . ."

"I could hear you all the way out in the garden." As Elsa spoke, abruptly that bit of Hubert fell back from the ceiling into his head.

Gerty put the tin of biscuits on the table. "It wasn't me· that started it, Else."

"No," said Dunstan, "it wasn't Gerty."

"Jiminee," Elsa said, "you ought to know better."

"Please don't be angry, Elsa."

"I'm not angry—"

"It wasn't Jiminee, either. It was Hubert."

Diana shook her head. "He was very naughty."

"He ought to be punished," said Dunstan.

Hubert didn't hear them. It was like a hurt, the way Elsa was looking at him. There were two little red spots on her cheek—the way there always were when she was very angry. But when she spoke, she sounded gentle.

"Pull up your stockings, Hubert."

He bent down. It took him a long time to pull the heavy wool stockings up under his knees and fold the tops down neatly over his garters. The blood pounded in his head. He was hot again and very weak.

"We must all remember," Elsa said, "to be very quiet."

"Yes," murmured Diana, "we mustn't disturb Mother."

Elsa faltered for a moment. "We mustn't disturb *anyone.*"

"Hubert ought to be punished."

"We can think about that tomorrow, Dunstan," said Elsa. "We've got work to do now. And it's your turn." She held out the spade. "Come on." She opened the back door for him.

"All right." Gripping the spade tightly, Dunstan gave a quick backward glance to Hubert and shut the door hard behind him.

Elsa gave Gerty a biscuit and sent her to bed. Then once again the waiting began. Each of them took one of the biscuits, which were usually reserved for Sunday. They were filled with hard cream. Hubert's mouth was dry and he could hardly swallow the crumbs. He scraped the cream off with his teeth and gave the biscuit part to Jiminee. He could not look at Elsa.

He sat on a kitchen chair and waited—for Dunstan, for Jiminee, for Diana, for himself. He did not remember going out or coming back in again. He was just there, sitting at the kitchen table, with the waves of hot and cold washing through him. The faces of his brothers and sisters merged and shifted and separated again, like a pack of cards being shuffled. The biscuit crumbs were dry on his tongue. It was a long time waiting. When he closed his eyes he could taste the deposits of cream between his teeth. Once, he opened his eyes and saw Diana reading from the book. And that seemed strange, for Diana was never the one who read. Perhaps he dreamt it. Yet he heard her, because out of the quiet, trembling flow of her reading, words would become individual bells and he would understand them:

. . . upon the hem of it thou shalt make pomegranates of blue, and of purple, and of scarlet, round about the hem thereof; and bells of gold between them round about: a golden bell and a pomegranate, a golden bell and a pomegranate, upon the hem of the robe round about . . .

Then it was his turn. He was alone again with the spade. But he couldn't find the rhythm of digging—there were magic words to help, but he couldn't remember. *Bells and pomegranates,* he tried, *pomegranates and bells.* His arms were filled inside with candy floss and the spade wouldn't come up. He lifted it weakly at last and a little cascade of earth and stones poured back into the hole. Hubert began to giggle. He sneezed—and the giggles were cold in his throat. He half turned round to the garden, waiting for it to pounce. But it was quite still and, even when he held his breath, it did not give itself away. It waited, moment for moment it waited with him. And it looked so peaceful—the grass freckled with moonlight falling through the leaves—but it was a trick.

And then he heard it—a creak from the garden door and a shuffling among the leaves. There were robbers come—robbers down there in the night. Hubert stood as stone-still as a garden statue, and the leaves moved slyly. A thousand knives flickered in the moonlight, ready and waiting.

They would win. He knew from the beginning they would win. He could not shout for help. Only his held breath and his open eyes kept them at bay. But inside his skull the blood struck rhythmically, harder and harder, and he could not hold his breath forever. He was dizzy with the noise of blood.

He could hold it no longer.

He dropped the spade and with one swift movement fell to the floor of the grave, crouching on his knees and elbows. He put his hands over his head and let his breath go. It didn't matter now. Nothing mattered. He waited for the knives to strike—for the thump on his back as the hilt smashed against his spine.

He pressed his knees and his elbows into the ground with all his force. If only he hurt himself enough, if only he could draw blood, perhaps the robbers would spare him. But he knew they wouldn't really. They would kill him down there in the grave with their knives. And then they'd draw their knives out and they'd laugh, because they wouldn't have to keep quiet anymore. They were merciless.

Hubert shivered uncontrollably.

He smelled the old hard earth where nobody had been for centuries.

He could not believe it when he opened his eyes and saw that it was green and bright with sun and not a black hole at all. The garden was so different he could hardly recognize it. It was filled with different greens—the borders high with green plants and grey plants and almost-blue shrubs and flowers blue and red and orange, like huge marigolds. And the grass was a lighter green and the leaves of the apple tree were very dark green, like watercress. Deep orange-red fruit hung from the apple tree—not apples at all. Hubert reached up and a fruit slipped into his hand. It was round and big and he laughed because all at once he knew it was a pomegranate. He picked another and, as he pulled it, the branch rang with the sound of tiny bells. They tinkled like fairy bells. He stretched to see them, but they were hidden deep in the leaves. Now that he listened, the wind blew the branch and the bells sounded all the time, and he knew they were made of gold. And suddenly, holding a pomegranate in each hand, he began to dance to the music of the gold bells. The grass was soft to his bare feet and the smell of the flowers and the spices rose around his dance to make him a coloured robe. He danced right to the edge of the pool in the centre of the garden and the water reflected the magnificence of his robe. It was so clear he could see each tiny embroidered pomegranate—in blue and scarlet and purple—as the robe swayed to the sound of the gold bells.

And on the surface of the water were big white lilies on green mats. Suddenly he flung off the robe and leapt into the cool water among the lilies. The heat of his dance was cooled and he swam gently between the broad leaves. With great gentleness he placed his pomegranates on one of them. He was free. He knew that he had been very tired, but now he was not anymore. He lay on his back, smelling the smell of the lilies, hearing the faraway bell music, and the bright sun shone down. His body was washed and silver, and smooth.

The sun was very bright in the sky and as he watched it seemed to grow. It enlarged in the sky and was no longer soft, but hard and yellow. Hubert screwed up his eyes and tried to turn his head, but the water was suddenly resistant. The light was so bright he cried out, and with all his strength he tried to turn over—but something held him back. He struggled against the hand on his shoulder and put up his arms to shut out the light and drag back the vanishing garden.

"Hubert, come on. Wake up, Hu."

"Don't shine the torch in his face, silly."

"But he won't wake up."

"Shake him."

The light went out, but someone was shaking him hard. He opened his eyes.

"That's enough—he's awake now." It was Elsa.

He saw nothing but blackness. He couldn't remember at all. He was lying on the ground and it was hard. He was wet still from the pool. He could feel the stickiness of his shirt and there was a raw wetness between his legs.

"Let him get up. Come on, Hu, get up."

He managed to whisper, "I can't."

Then a hand gripped his. It was Elsa's; he knew because it was strong. She pulled him to his feet.

"What you want to go and fall asleep for?" said Dun.

He was dizzy—as dizzy as when he'd held his breath. He blinked hard. "There were robbers," he blurted, "robbers waiting in the garden!"

"Robbers!" said Dunstan contemptuously.

"There *were* robbers!"

"Don't be silly, Hu," Elsa said.

"But there were, there were, there were!" As he said it he burst into tears and all the sleep-stilled shivers in his body attacked together.

His weeping silenced them all. Hubert never cried. Dunstan, or Dinah—even Elsa, yes. But Hubert!

They saw his bent head and heard the grate of indrawn grief and the cry of its expulsion, but none of them knew of any comfort.

He could not stop.

"Hubert?"

"Hu."

Their voices were puzzled and gentle.

He stood alone in the grave and wept.

"What's the matter, Hu?"

"Aren't you feeling very well?"

And then, quite abruptly, he was empty and could cry no more. There was nothing to feel or to be afraid of. He was hollow. He could see now. He could see that the garden was just dark. It wasn't sunlit, and there weren't any robbers.

There were no pomegranates and no bells. And there wasn't any pool—just an old hole in the lily bed. He put his hands on the sides and pulled himself out and stood up. He could hardly manage it, he was so weak. He was all right, except he couldn't stop shivering.

"Aren't you very well, Hu?"

"I'm all right."

Elsa put her hand on his forehead. "Why, you're frozen. You are a silly."

"Is he ill?" asked Jiminee.

"You're terribly cold, Hu," Elsa said. "I think you better go to bed."

"Why can't we all go to b-bed?"

"Don't be an idiot, Jiminee," Dunstan said violently. "We got to finish it, haven't we?"

"B-but, we have finished, Dun! It's big enough now, isn't it?" He shone his torch down into the trench. "That's deep enough."

"How do *you* know it's deep enough?"

Diana answered him, "It's deep enough, Dun."

"Well," he said, suddenly mild, "even if it is, we've still got to . . . got to fetch Mother."

"Yes," said Diana.

"But we need Hubert for that—and he's going to b-bed. We can't do it without Hu."

"Oh, yes, Jiminee, yes we can." Diana touched him gently on the shoulder as if to still his doubts. "Children," she said, "children—it's time now."

"You'll have to wait till I get Hu to bed," Elsa said.

He didn't protest. He let her put her arm round his waist and half carry him.

He could never have climbed the stairs by himself. And his fingers were so fat he couldn't even undo the buttons on his shirt. Somehow he didn't mind Elsa doing it—didn't even mind her undressing him and taking off his wet pants and putting him into bed. He was all hollow still—like a tree trunk with nothing inside.

She did it all in the dark. He was glad of that—he didn't want to remember that piercing sun. He just wanted to forget, to sleep.

But when Elsa had left him and said goodnight, he couldn't seem to sleep after all. He thought he'd been cold, but now he was terribly hot—so hot he flung the bedclothes off—and still he was hot.

Hot and cold—one moment nothing would cool him, and the next an icy wind froze him through the blankets.

It was while he was shaking with this cold that he became aware of Jiminee by his bed.

"Hu?"

He tried to nod.

"Hu—there *was* something in the garden. It wasn't robbers, b-but . . . wouldn't you like to know?"

Hubert could hardly hear him—he was conscious only of the great hand, the hand of a giant snowman, that gripped him and shook and shook and wouldn't let go.

"It was Blackie—it wasn't robbers at all. Just B-Blackie. Somebody left the garden d-door open, and Blackie got in. He was sn-sniffing round b-by the wall. Elsa wasn't half angry—b-but I didn't leave it open. You didn't either, d-did you, Hu. I think it was Dun. D-Dun's always going off d-down there by himself."

"But Dun's afraid of Blackie," Hubert managed.

"Well, he d-didn't *m-mean* to. It was just an accident, I 'spect."

There was a brief moment of peace for Hubert then. In a minute, he knew, he would be aflame. "Have you finished?" he said hoarsely.

"Finished? Oh, yes. It wasn't b-bad at all. The others are just p-putting the earth back. I thought I'd come and tell you about B-Blackie. I say, do you know what D-Dinah says?"

But Hubert couldn't answer. The heat had got him now. All he wanted was water, but he couldn't speak. He knew the silvery water of the pool was not far away, but he couldn't reach it. Struggle as he would, he'd never get it.

". . . to build a tab-taber-tab-b-b-ber—a t-temple . . ."

He could see the white lilies floating and very faintly he even heard the bell music, bells and pomegranates . . .

". . . like M-Moses m-made Aaron b-build . . ."

. . . pomegranates and bells . . .

". . . Dinah says we ought to d-do it for Mother, you see . . ."

. . . scarlet and purple and blue—and golden bells.

SUMMER

10

The garden was locked from the inside, although Hubert had been careful to leave it open when they went to do the shopping. He and Elsa stood outside in a patch of shade cast by the plane trees. It was very hot. The tops of the trees moved languidly in a tiny breeze. The tar of the road gave up shimmering waves of heat.

They looked at each other in silence. Hubert shifted his grip on the handle of the shopping basket—his palm was sticky and crinkled by the wicker work. They would have to go the long way round to the front now.

It was very quiet in the road. School had broken up the day before, but most of the children came from the other side of West Avenue. Not many lived in the big, still half-smart terraces that opened out onto the park, and those that did mostly went to boarding schools. In the summer a lot of them went away to the seaside. Anyway, they wouldn't mix with council-school children.

Monmouth Terrace and Ipswich Terrace and Abergavenny had a look of summer desertion. Even the dogs lying in the shade of the doorways were almost invisible.

"Well?" said Elsa.

Hubert nodded, and they began to move. He had a half-sense of gladness that they couldn't get in the back way. He knew Elsa felt it too. It gave them a little longer before they had to face Mrs. Stork. The constant fear that Miss Deke at school would find out had ended with the coming of the holidays. But there was still Mrs. Stork—old Talk-Stork, queen of Nosey Parkers. Every Thursday, Mrs. Stork's *day*, Elsa had to invent an excuse to stay away from school and look after Willy so that Mrs. Stork wouldn't get at him. Now that all the children were at home, Mrs. Stork would be bound to worm the truth out of one of them. She suspected something all right.

They should have got rid of her long ago. They shouldn't have let her stay on so long. *Never put off till the morrow what you can do today.*

Hubert pushed his sandals down hard on the unpaved strip that ran by the wall and dust puffed up over his toes. It was no good thinking what they *should* have done.

They turned the corner into Ipswich Terrace. Here there were no trees along the street, except at the end, by the park, where every evening four or five smartly dressed ladies would stand and talk. Even when it rained they stood there. Hubert had seen them once with their bright faces sheltered from the rain by red and yellow and purple umbrellas, like a fair. They weren't there now—just the sun. Hubert put his free hand on the top of his head and felt his hair. It was scorching.

The front door was shut, but as they walked up the path it opened abruptly and Gerty ran out to meet them. Two streaks of dirt framed her nose.

"Elsa! Dun says me and Willy mustn't swing anymore!"

Elsa frowned. "What do you mean?"

"He says we mustn't swing anymore—not in the garden. Tell him it's not fair! We can, Else, can't we?"

Elsa clenched the handle of her basket tightly and two small red spots showed on her cheeks, but her voice was calm. "Perhaps he had a reason, Gert. Didn't he say why? Perhaps the swing isn't safe anymore."

"He didn't say why, he didn't! He just said we mustn't."

"You're a little liar, Gerty Hook." Dunstan spoke from just inside the doorway, so that only the whiteness of his face showed up in the shadow.

Gerty twisted round and stepped backwards into Hubert. He put his hand on her shoulder and felt her plump little body press against his. He resisted his own inclination to step back too.

"Dunstan—behave yourself!" Elsa's chin was up, and the hesitancy of the last few weeks was gone. Suddenly Hubert was proud of her. "Go on," he murmured.

"I won't have you telling the little ones what they can do and what they can't do."

Dunstan stood unmoving in the doorway. Out of the dimness of the hall his words came clear and hard. "*You* won't have it. *You* don't seem to realise certain things. *You* don't seem to realise the garden is a place of rest—not the place for Gerty's silly shrieks and screams. *You* don't seem to realise that—do you, Elsa?"

Elsa stepped forward, squinting to see better into the shadow. "I don't want to listen to any more from you. You're cheeky and—"

"Exactly—you never do want to listen. *You* have to decide everything. Well, perhaps it would interest you to know Diana agrees with me. Put that in your pipe and smoke it!"

Elsa was trembling with rage. "I don't care what Diana says! It's none of her business. If it was decided in a meeting . . . but *you* can't go round giving orders. Who do you—"

"*Don't care!* That's just typical. I suppose you don't care what Mother thinks?" For a moment the scorn had gone from Dunstan's voice, then it returned redoubled. "Don't care was made to care!"

Elsa turned her head and spoke directly to Gerty. "You and Willy can use the swing whenever you want, Gert."

Gerty began to smile. She looked up at Hubert and slowly pushed his hand from her shoulder. With all the sedateness of a five-year-old she walked up the path and climbed the steps. As she passed Dunstan she looked him full in the face. "Yah boo!" she said, without breaking stride.

Dunstan lunged and grabbed her arm. He pulled her towards him and bent his face down very close to hers. "Listen, Gerty—you're a liar. That makes you a sinner, and sinners have to pay. If you swing once more, God will punish you. He'll tear out your insides, that's what he'll do—because you're a sinner."

Gerty struggled silently. For a moment Hubert was still, then he had dropped the basket and was running up the front steps. "Leave her alone!" he shouted. As Dunstan looked up in surprise, Gerty pulled herself free and vanished into the dark hall.

Hubert hit him in the face. Dunstan staggered back into the hall. The threadbare carpet slithered under his feet and he fell onto his back. The fall jolted the glasses from his nose and they hung swinging from one ear. Dazed and blind, but unblinking, he sat up, propping himself on his hands.

"It serves you right," said Hubert, feeling the soreness of his fist. But it was an excuse the way he said it, not a justification. Suddenly his anger was out of reach. He glanced about the hall as if he would find it on the silver letter tray, which Mrs. Stork had forgotten to polish again, or in the frozen joviality of the galloping huntsmen on the wall.

Dunstan rose slowly and fumblingly replaced his glasses.

"It serves you right," Hubert muttered again.

Dunstan stepped forward. "You knocked my glasses off," he said, staring intensely at Hubert.

And Hubert looked away—up, down, to the floor boards that still carried the bright impression of Flight-Sergeant Millard's boot.

"You knocked my glasses off." Dunstan paused. "I shan't forget that." He turned and went swiftly to the stairs.

He was halfway up when Hubert called, "What about what you did to Gerty?" Why did it sound so feeble, when he was right? Dunstan didn't even glance back.

Hubert stayed in the same position for a long time. Dunstan had hit Gerty and he had hit Dunstan. That was fair—

well, it *was* fair. Yet lately Dunstan had a way of making what was fair and unfair seem unimportant—silly, somehow.

"You shouldn't have hit him, Hu."

He half turned to Elsa. "It served him right."

"Perhaps it did. But we've got to stick together, Hu. We mustn't quarrel."

"He hurt Gerty. And he locked us out of the garden, didn't he?" He was suddenly angry with her.

Elsa sighed. She went over to the hall table and picked up a letter. She glanced at it casually and slipped it in the pocket of her dress.

"A letter?" Hubert asked.

She nodded.

"Aren't you going to read it?"

"Not now. There's Mrs. Stork. You go and find where she is. I'll take the baskets down to the kitchen." She reached out and picked up the brass lady bell that stood by the letter tray. It made no sound—it had been clapperless for as long as any of them could remember.

"Else—do you think Diana really said the little ones weren't to use the swing?"

Elsa shook the bell. "Of course. You know Dunstan never tells a lie." She laid it down carefully on the table and made a little dusting motion with her hand. "You better go and find Mrs. Stork now."

Hubert bent down and straightened out the rug. "All right," he said.

11

Jiminee was upstairs in Hubert's workshop. He sat at the table by the window, absorbed in his drawing.

Hubert watched. It was strange how all the awkwardness in Jiminee vanished while he drew. The nervous stutter of his limbs was gone, and his hand moved with steady exacti-

tude. Looking at Jiminee with a crayon in his hand, no one
could call him loony anymore. Best of all he liked to work
alone, but even when he yielded to the children's urging—
"draw for us, Jiminee, please draw us something!"—and sat
down with everyone looking on, the hesitant smile would
disappear and, like magic, he would become another Jiminee.

Hubert didn't want to interrupt. Watching his younger
brother made him forget about Dunstan. Jiminee's calmness
filled the room and made it a peaceful place. And suddenly
Hubert knew why Jiminee changed so when he drew—he
was safe. He wasn't running away, like he did when they
plagued him in the breaks at school, or standing, white-
faced and grinning, when they had cornered him at last; he
was just safe and . . . untouchable, that was it. And Hubert
remembered when Jiminee had first gone to school he
wouldn't go to the playground at breaks—that was before
Miss Deke had made him go out and "mix with your
fellows"—but would sit at his desk, drawing. One day,
Bill Chance—they called him "Fatty" behind his back—had
snatched Jiminee's pencil away and done a war dance round
the desk, holding the pencil just out of Jiminee's reach. But
no one else had joined in and eventually Fatty had handed
the pencil back and gone away. After that nobody—except
Miss Deke—ever bothered Jiminee when he was drawing.

Hubert drew in a deep breath, then let it out slowly and
gently. "Jiminee," he said, "have you seen Mrs. Stork?"

Jiminee paused, shook his head, and went back to his work.

"Who wants Mrs. Stork? Oh, it's you, love." Mrs. Stork
appeared in the doorway of the spare bedroom. "Just giving
this old room a bit of an air." She flapped a piece of blue
cloth that did duty as a duster and then raised it to pat at
her shiny forehead. "It ain't 'alf 'ot. What can I do for you?"

Mrs. Stork had a fat and jolly manner that her thin, but
heavily dewlapped, face belied. She was always sweating—
she smelt of cheese—and in off moments would wipe it away
with anything handy; Hubert had seen her do it once on the
lace curtains in the front room. He'd investigated afterwards
and found the curtain covered with little black streaks.

"Elsa wants to speak to you."

"She does, does she? Well, it's nice to know there's somebody round here who don't lock themselves in their room and won't come out even to talk to an old—" She caught the expression on Hubert's face and flapped her duster at him. "Oh, don't mind me, love, I don't mean no 'arm. Just this weather. I wouldn't want to disturb no one if they're sick. If they're sick."

Hubert said. "I'll tell Elsa you're here."

"That's right. Save my old bones. Berty—" she called out as he left the room, "you might ask her to bring me a cup if the kettle's on the boil. I could do with a sit down." She gazed round the room and spotted Jiminee. "Hello, there's a quiet one. What are you up to, Jimmy?" She came up behind him and peered at his drawing. "Artistic. What is it?"

Jiminee put down his pencil. "It's the seaside."

"Loverly. Is that supposed to be a man there?"

"He's fishing."

Mrs. Stork breathed out. "Well, I never seen the seaside with just one man fishin'. You want to put some more people in there, Jimmy—there's always a lot of people at the seaside, I should have thought you'd know that."

"This is a l-lonely seaside."

"Lonely! Well, I certainly wouldn't want to go there for a holiday—go there for a holiday. No. What's them yellow patches in the water?"

"D-don't you know how the sun shines on the w-water in the summer?"

"I expect I seen the sea a good bit more than you. I never seen it look yellow like that. A yellow sea. Meant to be China or something, I suppose?" Mrs. Stork laughed. "Chinese seaside."

Jiminee reached out and picked up his pencil. He held it, not attempting to draw, not saying anything.

Mrs. Stork's chuckles diminished to a mellow wheeze. "It's a lovely painting, ducks, all the same." She sighed. "My John used to like to sit and draw like you. Anything he'd draw—snakes and birds and—" Mrs. Stork gestured vaguely, "and trees. I always said he'd have 'ad a wonderful way with a paint brush. If he'd lived. A wonderful way. But he was taken from us—me and my Tiger. He was younger than you. Five he was. He was five." She shifted so that she could see Jiminee's face. "In the midst of life we are in death."

Mrs. Stork pressed the duster to her forehead. For a moment red pressure marks showed along the frown lines. "Tell old Mrs. Stork, Jimmy," she said, "is your ma real bad?"

Jiminee raised his eyes. He began to shake and a smile flickered at the corners of his mouth. "I think Elsa's c-coming n-now."

Mrs. Stork turned quickly as Elsa and Hubert came into the room. "Oh, Elsa love, I was wonderin' where you'd got to. Have you brought me my tea?"

"I put the kettle on. It'll be ready in a little while."

Mrs. Stork's face drew together at the mouth like a string purse. "Oh, dear, I was looking forward to a nice cup."

"Well, it won't be long. Mother asked me to tell you we won't be needing you for the next fortnight."

"Well, I suppose I can wait. Been waiting all my life I 'ave—waitin' to get 'ooked, waiting up nights for my Tiger, waiting by my little Johnny's bedside when he was sick. I ought to be used to it. What d'you say, ducks?"

Elsa hesitated, and Hubert moved a little closer to her. "I said we shan't be needing you for the next fortnight, Mrs. Stork. So could I have your key?"

Mrs. Stork blew out a quantity of air. "That's what I thought you said. Well, you will have your little joke, I suppose. I always said you kids had funny ways. But it ain't nice to tease a body my age—"

"But I'm not teasing, Mrs. Stork. We just shan't be needing you for a little bit, that's all."

"That's all. You come in 'ere and just ask me ever so calm to leave! And—"

"It's just for a fortnight."

"Fortnight—don't give me that one. I know this 'just a

fortnight, Mrs. Stork'—don't you think nobody ever tried to give me the sack before? Just a fortnight! An' who are you to tell me, eh? That's what I'd like to know. Why don't Mrs. Hook see me herself? Why don't *she* tell me?"

"That's just it. Mother's sick. She's very ill and she's got to go away. That's what the doctor says—she's got to go away to the seaside and—and we're all going with her so you see there won't be anyone here and—"

"Doctor! *Doctor!*" Mrs. Stork rose a pitch. "Since when 'as your mum taken to seeing doctors?"

"Since just the other day," Hubert said. "Dr. Meadows came to see her."

"That's a lot of tarrydiddle! That's a fine tale! You can't tell me Mrs. 'ook would ever ask a doctor to come round! She hates 'em—the whole breed of 'em. I *know*. Don't I just. You standing there as bold as brass. 'oo d'you think brought you into the world, eh? 'oo do you think nursed 'er and looked after 'er and run up an' down stairs for 'er and gave her the comfort the poor soul cried out for in 'er pain and sorrow? Me—Mrs. Stork. These 'ere hands held you when none of you weren't more 'an a second old, when you was crying and screaming for the breath you breathe so lordly now. Wasn't it these hands that boiled the water to wash you and clean you, that wrapped you and made you comfy? And wasn't it these 'ere you sucked on when you weren't 'ardly old enough to open your eyes and when she hadn't the milk left in 'er poor body? And wasn't it these eyes of mine that saw her groaning and screaming in agony and shame for 'er sin? For 'er sin? Yes, that's what you are, *bastards*—the 'ole pack of you! Did I ever blame 'er, did these lips ever remind 'er of her shame, did I ever let on? Never! *Mother*—she ain't so pure, she's 'uman like the rest of us an' the sooner you learn it the better. An' you, so proud and fancy now, you'll find out—"

With her full strength Elsa slapped Mrs. Stork across the face.

Mrs. Stork's mouth remained open. The mark on her cheek slowly filled with blood, until the outline of Elsa's hand showed bright on the sallow skin. Mrs. Stork glanced swiftly at the tense faces of the children. She looked down at her feet and after a while her fingers gently started to knead the blue duster. She began to speak again, in a low, expressionless tone.

"I'm not used to being hit. Fancy you 'itting me. I nursed you when you was a baby an' now you 'it me. My Tiger—'e don't never hit me, my Tiger don't. Once—just once he 'it me, a long time ago, when we was first married. We hadn't been married more 'an three months. It was at breakfast one mornin', suddenly he ups and give me a clout, just like you did—right on the face. Just like you did. An' he says, 'you ugly old bag, you,' that's what he says, 'you ugly old bag you, what do you think I married you for if you can't even fry an egg proper.' He never hit me again, not after that. My Tiger. We're a lovin' couple now we are. He's a kind man, he is; he'd do anything for anybody. But people don't want help nowdays." She lifted her head a fraction. "Nobody wants help. 'e liked to work at the garden 'ere—on the days he'd come 'ere, 'well, old girl,' he'd say to me, 'well, old girl, this is the best day in the week for me this is.' He liked to dig at that sunk garden—he always likes to do a proper job, 'e does. He was lookin' forward to putting all those bricks in, yes, he was. But Mrs. 'ook, she don't want 'im no more. An' now you gone an' builded that silly little shed. It don't 'alf look silly sitting there in the lily bed. But it ain't none of my business. I know that. Nothing ain't none of my business anymore. I been livin' in a foolish paradise. I thought I was welcome 'ere. A foolish paradise. Well, if she thinks she can get on without Mrs. Stork, good luck to 'er. If she thinks she can get on without Mrs. Stork." She sighed.

"Mrs. Stork," Elsa began, "it's only for a fort—"

"No. Don't say no more, love. What's done's done. I know when I'm not wanted. I've felt it coming. Just because I'm always cheery, doesn't mean I haven't been upset these last weeks with your mum shutting 'erself up in 'er room.

I don't expect she even wants to see me now. I don't 'spect she wants to see anyone much—*except the doctor*."

Hubert said, "It's true about the doctor, Mrs. Stork."

"If you say so, love. If you say so. Well, I'll be going down now. I'll put the key on the kitchen table for you. I don't— I don't suppose you'd mind if I had a cuppa before I leave? No—well, thank you, dear." Mrs. Stork sighed and the hand with the blue duster hovered towards her eyes. "I won't say no more. I won't say no more."

She went quickly to the door, then paused and turned round. Carefully she looked from one to the other. "Though I well could," she snapped, "though I well could." She stepped into the passage and pulled the door to behind her.

Hubert's knees were weak. He wished they hadn't had to tell her here—not in his workshop. To have to listen *to her* say all that about Mother . . .

"Isn't she awful?" Jiminee said suddenly.

Hubert nodded seriously. That was just it. She was awful—the most awful thing on earth.

"Sssh!" said Elsa, "she may be just outside."

Hubert moved quickly to the door and yanked it open. He looked straight across the landing to Mother's room. Mrs. Stork was at Mother's door, slowly turning the handle this way and that. Hubert thought, bending over that door handle she looks just like a big rat. Then she glanced up and saw him. At once her lips tightened—it was a smile. She cleared her throat as Elsa joined Hubert.

"I was just—just wanting to say goodbye to your mum." She straightened up and smoothed her skirt with her hands. "That's all," she smiled again, "just to say goodbye. But I 'spect she's asleep now, eh? Well, that's all right then, I won't trouble her. I'll be running along now."

The three children came out onto the landing. There was barely room for Mrs. Stork to get past to the stairs. Still smiling, she sidled by them.

They looked over the banisters and watched her go down the stairs. She was agile for a large woman. Almost at the bottom, she stopped and raised her eyes to where the children observed her. There was no expression in her face at all as she stared.

Then she disappeared. They heard her footsteps in the hall, and the sound of the door down to the basement. After that, silence.

"Well," said Jiminee at last, "w-what I say is—g-good riddance to b-b-bad rub-b-b-bbish." He grinned.

"Good riddance to bad rubbish," Hubert murmured. He grinned back.

After a moment's hesitation, Elsa grinned too. And they stood there smiling at each other, thinking of old Talk-Stork —gone at last.

12

Hubert stood close to the tabernacle. Diana was inside, he knew, for every so often he heard the small sounds she made. They were like gentle, low laughter.

He hesitated to call to her—"Tea's ready, Dinah!" It would be a kind of—a kind of *insubordination*. No, that wasn't the right word. It would be like what Jesus said about those money men in the temple. He touched the rough yellow brick of the tabernacle. The cement had never dried properly. He pressed his hand hard against the wall and drew it downwards. He examined the grazes—little specks of blood were growing in the white trackmarks the bricks had made on his skin.

He heard the noise from inside again. He sighed.

The garden was hot and close. The trees whispered. It would rain before long. Already there was a jungle gloom at the bottom of the garden where the yew and myrtle grew.

Last summer, down there, they had played the jungle game all summer long. "I'll be the lion—I'll be the tiger—I'll be the wolf—I'll be the elephant—and I'll be the hunter, the hunter, the hunter." They hadn't played jungles once this year yet.

Hubert raised his fist to his mouth and sucked at the beads of blood. Perhaps they'd play it tomorrow—now that Mrs. Stork had gone and the holidays had come so there was no need to fear Miss Deke with her eyes that could tell at once if you lied. Of course they wouldn't do it while Diana was there. Diana wouldn't want to play anyway. Nor would Dunstan.

Hubert felt a spasm of anger at the thought of Dunstan. It was all right for Diana—she'd always been different, dreamy. She didn't interfere really; all she wanted to do was to spend hours and hours in the tabernacle. With Mother. She got all excited when she read the words of the Bible to the children, but that was the only time she was what you'd call *funny*. Dunstan, though—always bossing everyone around and making up new rules. He never paid any attention to the rules himself. It was hard enough to get Gerty and Willy to obey, without having them always chant, "But Dunstan doesn't—Dinah never does." You could never *talk* to Dun either. He always knew best—he always made you look like a fool.

Hubert clenched his fist in memory of the blow he'd struck Dunstan that morning—it was the first bit of satisfaction he'd had in a long time.

But it wasn't any good really. Elsa was right. He knew that.

He moved away from the tabernacle into the bed of lilies of the valley. The cool leaves caressed his sandaled feet. The lilies were long over. He sniffed for a trace of lily perfume, but all he smelled was the dusty scent of the apple-tree bark. The swing hung from the branch as stiff as if the ropes were made of iron. The tiny breeze had stopped altogether, but it would be a little time yet before the rain started.

Hubert decided not to call Diana—it wouldn't be the first time she had missed tea. And besides, it seemed wrong to break the absolute silence and stillness of the garden where Diana communed with Mother in the tabernacle.

He turned and walked quickly to the back door.

"Can we have biscuits today, Elsa?" asked Gerty.

Hubert grinned as he took his place. Elsa grinned too—Dunstan was missing and there was a noticeable feeling of relief in the air.

"It's not really biscuit day."

"I know there's biscuits in the cupboard. There's lots of biscuits. I know there is."

"Well . . ."

"Oh, let's," said Willy.

"They're choc biscuits too," added Gerty.

"Go on, Else," Hubert said, "why not? After all, it's the first day of the holidays."

Elsa laughed. "All right then. We'll have biscuits. And as a special treat, Gerty can open them."

Gerty took triumphant possession of the packet. It was long and thin. Reverently her small plump hands removed the yellow wrapping, and then a layer of red corrugated paper, which she crunched in her fist to hear the crisp paper sound. Hubert thought, watching Gerty with food made everything taste better somehow. One by one she picked the biscuits out of their wrapping and laid them on the plate. "One for Gerty . . . one for Elsa . . . one for Hubert . . . one for Jiminee . . . one for Willy." She paused. "And another one for Gerty," she said, putting a sixth biscuit on the plate, " 'cause she's good." She looked up, grinning broadly.

Covertly they all looked at Elsa. Elsa was stern—one each was the rule—but her mouth wouldn't obey properly and, suddenly, she gave up the struggle and grinned back. Jiminee began to giggle, then Willy, then Hubert—taken with a froth of giggles and, above their noise, Gerty's crow of delight.

"Oooh, Gerty!" And they laughed the more.

"One for my black wife!" cried Willy.

"You and your black wife!"

"Two for everyone!" yelled Jiminee. And Gerty lifted the end of the packet and let all the biscuits pour out with a great whoosh. They mounted on the plate and toppled and fell off the edge and rolled across the table. The children put their heads back and bowed their heads and held their bellies and rocked and gurgled. Big rich tears rolled from their eyes.

The biscuits spun and tottered and fell. "Oh," said Elsa, "ooooh!"

Willy snatched at a biscuit rolling towards him and put it to his lips to lick the chocolate off. His mouth became a grinning chocolate smear, and the mirth gathered the children together and shook them until gradually they were exhausted.

The biscuits were passed round—one for everybody. Hubert began to eat. He looked down at his plate, watching the way the blue lines on the plate pranced and winced through the water in his eyes. If he breathed regularly and not too deeply, he wouldn't disturb that tremulous bell of laughter that hung poised somewhere in his chest.

"D-do you know this one?" asked Jiminee. "What's the d-difference between a t-tree in autumn and an aeroplane that's going to t-t-take off?"

Nobody trusted himself to answer. Already suppressed bursts of laughter surrounded Jiminee—old Jiminee with his stale riddles that everyone knew weeks ago.

"G-give up?" Jiminee enquired with triumph. "Well, a t-tree in autumn sheds its leaves and an aeroplane that's going to t-take off—c-c-c-comes out of its hangar!"

A shout of laughter burst out. "Jiminee, oh, Jiminee." Their tired stomach muscles could hardly bear it. Only Jiminee was not convulsed—what an audience! He sat admiring the laughter he had made; nobody ever laughed like that at his jokes. Nobody, nobody. He was dizzy, but calm—and he smiled steadily, without a flicker.

"Oh, Jiminee—you got it wrong again!"

"Comes out of its hangar!" The laughter blossomed and burst again.

Gerty held on to a deep breath long enough to gabble, "It doesn't come out of its hangar, silly, it leaves its shed!"

Jiminee's grin ebbed. "D-did I say it wrong?"

"It doesn't matter, Jiminee, it doesn't matter," Hubert managed to call out of the giggles that swept him.

Jiminee hesitated—for a moment he did not smile at all—but the looks the others gave him were not tormenting and the laughter did not hurt. He laughed too—embracing their happiness.

It diminished more quickly this time, and at last they were eating in a silence disturbed only by an occasional wash of giggles. Gerty grinned as she munched, cooing happily.

"Gerty's a d-dove," said Jiminee.

"I'm not a dove."

"I'm a tiger," said Willy.

"No you're not." The crumbs spilled out of Gerty's mouth. "You're a little boy."

"Don't talk with your mouth full."

Hubert listened to them. He was thinking, *this is how the holidays ought to be*, when Diana, followed by Dunstan, entered the kitchen. The little ones fell silent.

"Hello," said Elsa, "you're late. But there's still some tea left and—"

"We didn't come for tea."

Diana shook her head gently. "No, I'm afraid not."

"We came," said Dunstan, "to ask . . . someone . . . a question." He examined each of them with care and then, slowly, drew from his trouser pocket a small white leather purse. He held it up and the embroidered beads flashed. "Whose is this?"

There was a moment's silence. Then, "Don't be an idiot, Dun," Hubert said, "you know perfectly well it's Gerty's."

Dunstan smiled. "I just wanted to be sure, Hubert." He turned his glasses on the little girl. "It *is* your purse, isn't it, Gerty?"

Without a word, Gerty slid off her chair and ran round to Elsa. Elsa put her arm over the little girl's shoulder.

Dunstan raised his head, brushing away the lock of dark hair that shut out the light from his white forehead. He held the purse higher. "I smell a thief in this room." He was smiling. "Who smells like a thief?"

Hubert stood up. "You do! You got Gerty's purse."

"Give Gerty back her purse," said Willy, smiling smugly and looking round for approval. But no one else smiled.

"Willy," began Dunstan quietly, but Diana touched his arm. "Tell them, Dunstan," she said.

Slowly Dunstan lowered the purse, twisting it so the cheap mother-of-pearl beads winked in the light, and then snapped it open. "Look!" He pulled out a ten-shilling note and held it high above his head.

"Ten shillings! Now we know who the thief is, don't we?" He was grim. "Where did you get it, Gerty?"

Gerty stared at him with wide-open eyes and then hid her face against Elsa. Elsa looked down and stroked the little girl's hair. She turned her face to Dunstan with a frown. "Don't bully her, Dunstan. She's too little to—"

"Where did she get the money?" said Dunstan.

"She's too little," Elsa reiterated, "she—"

"Too little to tell, I suppose, but not too little to steal," said Dunstan sarcastically.

"How do you know she stole it?" said Hubert.

"How else would Gerty get ten bob?"

Hubert turned anxiously to Elsa.

She was still frowning. "I'll ask her in private," she said. "I'm sure she'll tell me when we're alone."

"That's right," said Hubert with relief.

"That's right, is it? Tell Elsa in private, so she can make up a pack of lies? There isn't anything *private* about stealing. She's got to be tried. We're going to give her a trial."

There was a whimper from Gerty.

"You'll be the judge, I suppose," said Hubert angrily.

"Oh, no, Hubert," Diana broke in, "Dunstan won't be the judge—none of *us* will be the judge." She smiled. "Mother will decide."

Elsa stood up; Gerty still clung to her. "I think," Elsa said, "that we should have a meeting. We haven't had one for a long time. I think this business about Gerty should be talked over in a meeting. There are other things, too, you all ought to know—"

"You and your meetings!" said Dunstan.

"Shut *up*," Hubert shouted, "other people want to talk occasionally!"

"—we ought to discuss this business about the swing in the garden. And there's another thing too. I won't—"

"Do you think meetings are really necessary now?" asked Diana gently.

Elsa drew a deep breath. "We've *always* had meetings." She looked at her golden-haired sister. "Ever since there was just you and me, we've—"

"And Mother," Diana interrupted.

"—and Mother—we've always had them. We should all know what's happening. We're brothers and sisters, aren't we? We should *all* decide, and I never heard anyone complain about that before. We never called each other names till lately. We all seem to have forgotten about counting ten. Mother always said we've got to keep up to the mark—"

"Oh, Elsa! She still does!" Diana said.

Elsa ignored the interruption. "And I don't see," she went on earnestly, "I don't see how we can keep up to the mark unless we have meetings. It's not Willy's or Gerty's fault they're so disobedient lately, it's because there's no meeting to tell them what to do. We've got to have . . . We've got to have—"

"An organization," Hubert put in.

"—an organization. We've got to abide by the rules. We can't all just do what we want because—because of what's happened. We're a family and a family's got to have meetings—there's things to decide, there's things to—"

"All right," said Dunstan, "you have your silly meetings. We're going to have a *trial* and—"

"Hush, Dunstan," Diana restrained him. "But, Elsa, we *do* have meetings. In the tabernacle. We have meetings every night and—"

"That's not the same," said Elsa.

Diana cast down her eyes and smoothed her skirt. Then she looked up. "They're only different because we have Mother there, Elsa. You're not saying you'd rather not have Mother there, are you?"

"Well—no," Elsa floundered. "But that's Mothertime you're talking about. Meetings are different. Dun thinks so—*he* said they were silly!"

"He only meant meetings without Mother were silly," Diana answered patiently.

Hubert stared at Elsa, waiting for her answer. But she had none.

"Then that's settled, isn't it?" said Diana. "Dunstan and I will go and prepare for Mothertime."

"And the trial," added Dunstan.

Diana merely smiled.

The two of them left the kitchen.

Elsa roused herself. "Tea's over," she said. "You can get down now."

"My black wife wants another biscuit," Willy announced.

"Willy!" said Hubert sharply. The little boy pouted.

"Get down now," Elsa repeated. "Jiminee, you take the little ones upstairs." She bent down and gently loosened Gerty's tight hug. "It'll be all right," she murmured.

Jiminee came round the table and put his hand into Gerty's. "Come on, Gert. We'll p-play p-piggy backs, if you like."

Gerty looked up at him. Slowly she raised her free hand and slipped her thumb into her mouth. No one had the heart to raise the usual cry, "No thumbs!"

Jiminee led her from the kitchen, Willy following behind.

Hubert and Elsa were left alone with the dirty dishes. They gazed at the desecration of the tea table. The red and yellow biscuit papers lay crumpled like discarded banners by Gerty's plate. The scrubbed table top was patched with spilled jam and splashed milk. Somebody had upset most of the sugar.

Hubert sighed and began to gather up the mugs. Without exactly knowing how, he thought, they had lost another battle.

13

The rain dripped through the cracks of the boards that covered the tabernacle. It was raining with summer persistence and already the tiny thump of isolated drops was giving way to a steady splash as the carpet gradually became waterlogged. The bright glare of the torch Dunstan held killed the rain-washed light that filtered through the boards over the doorway. The torch light reflected upwards from the pages of the book and illuminated the bottom half of Diana's face. Elsewhere the tabernacle was dark. Jungle-hot darkness, thought Hubert.

She was reading again from the Song of Solomon. Sometimes it was other places in the Old Testament, but mostly the Song. She never read about Jesus anymore.

The children sat cross-legged in the darkness and listened.

I opened to my beloved; but my beloved had withdrawn himself, and was gone: my soul failed when he spake: I sought him, but I could not find him; I called him, but he gave me no answer . . .

Hubert closed his eyes to shut out the tremulous vibrations of Diana's voice. Not to listen, in his mind's eye he surveyed the tiny chamber they were in. There was no Mothersmell, but in every other way the tabernacle was a miniature of Mother's room upstairs. The chest of drawers, its varnished top already beginning to warp and crack, took up most of the tiny space. On it were Mother's wigstand and the wig and comb, the wash basin, whose cracked edge was still unmended, and the soap dish, the broken watch and the unlit night light. To one side stood the copper jug filled with water. The only chair was Mother's basket chair in the corner, on which no one was allowed to sit. The carpet they sat

on, from Mother's room, had been carefully folded to fit the
tabernacle.

As a piece of pomegranate are thy temples within thy
locks. There are threescore queens . . .

Hubert rubbed the rainwater along his arm and massaged
the stiffness of his grazed knuckles. Soon they were raw
again with dampness, but the pain comforted him somehow
and he opened his eyes.

At last the reading stopped. Diana closed the book and
raised her head. There were tears on her face.

Then Dunstan switched off the torch, and slowly the figures
of the children emerged in the dimness.

"Does anyone want to speak to Mother?" asked Diana.

There was a long silence. Hubert turned his head and
looked at the white blob of Gerty's face. She sat on Elsa's
left, and Hubert was on Elsa's right.

"Does anyone want to speak to Mother?" Diana asked
again, without change of tone.

Hubert felt the movement as Elsa put her arm around
Gerty's shoulder.

There was no answer, and the sound of the rain seemed
especially loud.

"Gerty wants to speak." It was Dunstan. Hubert held
his breath hard, as if to escape detection.

"No she doesn't," came the frightened answer. "Gerty has
a tummy ache."

There was a faint giggle of relief. Abruptly Dunstan shone
the torch at Jiminee. Jiminee blinked and put his hand up to
his eyes. There was absolute silence in the tabernacle. The
torch went out.

Dunstan's voice came out of the dark. "Gerty has a
tummy ache."

"Gerty has a tummy ache," came the echo from Diana.

There was a pause and then in a gentle singsong came the
reply, "Mother says what has Gerty done wrong."

Hubert gripped his knee hard.

"What has Gerty done wrong?"

Gerty sniffed. "Nothink."

"Nothing?" chanted Dunstan.

"Nothing?" answered Diana.

The beam of light flashed out suddenly at Gerty.

"Think again," said Dunstan sharply. "Isn't there something you want to confess, Gerty? Isn't there? Isn't there?"

The little girl jerked away from the light and hid her head against Elsa.

"You cannot hide from Mother," said Diana gently.

"You cannot hide," said Dunstan.

"She's too little," burst out Hubert, "she doesn't understand. Let her alone, can't you?"

"She's old enough to know she's sinned," said Dunstan. "Look at her turn away in guilt."

The light shone on Elsa's hand stroking Gerty's hair.

"You stole the money, didn't you?"

Her face still hidden, Gerty almost imperceptibly shook her head.

"Oh, Mother," murmured Diana, "dear Mother."

"You stole the money from Mother's housekeeping, didn't you, Gerty?"

"You're making Mother so sad," said Diana.

"And angry," Dunstan added.

Abruptly the beam of light shifted down to the floor and picked out Gerty's white purse lying in the centre of the carpet. The shiny beads twinkled. Gerty's hand darted out to snatch.

"No!"

The hand hesitated.

"No!" The beam shot up to Gerty's face. "No!" barked Dunstan.

Gerty drew back as though hit. But she did not hide her face. "It's my purse," she whispered.

"You stole the money that's in that purse—didn't you?"

"Didn't you?" echoed Diana.

"You better own up or Mother'll be—"

"I didn't, I didn't," cried Gerty.

"Mother's waiting," Diana said.

"She didn't steal the money," Elsa broke in calmly. "It's all there. I counted it. And so did Hu—didn't you, Hu?"

"Yes."

The light wavered to Elsa's face. "But," said Dunstan uncertainly, "you must have made a mistake. There must be ten bob gone."

"Well, there isn't, so that's that. And it's no good accusing me of being a liar, Dunstan Hook. You're making a fuss about nothing—just because you choose to see wickedness in every corner." A sigh came from the children—a release of fear-pent breath. "I'm sick and tired of you trying to boss everybody about," she went on. "We're all fed up with it, come to that. Why don't you just pipe down for a change?"

"Elsa," Diana's voice quivered, "how could you be so unkind?"

"It's not unkind, it's true!"

"You've forgotten Mother," Diana softly accused.

Elsa flushed. "I have not forgotten Mother—what's Mother got to do with this? Mother's—"

A warning grip from Hubert stopped her in mid-sentence. She took a deep breath. "That isn't the point. The point is—"

"What's the point?" said Dunstan.

"The point is—the point is Gerty didn't take the money, so —will you stop shining the torch in my face?"

"The point is," Dunstan said quietly, without shifting the torch, "where *did* Gerty get the money?"

"She—she probably found it," Elsa's voice carried a hint of anxiety. "What's wrong with that?"

The beam swung to Gerty. "Did you find it, Gerty?"

The little girl stared unblinkingly into the light.

Hubert said abruptly, "Why don't you mind your own business, Dun? She didn't steal it—so what does it matter where she got it from?"

"It's not *my* business, Hubert," Dunstan replied. "It's Mother's business. Who says she didn't steal it? You haven't got much of a memory, have you, Hu? Didn't Gerty steal your silver threepenny bit? Don't you remember that? Didn't she steal Diana's special hanky that Mother gave her? Don't you remember that? Gerty's a little thief. There's lots of other places she could have stolen ten shillings from—not just the housekeeping." He turned on Gerty. "Aren't there, Gerty?" he said fiercely.

"It's mine," Gerty whispered sullenly.

"How did you get it then?"

"I think," said Elsa, "I think you better tell, Gerty."

Gerty turned her face up to Elsa, and gave her a long solemn stare. "It was a present," she said at last.

The children were silent with surprise.

"A present?" said Dunstan disbelievingly. "You expect Mother to believe that?"

"It was a present, it was!"

"Who from, then?"

"Who did you get it from, Gerty?" said Diana.

"Yes, who from?"

Suddenly Dunstan and Diana turned the question into a chant—"Who from? Who from? Who from?"

Willy's high-pitched voice joined in, and then, despite himself, Hubert found the words in his own mouth.

Gerty's obstinacy slowly dissolved at the drumming words. "Who from? Who from?" Her plump face reddened and she sobbed. She pushed away Elsa's attempt to comfort her.

"Who from? Who from? Who from?"

"Join in, Jiminee," Dunstan commanded, flashing the torch at him.

Jiminee hesitated. "B-but I know who f-from."

"What?" Dunstan's face thrust forward and the torch reflected dazzlingly in his glasses. "Shut up, children. Who gave her the money?"

Gerty's sobs grew louder.

"Come on, Jiminee—out with it!"

Jiminee shifted his eyes away from the light. "I p-promised I wouldn't t-t-tell," he muttered.

Diana spoke gently. "Mother wants to know, Jiminee."

"You don't want Mother to be angry with you too, do you?" said Dunstan.

"N-no . . ."

"Tell us then."

"Well . . ." Jiminee's smile ebbed and flowed uneasily.

"Come on!"

"Well—it was the g-g-g-"

Gerty's sobs rose high. "Sneak!" she wailed. "Sneak—you promised!"

"Don't pay any attention, Jiminee," said Dunstan quickly. "Tell us—tell Mother."

Jiminee's shoulders began to quiver.

"Sneak!" wailed Gerty again in her last rage of despair—and then her weeping choked her.

"Mother wants to know, Jiminee," said Diana.

Jiminee stared straight at the light. He wasn't smiling anymore. He pressed his lips tightly together.

"Come on, Jiminee."

"Tell us."

His breath burst and, through a rush of tears and stammers, he told them. "It was the g-g-g-garage m-man."

The light hovered uncertainly and then settled back on Jiminee. "When did he give it her?"

"Last week."

"Did you see him give Gert the money?"

"Yes . . . I mean n-n-no." Jiminee's sobs came in hiccups. "She had it when she come out. I know 'cause she showed it to m-m-me. B-but I didn't really see him g-g-give her the m-m-money."

"If you were there, why didn't you see it?"

"Well, you see, I stayed in the f-front. The g-garage man said they wouldn't be long—him and G-Gerty. He said—he'd t-take me for a ride in Halby's D-Daimler if I didn't tell." Jiminee put his head down and clasped his knees as if to stop the hiccups from shaking him to pieces.

The beam of the torch swung slowly away from him and came to rest on Gerty's tear-bruised face.

"Why did the garage man give you the ten bob, Gerty?" Dunstan asked quietly.

Gerty did not stir. She had stopped crying, but her eyes, afraid and watching, glistened with tears.

"He took you in the back room, didn't he?" Dunstan coaxed. "We know he did, Gerty—Jiminee just said so. You might as well admit it. He took you into the back room by yourself, didn't he?"

"Yes." Gerty's whisper was as small as the rustle of an autumn leaf.

Dunstan cut off the light. At once the darkness seemed physically to touch them. The mild dry sobs of Jiminee ceased and in the sudden silence they heard the reluctant drip of the last of the raindrops outside.

"Ah!" It was hard to know who made the noise—soft and gentle, it made Hubert shiver for a second in the heat of the tabernacle.

"Ah!" Dunstan. He paused. "What did you do in the back room, Gerty?" His voice was low-toned—stealthy.

There was no answer.

Sitting straight up on his patch of damp carpet, Hubert felt the blood beat on each side of his forehead. His fingers found the sore place on his knuckles. He dug his nails in and pressed hard.

"What did you do in the back room, Gerty?"

Hubert shut his eyes tight. The stars moved dashingly behind his eyelids, slowed, merged, separated and were still. They were bright marks on the dark surface—scars on a polished floor board.

"Stop it!" he cried. "Stop it!"

"But, Hu," murmured Diana, "Mother wants to—"

"Stop it! stop it! stop it!"

"Yes—why don't you leave her alone?" It was Elsa.

"Leave her alone?" Dunstan was incredulous. He waited a moment, and then the light flashed out at Gerty. "Did the garage man leave you alone, Gerty?"

The little girl gasped.

"Did he leave you alone?"

"You must answer," said Diana.

"He didn't—did he?"

Mouth open, Gerty drew a long trembling breath.

"He touched you—didn't he? Didn't he, Gerty? Didn't he?"

"Oh shut *up,* shut *up!*" Hubert wrenched his coiled legs apart and stood up—his head met the boarded roof with a crack. Half-stunned, he fell back.

"You all right, Hu?" whispered Elsa.

He touched the top of his head and it was wet. Water? Blood? All he was aware of was the agony of pins and needles in his legs. The stars were whirling and exploding in his knees and thighs. "Oh," he said, "oh—you don't understand!"

"I understand!" said Dunstan fiercely. "Diana and I understand—even if you don't. We know Gerty was *vulgar!*"

"I wasn't vulgar—I wasn't!" Gerty wailed.

"Prove it!"

"I wasn't, I wasn't."

"Why did he give you the ten bob then? It was a reward, wasn't it? What was it a reward for? What did he make you do? Answer, Gerty, answer!"

"I . . ."

"What did you do?"

Gertie began to cry with choking sobs.

"What did you do?"

"It . . . was only . . . pretend," she heaved the words between her sobs. "He said . . . to pretend he was . . . my daddy."

"What did you *do?*"

"I—I took off my clothes."

The whispered words fell. There was a stillness as if everyone had ceased to breathe. The beam of light travelled slowly down Gerty's body, onto the carpet, and settled on the white purse.

Then Dunstan uttered one word. "Harlot!"

"Oh, Mother," mourned Diana, "Mother!"

"Harlot!" Dunstan burst out into passion. "Vulgar beast! Whore of Babylon! Filthy little guttersnipe!"

"How could she be so wicked?" cried Diana.

There was a moment of silence, broken only by Gerty's fearful sniffle. Dunstan cut off the light.

"She must be punished," he said.

There was a long pause. Outside it had begun to rain once more.

"Punishment is pain." Diana's voice had gone into a singsong chant. Hubert gripped his knee.

"Punishment is pain," Dunstan repeated.

"Pain is punishment."

"Pain is punishment."

Hubert gripped tighter. "Mother doesn't say that," he whispered out of a dry mouth.

The light flicked on full in his face.

"Pain is punishment," came Dunstan's voice hard and flat.

"Punishment is pain."

Hubert tried to unlock his cramped knees, but Elsa's hand slipped into his and pressed him down firmly. "Mother . . ." he tried again, but his voice wasn't working properly.

Dunstan shone the torch steadily.

"Punishment is pain," chanted Diana. "Gerty is wicked. Mother is hurt."

"Gerty must pay."

"She must pay for her wickedness," Diana's voice rose high.

"She must pay with pain."

"She must pay with pain," chanted Diana, "for the pain she has given to you, Mother."

Gerty gave a single whimper of fear.

"What shall be her punishment?" cried Dunstan.

Diana did not answer at once. Instead, there came an odd gurgling sound from where she sat. Hubert stared hard into the darkness, but the bright eye of the torch protected her from all sight. In his stomach he grew suddenly afraid. The gurgling rose to a higher note as though his sister was being strangled.

And then, it seemed to be from the corner where no one was, the basket chair creaked. It was the creak of somebody

sitting down. From the same corner there was a little yelp—
and silence.

The torch went out; but the image of light still blocked
the children's sight.

Then it came out of nowhere—tiny and high-pitched, the
tinkle of an ancient gramophone: "Take away the comb."

There was a rasping breath. "Take away the comb and
cut off her hair. Cut off her hair and destroy her vainglory.
She must be punished."

The voice wheezed. Then it started again: "Punish her
with silence. Leave her alone. None must be touched by
her vainglory and her deceit. Punish her." It paused, and
then, in pain of a great tiredness, it went on. "Do not speak
to her, nor touch her—until her hair is grown long again
and she has repented of her wickedness. Punish the sinful
daughter . . . daughter. Daughter of sin."

The voice deepened and faded, as if running down at last,
"of sin . . . sin . . . sin."

No one spoke or thought of speaking. Outside the wind
blew a gust of rain against the roof. Hubert listened to it,
trying to forget the voice that had not come from Diana
nor from any one of them sitting still in the tabernacle of
fear.

After a while Dunstan spoke. "Thank you, Mother."

It began to rain harder.

14

Dunstan watched from the stairs as Elsa gave them a last
inspection. "Turn them over, Jiminee," she said. She lifted
his hands and looked at the fingernails. "Passed." Jiminee,
Hubert, Diana, Willy—they all passed.

"Well, I think we're ready now," she said, and she gave
Willy's head a light pat. "Come on, children."

As they walked down the path and out onto the street,

Hubert caught up with his eldest sister. "What d'you think he asked us for?" he said.

"Who?" Elsa asked curtly.

"Old Halby—why'd he ask us to tea?"

"I expect he's trying to be kind."

Hubert was troubled. "You don't think he suspects anything?"

Elsa glanced down at him as they climbed the steps to the Halberts' front door. "Don't be a silly," she said. She reached up and pulled the bell. Inside the bells rang—one, two, three-four—each on a different note.

"Chimes," Hubert announced.

Willy smiled. "Do it again, Elsa."

Elsa shook her head. "It's not polite to ring more than once."

Suddenly Hubert thought of Flight-Sergeant Millard—he'd rung more than once. He'd rung again and again and again. *He* wasn't polite, but then, the phrase fell into Hubert's mind, he wasn't a gentleman. He started to speak when the door was opened by a small mouse-brown woman in an apron and cap.

"Hello," she said, "you must be the Hook children. Will you come in?" She held the door wide and one by one the children stepped inside. It was cool in the house and dark when the maid shut the door. "My name's Joan," she said. "Mr. and Mrs. Halbert are expecting you in the garden. Would you like to wash your hands before I show you the way?"

"No, thank you," Elsa said.

"We're all quite clean, thank you very much," added Willy.

Joan grinned. "Well, you look lovely." She put out her hand to touch Willy, but he ducked quickly. Joan's grin broadened. "Would you follow me, please," she said, suddenly solemn again.

Hubert waited for the others to go first. He peeped quickly into the drawing room as they went past. It was a beautiful house. The carpet in the hall was rich and so thick he couldn't hear anything, even when he surreptitiously stamped. And the floor boards were bright as mirrors. As they went by the window at the end of the hall, he reached out to touch the heavy curtains—they were dark red, with a leaf pattern in gold thread, but so fine that he wouldn't have noticed it unless he'd looked closely. As they stepped out onto the terrace, he wondered what the point was of having something beautiful that you couldn't even see.

Mr. Halbert rose slowly from his deck chair, but Mrs. Halbert was already darting forward to greet them. "How nice of you to come. Dear me now, you must introduce yourselves—we've never been properly introduced, have we?" She drew in a quick, gasping breath—Hubert noticed at once that she never seemed to breathe out—only in. He wondered what she did with all that air. "I'm Lily Halbert— Mrs. Halbert, that is—and this is my husband—Mr. Halbert."

Mr. Halbert nodded. "Samuel," he said—as if he liked to have everything straight. "You're Hubert, aren't you? I know you—you're the chap who opened the door to me yesterday."

Mrs. Halbert laughed on an indrawn breath. "And I know Elsie, don't I, Elsie?"

"Elsa."

"Elsa—oh, dear, I am sorry. Well now, Elsa, you must introduce us to the others. Now you're the pretty one, so you must be—"

Hubert caught the frown that passed quickly across old Halby's forehead. He made up his mind to try and sit next to Halby at tea. He was suddenly quite sure that Mrs. Halbert had nasty-smelling breath. Lily—what a silly name. Silly Lily. But, more than that, he had to find out if Halby suspected anything.

The introductions were over, but Mrs. Halbert was hurrying on, "—waited so long for this moment. And now it's come. It does seem so silly for us to have been neighbours all this time and never to have said two words to each other—well, except 'good morning'—I suppose that's two words." She breathed in a giggle that sounded as though she was about to burst into tears. Elsa was trying to speak, but Mrs. Halbert went straight on, "How sweet of your mother to let you come. But I thought perhaps she might be a teeny-weeny bit relieved to have an hour or two of peace and quiet on a hot Sunday afternoon?" She arched her eyebrows. "Not that, of course—oh, dear, no—we didn't want you to come. Oh, we're delighted, aren't we, Sammy?"

Halby made an indistinct noise in his throat. "Why don't we all sit down and get on with the real business—tea, eh?"

"I'm sorry," Elsa began almost desperately.

"What is it, my dear?" Mrs. Halbert looked suddenly pained.

"I'm sorry the others couldn't come. Only Gerty isn't feeling very well, and Dunstan stayed to look after her."

Mrs. Halbert's pain was somewhat less. "I hope it's nothing serious?"

"No, just a tummy ache."

"Oh, well then—we must remember to send her a piece of cake, as a token of good will, mustn't we? And Dunstan too, of course. How sweet of him to stay to look after her. What little dears children are. Now, you will remind me, won't you?"

Elsa nodded. "Yes, thank you, Mrs. Halbert."

"Well then—" Mrs. Halbert drew in a big breath and was off again.

Mr. Halbert led them over to the large teak table in the middle of the garden. It was covered with a white cloth on which were endless arrays of dishes with silver hats over them. Mr. Halbert sat at the end of the table, with Hubert on one side of him and Jiminee on the other.

Hubert found his hands sticky with the sweat of apprehension. Halby didn't seem very talkative, so he realised that conversation was up to him. "Your garden is much nicer than ours," he said abruptly.

Halby glanced at him, then held out a plate. "Have a sandwich—sardine, I think." He took one himself and pushed the plate towards Jiminee. "Oh, I don't know about that. It's neater, perhaps. But sometimes I think it looks a bit handmade." He stared at the neatly trimmed hedges and the perfectly aligned rose bushes. "A garden's a place to have fun in. You have fun in your garden by—well, messing it up. I mean, you wouldn't get any kick out of it if you have to keep worrying about keeping off the borders and that sort of thing, would you? No. Well, my sort of garden—that's different. I get my fun out of keeping it all in order, worrying about the blight and the frost and the birds eating the sweet peas. I like order, that's what it boils down to—and you don't. There's no reason why you should—plenty of time for that later."

Hubert finished his sandwich. "I like order, too," he said. Halby sounded all right to him.

"Help yourself to the sandwiches," said Halby. "Those over there are chicken and ham." He passed the plate. "Take a couple. Besides," he said, "I'm not sure I agree with you anyway. I've got nothing as exciting in my garden as that little house you've built in yours."

Hubert's sandwich dried up in his throat. So Halby did suspect, after all. He waited for the next inevitable question.

But it didn't come. Halby ate his sandwich very slowly, as if he didn't care for it much, then he said, "Tell me what you like to keep in order."

"Things," said Hubert, accepting a cup of tea from Diana on his left. "I mean—things like the wireless. I mended the wireless when it broke and I wanted to have a shot at Mother's watch that broke, but . . ."

"But?"

"Well, I . . ."

Halby took a sip of tea. "Too difficult, I expect. Watch repairing is a specialised business. Needs years of training."

At the other end of the table, Elsa and Willy were being subjected to Mrs. Halbert's rush of solicitude. Hubert saw Willy wasn't paying any attention. He was just eating. How Gerty would have enjoyed herself. Seven different sorts of sandwiches and scones too.

Mr. Halbert turned towards Jiminee. "Jiminee," he said, "that's a curious name—how did you come by that?"

Jiminee blushed scarlet.

"It was when he was small," said Hubert. "He couldn't say his name properly—Mother used to call him Jimmy. All he could say was 'Jim-im-im-eee,' so we called him 'Jiminee.' Jiminee stutters, you see."

"What a nuisance." Halby stroked his polished forehead. "Still, you mustn't let it stop you talking, you know." He smiled at Jiminee—and Jiminee's face broke into hurried and convulsive grins.

"Oh, he doesn't," Hubert said quickly. "He talks a lot really—don't you, Jiminee?"

Jiminee nodded. He opened his mouth to speak. For a long time it seemed as if nothing would come out, and then it came in a rush. "At home," he said, earnestly leaning forward, "we drink out of m-mugs!"

Halby looked grave. "There's a lot to be said for that. I often wonder what the use of saucers is. After all, we don't drink wine out of glasses with saucers—or beer, for that matter. And, looking at it logically, I should have thought one was much more apt to spill wine than tea. Odd, really—just one of those conventions, I suppose." He gazed thoughtfully at his cup of tea.

"I think saucers are very nice," Hurbert said, "for a change."

Halby nodded. He was watching his wife at the other end of the table. He's always looking at her, Hubert thought, and she isn't much to look at really.

It was later, after Mr. Halbert had made several unsuccessful efforts to get Diana to talk, that Hubert plucked up courage to ask about the car.

"Interested in cars, are you?" said Mr. Halbert. "Tell you the truth, I don't use it much. Try to give it a run at the weekends—but there's not much point in having a car in town, you know."

"Have you driven your car this weekend?" Hubert enquired.

"No." Halby rubbed the top of his head reflectively. "I say, would you like to go for a drive after tea?"

Hubert grinned. "Yes, please."

"You too, eh?" said Halby, glancing at Jiminee, who nodded his head vigorously.

"Well, we'll all go." Halby got to his feet.

"Where are you going, dear?" called Mrs. Halbert from the other end of the table.

"I thought we'd all go for a drive after tea. I'm just going to have the car brought round."

"But there won't be anyone at the garage on a Sunday afternoon."

"George'll be there. You'll come, won't you, my dear?"

Hubert hoped she'd say no.

She took a quick sip of tea. "A drive on Sunday afternoon? There'll be so much traffic, Sammy. I thought we'd all have a nice talk after tea. Wouldn't," brightly bleak, she smiled at them, "wouldn't you like that, children?"

Watching Halby, Hubert caught the momentary frown that wrinkled his placid, gleaming head. "I think they'd probably rather it was a drive—just a little jaunt round the park."

"Oh, well," Mrs. Halbert murmured. "I don't think I'll come, dear, if you don't mind."

"Very well." Halby turned and walked towards the house. "I shan't be a moment," he called over his shoulder.

Mrs. Halbert smiled. "Won't you have another sandwich, Willy?"

Willy shook his head. "Full up to dolly's wax," he said.

She burst into laughter, "Oh, it's such ages since I've heard anyone say that. Why, that's what we used to say when I was a little girl. What a sweet little boy you are." She sighed. "I remember a very proper little girl we had to tea once when I was small. Oh, very proper she was. When my mother asked her if she wanted anything more to eat, she said, 'No, thank you very much, I am replete—when I'm at home I stay stuffed!'" The children smiled politely.

Elsa said, "That's what our youngest sister, Gerty, always says—'stuffed.'"

"Does she? How charming—does she?" Mrs. Halbert's smile gleamed on and off like a faulty torch. Just like Jiminee's, thought Hubert. "Well, if you've all had enough, I expect you'd like to get down and run about in the garden."

They stood about on the smooth peninsulas of lawn, waiting for Mr. Halbert to return. Joan was clearing away—every so often snatching a quick glance at the children. Mrs. Halbert talked.

Suddenly Willy lay down on the lawn and closed his eyes. "Willy," whispered Hubert, "get up at once." But Mrs. Halbert had already noticed.

"Oh, dear, oh, dear. You're not feeling sick, Willy? Is he ill—oh, I do hope not. Perhaps that cake. Willy?" She bent down.

"I'm a tiger and I'm asleep," Willy announced.

"Oh, what a funny little boy," Mrs. Halbert beamed.

"Willy, get up!" said Elsa.

"I'm a tiger, and I'm asleep," Willy said sternly.

"Oh, what an idea!" said Mrs. Halbert.

Hubert said, "He thinks he's playing the jungle game."

"I'm the tiger, the tiger, the tiger," chanted Willy.

"Get up, Willy," Elsa repeated.

"The 'jungle game'!" Mrs. Halbert pealed with giggles. "But there's no jungle here!"

"Yes there is." Willy opened his eyes briefly. "It's all jungle."

Hubert decided that Mrs. Halbert was an ass.

"Willy, if you don't get up at once, you'll go straight to bed when we get home."

"Tigers don't go to bed." Willy growled softly.

"Tigers don't go for drives in cars," said Mr. Halbert from behind their back. He was smiling. "Come along, children, the car's outside."

Willy bounced to his feet at once.

They followed Mr. Halbert through the house. Hubert kept anxiously close to him.

"Children!" Elsa said warningly as Halby opened the front door. Hubert turned as Elsa stepped towards Mrs. Halbert. "Thank you very much for a lovely tea," she said. "We enjoyed it very much."

Mrs. Halbert fluttered a hand up to her mouth. "Oh, but you're coming back, aren't you? You must come back after your drive!"

"Thank you very much, but I think it will be Willy's bedtime by then."

"Oh—oh," Mrs. Halbert sucked in the air. For a moment Hubert thought she was going to cry. "But—but you will come just to collect some cake for your little brother and sister who didn't come, won't you? We mustn't forget them, must we?"

Elsa considered. "All right," she said, "but we really can't stay long."

"How charming—how sweet—what delightful children you are." She came to the front door to see them off, still chanting their praises.

Hubert stood back on the pavement to admire the black magnificence of the Daimler. It made Mr. Halbert seem small by comparison—it even made the huge figure of George, the garage hand, seem small.

"Thank you, George," Mr. Halbert said, "I'll put it in myself—no need for you to wait."

George nodded and blinked. "Thank you, Mr. Halbert," he said as he opened the door.

Mr. Halbert turned to the children. "I think we better pack you in first. Now who'd like to go in front?"

"Me," said Willy.

"Willy's never been in a car before," Hubert said.

"Well, then, it'll be Willy and—let's see—you better come in the front too, Hubert. After all, the trip was your idea." Mr. Halbert smiled. "Elsa and Jiminee and—Diana, isn't it?—you climb in the back."

"I don't want to go, thank you very much."

"What?" Halby was already lifting Willy into the front seat and he looked back with surprise.

Diana was straight and white. She repeated what she'd said. "I don't want to go, thank you very much." The dreamy look was gone from her eyes.

Mr. Halbert set Willy firmly in the front seat and turned to Diana with a puzzled look. "Why don't you want to go?"

"I would prefer to go home, please."

She was always like that, thought Hubert. People never noticed Diana at first much, even though they all said she was so pretty. But she just wouldn't open her mouth. And then suddenly she'd say something that surprised everyone— and then they didn't forget her anymore. They just looked puzzled, like old Halby.

"I'd prefer to go home, please, if you don't mind."

"Don't be so rude, Dinah," Elsa whispered fiercely at her.

Mr. Halbert frowned. "Perhaps you want to wash your hands?"

"No. I would just like to go home, if you don't mind."

"Very well," Mr. Halbert nodded curtly. His face was red and his voice was full of inexplicable grownup anger. Hubert felt the disappointment in his chest—somehow he'd thought that Halby was going to be different.

"Thank you for a lovely time." Diana paused. She turned her eyes and looked at the garage man, still standing with his hand on the door of the car. He looked back at her, and then he began to blink rapidly. She kept staring at him even after he looked away. He wiped the palm of his left hand slowly against the thigh of his khaki dungarees.

"Goodbye," Diana said.

They watched her walk stiffly back to number 38.

"Well, let's get going," said Mr. Halbert, not sounding very pleased.

Hubert tried his best to talk during the drive, but Mr. Halbert was not in a talking mood. But it didn't matter really. The car was better than anything Hubert had ever dreamed. They turned on to the main road at the bottom of Ipswich Terrace and in a few minutes were in the park. It seemed as if they were going very very slowly, yet the big Daimler did all the passing and was never passed itself.

"Can it really do ninety?" asked Hubert, looking at the speedometer.

"Not in the park," said Mr. Halbert.

"But if you really wanted to, I expect you could, couldn't you?"

"I expect so."

The grass was greener than usual for August. With only a few days of shade-killing brightness, the summer had been one of almost tropical heat—rain, steaming suffocation, and more rain, but very little sun. But today the park was happy with sunlight. Every green chair was occupied and the bell of the ice-cream man tinkled. Already the car had carried the children far beyond the limits of their walks with Mother. Hubert tried to turn his mind away from those days before Mother was sick and before her edict that they "must never go in the park without a grownup" had become an iron law that only permitted them the trip to school or to do the weekly shopping.

Mr. Halbert slowed the car and turned into one of the smaller car parks. "What about an ice?" he asked. "There's a Walls' man over there."

"Oh, but we had such a big tea," Elsa said doubtfully.

"Well, I don't suppose an ice would do you any harm." Mr. Halbert seemed preoccupied.

They ate them sitting on the running board of the car. The smell of the ice and the hot rubbery smell of the running board and the dust and the grass and the petrol filled Hubert with delight, so he wanted to skip and dance and yell. But somehow, he didn't—perhaps it was the presence of Mr. Halbert that stopped him. But that wasn't really the reason; instinctively he knew that if he showed his joy, something bad would happen. You have to pretend, he thought, that you're not really enjoying yourself too much, or perhaps you won't. And suddenly he didn't want to go home anymore. He wanted to stay in the park forever, sitting on the running board, eating ice cream, and with Mr. Halbert standing there jingling the change in his pocket.

Maybe Mr. Halbert didn't want to go home either, for he drove back more slowly and didn't seem to mind if other cars overtook them. Hubert half closed his eyes so that the trees flowed past like a green river. He opened them as they turned into Ipswich Terrace, just in time to see the ladies standing at the end of the road.

"Mr. Halbert?"

"Yes?"

"What are those ladies standing there for?"

Mr. Halbert hesitated. "Women of ill repute," he said in a tone that stopped Hubert asking any further.

He parked the car outside number 40 and led the children into the house. "Well," he said as Mrs. Halbert greeted them, "I hope you liked the drive."

"Oh, yes!"

"It was super!"

"Wizard!"

"And thank you very much for the ices."

"Oh, Sammy, you didn't give them ices too?"

Halby nodded, as if in answer to quite a different question. Then he turned and went down the hall into the room that overlooked the garden. He closed the door and drew a deep-blue velvet curtain over it to shut out the noise. Then he went to the large desk by the window. He sat down and took a cigarette from the silver box. He lit it with a mono-grammed leather cigarette lighter. He replaced the lighter carefully so that it aligned with the cigarette box and the letter scales and the ink stand. He looked out into the garden. The tea things and the white cloth had been removed from the teak table. Joan had even remembered to shift the table itself a little, so that the grass under its feet would not wither and die.

Slowly Mr. Halbert blew a long stream of cigarette smoke towards the window.

15

As the others went on into the house, he closed the gate of number 38. He took a last look at the Daimler and sighed.

"Hu." Jiminee had come back to stand beside him. "Hu, it was *him*—the g-garage man."

"Yes, I know." The sun shone on the car and Hubert wondered whether Halby would ever take them for another drive in it.

"It's super, isn't it."

He didn't answer. Once, long ago, he remembered Mother telling them, "Never take lifts from strangers." If he remembered it, Dunstan would too. But was Mr. Halbert really a stranger? He was sure Mother didn't mean people like Halby—but, well, how could you explain that to . . . to the voices in the tabernacle?

"Hu, it was very nice of him to take us out, wasn't it?"

Hubert nodded.

"It would be wizard if he was our d-dad."

Hubert clutched the two pieces of cake wrapped in grease-proof paper closer to his chest. "Well," he said, "he isn't." He clicked the gate finally shut, and walked up the path.

Jiminee followed him. "But if he was—it would b-be super, wouldn't it?"

He gripped Gerty's cake hard and his fingers dug through the paper to the moist crumbly surface. "Oh, shut up, Jiminee."

Elsa was arguing with Willy in the hall. "You just go straight to bed, Willy."

"I want my supper first." Willy was in his stubborn mood.

"You've just had an extra big tea and an ice too. Now you do as I say."

As Hubert watched, Dunstan and Diana came through the swing door that led down to the kitchen.

Dunstan said, "You're late for Mothertime."

"There's no Mothertime for Willy tonight," Elsa snapped.

"There's always Mothertime for everybody. No exceptions. Except anyone who has been very wicked."

"Don't want Mothertime," said Willy. "I want supper."

"Willy dear," Diana murmured, "how do you know Mother doesn't want to speak to you?"

"I don't care if she wants to speak to me. I want supper."

"Willy," Dunstan warned, "remember what happened to Gerty."

"Come along, Willy," Diana said.

"I won't." He stood with his fists raised ready to punch anyone who came near. "I hate Mother—she's cruel. I want supper." The enormity of his words was beyond him.

They were all silent, watching Willy. Even Elsa could find nothing to say. Hubert half expected the little boy to vanish, or fall down dead. But only the clock ticked in the hall.

Dunstan pointed one finger at Willy—a finger that trembled. "Blasphemer," he said.

"Blasphemer!"

Dunstan took a step forward, but Hubert knew he wouldn't risk touching Willy. Willy went mad when he was in a rage like this—he'd bite and kick and hit, and he was strong. It would take three of them to handle him.

Elsa said, "I think you'd better go to bed now, Willy— that's enough for one day." Hubert was surprised at her voice—it didn't sound like Elsa; it sounded kind of . . . *tired*, more like Diana.

"Yes," said Dunstan. "Yes—you're much too wicked to come to Mothertime now. But tomorrow you'll come all right. Tomorrow, Willy."

Suddenly Willy darted towards Dunstan, but turned just before he reached him and rushed at the stairs. He stumbled once before he reached the corner, then he was out of sight. The children stood with their heads raised, listening to the dwindling scamper of Willy's feet. At last, at the top of the house they heard the door of his room slam. He would bolt it and stay in there and cry alone, Hubert knew, as he always did.

Dunstan brushed the lank hair from his eyes. "Mother will punish," he murmured. He coughed. "Now," he said, "we will have Mothertime."

Hubert hesitated. "Can I go upstairs first?" As he pressed the two pieces of cake tight to his chest, he realised that this was the first time he'd ever asked Dun permission for anything.

There was a pause while Dunstan, his head set a little to one side, observed his brother. "Yes," he said in a soft tone, "yes, you may, but hurry up. Mother is waiting."

Hubert moved towards the stairs.

"Hubert—what's that you have in your hand?"

He turned back. "Oh, nothing," he muttered.

"Nothing?" said Dunstan. "Let's see."

Hubert glanced up the stairs. If he ran, he could be in Gerty's room with the door locked before they could catch him. He shook his head. *Don't be barmy*, he thought. He looked at Dunstan and extended his hand with the grease-proof paper parcel.

"Funny-looking sort of nothing," said Dunstan.

Hubert stared. There was something unfamiliar about the tone of Dunstan's voice. "It's cake," he said.

"But I thought you said it was nothing?"

"Well, I—I made a mistake." He felt a fool—and suddenly he knew that was what Dunstan intended. That was what Dunstan enjoyed. He drew breath. "I—I shan't be long."

There was nothing to be afraid of. He wouldn't *talk* to Gerty—just give her the cake and come straight down again. He wondered that Dunstan had not warned him against breaking Gerty's Coventry. Dunstan loved to warn.

He pushed open the door of Gerty's room. She lay curled, knees up and face buried down into the pillow. The sheet she wrapped about her head had slipped to reveal the white scalp and the chopped tufts of hair. She had not struggled against the operation of the kitchen scissors. She'd sat with head bowed while Diana did her work. But now

Gerty would start away in fright if anyone tried to touch her head.

He sat down gently on the bed. All at once, it didn't matter that he was going to break the vow of silence and speak to her, that he was going to bring her back from Coventry.

"Gert?"

Her head moved a little.

"How do you feel, Gert?"

Her nose was stuffed and she breathed through her mouth. She'd been crying again. She turned a little more and looked at him without interest.

"I've brought you some cake." He began to unwrap the greaseproof paper. The cake was all different colours—swirls of green and pink and yellow and chocolate. The slices were squashed where he had held them against his chest. "It's called Russian cake," he said.

Slowly Gerty looked down at the cake and for a moment Hubert had a wild hope that her eager hand would reach out from under the sheet and seize a piece. But this wasn't the old Gerty. She just stared at it for a long time, then turned her head away.

"It's lovely. Really it is, Gert. You'd love it." He waited for her to look at him again, but she wouldn't. "I wish you could have been there. There were seven different kinds of sandwiches. Chicken and sardine and cucumber and marmite. There was scones and jam too, and lovely thick cream to go on top. It's a shame you couldn't come. But you'll be better soon."

Gerty didn't move. Hubert broke off a corner of cake and held it out to her. Imperceptibly she shook her head. "It's good," he said. "It's called Russian cake." He put the piece in his mouth and chewed. It didn't taste the same as it had at tea.

He laid his hand on Gerty's forehead. It was terribly hot. "You'll feel better soon," he murmured. He knew she was very ill.

He turned abruptly to the doorway. Willy stood there looking at them. "What you want?" said Hubert.

Willy raised his arm and pointed a solemn finger at Gerty. "She screamed in the night," he said. "She screamed and screamed. Small screams so nobody could hear. But I heard," he said impressively. He lowered his arm. "It must have hurt an awful lot."

"You should have woken Elsa," said Hubert.

Willy ignored him. "She wanted a drink of water. I heard her. She kept asking for it."

"Well, why didn't you get her some?" asked Hubert irritably.

Willy looked disdainful. "She's on Coventry."

"You . . ." Hubert clenched his fist and counted ten rapidly. It was only Willy. Willy was too young. Willy didn't understand. He took a deep breath. "Go away, Willy."

"No." The little boy shook his head.

After a moment, Hubert shrugged and turned back to Gerty. Suddenly he didn't care if Willy sneaked on him to Dunstan.

"Gerty," he moved his hand softly over her hunched body, "how's the pain now?"

The little girl pushed her head deeper into the pillow. Her lips moved. "It hurts," she whispered. And when he touched her stomach, she winced.

They ought to get a doctor. This time they really ought. Elsa would agree and then he'd run down the road and get Dr. Meadows and everything would be all right. He frowned —*if* Elsa would agree. She didn't . . . she wasn't . . . like the old Elsa anymore—not quite. He folded the two slices of cake back into the paper. "Nothing's changed"— that's what Elsa had said. Well, it had. She had. And Dunstan and Diana. And now Gerty. Just me, thought Hubert, just me and Jiminee are the only ones that have stayed the same.

He stood up, looking down at Gerty and smoothing the paper over the cake. He glanced at Willy. "Do you want a piece?"

Willy nodded and came forward. He held out his hand.

"I want two pieces," he said as Hubert started to unwrap the parcel. "One for my black wife."

Hubert frowned. The other piece was Dunstan's really, but he wouldn't want it. He gave Willy the cake.

Willy smiled. "Now I won't tell Dun I saw you talking to Gerty," he said.

"You little . . ." He could think of nothing to say in his fury. And then it was too late, for Willy had run back to his own room and slammed the door.

Gerty had completely covered her head with the sheet now. She'd be all right when Doctor Meadows came. "Cheer up, Gert," he said brightly to the sheeted form on the bed, "you'll feel better soon."

At the door, he suddenly remembered. He turned, smiling. "I nearly forgot," he said. "I nearly forgot to tell you. Old Halby took us for a drive in his Daimler."

There was no response.

"Old Halby," he tried again, "took us for a drive all round the park." Suddenly he felt the tears in his eyes. "And he gave us ices and—and things."

The small figure on the bed made no movement.

"It was wizard," he said.

16

The house was quiet. Down in the kitchen, with two doors separating it from the upstairs, it always was quiet—and cool.

Hubert dozed in the only comfortable chair—a large wooden frame with an adjustable back and two brown corduroy cushions. His leg was cocked over the arm of the chair, and the bite of the edge into the flesh below his knee was comforting.

Sitting in "Mrs. Stork's corner," he didn't think about

upstairs. Or outside. Even with the door open, the kitchen coolness kept the hot outside at bay.

The red second hand moved round and round. Hubert shut his eyes. When he opened them again, the minute hand had hardly advanced at all. There was still almost half an hour till tea.

He shifted, and the bag of sweets on his stomach rustled.

"Want a sweet, Jiminee?"

Jiminee looked up from his drawing. He put down his pencil and slid off the chair. "What kind have you got?"

"Liquorice all-sorts." Hubert opened the bag and displayed them. "Take two."

Jiminee hesitated. "C-can I really?" He'd been caught this way too often—the generous offer, the sweets under his nose and then suddenly the bag whisked away with shouts of laughter. Or perhaps there wouldn't be sweets in the bag at all—just stones.

"Go on," said Hubert.

Jiminee dipped his hand in. He took two of the thick white wheels with only an axle of liquorice. They were the best in the bag. But he frowned, holding the sweets in the palm of his hand. "May I really? There aren't m-many left."

Hubert said, "I don't want any more." He'd eaten seventeen since dinnertime.

Still unsure, Jiminee said, "I know you always save the best ones till last."

"It doesn't matter." He hadn't saved them this time anyway. He'd just put his hand blind into the bag and taken out the first one he touched. He hadn't even tried to guess what kind it was from the way it felt in his mouth. It was funny—he'd never done that before. And he'd never eaten seventeen at one go before—it was almost the whole week's ration. He didn't care one bit.

Jiminee still hadn't eaten the sweets. He held them as carefully as if they were half-crowns. "What do you want me to d-do?"

"Nothing."

"You sure? You sure you d-don't want me to run up-stairs?"

"No." Hubert shook his head emphatically.

"They're a p-present?"

Hubert swung his leg off the arm of the chair. "Yes, they're a present."

Jiminee went slowly back to the kitchen table and climbed onto his chair. He put the first sweet into his mouth; it made a great lump in his cheek. He looked at Hubert, without going back to his drawing. "I think," he said at last, "I think you ought t-to save them."

"Why?" He was sitting up now and wasn't sleepy anymore.

Jiminee didn't answer. He switched the sweet to the other cheek.

"Why?" Hubert repeated.

"F-fair shares."

Hubert stood up. He put the bag on the table and looked at it. You could tell there were only three or four sweets left now. "It's too late," he said, "there aren't enough." He'd tried to give one to Gerty—offered her the pick of the bag. But she'd just turned her head away as she'd done to all food ever since he'd given her Mrs. Halbert's cake. She went on asking for water, but she didn't cry now.

"Anyway," Hubert said suddenly, "fair shares doesn't count anymore."

"B-but . . ." Jiminee blinked with effort. Then he gave up and began to chew the sweet in his mouth.

It seemed to Hubert as if they were both waiting for something. The foreverness of the afternoon had gone. Long ago, this had been the time when Mother would come bustling into the kitchen to start the tea. At school it was the moment when expectation of release would conquer boredom. Now . . .

Now it was the knocker—thunder at the front of the house.

"Wh-who c-could—"

But Hubert had already crossed to the door. He wasn't going to wait for the next knocks this time. He climbed the stairs and pushed open the door into the hall. He knew what to do now. He knew what to say this time.

He stopped at the front door and took a deep breath and held it in his lungs. He reached up slowly and clicked back the latch.

The door opened with a sticky sound from the rubber lining the jamb.

"Why hello, Hubert." A smile and white gloves. "You remember me, I'm sure."

He just stared at her. It couldn't really be her. It . . . and then he remembered Miss Deke's summer visits. She always came in the middle of the summer holidays and . . .

"Aren't you going to ask me in? You were always quite the little gentleman, Hubert—*weren't* you? I've come to call on your mother."

Miss Deke's smile succeeded merely in straightening the naturally down-turned corners of her mouth into an edge that had menaced far more children than it had ever comforted. She began to loosen the fingers of the glove on her right hand. "Well?" she enquired.

"Come in," Hubert said. His throat was thick.

"Thank you." Miss Deke stripped off her glove and stepped across the threshold. Involuntarily Hubert looked down at the floor where that other imprint was still clearly outlined.

Miss Deke caught his glance and raised one eyebrow. "You needn't worry—my feet are quite clean."

He closed the door and, still with his eyes down, led her along the hall. In his head the blood banged out the warnings: *I've got to tell Elsa—I've got to warn the others— I must . . .* He pushed open the door of the front room, and let Miss Deke go ahead of him.

"How lucky you are to live in one of these houses. So good and solid."

She turned on him so abruptly that he blushed. "Aren't you pleased to see an old friend, Hubert?"

"I—" Then he knew he couldn't manage it. Nobody could lie to Miss Deke, not even one of her favourites.

She had removed her left glove, and now she began to massage the middle joint of her ring finger, while she watched him thoughtfully.

He said, "Excuse me, Miss Deke, I'll go and get Elsa." Then he fled.

He ran up the stairs, stretching his thigh muscles to take two at a time. She'd be with Gerty, he was sure of that. He ran past Mother's empty room and up the second flight and all he could think was that it was like a dream—a horrible dream of chase and terror that never ended except by waking up into the real world. And this was the real world.

"Elsa! Elsa!" He burst into the room.

Elsa looked up from the book she was reading to Gerty. She was just turning a page and Hubert could see the illustration of the wicked fox with the big bag over his shoulder. It was *The Little Red Hen* she was reading from.

"Shshsh, Hu—she's nearly asleep." Elsa frowned at him.

"But it's Miss Deke!"

Her frown deepened. "Miss Deke?"

"Yes—she's downstairs, in the front room."

Elsa turned the page and smoothed it down carefully. "Well, why don't you tell her Mother's too ill to see her?"

"But Elsa . . ." He didn't understand. "She won't believe me."

Elsa's eyes went back to *The Little Red Hen*. "I don't expect she'd believe me either."

He was frightened. The dream wasn't ending at all. "Of course she'd believe you, Else. You've *got* to come!"

The older girl drew in her breath. "I'm reading to Gerty. She's ill. She needs me. So I can't come."

"You've got to come, you've got to!" He wiped the stickiness of his hand down his trouser leg. "I *said* you'd come!"

She didn't answer and he saw the stubbornness of her mouth.

"Elsa—please, Elsa. Only for a minute. You can come back to Gerty as soon as Dekey Bird's gone. Please. Otherwise we'll all be found out."

Elsa shook her head and he knew that she wasn't really listening to what he said. She didn't care anymore. It seemed to him then that she hadn't cared for a long time. If Elsa gave up—then there wasn't anyone else at all.

"You're a coward, Else. That's all. You're just afraid. You're just afraid to talk to old Dekey Bird." He forced the tears back into his eyes. "You're a cowardy cowardy custard."

No one could ever have said that to Elsa before. A week ago even he wouldn't have dared himself. He didn't know how he dared now.

Elsa raised her head. She gazed away from him, out of the window. All at once Hubert saw how like Mother she looked—like Mother had been just before . . . He waited. No one could tell what she was thinking.

"Gerty is very ill," she said.

Hubert nodded. He knew that. He knew Gerty needed a doctor, but up to now Elsa had just shaken her head when he mentioned it. "She'll be better soon," she'd said. But Gerty wasn't getting any better—she was hardly recognizable as the fat, smiling Gert. There were dark patches under her eyes and her face was thin and very red—not a proper red though. And she moaned almost the whole time.

"All right, I'll come." She stood up, hesitating a moment as to what to do with the book. Then she laid it face down on the blanket.

Gerty started to cry.

"It's all right, Gerty, I'll be back in a minute." She bent down and kissed the little girl on the forehead.

Gerty's whine started up again as Elsa left the room. Hubert followed close behind her down the stairs.

Elsa paused on the landing and turned to him. "We've got to get Gerty a doctor."

Hubert sighed with relief. "All right, I'll run round to Dr. Meadows as soon as Dekey Bird goes."

Elsa said, "He'll never let you."

"Who?"

"Dunstan. Dunstan'll never let us get a doctor. He doesn't care what happens to Gert."

"It doesn't matter what Dun thinks. We won't tell him."

It was hard to see Elsa's expression in the gloom of the landing. She said, "He'll say Mother wouldn't want it. That's what he'll say. Mother doesn't like doctors."

"But Mother . . ."

"It's true. You know it's true. Mother would never have a doctor in the house. Look what Mrs. Stork said."

"But you just said we'd got to get a doctor."

She started down the stairs. She'd taken two steps when she stopped and looked up at her bewildered brother. "Yes," she said. "Yes, I did."

Miss Deke was sitting in the same chair when they entered the front room.

Miss Deke nodded. "Hello, Elsa. How are you?"

"Very well thank you, Miss Deke. I'm sorry Mother can't see you today. She's not very well, you know."

"Yes, I knew she wasn't well. I rather hoped she'd be better now."

"I'm afraid she isn't. She's asleep."

"Oh, well, we mustn't wake her up, must we?" Miss Deke gently rubbed at her finger joint, but didn't stir from her seat. Nor did she shift her gaze from Elsa. She just stared and stared with her Dekey-Bird eyes that made everything go out of your mind so you couldn't think what you were going to say next. Elsa's hands were clenched so that her knuckles were white.

Miss Deke laid one glove on top of the other and smoothed them out together. "I was rather looking forward to meeting your little brother—William I think his name is, isn't it? He'll be coming to school next term, I hear."

"Miss Deke."

"Yes, Elsa dear?"

"Miss Deke."

He knew. She was going to tell Miss Deke about Gerty. He could almost hear the words being formed in her mind.

"Elsa!" he cried.

"Miss Deke—"

"Hush, Hubert!"

"Miss Deke, it's Gerty."

Miss Deke's hands were still for the first time that afternoon. "Yes, dear?"

"Gerty's—Gerty's . . ." She couldn't go on. She was weeping—the tears came straight down her nose and down the corners of her mouth. And she didn't make a sound.

Miss Deke stood up.

"Gerty's not very well, either," said Hubert desperately as though his words would drive the schoolmistress back to her seat. "But she's going to be all right."

Miss Deke stepped forward.

"Oh, yes, Gerty's going to be quite well again soon," said Diana from the doorway.

Miss Deke halted in surprise.

"She's only got a little tummy upset—hasn't she, Hu?" Diana put her head to one side and smiled. "Hello, Miss Deke."

"Good afternoon, Diana." But Miss Deke did not smile back. "Elsa doesn't seem to agree with you about Gertrude—do you, my dear?"

"Oh, yes, she does," insisted Diana gently. "She's just a bit upset herself, you see—aren't you, Elsa? You see, Miss Deke, she had to sit up with Gerty all last night. So, of course, she's tired today."

"I see," said Miss Deke, her voice neutral.

Still smiling, Diana went on, "Oh, yes, Gerty will be quite well in the morning. Mother thinks so, and the doctor does too."

Imperceptibly Miss Deke relaxed. "You have a doctor?"

"Oh, yes, of course. He's the doctor at the end of the road—what's his name, Hu?"

Hubert looked at Elsa—she held her head down and the tears were falling directly onto the floor. "Dr. Meadows," said Hubert slowly. He didn't understand. He'd never seen

Diana like this before. She hated strangers—if Miss Deke could be called a stranger.

"Dr. Meadows," Diana echoed happily, "that's right. So you see, there's nothing to worry about really, Miss Deke."

"Yes, I see." Miss Deke drew on one glove. She glanced at each one of them. Then she turned directly to Elsa. "Are you quite sure there's nothing else the matter, dear?"

Elsa didn't move, but she lifted her head as though it was very heavy. Her eyes were quite red. She didn't really look at Miss Deke. "No," she whispered.

Automatically Miss Deke's hand went out to the girl, but Elsa stepped back. "No," she said, more strongly this time.

For a while no other word was spoken. When Hubert turned his eyes away from Elsa to Miss Deke, he saw she had both gloves on again. But still she didn't move. Hubert thought, *she doesn't know what to do.*

The silence was broken by a knock at the door. Even Miss Deke jerked in momentary alarm. Then she smiled the smile that wasn't a smile. "Well," she said, "that is my signal to leave. Perhaps it's the doctor come to see Gertrude."

Hubert went ahead of her to the front door. He heard her say goodbye to Elsa and to Diana and then her footsteps were behind him. He opened the front door.

Mrs. Stork didn't see Miss Deke at first. She grinned at Hubert. "Hello, dearie—remember me?"

"What are you doing here?"

"Well, that's a nice welcome, I must say!" Mrs. Stork made a mock wry face. "I come to fetch my apron if you must know. You remember the flowered apron I used to wear —when I was workin' here? I must of left it in the kitchen—why don't you be a duck and run down and 'ave a look—"

The emergence of Miss Deke from the shadowy hall quenched Mrs. Stork's flow abruptly. "Oh—beg pardon. I didn't know you had visitors."

Miss Deke nodded slightly and turned to Hubert. "Please tell your mother I was so sorry she wasn't able to see me.

I do hope she is better soon. Goodbye—I expect I shall see you at the beginning of next term, shan't I?"

"Yes. Goodbye, Miss Deke."

"Miss Deke!" Mrs. Stork's meagre lips opened in a smile. "Oh, I've heard ever such a lot about you. You're the teacher, aren't you? I'm Mrs. Stork—I used to be Mrs. Hook's daily help before . . ." She sighed suddenly.

For a moment Miss Deke hesitated; then she held out her hand.

"How do you do, Mrs. Stork."

"Pleased to meet you, I'm sure, Miss Deke. I've always been 'oping I would. My, you're a regular household word in this house." She fumbled rapidly in her bag and pulled out a handkerchief.

Miss Deke said nothing.

"Oh, yes," said Mrs. Stork, patting her throat, "ever since Di was in your form, I've heard about you and what a wonderful person you was. You won't run out of love in this 'ouse, Miss Deke, I can tell you that. I was 'ere nine years, I was."

"Really?" Miss Deke coughed. "Er—you must know the children very well."

"Me? Like a second mother to them, I was. Ain't that true, Berty?"

Hubert forced a smile.

"There you are! Oh, Berty, don't bother about that apron now. I'll fetch it another time," she wiped the patch of flesh beneath her chin, "if you're not away at the seaside, that is. Was you just going, Miss Deke?"

"Yes," responded Miss Deke. "I was on my way out, when we heard you knock. We thought it might have been the doctor."

"The doctor—oh, my Lor—the doctor! I 'spect you're walking up the terrace, aren't you? That's just on my way 'ome too."

Suddenly the two women were smiling at each other.

"Well, goodbye, Berty." Mrs. Stork dropped the hand-

kerchief in her bag and snapped the lock shut. "Be sure an'
tell your mother I called."

The two women descended the steps together. As he
watched them walking down the path, on a sudden impulse
Hubert called out, "Goodbye."

They stopped and turned. For a moment they stared up
at him and then their heads came together again. As they
moved on, Hubert caught a snatch of a sentence. "Tell me,
ma'am," asked Mrs. Stork, "how *is* Mrs. Hook?"

Then the gate clicked to behind them and they were
hidden by the front hedge.

17

It was the worst thing that could have happened. As he
watched Miss Deke's hat bobbing over the hedge, he knew
that.

They were in real danger now.

He closed the door and walked back to the front room.
But he didn't go in as he had meant to. Through the crack
in the half-open door he saw Elsa and Diana. He watched.
Elsa was sitting where Miss Deke had been, and Diana was
kneeling beside her chair. He heard Diana's voice.

"What does it matter, Elsa, about Miss Deke?" She was
stroking the older girl's head. "Mother will always look after
Gerty."

There was no protest from Elsa. Face between her hands,
she submitted silently to the other's gentle caress. At last she
lifted her head and seemed to stare directly at the crack
through which Hubert looked. But she stared as though she
didn't see anything at all, as though she were listening, maybe,
to something very faint and distant that was more important
than anything else in the world. Perhaps it was Mother's
voice . . . perhaps . . .

Hubert turned away.

He went briskly to the stairs and began to climb. On the landing he halted. He knew quite well what he was going to do.

He entered his workshop. Willy was sitting on the floor playing with the top Hubert had made for him for his last birthday. The little boy did not even glance up. He muttered as he wound the string of the top. Probably talking to his black wife, thought Hubert.

He went over to his workbench and looked at his tools. He hadn't used them much lately. They'd never let him have a workshop like this at the orphanage. He selected a medium-sized chisel.

He left Willy sitting on the floor and walked across the landing to Mother's room. These days the door was unlocked and the key on the inside. He shut the door behind him and twisted the key.

It was easy to press the lock of the desk down with the blade of the chisel. He pulled the lid back carefully. Inside the papers lay just as Elsa and he had left them that morning long ago. He took out the sheaf of letters. "89216 L/C Hook C. R." It was the right bundle. He even remembered some of the words. He undid the string and spread the letters on the desk.

It would be the last one in the bundle. It was. It was dated last year, and, what was much more important, it had an address in the top right corner. The letter was short:

My dearest Vi,

As ever to wish you well and comfortable on your birthday. Many happy returns, old girl.

How are the kids?

I'm fine and I've even got a steady job—I won't tell you what as it might offend the ancestral sensibilities and all that. However it pays well. If you ever want any extra clover, you know you've only got to drop your old Charlie 'ook a line.

I suppose it's no use asking you the same old question again, is it, my old dear? Still, here goes. How about

it? I'm ready and willing and will promise to be as ever
loving and faithful as human nature permits. I can't say
more, can I? I admit, it don't sound very good. But
those kids need a dad—even me. Remember that, Vi.

Think it over and let me know. Present address will
find me until the bailiffs come.

                    Your tender-hearted spouse
                    Charlie

Hubert read it over and then pulled the pad of writing
paper to him. He picked up the pencil and licked it. Carefully
he wrote the address in the right-hand corner, as should be
done. He stopped. After a minute he put the pencil down and
crossed to the window.

The room was stuffy and all the scent of Mother had gone.
He looked down at the garden. Already the lilies had begun
to cover the mound of earth at the base of the tabernacle.
Come the autumn, the plants would be lapping against the
walls. He looked across at the Halberts' garden. It was im-
maculate as ever. It was empty. Hubert wondered if Halby
was indoors or whether he had gone for another drive. Halby! He had a momentary wild idea. Halby might . . . but it
died almost at once. Mr. Halbert was very nice, but, deep
down (and why he was so sure of this he didn't know), Mr.
Halbert didn't like children.

Hubert went back to the desk and sat down again. He
picked up the pencil. He hesitated, and then his pencil came
down on the paper.

"Dear Dad," he wrote.

AUTUMN

18

He had been kept in for not "paying attention," so he had missed the others at the school gate.

He was alone and he hurried.

The greyness of the day was already turning to dark. The roof of the sky had sunk to a level just above the neon lights, making greenish tunnels of the streets, dusky with autumnal mist. Except in the lesser roads, still lit with old-fashioned street lamps, night had been abolished. Nothing could lurk in the main streets.

Hubert halted at the mouth of Hatton Alley. It was a short cut, but there was only a single lamp in the whole length of it. He listened. He heard the shifting of the dead leaves that had fallen from the trees arching over the alley walls. Leaves—footsteps. Cowardy cowardy custard. He took a breath and plunged in.

Footsteps, yes—always that metallic echo of other feet running behind him. He crunched the curled leaves faster. He ran.

"Whoa up, sonny!"

The hand on his shoulder stopped him and steadied him in one movement.

The policeman stood bang under the light. He must have been in the alley when Hubert started down.

"What's after you, son?"

He looked up at the policeman's face. The eyes were shadowed by the peak of his helmet, and only the mouth and half of the nose were visible.

Hubert glanced back the way he had come. There was no one behind him. The leaves lifted and scattered a little and lay still. He turned back to the policeman. They stood together, silent in the lamplight. Their cold white plumes of breath met and mingled. He was quite safe now.

He moved to lift the hand from his shoulder. Momentarily their flesh touched and he felt the hair on the back of the man's hand. The policeman dropped his arm.

Hubert didn't move. There in the dark alley with this man it was suddenly better than anywhere he was going, and at once he had the temptation, which had come to him often lately, to just go up to a policeman and say . . . He opened his mouth to speak.

And then he was running on down Hatton Alley. He stopped before he reached the terrace and stepped into the shadow of the alley wall. Swiftly he rubbed his sleeve against his eyes.

When he looked back, the policeman was gone.

He moved out into Ipswich Terrace. To push the thoughts away, he watched the slabs of the pavement beneath his feet. He didn't try to avoid the cracks—step on a crack and kill your mum, they said. But that was a child's game. He let his feet fall where they would. Soon he was hurrying again. No matter what he did, he couldn't get rid of the thoughts . . .

The Day he'd Posted the Letter. He had hurried back then, too. No one had seen him go out and the streets had been deserted, although it was a warm evening of summer. When he had posted the letter and started on his way back, he had thought of his white envelope lying among all the others due to be picked up at 5:30 P.M. It was as if all the effort of hope had been deposited in the red letter box—and a great relief had come over him.

Nevertheless, he had hurried. When he got back, the

house seemed deserted. He had gone from room to room, running at last, until he had found them all, standing in that room so quiet that he didn't know they were there until he entered. And when he did, no one looked at him. No one looked at him now. None of the children looked at each other much now. . . .

As he reached up and pulled the latch of the gate back, he glanced up the road. He could see the ladies—four of them—standing there as always, waiting. What did they wait for? It would be cold to stand out there on a night like this. "Women of ill repute," Mr. Halbert had called them. Perhaps that meant they didn't have anywhere to go. Suddenly, Hubert imagined himself going up to them and saying, "If you haven't got anywhere to go, you can come and stay at our house." Silly, don't be silly.

He pushed open the gate and let it slam behind him. He thought of the policeman and of Mr. Halbert. Mr. Halbert had hair on the back of his hands too—brownish hair that looked gold in the sunlight when he had his hands on the wheel of the car. Flight-Sergeant Millard had had it too. Mr. Roster, the headmaster, didn't though, nor did Miss Deke, though she had a moustache, just a little one. He wondered if the ladies on the corner of Ipswich Terrace had moustaches too—he'd never been close enough to see. And then he thought of Him—he was sure He had hair on his hands, and most probably he had a moustache too. But why didn't he answer the letter? Perhaps he was ill. Perhaps he had never got it. Perhaps he didn't answer because he was a "bad lot." Perhaps . . .

He was crying again as he stood before the front door. He didn't know why—it was something to do with the policeman and the "women of ill repute" and Mr. Halbert and Him . . .

Cry-baby bunting! He pulled the key from his pocket. He was as bad as Willy, always crying nowadays. He sniffed.

Be a man, Hubert, be a man!

He turned back to look at the street. There was no one there. He lifted the key and turned it slowly in the lock.

19

They had stood round Gerty's bed and no one had looked at him.

"What's the matter?" he said. He was hot with running.

They didn't answer, and he pushed through the group of children round the bed. Gerty was lying quite still with her eyes open. She wasn't flushed anymore. She was gazing at Elsa, who knelt on the floor beside her.

Hubert drew a deep breath. "She must be better," he said. He touched Elsa's shoulder. "She's better, isn't she, Else?"

The girl turned a frowning face up to him. "Sssh—she's trying to say something!"

Hubert stepped back a pace and glanced round at his brothers and sisters. He gripped Jiminee's arm. "What is it, Jiminee?"

The boy looked quickly at Hubert and hesitated. "She started to sc-scream," he whispered.

"She's not screaming now."

"N-no—then she w-went all quiet."

"Ssshh!" Another hiss came from Elsa. "She's trying to say something."

The little girl's unformed lips moved clumsily, but there was no sound. Her eyes were very big and brown. And there was something about her face—perhaps the thin exhaustion of the flesh—that suddenly reminded Hubert of his last sight of Mother. He looked up and caught Dunstan watching him. As he looked at his brother, he wondered why Dunstan had come upstairs with the others. Nothing happy ever happened when Dunstan was there.

Gerty was still struggling with the words that would not come out. But at last she managed something—a sound like a worn-out needle on a very old gramophone record. Elsa bent lower. The noise flickered and died, then flickered again.

"What does she say?"

Elsa turned her puzzled face to the children. "I can't make it out," she said. "Something about a rabbit."

"I know!" Willy pushed his way to the bedside. "She wants a rabbit—a cheesy rabbit, of course. Don't you, Gert?"

The little girl closed her eyes and nodded faintly.

"There you are!" Willy announced with pride, "I told you so—she wants a cheesy rabbit."

"A *Welsh* rabbit," corrected Elsa, but she could not help smiling.

"She *is* better then," Hubert said.

"Of course she's better!"

And then they were all smiling at one another. And they turned to Gerty—and suddenly she was grinning her old Gerty grin again.

"Well," said Elsa, standing up and brushing her skirt, "who's going to get it?"

"Me!"

"Me!"

"Me!"

"Jiminee," said Elsa in her sedate voice, "you're best at making Welsh rabbits. You go." And Hubert knew that it was the old Elsa speaking. "And Hu will help you."

"Come on," said Hubert.

At the head of the stairs, Jiminee said, "Race you, Hu!" Hubert was filled with joy as he ran merrily down the stairs which so few minutes ago he had run up with such fear.

He timed them by the kitchen clock. Toasting the thick hunk of bread that Gerty always liked, grating, mixing, spreading and grilling the cheese, and warming the plate. It took them exactly seven minutes.

"It's a record."

They gathered up knife and fork.

"Won't she want to d-drink something?" Jiminee asked.

"Milk," said Hubert decisively. He filled Gerty's yellow mug to the brim. "I'll carry it," he said.

Again Jiminee went ahead of him. He had to climb slowly so as not to spill a drop of the milk. He was grinning in triumph as he entered the bedroom.

They were silent, staring.

"What's up?" he asked anxiously.

"What's the m-matter?" Jiminee murmured.

The milk slopped as Hubert moved further into the room. Elsa was kneeling by the bed again, but this time her head was bent all the way down to the pillow. And Gerty's eyes were closed.

"What is it?" Hubert almost shouted.

"Hush, Hu." Diana turned slowly towards him and her face was filled with the faraway look of Mothertime. "Gerty has passed on."

"But . . ." He looked down at the mug in his hand. The milk he had brought for her had slopped over the edge and three lines of it ran down the yellow sides of the mug. It's not fair, he thought, it's not fair.

He raised his eyes to Diana. "You said," he spoke carefully, wanting to remember the words just right, "you said Mother would look after Gerty."

"But she has, Hubert dear." Her voice was filled with gentleness. "She is looking after Gerty—now." She shook her cap of golden hair with a soft movement of her head. "They're together now. They're happy together now." She paused, then, "I must go to them," she said.

They heard her going down the stairs, and for a moment Hubert thought of the brick tabernacle in the garden.

"We'll have to bury Gerty in the tabernacle." He couldn't think of anything else to say.

"No!"

Dunstan waited for them all to turn to him. Only Elsa remained by the bedside with her head down.

"Gerty won't be buried in the tabernacle." One of Dunstan's socks had slipped down to his ankle, exposing a skinny, hairless leg—but he didn't look at all silly. "Gerty isn't fit to be buried with Mother."

"B-but Dinah said—" Jiminee started.

Dunstan cut him short. "Gerty was punished. That's why she's dead—because she's wicked. She betrayed us—that's what she did. Gerty died because she was a traitor to Mother." He spoke the last words with great precision.

Elsa raised her head. She glanced at Dunstan and then stared out of the window. She didn't say a word. After a while she let her head drop down to the pillow again. A tuft of her thin hair fell across the dead girl's puckered mouth.

Hubert's hand shook convulsively and he felt the milk spilling on his skin. He bent his knees and set the mug down on the floor. He remained there, squatting, watching the yellow mug in the pool of milk. Behind him someone began to cry—and then someone else.

At last, the whole room was filled with weeping.

Hubert reached up his milky hand and the tears and the milk mingled on his face.

20

There was only Jiminee in the kitchen when he entered.

"Hullo, Hu. I thought you were n-never c-c-coming."

Hubert nodded vaguely.

"I put the k-kettle on."

He'd put the kettle on. That was something. Hubert slipped off his jacket and rolled up the sleeves of his grey wool shirt. Once, everybody had a duty. But that was a long time ago. It didn't work nowadays—not since Gerty'd died and Elsa had . . . *Had what?* Hubert asked himself as he lit the Ascot and watched the hot water pour onto the dirty breakfast things in the sink.

"What's for tea, Hu?" Jiminee asked cautiously.

They always asked him now—not Elsa anymore. "Marmite sandwiches, I 'spect." Jiminee wasn't much help, but at least he did try. None of the others did—although they ate what he gave them all right, even Diana and Dunstan.

He picked up an egg cup and scraped away the remains
of the yolk with his fingernail. He couldn't do it all, though.
The whole family to feed, and the house to clean, and the
shopping to do. He laid aside the egg cup and rinsed a plate.
If only Elsa would help. If only . . .

He turned off the hot water. Only ten minutes ago—he
glanced up at the clock—he had promised himself to be a
man and now he was thinking of *ifs*. *"If" is the silliest word
in the English language.*

"I 'spect," he said reluctantly, "I 'spect we could have
some cake. After all, it's nearly Friday."

If only he could talk to Mother properly. *There,* he was
at it again. But this was different—Mothertime was real.
Mothertime was the only thing they had left really. He
rinsed the china toast rack. If only Dunstan weren't there—
listening, listening. He didn't mind about the others.

"Come on, Jiminee, give us a hand with the drying."

As each plate was dried Hubert put it back in place on
the kitchen table. It was the easiest way—not to have to
bother with putting the things in the cupboard and taking
them out again. He turned down the light under the kettle
as it began to whistle. The puffs of steam that pouted reluctantly from its head made the kitchen seem warmer.
Hubert started to cut the bread, spreading each slice with a
thin layer of margarine before it was sliced from the loaf.

"Jiminee, get the cake tin out." He measured the width
of a slice carefully—the slices he cut were neat and accurate
—and drew the knife steadily back against the hard crust.
Saw, don't push.

"Okay, Hu." Jiminee lifted the half of the cake that was
left onto the table.

"Cut it like this," Hubert said, running his finger to demon-
strate a thin wedge. "Put them all on the willow plate."

He went back to the loaf, keeping an eye on Jiminee.

Spreading and cutting, cutting and spreading. It was a
hot job. He stopped for a moment. The curtains across the
windows were undrawn and the blackness of the garden outside looked coldly in. It would be at least three weeks be-

fore they could have the stove lit in the kitchen—November
first. It would be winter then. It almost was now. And
they'd need coal, for the cellar was pretty well empty. Hubert wondered if the coalman just brought it automatically,
or if you had to tell him to come. Elsa would know—if she
would tell him. Yes, of course she would. Elsa wasn't spite-
ful.

He cut into the loaf again, not thinking what he was
doing, and the slice was ragged. He laid it on the plate
with the others. Waste not, want not. He'd eat that one
himself.

"Finished, Jiminee?"

Jiminee ran his finger along the blade of the knife,
gathering a small pile of yellow cream and crumbs. He put
the finger in his mouth and pulled slowly; it popped as the
finger came out. Jiminee grinned.

"Finished?" Hubert felt unreasonably angry.

"Oh—yes."

"About time too." He deliberately looked away from his
brother. "You're such a slow coach," he said. Stupid, stupid,
stupid—why was Jiminee such a fool? Couldn't he do anything by himself? He thought, *what's he going to do when he
grows up?* To absorb his irritation, he counted the pieces of
cake that Jiminee had cut.

"Jiminee!"

Jiminee smiled tentatively. "What's wrong?"

"There are *seven*—you've cut *seven* bits!"

"I'm s-sorry."

Hubert reached over and put a piece of the yellow cake
on his palm. "How could you?" he shouted. Suddenly he
was beside himself. He thrust the cake under Jiminee's nose.
"How could you?"

Jiminee blinked. "But—b-but—"

"But what?" He pushed the cake at Jiminee, so that the
breath from the younger boy's nostrils dislodged crumbs
of cake and blew them onto the floor.

"But it isn't what you th-think."

"You forgot, didn't you?"

"I d-d-didn't—I d-d-didn't." Jiminee's lips fluttered. "I didn't forget. It wasn't that. It was for Willy's b-b-black wife!"

Hubert lowered his hand. His anger was gone. He put the slice back onto the willow-pattern plate. He was ashamed. It was he who had forgotten—forgotten Willy's black wife.

He wanted to apologise. "I'm so—"

"And b-besides," Jiminee added, "besides—there might b-be somebody else who'd like a p-piece of c-c-cake, mightn't there?"

Like the hour hand gone mad, a wild swing of hope spun within Hubert. "Who?" he whispered. Perhaps He had arrived—hiding behind the chair, waiting to jump out. He glanced round the room. A surprise.

"S-someone," said Jiminee, smiling.

There wasn't anyone in the kitchen. In the garden. Perhaps He was in the garden. "Who?" he cried.

Jiminee flinched at his shout. And suddenly Hubert knew there was no one.

"S-somebody," said Jiminee, his smile wavering, "just some-b-b-body."

There was no one. For a moment the looseness within almost overcame Hubert. Then he shook his head. Ask a silly question, get a silly answer. He sighed.

He went slowly back to the table and picked up the bread knife.

"Go and call the others," he murmured. "I'll finish cutting the bread."

When Jiminee was gone, he glanced up at the black winter windows, which were beginning to steam up with the warmth of the kitchen.

Perhaps, he thought, perhaps the letter will come tomorrow.

21

The postman came up from the direction of the park. He didn't have a bicycle. He liked to walk. He was a small man, precise in his movements. His free arm swung straight at the elbow and he held his head so high that the peak of his cap cast a shadow halfway down his nose. He whistled as he came, always the same abrupt series of notes that must have made a melody somewhere in his mind. He had four medals from the War.

He halted in front of number 36, shifted three letters from his left to his right hand, clicked open the gate and marched up the path.

From the window of his workroom, Hubert watched.

Back down the path came the postman. Gate open, gate shut. Pause, then whistle and march again. As he approached number 38, Hubert leaned forward at the window.

The postman stopped. He looked down and shuffled the letters in his hand. He looked up, then down again for another quick shuffle. When he raised his head once more, the whistling ceased. He examined the house, and Hubert thought their eyes must have met. But it was hard to tell because of the shadow over the postman's face.

Suddenly he cocked his head on one side. After a minute his right arm straightened, he turned smartly, and with head straight and erect, he stepped out towards the Halberts'. As he passed the dividing line of the front gardens—the ragged yew of number 38 and the trim box leaves of number 40—he started to whistle again.

He halted in front of number 40 and began to sort through a thick sheaf of white envelopes. Hubert thought, *he's made a mistake, in a moment he'll come running back with the letter.*

But this postman never made mistakes. He went up the path of number 40 and the front door opened for him.

Through the clarity of the autumn morning, Hubert heard his greeting. "It's a nice day again," the postman said.

There was no letter.

22

They had got up the steps at last.

Somebody had forgotten to turn on the porch light. The two boys stood quite concealed by darkness. The white fountains of their breath did not reach beyond the shadow of the house.

The sounds of the park road at the end of the terrace fluctuated gently. It was misty now. In a few hours it would turn to fog. The boys held hands.

"It's quite safe. I p-promise it is."

As he spoke, Jiminee felt the hand in his tighten.

They waited again, looking down into the street. Nobody passed. Anyone going to the pub would have been there long ago. The last post had gone.

No sounds came from inside the house.

Jiminee's feet were frozen. He did not feel them. All he felt was the other hand in his. It didn't move, except to tighten and then slowly relax. Once it had wriggled so that their fingers interlaced.

"All right? I'm g-going to knock now."

The fingers clamped hard against his.

"It's all right."

He didn't have far to reach. He lifted the knocker and let it fall once. The flat sound was buried immediately in the mist.

"It's all right. It's all right."

It was a long way from the kitchen. At last they heard the footsteps hesitating in the hall.

The door opened with the sound of perished rubber pulling free. Hubert's head appeared.

"Jiminee? Where you been?"

Jiminee let go the hand and moved into the light from the hall.

"Where have you been?" Hubert was whispering. "It's nine o'clock."

"I kn-know."

The mist was caught by the light as it was slowly pulled into the hall by the warmth of the house.

"Well?" said Hubert. "Come on. It's cold out here."

"I got someone with m-me."

Jiminee moved back and took the hand in his again. Already it was cold. It held hard to his.

He half pulled the little boy into the hall with him. "Shut the door, Hu." He turned to his companion. "It's all right, we're in. G-go on, Hu."

Hubert put his back against the door and it shut. He stared at the other boy. "Where have you been?"

"Walking."

"Who's this?"

"This is Louis." Jiminee smiled. "It's all right. Nobody saw us. The whole way from school. D-did they, Louis?"

The boy looked at Hubert. His large eyes never blinked. He tightened his grasp on Jiminee's hand.

"There you are!" said Jiminee.

"What's he doing here?"

Jiminee's smile widened as he glanced from Hubert to Louis and back again. "Louis has c-come to live in our house."

Hubert turned his eyes away. The mist was still faintly visible in the hall. Unpolished and letterless, the silver tray lay on the table.

"He can't stay here," he said briefly.

They said nothing.

Hubert wouldn't look at them. He wouldn't. He had thought Jiminee had been run over, or kidnapped. But instead, Jiminee had kidnapped someone else. You can't just kidnap somebody and expect no one to find out.

He said, "You kidnapped him."

"I d-didn't k-k-kidnap him. He wanted to c-come—didn't you, Louis?"

Hubert couldn't keep it up. He looked at Louis. Louis stared back. He wasn't the sort of kid you'd notice much, really. His face was very thin, and it made his eyes seem huge. They were brown eyes. What would his mother and father do when they found out? He was like a deer at the zoo. He had the same big nose.

"Have you had any supper?"

"No," said Jiminee. "Can Louis stay?"

Hubert gave the door a final shove with his back to make sure it was closed.

"You better come and have some supper," he said, taking a step towards them. Louis flinched back, pulling Jiminee with him.

"It's all right," Jiminee said quickly.

Hubert stopped dead. He took a sharp breath and suddenly the smell of the mist was very strong in the hall. Somewhere under his feet was the scar on the floor board, but he hardly thought of that now. There was a turbulence of mist from which the little boy, backed against the table and half hidden by Jiminee, stood out as though cut with a fret saw. There was a look on Louis' face . . . perhaps it had been a stranger in Hubert's cup that morning, not a letter after all. Louis reminded him of someone, of . . . he closed his eyes against the mist and for a fraction of a second he saw Louis lying wounded on the carpet . . .

Hubert shook his head and opened his eyes. The mist was gone. He raised his hand as gently as if it held the letter of relief. "Yes," he murmured, "it's all right."

They stood silent. Upstairs a door opened.

Hubert walked to the door to the basement. "Come on," he called over his shoulder.

One by one, each of the children had come down to the

kitchen, as though summoned. Each had asked and been answered.

"Louis. He's going to stay with us."

"Louis—Louis Grossiter."

"Louis has come to live with us."

Through it all, Louis sat straight against the chair back, his fists clasped tightly on his knees. He looked mostly at Jiminee, only occasionally at anyone else. He hadn't said a word.

"Where did you get him from?" Hubert asked.

"He's in my form," said Jiminee. "He sits at the b-back."

"How old is he?"

"Eight."

"I know everyone in your form," said Dunstan. "I've never seen *him* before."

"He's n-new. He doesn't come from here." Jiminee glanced at Louis. "He c-comes from M-M-M-Manchester."

"Manchester," Hubert murmured. That was hundreds of miles away. Hundreds. No wonder Louis was—it must be like a foreign country to him.

"Why doesn't he eat anything?" Willy asked.

The plate of biscuits lay untouched in front of Louis. The mug of warm milk already had a thick crinkled skin on top.

Elsa moved round the table to be beside Louis. He turned his head to look at her. She reached down and touched his hand.

"He's cold," she said. "The poor little thing is almost frozen to death."

She rubbed his hand for a few moments and then lifted it and, carefully uncurling Louis' clenched fingers, put it round the yellow mug. "Hold it," she said quietly. "You'll soon be warm again." She smiled at him. "Isn't that better?"

Louis didn't answer. His thin fingers were hooked awkwardly round the mug.

Hubert stood up. "Elsa!" He had been sitting on the edge of the chair, watching the children watch Louis and trying to think of something to do. "Elsa!" He called again, yet he didn't know what he wanted to say.

Her head was turned to him enquiringly. From the momentary animation with Louis, her white peaked face had returned to its customary expression of—nothing.

Hubert searched in his mind for something to say, as she waited in the calmness of the numb for him to speak. He felt himself blushing. He knew it was tremendously important, if only . . . then suddenly it seemed to burst inside him.

"We've run out of coal!" he shouted.

It was a shout. He hadn't meant it to be. Out of the corner of his eye he saw Dunstan's startled jerk.

He hadn't meant to shout. He tried again. "We've run out of coal."

The children remained still as if they had been struck by lightning.

"We've run out of . . ." It was no use. They didn't understand, they didn't . . .

Elsa turned back to Louis. "Is that better now?" she asked, touching his finger with her own.

As she spoke the children moved.

"We should have a fire, if Louis's cold," Jiminee said.

"A fire!" Willy cried.

"A fire!"

"It's too late for a fire," said Elsa, without glancing up.

Her decisiveness silenced them.

It isn't too late to have a fire, Hubert thought, it's too early. We never have fires before the first of November. Anyway, we haven't got any coal.

He said, "What are we going to do with him?"

"He's got to go to bed—we're going to put him to bed, that's what we're going to do," said Elsa.

"But Else—"

"Can he sleep in our room?" asked Willy.

"But, Else, we've got to decide what to do with him." Hubert's voice was urgent. "We can't just keep him. His mother and his dad will be looking for him and—"

"Hubert's right," said Dunstan.

Hubert gaped. "What?"

"Hubert's right. Of course he is. Not everyone's like us. How do we know he isn't a traitor?" He darted a finger at Louis.

"But that's not what I meant," began Hubert, "I meant—"

"It doesn't matter what you meant." Dunstan stared at Hubert and suddenly something started to move in Hubert's mind.

"Dun—" he said.

"It doesn't matter what you meant," Dunstan repeated. "just 'cause we found one traitor out, doesn't mean to say there aren't more." He brushed a flap of black hair from his forehead. "Anyone can be a traitor." He looked only at Hubert. "Anyone. *Him*—how do we know he isn't a traitor—a traitor in the gates?"

Diana reached out and touched Dunstan's arm. "We'll find out, Dunstan. We'll ask Mother."

Dunstan's rigidity relaxed. He nodded. "Yes. That's what we'll do."

"Mother will tell us," Willy asserted.

"Mother will tell us," said Diana.

"I don't mean that—I don't mean it." Hubert banged the table.

"We mean it," Dunstan said calmly.

"Don't you see it doesn't matter? Supposing he is all right. Just supposing—what about his mother and his dad? They're going to be looking for him, of course they are. And the police—do you think they won't tell the police their little boy's gone? And then they'll all be looking for him. They're bound to find him in the end. How's he going to come back from school without people finding out where he's going?"

"He won't g-go to school then," said Jiminee.

"Don't be silly. Of course he's got to go to school."

"Why?"

"Because—because we all go to school. That's why and what's more . . ." Hubert glanced at the faces around him and he knew at once that he wasn't convincing anybody. "Elsa!" he said. But Elsa didn't seem to be listening even.

He sat down and lowered his head. "They'll find out about us too," he murmured, almost to himself.

There was nothing more to be said.

Diana spread her hands. "Come, children. Let's go and ask Mother."

"Can Louis c-come?" asked Jiminee.

"No," said Dunstan. "He must stay here, till Mother decides."

Jiminee blinked. "You won't run away—w-will you, Louis?"

Almost imperceptibly Louis shook his head. It was the first sign that he understood what was happening to him. The children had been talking about him as though he were not there. As though he were a piece of property. But the tiny shake of the head had shown that he was among them. The children were more startled than by Hubert's shout.

There was a long pause. Then Diana said, "We shan't be long."

Hubert kept his head down.

"Come on, Hubert."

"I'm not coming."

Without looking, he knew that Dunstan was the last one, waiting at the kitchen door.

"Hubert!"

He didn't answer.

"All right then," sharp and crisp, the night air and Dunstan's words came into the room together. "I shall remember this, Hu."

The door shut and the glass shivered in the frames.

The two boys were alone.

Hubert raised his head, without looking at Louis. By holding himself quite still, he hoped to stop time and the thoughts that ticked in his head. But the clock hummed just the same. The smell of cooling milk was just the same. Hubert sniffed at it. Perhaps it would be for the last time. "I shall remember this," Dunstan had said. Didn't he know that if they kept Louis they would be found out, didn't he realise that then all they'd have would be just to remember because—because . . .

He faced the clock. It wasn't forever they could hide.

Suddenly he knew there wasn't much time at all. He knew now that there never would be any letter, and he wished he'd gone with the others. He wanted the watch. He wanted to take it out of the tabernacle and keep it for his own. It didn't matter if it didn't work. It didn't matter if it never worked.

Turning slowly to Louis, he realised too that it didn't matter if he stayed or not. Reluctantly he tried to smile.

The little boy made no response.

Hubert grated his chair back and walked carefully round the table. He picked up the teaspoon beside the cup and inserted it under the white skin on the milk. Steadying the mug with his other hand, he skillfully twisted the spoon, gathering the skin, turning it and lifting it clear in one piece.

"There," he said. "You'll be able to drink it now."

He went over to the sink and put the spoon under the tap. The cold water gripped the milky flesh and pulled it free. He turned off the tap and put the spoon on the wooden draining board. He leant his back against the sink. Louis' profile was towards him.

"Do you have a dad?" he asked. He paused to give Louis a chance to answer. Louis gripped the yellow mug a little tighter, but that was all.

"We don't," went on Hubert. "At least, I don't think we do. But I 'spect you do. Don't you?"

Louis just looked steadily in front of him.

"You can drink your milk now. It's quite all right."

The clock hummed.

"They won't be long now. At least I don't think they will. They've just gone to the tabernacle, you see, to ask . . . about you. I'm sure it'll be all right. I could warm that milk up for you again, if you like?"

It would be almost over now. In a minute they'd be coming in. It wasn't a proper, full-length Mothertime.

"That's Gerty's mug you've got. The yellow mug. Gerty was five. She was the second youngest next to Willy. She died. She got ill, then she died. Now there are only six of us. Gerty wasn't like you. She was fat. She talked an awful lot."

Louis was staring at the mug now. Hesitantly his right hand came up and closed round the other side of the mug. He pulled it a little closer to him.

"It's yours now," said Hubert.

Before the door opened, he could hear them talking. But they were silent as they entered.

It was all right, he knew that at once.

Jiminee danced across the room, his smile coming and going, and stood close over Louis. Willy strode, his chest out. All of them had grins at the edge of their mouths.

"G-guess what?" said Jiminee.

"Shhhh!" Dunstan held up his hand. "Let Diana say."

Frowning slightly, she waited for them to be quiet. Her Mothertime face had not worn off yet, and though she was looking at Louis, she hardly seemed to see him. Louis turned his eyes to her and held her gaze.

"Mother," she began. She shook her head, as if to make the words fall together in her mind. "Mother says—you can stay."

"You can stay!"

"You can stay!"

"You're going to stay!"

Jiminee and Willy, even Elsa, burst with cries. Dunstan was smiling, and suddenly he laughed.

But Hubert watched Diana. Her face was whiter than ever and as she brushed her hair back with a small, trembling gesture, she shivered suddenly. She must have felt him looking at her, for she turned. For a second they stared at each other. As he opened his mouth to speak, Diana looked quickly away.

Hubert forced himself not to move. Something had happened. Diana was frightened. The hubbub of the children around Louis did not touch him. Something must have happened in the tabernacle.

The others weren't scared. Only Diana. The fear that a

little while ago he had put aside returned to Hubert's stomach. He felt the wings moving, gentle as caresses. He took
a deep breath and the bird poised. In a long gliding stream
he let it out, until his lungs were dry and his head dizzy. In
his trouser pockets his clenched fists felt the tremulous
warmth of his thighs.

"Aren't you glad, Louis?" Willy leaned forward. "Aren't
you glad?"

Hubert took his hand out of his pocket and touched the
cold stone of the sink.

"Of c-course he's g-glad," said Jiminee.

Still the boy did not move except to turn his head from
speaker to speaker.

"I think he can't talk. I think he's dumb."

"Willy!" Elsa admonished quickly. "You must drink your
milk, Louis. It's good for you."

"Perhaps he doesn't like milk," Willy said.

"Would you like some tea?"

"Lemonade!"

"Cocoa!"

"Bovril!" Willy shouted triumphantly.

"Oh, yes, bovril!"

But Louis gave no indication—it was as if there were an
invisible curtain separating him from all that was going
on.

"Do you think he'd like bovril, Jiminee?" asked Elsa.

Jiminee screwed up his face, and somewhere the smile
hovered. "I-I-I . . ." His eyelids fluttered. "Um-um-um . . ."
The sound stopped, though his lips still opened and closed.
His whole body quivered.

Then slowly Louis' hand left the mug and reached up
and gripped Jiminee's. Jiminee stopped shaking at once. His
face cleared. "I d-don't know," he said, with a wide smile.

There was silence.

Dunstan stirred. He nodded to himself and went over to
the sink. He took a glass from the draining board and filled
it with cold water. Standing close to him, Hubert could hear
Dunstan's breath. Their bodies almost touched. As he

looked, Hubert suddenly knew why Louis seemed familiar—
he was like Dunstan, Dunstan without his glasses. The same
dark-brown, almost black eyes; the same color hair; the
same look—as though each had something special which no
one else could ever share.

Dunstan went back to the table. Carefully he put the
glass down in front of Louis. Cold beads of water trickled
down the sides of the glass. Almost reluctantly, Louis let
go of Jiminee and raised his hands to the glass. He gripped
it tight and lifted it to his mouth.

He drank.

In the stillness, each gulp in his throat was loud. He drank
all the water.

He returned the glass to the table, looking at it as if to
make sure that every drop was drunk. He took his hands
away and looked up at Dunstan.

"Thank you," he said. He smiled.

There was a soft rustle of sighs from the children.

"He does talk, after all," said Willy. And they all laughed.

Dunstan was the first to stop. "You'll stay then, Louis,
won't you?" he said quietly.

Louis looked shyly down. "Yes, I'd like to stay very
much."

"And you ought to go to bed, too," Elsa said. "We all
ought to go to bed. It's late." She hesitated. "You can sleep
in my room, if you like, Louis."

"No!" said Willy. "Louis's going to sleep in my bed."

"But, Willy," Elsa said, "there wouldn't be any room for
your black wife."

"I don't care about her!"

Elsa smiled. "Let's ask Louis who he wants to sleep
with."

Louis glanced at each one in turn.

"I'd like to sleep with Jiminee, please."

"That's right," said Dunstan, "Jiminee's the one who
found him"

Hubert moved into the circle round Louis. "You don't
know any of our names yet, Louis—except Jiminee."

Louis nodded gravely. "Yes, I do. Jiminee told me. You're Hubert."

"Yes, I . . ." Hubert faltered. He raised his eyes and saw Diana staring at him.

"Louis," said Dunstan. "I'll lend you my pyjamas."

"Bed."

"Yes, bed."

"Tomorrow," Dunstan said, "we'll show you the house. And the tabernacle." He went over to the door and held it open.

"I'll tell you a story when we're in b-bed," whispered Jiminee, as he and Louis and Dunstan left the room.

Elsa stood at the door. "You coming, Diana? Hubert?"

"In a minute," said Hubert. "I've got to lock up, you know."

Elsa stared somewhere above his head. "Oh, yes." She stepped into the passage and the swing door closed softly behind her, hissing for a moment and then relaxing.

"You want to help, Dinah?"

He knew she was still looking at him, but he kept his own eyes averted. Idly, he saw that the skin had formed once more on Louis' milk. "You want to help lock up?" The wings had begun to beat again in his heart.

"Yes."

She moved. Across the kitchen to the back door. She stared out into the garden. Hubert knew that she couldn't see anything; the reflection of the kitchen light would blind her to the dark world outside. But she went on staring. He watched her, waiting for her to swing round, yet knowing that he did not want to face her. He wanted to think of tomorrow—Saturday happy with Louis. Just tomorrow. One tomorrow.

Diana turned the key in the lock.

As she did so, Hubert reached out for the mug and turned swiftly to the sink. The milk slopped, falling cold onto the piece of flesh joining his forefinger and thumb.

He knew that she had turned too.

"What's wrong, Dinah?"

She was leaning against the locked door and staring at the back of his head.

He put his hand on the tap.

"Nothing. Nothing's wrong, Hubert dear."

In a spout of anger the cold water dashed from the tap, sweeping the milk from his hand, plunging into the mug, discharging milk and water and skin into the stained floor of the sink. In a swinging rush it sunk itself, gobbling the holes in the brass drainer.

He let the water run for a good while after the mug was clean.

23

Hubert put the sandpaper down on his worktable and blew the dust from the side of the little box. The tiny motes of wood shot out of the shadow of his body into the dancing sunlight that filled the room. Hubert smiled. Behind him the voices of Louis and Jiminee were hushed in the concentration of drawing.

He ran his thumb along the wood. It was smooth and handsome. Now only the lid remained to be done, and then he would oil the whole thing.

He was proud of the box. The corners were perfectly dovetailed and the lid fitted exactly. It was the best thing he'd ever done. He twisted the tiny key, backwards and forwards—no trace of obstruction.

Originally it had been intended for Mother's birthday. Three-quarters finished, it had lain on his worktable for months. Now it was for Louis. Everyone was going to give Louis a present.

Hubert picked up the sandpaper and started on the lid. He'd have to stop at half-past ten to do the shopping. But he'd have the box finished by suppertime, except for the oiling. That would take two or three days, but he was sure

Louis wouldn't mind waiting. He paused in his sandpapering. Two or three days did not seem so ominous as it had last night. Two or three days was safe. And besides . . . he had promised himself last night just before he went to sleep that he would not think of the future—as if there were no God. As if there were no Mother. Anything beyond two or three days was *their* job.

Into his mind spun the last-night face of Dinah. He closed his eyes and opened them again quick. Don't think of her. He gave a preliminary scrape with the sandpaper as if to erase the memory. And then he heard Jiminee's voice.

"What's it like to have a d-d-dad?"

Hubert held his breath.

"Well. I don't see him much." Hubert noticed for the first time the funny way of saying things that Louis had. It wasn't "much," it was "mooch."

"Where's he away?"

"Well, all over the place. He's a traveller."

"A t-traveller? Like M-M-M-Marco P-P-P-Polo?"

"No. He sells things. He has a big case. It's called a sample case. He takes it wherever he goes and people look at it and then they buy things."

"Like the l-lady who sells M-M-M-Mansion polish?"

"No, I don't think so."

There was a pause, and Hubert heard the scratching of Jiminee's pencil.

"What's that?"

"It's a b-bear."

"It's not a very big bear."

"N-no!"

"It's a baby bear!"

"N-no!" There was a note of triumph in Jiminee's voice. "It's a b-baby b-b-b-b-bearess!"

They were struck with instant giggles.

"Bearess," said Louis.

"B-bearess!"

The pencil scratched again. "There!"

Downstairs the clock struck half-past ten. Hubert lowered the sandpaper and started to open the drawer where he kept the box.

"Still," said Jiminee, "you got your m-mother."

"My mum. Yes."

"I seen your m-mum. Rem'ber?"

"Yes."

"At the g-gate. Old Fatty Chance was b-b-b—hitting you. It was your first d-d-day. Your m-mum come to c-c-collect you."

"Yes."

"I d-don't like your m-mum."

Hubert gripped hard on the box.

"No," came the answer at last, "nobody does very much."

"D-d-do you?"

There was a long pause. The pencil stopped its travels.

"No."

Almost at once Jiminee was drawing again. "Well," he said, "you don't have to worry ab-b-bout that n-n-now."

"No," said Louis. "No. I don't."

Hubert dropped the box into the drawer and shut it quietly. He slid the old sandpaper among the other pieces in the packet and let the elastic band holding them snap slightly.

When he turned round, Jiminee and Louis were entirely absorbed in the drawing. Hubert walked softly out of the room, so as not to disturb them.

He hesitated for a second and then went down the stairs. He knew he would most likely find Elsa in the front room. That's where she spent most of her time these days. At night sometimes she'd sit there without any lights on at all.

In the hall he glanced at the table. The silver tray lay bright and shining. He'd polished it before breakfast this morning. But there was no post. Not even a circular.

Hubert pushed open the door of the front room and stepped in.

She was there. He saw a quick movement as she covered something white in her lap with her spread hands.

"Coming shopping, Else?" Perhaps he should have knocked, he thought.

The room was sunny, but Elsa sat in the shadows. Beside her on the table was her workbox. She's sewing, thought Hubert, sewing something for Louis, I expect. She wouldn't be darning—she hadn't done any of that for weeks. He wriggled his toe in his shoe and felt the big hole in his sock. They were all like that, and so were Jiminee's and Dunstan's and Willy's. He sighed.

"Else?"

"No," she said.

"Oh, come on, Else."

This time she didn't even bother to shake her head. He stood watching her for a moment. He had hoped the coming of Louis would change her somehow back into the old Elsa. He sighed—he couldn't really be cross with Elsa. He turned back to the hall.

He took his coat out of the hall cupboard and buttoned it methodically. Then he lifted out the big basket with wheels and a walking stick attached. He had bought it two weeks ago, because he couldn't manage all the shopping by himself otherwise. Once he'd had to make three trips—and it took so long there was hardly any time left to do cleaning. But the big new basket took everything easily. Seventeen and six —for many weeks the price had frightened him, but there was plenty of money. He cashed the cheques in Marlowe Street now and there was always some over at the end of the month. More than four pounds at the end of September. He kept it at the bottom of the nail box in the drawer in his worktable. No one would ever look there without asking his permission.

He took the latest cheque and the shopping list out of his pocket. He turned the cheque over and saw Jiminee's endorsement on the back—*Violet E. Hook* in Mother's exact writing. Hubert thought, not even an expert could tell the difference. In the dim light that filtered through the dusty transom he read over the shopping list. It was almost the same every week, and he knew it by heart by now. But there was one thing added this week—lavatory paper. He'd wondered for a long time how he could ask for lavatory paper. At last he'd solved it by handing the list to the grocer with everything crossed out but that.

And coal! He ought to ask Elsa how to order coal. He looked back down the hall. No, he didn't want to disturb her again. There was plenty of time anyway. It wasn't what you'd call cold yet.

He opened the front door. No, it wasn't cold.

There were people in Ipswich Terrace. Two women coming back from early shopping. The milkman further down the road. The gentleman in the brown coat and the black hat who lived at the end house and was always bustling to the post box. A man in his waistcoat cleaning a car. A tiny Hillman—not much of a car, but it always shone.

Hubert stood at the top of the steps and breathed in the milk-white light of early autumn. Two or three days was forever. He blew out a long frosty breath.

He decided to buy two different kinds of biscuits. The coloured ones with faces and jam eyes, and chocolate fingers. A treat for Louis.

24

He set the wheels against the curb of Monmouth Terrace and heaved. Pounds and pounds. Three stone, perhaps four stone. The basket was filled with ammunition that might go off any moment if it was jolted. Slowly he exerted his strength; it ran down his arms into the handle of the basket, down to the wheels that rose gently. Suddenly the weight was gone. He'd done it!

The battery would have its ammo now. No more curbs.

He rested for a moment, looking down the tree-lined terrace. He remembered the summer when he and Elsa had walked down Monmouth to the garden door and found it locked. The summer leaves were brittle and yellow now and filled the gutters and mounted high against the garden walls. It had been years ago.

Years ago.

He heard their laughter and glanced up.

"Look at Ma! What you got there, Ma—milk for de lickle babies?"

They stood high on the limbs of the tree and yelled down at him. Hubert squinted up at their sun-haloed bodies. Fatty Chance and two others he didn't know by name—just suckers-up to Fatty. He moved closer to the tree.

"Mind you don't spill that milk, Ma!"

Head craned back, Hubert grinned. They were great birds up there in the magnificent altitude of triumph.

"Can I come up?" he called.

"What do *you* think," Fatty shouted back. "We don't want no Mas up here."

The giggles of his companions grated on the autumn air like mirthless mating calls.

"Knees up, Mother Hook!" The branches were filled with their echoless screeches.

"Please! Let me come up!"

Fatty leaned over his branch. It wasn't funny anymore. "Scram, face-ache!"

"But—"

Fatty worked his cheeks and suddenly pushed his lips into a fishlike snout. A fat accurate gob of spit splashed heavily at Hubert's feet. It lay glistening on the pavement. Hubert put his foot on it and smeared the saliva on the stone.

Fatty was preparing to spit again.

Hubert gripped the handle of the ammo basket. There were other trees. There were trees in their own garden. But, looking up, waiting for the spit, Hubert found no enticement in the thought of other trees.

"You and your silly old plane tree," he called halfheartedly.

The second blob of spit landed on one of the lower branches.

Hubert had started to move away. He turned, head up to

the boys black against the sun. He wanted to knock them out of the tree—smack, smack—and see them smash like the spit on the pavement. "Missed!" he shouted. "Missed, fat pig!"

Fatty Chance moved so fast he seemed to slide down the tree. He dropped, one, two, three branches, swung by his hands and fell with his feet planted wide apart, his knees bent. He bounced forward at Hubert.

"What you call me?" His lips were still wet.

He is a pig, thought Hubert. He is fat. He nerved himself to utter the word which hardly anyone at school, certainly nobody from Hubert's form, dared say to the fat boy's face.

"Fatty—that's what I called you. And what's more—that's what you are."

Far away at the park end of Monmouth, the postman had begun his delivery. His whistle came faint but clear.

"Why, you little—little insect. I ought to clock you." Fatty raised his arm.

Hubert watched the postman halt with a smart military movement. The whistling ceased.

"I ought to—" Fatty lowered his arm.

Hubert glanced at him in surprise.

The fat boy's face was red and white, and his blue frog eyes added a touch of macabre patriotism to the plump flesh. "But I won't," he said. He was smiling.

"I won't. You want to know why?" He relished the question with his lips. " 'Cause you're going to get something that's far worse than what I could do."

Hubert stared at the eyes. "What do you mean?"

Fatty chuckled. "Ah, that would be telling, wouldn't it?"

"You're just pretending!"

Fatty was unmoved by the accusation. "I know what I know. You're going to get it! You and all them meat Hooks!"

"You're lying, you're just—"

"You're going to catch it!" Fatty was suddenly fierce. "I seen! I got eyes in the back of me head! I seen! I *know!*" He pushed Hubert in the chest. "And I'm going to tell!"

"You don't know nothing!"

"No?"

"No!"

The postman was closer now. His old army boots were lustrously black even from a distance. Snap, snap! he halted metallically.

"All right," said Fatty, "now scram." He gave Hubert a final shove.

Hubert examined the invulnerably confident Fatty. He turned away with as much dignity as possible. He felt silly with the basket of shopping. Shopping! He lugged at it fiercely.

"And don't forget," the fat voice called, "you're going to get it!"

He turned the corner of Monmouth, then Ipswich. Sweating with effort, he concentrated on pulling the basket. It wouldn't do any good to think about what Fatty Chance said.

Threats were always idle, that's what Mother used to say. Sticks and stones may break my bones, but words can never hurt me.

Pulling the basket up the front steps, through the hall, and easing it down the kitchen stairs, controlling the wheels so the basket would not jolt, Hubert thought there must be an easier way. The muscles of his arms trembled with tension as he pushed into the kitchen. It wasn't enough that he had to do all the shopping himself, but they wouldn't even leave the garden door unlocked for him.

He emptied the basket with precision, trying not to let his anger burst. Lux, butter, a tin of salmon. They never even said thank you! Sardines, marmite, baked beans. What would happen if he got ill? What would happen if he sat in the dark like Elsa? Or prayed all the time? Or read books?

He picked out the packet of chocolate fingers. He screwed up his eyes and the blue and silver foil glimmered with lashes. Inside were layers and layers of deep chocolate fingers, separated by strips of crinkly red paper. Closing his eyes completely, he saw the crushed red paper, discarded on the table, the heap of biscuits pouring over the plate, spinning and twisting, and the laughter and Gerty's voice—"One more for Gerty!"

He smashed the packet on the table. *I won't cry, I won't.* He was in his own eyes, fighting with the big beads of water that wanted to get out.

He knew he would win. He knew he wouldn't cry.

The packet wasn't too badly dented. Inside, some of the fingers would be broken, but that could have happened anyway if he hadn't been so careful with the basket.

He touched the top of the table. It was smooth and soft with scrubbing—velvet wood. He stroked it for a moment, gaining an obscure comfort.

He lifted his head as he heard the shout from the garden. He dashed to the door, expecting . . . But as he gripped the handle, he saw through the glass the group by the swing. It had been Louis' voice. He was high in the swing, his body pushed forward, his head twisted back to look at Elsa and Jiminee. His mouth was shaped with delight.

Hubert started to pull at the door and then slowly he let his hand fall away.

They were laughing. He hadn't seen Elsa like that for . . . They hadn't seen him. They weren't looking at the house. Louis' cry came again.

He would just be an interruption. If he opened the door, he would see that look of children in the playground disturbed in their absorption. A million times he'd seen those closed faces stare up from marbles at other children. And now he knew it would be him. He didn't have the heart to pretend not to notice. Not to Elsa, whom he'd never pretended to before. Not to himself. Not today.

Behind him the clock hummed and he turned back to the half-filled basket. He emptied methodically, unwrapping each packet and putting it away. He left the bag of potatoes till last. Opening the bag, he lifted out the orange-purple fruit that lay on top.

His hands were not big enough to go all the way round the pomegranate, but he held it close. Just one. It had been impossible to resist buying it. He tapped it and it sounded

hollow. He polished it on his sweater. It had tiny purple
veins all over its surface, like an old man's nose. Hubert
smiled and rubbed it backwards and forwards against his
cheek.

He'd never had a pomegranate before.

It was too big for his pocket. He tucked it under his
sweater and pushed the bottom of the sweater into his
trousers, so the pomegranate was held safe.

Hubert mounted to the hall, dragging the basket behind
him. As he put the basket away in the cupboard and
straightened the silver tray on the hall table and climbed
the stairs to his bedroom, he was filled with stealthy delight.
He had forgotten the garden and the trees and Fat Chance.
He had no eyes for noticing the house or the tarnished brass
handle of Mother's room.

He went silently, step by step, purpose and pomegranate
safe together under his sweater.

The top of the house was his.

The noise was so tiny it could have been the scratch of a
mouse. There were mice in the house, perhaps more now
that there were many corners untouched by broom or
sweeper. But they didn't come out in the day.

He waited by the door of his room. It came again. From
Diana's room. And then Hubert knew what it was and he
frowned. Diana was up here. Diana was crying.

He didn't want to see her. He pushed the door of his own
room and then halted. He could tell by the sound that they
were not just ordinary Diana tears. Something was badly
wrong. Reluctantly he turned and went down the passage to
her room.

"You haven't made the beds!"

It was somehow the most important thing about the
room. More important, at first, than Diana's figure, lying
head turned into the pillow with sobs. Of all the children's
rooms, Elsa's and Diana's was always the tidiest. He gazed
at sheets and blankets crumpled from last night, from many
nights, he knew suddenly. And he felt again the preliminary
shiver of wings in his chest.

Outside Elsa was playing and here—here was untouched disorder, the smell of nights between dirty sheets, a pair of knickers over the brass bedstead. They hadn't even drawn the curtains properly.

He almost turned from the room of despair then, where the battle he fought for the regular and the orderly and the normal and the ordinary was so obviously lost.

"It won't do, it just won't do," he seemed to hear the anonymous schoolteacher's voice judiciously blighting hope. He gritted his teeth against it.

The sound of his grating teeth turned Diana's head to the door. Her cap of hair was matted and it shone no longer.

"What's up, Dinah?" he tried.

She did not answer.

He moved into the room and knelt down close to the bed.

"What's wrong?" But as they stared at each other he knew that he would have to be exact in his questions if she were ever to tell him.

"Is it about Mother?"

She just looked at him steadily, but all the while increasing the bat wing beats. It had been directly after last night's Mothertime that she had changed and started to stare at him. But the others had not been upset. So it must . . .

"Is it about Mother and Louis?"

She bit her lip.

"Didn't . . . didn't Mother really want Louis after all?"

The tears mounted in her eyes and fell of their own free will, as if she had nothing to do with it. "No," she whispered.

But it was nearly right. "It *is* about Mother and Louis, isn't it?"

He gripped her hand gently.

"Yes," she said.

"What did Mother say about Louis?" he asked.

Diana turned her face into the pillow. He let her lie there for a little. Then he reached down and turned her head back to him. "Don't be so sad, Dinah. Tell me."

She didn't resist him. Her lips moved and, as she spoke, he realised that the bird was inside her too.

"Mother wouldn't answer!"

Mother wouldn't answer. The words and her fear flew up at him so that he was almost stunned for a moment.

"What do you mean?"

"She wouldn't answer!" Her voice rose.

"But she—"

"No! No—she didn't say anything. I made it up." She held his hand tight so as not to let him retreat before her vehemence.

"But—" Hubert shook his head. He could not believe it.

"I did." She was excited. "I asked and asked and nothing came. It wouldn't work. And they were all waiting and waiting. So I lied, Hu. I put on Mother's voice and I told them a lie."

He knew she was telling the truth—the rush of it smothered his mind.

"What am I going to do?"

"Do?" He tried to focus beyond her immediate entreaty. "Do?" But there was a more urgent question that must be answered first.

"Have you told Dun?"

Her grip on his hand tightened again. "No," she whispered. Hubert breathed with relief. "Don't," he said.

"All right," she said eagerly. He was surprised. She was so close to him, so different from the grave, cool Diana of the tabernacle. Her hand was heavy in his, but he did not think of moving it. She was waiting for him to tell her what to do.

"You mustn't tell anyone."

"But—but at Mothertime tonight?"

"You must pretend again," he said.

"But I can't, Hu, I can't!"

He looked up, blinking his eyes from the closeness of watching her. "It'll be all right. I'll be there." He paused. "If you don't pretend—if you don't go on pretending, Dun will know something's gone wrong. Then Louis—"

Louis would have to go. But it was more than that. The children would be lost; without Mother, there would be no controlling them. Anything could happen. "Besides," he said, "Mother might answer tonight."

"She won't, I know she won't."

Hubert knew too. "Perhaps she was just—asleep last night."

"She never sleeps. You know that, Hu. No, she just didn't answer."

Why hadn't she answered? She could have said no. "Do you think she doesn't want Louis?"

Diana shook her head doubtfully.

"You want Louis, don't you?" he asked.

"Yes."

"Then that's why you lied—pretended Mother did too."

"Yes."

"Then we must keep on pretending." Perhaps, he thought, perhaps Mother didn't understand. It was almost inconceivable. He thought of Elsa's wanting a doctor for Gerty, despite Mother's contempt for doctors. He knew, beyond doubt, that Elsa had been right. Perhaps Diana was too. Perhaps Mother didn't—didn't *know*.

"Do you think she's gone away for good?" he said.

"Who?"

"Mother."

He looked down at the horror in Diana's face. "Oh, no, no," she said, "how could you say that?"

"I don't know. I just wondered. Perhaps—"

"Perhaps what?"

He shook his head. "Nothing."

Because it did not matter anymore. They had to keep Louis, that's what mattered. That was the only thing that mattered. At once the wings stopped. It didn't really matter what happened tomorrow, or the next tomorrow, or the day after. He felt full of calm and he smiled at Diana.

"It's all right," he said. He still had to finish the sandpapering of Louis' box. There might just be time before lunch. "What are you going to give Louis?" he said.

Diana had smiled back at him hesitantly, but at his question she seemed about to cry again.

"Haven't you got anything?"

"No," and he felt her hand tremble in his.

"Well," he said, "well, I've got something you can give him." He pulled his sweater up and brought out the pomegranate. "There," he said. It was as beautiful as ever. "It's a pomegranate."

"A pomegranate." She let go of his hand and took the fruit from him. "A golden bell and a pomegranate, a golden bell and a pomegranate, upon the hem of the robe . . ."

"You remember!"

"Yes," she looked up at him smiling, "I remember. It's a lovely present. Can I really have it?"

"For Louis."

"For Louis."

"Yes."

"It'll be the very best present of all!" She sat up.

"Yes," said Hubert. "Yes, it will."

"Thank you, Hu."

"That's all right." Her tears were forgotten. It seemed to Hubert a very long time since he had seen Diana smile like that. He stood up, watching her. He put out his hand and brushed her hair back a little. Then he went to the door.

"Dinah," he said.

"Yes?"

"Dinah, why don't you make the beds."

She looked vaguely round the room and then back at him. "Oh, I will. Of course I will."

He left her and went slowly along the passage to his own bedroom. He was glad he'd given her the pomegranate. It was much better really than hiding it away in his drawer.

He entered the room and crossed to the window and looked down. In the garden they were still swinging. It was almost no surprise to Hubert to see that Dunstan had joined them. A few days ago, hours, minutes even, how strange that would have seemed: Dunstan swinging. But now . . .

He looked over to the Halberts' garden. Luckily there was no one there. Just rose bushes rising out of the hard earth and the lawn still white with dew where the shadow of the

house shut out the sun. The Halberts wouldn't come out
in winter. Old Halby would be safely inside in front of the
fire. Instinctively Hubert knew that the Halberts wouldn't
wait till November to have fires. It was still a nice garden
though. But not, he thought, glancing down again at Dunstan and Elsa, who were now both pushing Louis on the
swing, not as nice as ours.

Dunstan and Elsa. Hubert and Diana. But they'd all give
presents to Louis at supper. They'd all be together then.
And . . .

He stepped back into the room. He'd better start thinking
about lunch.

25

"Oh, Mother, you are always with us," murmured Diana.

"Oh, Mother, you are always with us," the six voices
echoed.

"indoors and outdoors,"

   "indoors and outdoors,"

"when we are awake and when we are asleep,"

   "when we are awake and when we are asleep,"

"to protect us and guard us,"

   "protect us and guard us,"

"to watch us and love us,"

   "to watch us and love us,"

"at school and in the streets,"

   "at school and in the streets,"

"but most of all in your house,"

   "but most of all in your house,"

"and in the tabernacle,"

   "and in the tabernacle,"

"look after us, Mother,"

   "look after us, Mother,"

"and make us good,"

"make us good,"
"and strong,"
"and strong,"
"and obedient."
"and obedient."

Dunstan turned the torch on. He covered the naked light with his handkerchief, so that only a dim glow filled the tabernacle. Diana leaned forward to the table and began to comb Mother's wig. The half-darkness blurred all detail. The children's attention was fixed upon the priestly motion of the combing and the rustle of comb against hair.

"We comb your hair," said Diana. "And bring you lilies in the spring," her voice quivered momentarily, but held. "We love you."

"We love you," they answered.

"We have been . . ." she stumbled again. "We have been . . ."

"Wicked," said Dunstan.

"We have been wicked. Please help us to be good."

The tabernacle had never dried out since the summer rains. The dampness permeated the rug on which the children sat and the mould greened the corners of the chest of drawers. Even in the heat of their closeness, Hubert shivered.

"Are there any questions for Mother?"

Willy said quickly, "Ask Mother if she's glad to have Louis."

There was a moment of silence. "But we know Mother wants Louis," said Diana. "We asked her last night."

"I want to hear it again," Willy persisted.

Hubert drew in his breath. "Go on," he said, "ask her again."

He waited, wondering if she could do it. He closed his eyes and tried to imagine himself far away. But, turn where he would, the far away became tomorrow's school. It was the last lesson in the late afternoon, and the blackness of the windows and the brightness of the light bared the room of any comfort. There were no giggles, only the sound of the pens scratching at the silence. And in the doorway stood Miss Deke, tall and severe, looking at each child in turn, searching for Hubert, searching for the truth.

"Louis . . ."

Hubert opened his eyes at the authentic voice of Mother.

"Louis is one of the family."

He breathed carefully so no one would hear his sigh of relief.

"Mother loves Louis."

She had done it!

"We must all love Louis."

There was a stirring and a movement of feet in the tabernacle. The shadows were set to dance.

But Diana had not quite finished. "Louis," the voice was struggling at the top of an immense slope, "Louis . . . loves us."

She had mounted and triumphed. The bird in Hubert's chest was a big eagle flying straight and magnificent, up towards the sun.

"Thank you, Mother."

"Thank you."

"Thank you."

It was over.

One by one they crawled out of the tabernacle.

Hubert stooped as he entered the kitchen to brush the earth from his knees. He put his hands under the tap and let the cold water run over them, washing away the dirt and the stickiness of his fear in the tabernacle. His hands were small and cool as he dried them on the dish towel. He lit the gas under the saucepan of milk and water and turned the light low.

The table was laid, a spoon and a plate at every place and a dish of the biscuits left over from tea in the middle of the table. The coloured mugs were lined up on the draining board ready for cocoa.

All the children sat down. There was complete silence— this was the moment. As Louis glanced round, perplexed at the lack of talk, the children could no longer contain their smiles.

"It's time," said Elsa, grinning, "it's time to give Louis his presents."

Louis' look of dismay was tinged with the expectation of trickery—the silver paper wrapping round a stone. His hands tightened.

"It's all r-right, Louis," said Jiminee quickly.

Elsa had already opened the drawer in the sideboard where the presents were stored. She lifted out a flat parcel and brought it over to Louis and laid it in front of him.

"For Louis," she said, "with my love."

Louis watched the small tissue-paper package as though it might suddenly leap up at him.

"Go on, it's for you. Open it."

He raised his hand and touched it gingerly. Looking up at her, he asked, "What's in it?"

"It's a surprise. A present." She smiled.

Reluctantly he unwrapped it. He turned the last fold of tissue paper and exposed the plain white handkerchief.

"It's a hanky," he said wonderingly. So simple a thing could be no trap.

"Turn it over," said Elsa.

On the other side, carefully placed slantwise in the corner, were the initials *L. G.*, the *L* in brown, the *G* in orange.

"It's mine!" he cried.

"L. G. Louis G-G-Grossiter," said Jiminee beaming.

Louis touched the threads delicately. He raised his head. "It's beautiful," he said.

And Elsa blushed.

"It's the best present I've ever had."

Slowly she went back to her seat and sat down. She touched her cheek with her hand. "I'm glad you like it," she murmured quietly.

"I love it," he answered.

He hushed them all.

"Next," said Willy. "Dinah's next."

She brought the pomegranate carefully in her two hands.

The polished hide shone orange against the white-scrubbed wood of the table.

"It's a pomegranate," said Hubert.

Louis nodded. He traced the veins on the fruit with his finger, and then he looked up at Diana and smiled.

A book from Dunstan—*A History of the City of Manchester and Its Environs* by the Reverend T. Shand. Hubert's box. From Jiminee, a drawing of a deep green valley, filled with strange animals and surmounted by purple mountains skirted with snow. A strong blue river ran through the centre.

And Willy presented his best possession—an 1842 bun penny, which he had spent all morning polishing.

Louis' plate and spoon had been pushed to one side to make room for the gifts. Louis put out his hand and touched each one in turn.

"I've never had so many presents," he said at last. "Never ever."

He picked up Hubert's box and held it in his hand. "I'm going to put it in here," he said slowly.

"What are you going to put in there?" asked Hubert.

"My ammonite." Louis opened the box.

"He's g-got a f-f-fossil," Jiminee said. "That's what he m-means."

"An ammonite. Not just any old sort of fossil." He smiled at Jiminee. "It's a little sea animal that died millions and millions of years ago. A special one. It's stone now—like marble, only it's orange-coloured."

"How can it be stone, if it's an animal?" said Willy.

"That's what happens. It dies, then slowly it becomes pet-pet-"

"Petrified," Dunstan said.

"Petrified. It's the most beautiful thing you ever saw."

"Let's have a look," said Willy.

"I haven't got it here. It's at my mum's place." Louis frowned. "But it's quite safe. She'll never find it."

"How are you going to get it back?" Elsa asked.

"I'm going to fetch it."

Hubert said quickly, "But they'll catch you if you go back."

"No they won't. I'll go on Friday night—Mum's always out on Friday night. She gets paid on Fridays."

"But somebody's bound to be there—maybe the police. They'll be expecting you to come back, Louis."

"Yes," said Dunstan, "Hubert's right. You're a missing person, Louis."

Louis looked from Hubert to Dunstan and back again. For a moment they thought he was going to cry. "All right," he said, "I won't go back then. I'll go back when I'm grown up and nobody'll be able to hurt me then, will they?"

"No," said Hubert, "everything will be okay when you're grown up."

"Besides," Louis said, "it's quite safe—she'll never find it."

The milk and water began to fizz in the pan and Hubert got up to attend to it.

"Anyway," said Louis—and Hubert half turned from the stove to listen— "Anyway, even if she does find it—I don't want to go back. I want to stay here."

Hubert mixed the cocoa and poured it into the mugs with a steady hand. He paid no attention to the wave of chatter that had swept the children behind him. Louis really wanted to stay. Now they were all together, just as he'd thought they would be this afternoon when he'd looked down into the garden. Nothing else mattered.

The hot steam of the cocoa rose to his face. The talk of the children and the gurgle of the liquid as it swirled into the earthenware and, somewhere underneath it all, the soft purr of the electric clock swelled inside him into a pure sense of contentment. The rising smell of the cocoa reminded him suddenly of the perfume of the lilies of the valley and of the scent that they had always called Mothersmell—but this was not a hurtful memory. For a moment it seemed to him that Mother was more alive than ever.

He filled the last mug. He took the empty pan to the sink and put it under the cold tap.

He turned to the children. "It's ready," he said.

26

Hubert pried open the lid of the tin with a sixpence.

"It's a funny-looking colour," said Louis.

Hubert heard the disappointment in his voice. "That's all right. It's light-blue enamel, like it says on the tin. It's just got to be mixed first." He opened the drawer of his worktable and selected a clean stick. "All the colour goes to the bottom, see—but it comes back when you mix it."

He dipped the stick into the paint and stirred in slow circles. Swirls of colour appeared in the liquid and gradually integrated until the whole surface was blue. "There," said Hubert, "you'll want to give it a stir every so often."

Louis smiled. "It's just right, isn't it? Can I start now?" He held the brush poised.

"Okay," Hubert nodded. "Don't take quite so much or it'll drip. Wipe some off on the edge."

Louis drew the brush across the lid of the little box.

"Do it all in the same direction," said Hubert.

For a while Louis painted steadily. He picks it up fast, thought Hubert, as he lowered the brim of the lamp to keep the light out of Louis' eyes. "That's right," he said. The little boy was quite absorbed. He wasn't afraid anymore. He'd been a little shy again at first when they'd all come home from school and found him and Willy playing in the kitchen. But the shyness had worn off at teatime.

"It's going to look nice, don't you think?" Louis asked.

"Yes—smashing." Nobody had said anything at tea about Mrs. Grossiter's visit to the school that Monday morning. It had seemed better not to. But Hubert wondered again whether he should tell Louis.

"Light blue—that's my favourite colour. Cambridge." Louis paused in his painting. "I'm Cambridge. What are you?"

"Oxford," said Hubert. It was bound to upset Louis to

know that his mother was looking for him. Standing on the platform in front of the whole form, Mrs. Grossiter had been a monstrous figure—fat, but fat-nasty. She had sweaty skin and smallish eyes; it was difficult to think of her as Louis' mother. *Will anyone who saw Louis Grossiter at any time after school on Friday night please stand up.* Mrs. Grossiter had muttered something. *That is, any time since Friday—any time over the weekend or today. Nobody?* Nobody.

Louis was saying something. "What?" said Hubert.

"I said perhaps Oxford will win next year," he smiled up at Hubert.

Hubert grinned. "I bet you sixpence they'll win!"

"All right." Louis laughed.

No, he couldn't tell Louis—it wouldn't do any good. It would make him afraid again, threatened. Like Fatty Chance's threat, *you'll catch it.*

"What's Elsa?"

"Cambridge."

"I bet Dunstan's Cambridge, too."

"Yes."

"And Diana—no, let me guess." He half closed his eyes. "She's Oxford."

Hubert nodded. It had always seemed odd that Diana and Dunstan weren't the same.

"I know Jiminee's Oxford. I'll bet Willy is Oxford too."

"Yes."

"That makes us three and four—four on one side and three on the other."

"It takes eight to make a boat," said Hubert, but Louis had gone back to his painting and didn't hear.

Hubert wandered to the window and peeped between the drawn curtains. The front garden was a dark hole. Robbers or anything could lurk there easily undetected. He made sure the window catch was fastened and let the curtains fall back into place.

He wondered what all the others were doing. He was

restless. Perhaps it would be good to make sure all the doors and windows were locked.

It was very quiet in the house. He held his breath but heard nothing but the tick of the hall clock—backwards and forwards it went, backwards and forwards, forwards and backwards. You could make the clock follow almost any rhythm if you wanted to.

The front door first. He reached the bottom of the stairs and turned into the hall. He went past the front room and stopped at the table. He ran his finger lightly along the edge. Dusty and a little damp. Nobody'd had time over the week-end to do any cleaning. But now Louis was here all week, they could have the place spick-and-span in no time. It would be like old times, except for Mrs. Stork.

He walked slowly towards the front door. The catch looked fast. He raised his hand to test it, and then suddenly held still. He had heard a scraping sound outside, as though someone were mounting the steps. His instinct was to turn off the hall light and run. It was too late for that. He held firm.

It seemed to him then that he heard someone breathing on the other side of the door. His startled imagination puffed the stranger into a figure of unknown menace—Mrs. Grossiter gigantic with rage, Mrs. Stork, Flight-Sergeant Millard . . . No visitor was welcome—unless it was Him, unless it was Charles Ronald Hook.

The unknown hand struck two sharp blows on the knocker.

Hubert's stomach moved convulsively. He did not look down, but it seemed to him that the prints of the boot on the floor had become individual glinting eyes that stared up at him. They challenged him to look down and observe the triumph of their threats.

Fighting, he told himself that it was not Millard, that it was the postman, or the coalman come to deliver at last . . . or Him. Yes, it was Him. But he did not move to open the door, for in his inward heart he knew that He was not the caller. That would be a miracle. There were no miracles.

It was years since the sounding of the first knock. The second would come at any moment. He prayed, *go away, please go away*. He shut his eyes and suddenly he was on the end of a long plank. The sea below him was cold and green, not the azure inviting ocean of the pirate picture books. The wood trembled under his feet. The next knock was the signal for execution. It would seal his doom.

Hubert turned to run. At the same moment the knocker sounded *crash-crash*.

"Who is it, Hu?"

He almost lost his balance as the rug slid on the hall floor.

"Who d'you think it is?"

All of them stood at the bottom of the stairs—and their questions of fear pushed at him, thrusting him away. He clutched at the table to steady himself.

"The police?"

"Miss Deke?"

"Louis' mum?"

The whispers trembled towards him for an answer. The shame that he had been going to run away was replaced by anger that they did not see he was afraid too.

"Are you going to answer, Hu?"

Once again the knock came.

"Wait," Hubert called over his shoulder. The sound of his unhushed voice made the children flinch. He was angry with them for their fear and then he was angry at himself for being angry. *He* was the one they depended on, *he* was their shield—that's what they were telling him. But he had known it himself—oh, for ages. Without him the house would collapse.

It wasn't Dunstan.

It wasn't Mother. Mother was dead.

It wasn't Elsa anymore.

It was him—Hubert Hook.

He took his hand from the table. "Jiminee, take Louis to the tabernacle. Willy, you go with them. The rest of you stay where you are."

He waited until the three youngest had disappeared down the kitchen steps. "All right," he said, "I'm going to open it."

He turned and walked resolutely to the door. He tugged it open and the autumnal night rushed in.

"Miss Deke!"

"Yes—Miss Deke." This time she did not wait to be invited, but stepped inside at once and closed the door herself.

"I want to speak to your mother, Hubert."

"I'm sorry, Mother's asleep, Miss Deke."

"Then I'm afraid you'll have to wake her up." She patted her gloved hands together with a gesture that meant she would stand for no delays.

"Won't you come and sit down?"

"No, thank you. I came to see your mother and that's what I intend to do." She was completely the crisp-worded, cold-faced Miss Deke of the schoolroom who spoke from the winter within her.

"The doctor says—"

"Never mind what the doctor says. What I have to say to your mother can't wait." She looked away from him for the first time and saw Dunstan, Diana and Elsa at the foot of the stairs. She gazed at them, then nodded and made a little throaty noise, as if to indicate that this was exactly what she'd expected.

Hubert looked at them too, but the sight of their wavering smiles did not make him angry against them now—he was angry for them. Himself, he was no longer afraid.

"Miss Deke!"

She glanced back at him.

"Miss Deke. Mother is ill. The doctor says she is not to see anybody. So I think you better go."

The blood of outrage rushed to Miss Deke's white face. "You *dare* to speak to me like that?"

Hubert lifted his chin. "This is our house, not yours."

"It's your mother's house, young man, and it's her I have come—and am going—to see, even if I have to find her room myself."

"That won't do you any good—it's locked!"

Miss Deke put her head to one side. She examined Hubert with her wily bird look, as if listening to his inmost thoughts. "It's locked," she repeated softly.

Something had gone wrong. He searched desperately for words to repair the damage.

"You say the door of your mother's room is locked?" The sudden gentleness of her voice did not conceal her incredulity.

"I mean . . ." He looked down, catching a glimpse of the boot prints, of Miss Deke's large outward-turning feet, of Diana and Elsa and Dunstan, waiting in petrified whiteness for the contest to end. "I mean . . ."

"I think I'll accept your invitation to sit down now, Hubert." She struck a brief tattoo from her gloves and walked swiftly to the door of the front room. She paused for a moment and glanced to the end of the hall. "Come along, children."

As Hubert led the others into the room, Miss Deke had already turned on the lights and sat down. Her thin, knife-like body seemed to cut into the heavy black leather of the chair.

"Sit down, children."

"It's no good, Miss—"

"Sit down," she commanded. She watched them as they reluctantly placed themselves around the room. She let the silence increase, focussing her attention on stripping off her gloves. She folded them neatly in her lap and looked up.

"Now, children—where is Mrs. Hook?"

Hubert touched his bare knees, rough with goose flesh. Cold emanated from Miss Deke and the room was chilly. The constant tick of the hall clock was just audible, but, try as he would, he could fit it to no rhythm now. He gazed at the empty gloves on Miss Deke's lap, taking a comfort in the concentration as if it made him invisible or, at least, untouchable by her words.

"Where is Mrs. Hook?"

He roused himself. "She's upstairs in her room."

He was aware of Miss Deke's movement towards him. "Do you really expect me to believe that, Hubert?"

She leant towards him, her interrogatory bird head tilted. "Why not?" he said.

Miss Deke smiled faintly at this last feeble retort to defiance she knew so well. "What about you, Elsa, don't you want to say anything? Diana? Dunstan?"

Diana cleared her throat.

"Yes?"

Diana managed a trembling whisper, "Mother is with us."

Miss Deke smiled briefly. "Won't we tell the truth?" she enquired.

Hubert blinked. He grappled with the knowledge that what Miss Deke—or any grownup—called the truth was only what she wanted to hear. He said, "We are telling the truth."

Miss Deke worked the joint of her thumb between her fingers. She glanced rapidly round the room, the dust everywhere proclaiming its lack of care. "Very well," she said, suddenly decisive, "if you will not answer me, I shall have to report you." She paused, waiting for a response. "I mean —report you to the police." A slight indrawing of breath from the children was the only acknowledgement of Miss Deke's words. "You cannot," she went on, "keep your mother incommun——without communication from the outside world. If she is as seriously ill as you say, it is not to be hidden. She must have expert medical attention. I happen to know she is not getting it. I was forced to take it upon myself to make enquiries of Dr. Meadows and he tells me that Mrs. Hook has never been a patient of his. I am sorry you lied about that . . ."

Hubert made a supreme effort. "It wasn't Dr. Meadows. It was another doctor. We made a mis——"

"No, no, Hubert, please." Miss Deke swiftly waved his words away. "Let it be. It was, as a matter of fact, quite another matter I called about. One which I should like to have raised with your mother. However, as she is—not available, I shall have to put it straight to you." Her head straightened and her hands lay still in her lap. "Where is Louis Grossiter?"

Hubert stood up, clenching his fists. Miss Deke opened her mouth as if to command him to be seated, but she thought better of it.

"I have it on the best authority that Louis is in this house."

"Fatty Chance!" said Hubert contemptuously.

Miss Deke gave him a curious look. "Yes," she admitted, "Billy Chance came to me after school and told me that you had Louis here."

"He's a fat liar!"

"No, Hubert," she shook her head, "I'm afraid not. Not this time. You must give Louis up at once. Perhaps you do not realise what a serious offence it is to keep someone against their will—" Something in Hubert's face caused her to hesitate. "Or even with their consent. It's kidnapping, and I do not have to tell you—"

"Fatty's a liar!"

"Hubert!" Her voice struck hard at him, slipping the gentle tether she had imposed upon it.

Deliberately he took a step forward. "Fatty's a liar!"

Miss Deke rose, her hand gripping tight to her gloves. "Stop it!"

"Fatty's a liar—and what's more you've no right to come here." He sensed that behind him the other children had risen too. "Why don't—"

"Stop it at once!" Dekey Bird twitched her head in the manner that had earned her nickname. "This minute!"

"Go away!" said Hubert.

"Go away . . . go away," the voices behind him rose.

". . . quiet this instant . . ."

"Go away, go away, go away." They made it into a chant of violence that swept Miss Deke's words away.

Straight as a sword, she watched the four faces of hate that cried out against her. She did not attempt to silence them. She had lost. They would drive her from the house. But it was not her defeat—she had known a thousand in her time—nor the children's resistance to her words that caused Miss Deke to feel an intense and melancholy unease. She was afraid—not for her own safety in that dark, drab room—but of the cause of their murderous fury. Whatever it was, and her mind skirted it quickly, it had given them a power of confident rage that made them—she murmured the word to herself—*unnatural*.

"Go away—go away—*go away!*"

She had started to move, when the children's chant was interrupted by another sound. Someone was knocking at the door with a confident briskness that made Miss Deke's knocks seem like delicate taps—*bam-bam, bam-bam, bam-bam*.

". . . awaaaay . . ." Their cries dwindled.

There was a long silence in the room.

Miss Deke singled out Hubert. "Well?" she said, pulling on one of her gloves.

"I'll . . . I'll answer it," he said. He walked to the door; his knees were so weak he felt at every step he must fall down. He was thirsty too. He stepped into the hall and looked for a moment at the door that opened down the steps to the kitchen. He could rush down there and drink water forever at the sink.

But he turned towards the front door. Briefly the thoughts he'd had before Miss Deke's entrance slipped through his mind. Now they did not deter him. It didn't matter who it was. The temporarily engulfing rage of the front room had washed him clean of fear or expectation. "It's over now," he repeated to himself under his breath. "It's over now."

Reaching up, he twisted back the latch and pulled open the heavy door.

27

He was a big man. The porch light shining behind his head and the hat resting low on his forehead made it difficult to see his face. He stood quite still. His hands were thrust in the square pockets of his camel's-hair coat, so that only the thumbs protruded.

"Yes?" said Hubert.

The stranger did not move for a moment—it was as if he did not have to hurry. Then slowly he lifted a hand to his face and rubbed his upper lip caressingly with his index finger.

"Well," he said at last. Then he laughed. It was the laugh of a man who enjoyed himself, and immediately it dispersed the shadows of menace that had floated into the hall with the evening mist. "Well." With a quick movement of thumb and finger the stranger flicked back the brim of his hat so that the dim hall light fell on his features.

He grinned. "I'll bet you're Hubert the letter-writer." His laugh burst out again.

"Who—" Hubert began, "what . . ."

The man reached out and tilted Hubert's face. "The dead spit of Vi."

Hubert caught the whiff of nicotine on the man's fingers— the scent of comfortable manliness filled him with a sudden, surprised confidence, like flowers caught unawares by a burst of artificial sunlight. "You're, you're—you must be—"

"That's right." The man bent his knees so that he was on a level with Hubert. "Sorry I'm a bit on the late side— had a spot of . . . unfinished business to clear up."

"Dad! Oh, Dad!" He flung his arms round the man's neck. He felt the stubble on the cheek and the warmth of the coat against his face. The smell of tobacco and tweed and man was strong.

"Quiet down, old boy, quiet down."

"Dad, Dad!" Clasped in those arms, his eyes pressed tight against the shoulder, Hubert knew that he never wanted to move. He began to sob.

"Hey, it can't be as bad as all that." There was a hint of a question in the gentleness of his tone.

But Hubert could not be quieted for a while. The birds of disaster that had soared and trembled within him for so long were struggling out at last. And the pain and the cries as they left him were nothing but joy. The strong hand lifted his face again.

"I'm all right," murmured Hubert, his eyes filled with the diamond light of his tears, "really I'm all right, Dad."

" 'Ere—not so much of that 'Dad' stuff. *Dad*—makes me feel like an institution." He chuckled. "Call me Charlie— Charlie 'ook. Nobody ever called me anything else. Least, not my friends."

"But—but you're—"

"Charlie 'ook."

Tentatively, Hubert tried. "Charlie 'ook?"

"That's it." They grinned at each other.

"Well," said Charlie 'ook, standing up, "and how's Vi— your mother?"

"But, but—" Hubert was bewildered, "she's dead. I told you in my letter!"

"Ah—yes," Charlie 'ook rubbed his upper lip. "I forgot. Who looks after you then?"

"No one. We do."

Charlie 'ook listened without interruption until Hubert glanced into the hall. "Well, let's make ourselves at home, eh?" He started to move forward, but Hubert grabbed his hand quickly.

"No," Hubert whispered hurriedly, "we can't go in yet. Miss Deke's there." He pulled Charlie 'ook out onto the front step and drew the door almost shut behind them. The urgency of what he had to tell Charlie 'ook overcame him for a moment; then, in a rush, he told him: about Miss Deke, her suspicions about Mother, about Louis, about Gerty . . .

Charlie 'ook listened without interruption until Hubert had finished. Then he was silent for a little, as if waiting for the echoes of Hubert's news to diminish.

"What do you live on?"

The question startled Hubert. "Well—we live on . . . I don't—"

"I mean where does the money come from?"

Hubert almost laughed with relief. "The cheque. Mother's cheque—it comes every month."

"But she's—ah, I see." Charlie 'ook removed his hat and ran his hand over his thin blond hair. "How do you cash the cheque?"

"We take it to the bank."

"And they cash it, do they?" He spoke slowly. "What about the endorsement—the signature on the back?"

"Oh, that! Jiminee does that—he's very good at drawing, you see. He can copy almost anything."

"Pretty sharp." Charlie 'ook stretched out his hand to rumple Hubert's hair. "Pretty damned sharp." He laughed again. As Hubert realised that what they had done was, in some inexplicable way, rather clever, he laughed too.

"And nobody knows, eh? About Vi—or Gerty?"

"No."

"Blimey! Except this Miss Deke—she suspects?"

Hubert nodded. "She said she'd report us to the police— for not letting her see Mother."

"But she hasn't got anything concrete to go on." He thought for a moment. "Schoolmarm. What about Louis— she knows you got him?"

"Yes—Fatty Chance sneaked. He saw Jiminee and Louis coming here."

"What's Miss Deke want to do about it?"

"She wants to take Louis back to Mrs. Grossiter, I think."

Charlie 'ook half turned to the neon glare of the street. His profile was outlined against the light. Hubert had a sudden fear that he was going to leave. Then Charlie 'ook said, as if to the deserted street, "We'll 'ave to let her take Louis."

"But you can't. Louis—we've adopted Louis. This is his home now!"

"It doesn't make any difference," said Charlie 'ook, still to the street; then he glanced down at Hubert. "Look—it doesn't matter what you want or what Louis wants. Louis belongs to his mum. That's the law. There's nothing we can do about that. If we go against the law, you know what happens? Prison! Prison—not for you. For me, because I'm responsible for you, see? And if I go to jug, that's the end of the game. The police'll find out about everything—Vi, Gerty, the lot! We'd be done for then."

"But we can't give up Louis—we *can't!*"

Charlie' ook twisted his hat in his hand. Hubert watched the orange-coloured feather in the hatband come round and round. "We got to," said Charlie 'ook earnestly. "Look, he can come and play with you, can't he? And if he's really unhappy, perhaps we can adopt him—legally—who knows? But if we hold onto him now, we'll be in the soup. All of us. There won't *be* no home for any of us here, let alone Louis."

"Yes but . . ." The force of Hubert's logic was muted. Charlie 'ook had arrived. The miracle had happened. He didn't meet Charlie 'ook's eyes as he asked, "Can he take his presents with him?"

"His presents?"

"We gave him presents. I gave him a box. If he can take the presents, then—then he'll have something to remember us by."

"Of course he can take the presents. Of course he can. But you'll see him again."

They stood quietly. Charlie 'ook stopped turning his hat. "It's settled then?"

Hubert nodded. It was worse than sneaking, he knew that. Worse than anything Fatty Chance had ever done. But there was nothing else to do. Nothing.

"Well—now we better go and deal with this Miss Deke, eh?" He laid his hand gently on Hubert's shoulder and pushed open the front door. They stepped together into the hall.

Charlie 'ook dropped his hat on the table. With deliberate motions he unbuckled his camel's-hair overcoat and took it off. "Where is she?" he asked in a low voice.

"In there," Hubert indicated the front room.

Charlie 'ook started to fold his overcoat, then, changing his mind, tossed it carelessly onto the hall chair. "By herself?"

"No—Dinah and Elsa and Dun are in there too."

"Ah." He nodded. He was patting his pockets with little delicate taps. All the while he was looking around the hall. He seemed unwilling to move. He glanced at the clock and then at his watch. "Well," he said, "well." He drew a packet of Players half out of his pocket, then slipped it back again.

A murmur of voices came from the front room.

"They're talking," Hubert whispered.

Charlie 'ook's movements ceased as he listened. "Not a good sign, eh?" He hesitated one moment more, then, "Come on," he said, "we got to break that up." He walked to the front room and pushed the door wide.

They were standing in exactly the same position as when Hubert had left them—such ages ago, he thought. They were silent now, watching Charlie 'ook as he stood in the doorway. Miss Deke, thin and white-faced, was small beside him, almost insignificant. The old house, with its high ceilings and wide doorways and heavy furniture, had someone to fit it at last.

"Well," said Charlie 'ook, "this is a nice surprise." He surveyed the children benignly, but quickly switched his glance to the schoolmistress. He smiled. "And you must be Miss Deke." He came into the room and held out his hand. "Pleased to meet you—always wanted to."

Miss Deke wavered for a second.

"Anything wrong?" said Charlie 'ook.

"No," she extended her hand. "Yes, I am Miss Deke. And—"

"Just a goose walking over your grave, eh?" He chuckled and grasped her hand firmly. "How do you do?"

"How do you do?"

"Never better, thanks." He turned to the children. "Now kids, why don't you trundle off for a bit? Hubert's got some news for you, haven't you, Hu?" Laughing, he ushered them to the door. "Miss Deke and me wants to have a little natter."

"Come on," said Hu, "come *on!*"

Bewildered, they looked anxiously from Hubert to Charlie 'ook. But they went.

Charlie 'ook closed the door and turned to Miss Deke.

"Have a seat, Miss Deke." He leaned back against the door and pulled the packet of Players from his pocket. "Sorry I wasn't here when you came. Just got back from the North—had to spend the weekend up there. Business, of course." He lit a cigarette and blew a cone of grey smoke into the room. "Business, business—never get away from it. How I envy you schoolteachers."

Miss Deke did not move. She said slowly, "As you mentioned, we haven't met before, and I don't—"

"Pity, isn't it? We'll just have to make up for lost time, eh?" He chuckled.

"I'm afraid, you know, that I am at rather a loss." Miss Deke attempted an apologetic smile. "I just don't know who you are."

"Good Lord! I say, I am sorry." Charlie 'ook started to slip the packet of cigarettes into his pocket and then jerked it out again. "Smoke? No? Well," he said, moving into the room, "I'm Charles Hook—Charlie 'ook. Mrs. Hook's husband—the paterfamilias, as my dear father-in-law would have said."

"Oh!"

He watched her gravely. "Why don't you sit down, Miss Deke?" He went over to the black leather chair and brushed the seat with his hand. "There. Everything's in a bit of a mess, I'm afraid—but with Mrs. Hook away—"

"Away!" Miss Deke was unmistakably surprised. She sat down indecisively on the edge of the chair.

Charlie 'ook grinned. "I expect the kids told you differently, eh? Well, you know how they are—don't like to admit she isn't here, even to themselves. No, I had to send her to my sister Molly in Folkestone, you know."

"I see," Miss Deke said blankly.

"She's not a well woman, you know. Not well at all."

Miss Deke tilted her head politely—it might have been in sympathy or in enquiry.

"TB," he caressed his chest lightly. "We didn't find out for a long time. You know how Mrs. Hook is about doctors. By that time, Gerty had got infected too. But they'll be right as rain soon—both of them." He smiled with deliberate lack of conviction.

"I *am* sorry—I didn't know. Of course, I knew Mrs. Hook wasn't well, but . . ."

"Oh well. Bit of sea air will put 'em on their feet in no time." He bent low to stub out his cigarette on the inside of the fireplace. "I blame myself about it," he said, straightening up. "Perhaps I ought to explain . . ."

"Oh, please, no, Mr. Hook. I by no means want to pry."

"No, no. I'd like to—" He waved his hand, vaguely taking in the room, "I'd like to get it off my chest. After all, after Mrs. Hook, you know the children best. You see—well, Mrs. Hook and me have had what you might call a *spotty* marriage. I had to be—"

Miss Deke started to protest, but Charlie 'ook held up his hand. "No, I'd like to go on. I had to be away a lot—on business. And, well, we began not to get on so well. You probably knôw how it is. So we separated. Not legally or anything like that, of course. But we didn't see each other for—two or three years. It was difficult—my being away from the children, you know. Hard on them, I mean. Children need a father. Yes, yes. Vi—Mrs. Hook—wrote me every so often. But she never mentioned anything about being ill. I had no idea about it till I got a letter from Hubert. He wrote on his own." He stopped to light another cigarette. "Of course I came back at once. It was a struggle to get Mrs. Hook to see a doctor. Christian Science, you know, that sort of thing. But I got her to see reason at last. She couldn't do anything for the children—she was that weak. And of course they couldn't look after themselves, could they?"

Miss Deke nodded. "No. I don't suppose they could. No."

Charlie 'ook flicked the lampshade by the fireplace and a whirl of dust rose. He smiled. "Didn't even have a daily woman."

"I see. Then I suppose that was after Mrs. Stork left?"

"Mrs. Stork?" Charlie 'ook said sharply.

Miss Deke was embarrassed. "Yes—I, I happened to run into her one day, after she left you that is, and—"

Charlie 'ook frowned. "I'd rather not say anything about Mrs. Stork, if you don't mind, Miss Deke."

"Oh, yes. I quite understand."

"Yes, well," he rubbed at his upper lip, "with her—Mrs. Hook—in bed, they tried, the nipp—— the children that is, tried to make a go of it. But—well, you see what happens even when I have to be away for a few days: with this Louis, I mean."

"You *know* about Louis?" Miss Deke half rose from her seat.

"Oh, yes. Hubert told me as I came in. They don't have any secrets from me, Miss Deke."

"But Hubert told me that—"

"That Louis wasn't here? Yes—I expect he was afraid you'd want to take Louis away."

"But that's exactly what I *do* want, Mr. Hook—what I must do."

Charlie 'ook sat down on a ladder-back chair opposite Miss Deke. He stared into the empty fireplace. "Yes," he said, "I see that. But what I don't see," raising his head, "what I don't see, Miss Deke, is why Louis came here in the first place. He's not a prisoner, you know. He *wants* to be here, to stay here."

Miss Deke slowly massaged her thumb joint. "I think I can—I am afraid I can answer that, Mr. Hook. Louis is not a happy boy. He is not—in confidence—I think very happy at home. His father is away a lot and—" She halted in mid-sentence and flushed.

"Like me, you mean," said Charlie 'ook with a smile.

"I'm sorry, Mr. Hook. Your children are—well, perhaps they are the exception that goes to prove the rule."

"But I'm afraid they were rather rude to you tonight."

"No children of any calibre are invariably polite, Mr. Hook." She spoke with a decisiveness that had been missing from her voice all evening. "Apart from that—usually, *usually* the continued absence from the home of the father is not good for a child. And Louis, Louis is no exception."

"And how about his mother—doesn't she care for him?"

"Oh, of course she cares for him. But she's—different, Mr. Hook, frankly, from the sort of person we're used to dealing with. She's a Mancunian, of course; perhaps that partly accounts for it."

Charlie 'ook laughed, choking on the smoke of his cigarette.

"Is that funny, Mr. Hook?" Miss Deke asked, surprised.

"No," he coughed, "no—you must excuse me. I have a lot of business dealings up North. I quite understand what you mean."

"Oh, I see."

"But why are *you* here, Miss Deke—not Louis' mother?"

Miss Deke opened her fingers. "Mrs. Grossiter doesn't know where Louis is."

"Why not?"

"Because I didn't tell her," she answered simply. "I thought it would be better if I could take Louis back myself."

"And not tell her where you found him?"

"Of course I would be bound to tell her that, Mr. Hook. But I think she will be likely to make less fuss—than if she had discovered him herself."

"Isn't she likely to make a fuss—I mean, she could be rather nasty about the whole business, couldn't she?"

Miss Deke did not answer and he leaned forward and repeated his question.

"Perhaps," she said at last.

"I get it." Charlie 'ook stood up. "She's cruel to the little blighter—is that it? *She* couldn't stand the talk."

"I didn't say she was cruel, Mr. Hook. I do not know that." She looked down at her hands.

"But she won't make a complaint?"

Miss Deke raised her head. "No, I don't believe she will."

Charlie 'ook thought for a moment. "All right," he said. He tossed his cigarette stub into the fireplace. "All right, I'll fetch Louis."

At the door he turned. "Thanks, Miss Deke."

She gazed at a spot above his head. She smiled briefly.

He stepped out into the hall and closed the door of the front room behind him.

With great care he took out a cigarette. His fingers trembled only slightly as he lit it. He let the dead match fall to the floor; then he allowed himself to lean against the wall. He took a deep breathful of smoke and closed his eyes. "Blimey," he murmured.

It was some time before he opened his eyes again. His first action was to check his watch. Then he went to the bottom of the stairs and listened. Except for the sound of the clock, the house was noiseless. He pulled open the door at the head of the kitchen steps. Voices—high-pitched, angry?—came from below.

He descended swiftly, found the kitchen door and pushed it open.

They were all seated at the table, except Hubert. Hubert had his back to the door that led to the garden. His cheeks were red and he was angry. They were all angry.

Charlie 'ook stood, rubbing his upper lip with his forefinger. Behind him the door was swinging softly to a standstill. He had interrupted, not ended, their argument.

"Hello," he said, "I'm Charlie 'ook."

"Yes," said Elsa, "we know."

"I told them," Hubert said.

Charlie 'ook frowned. "Elsa?" he asked.

"Yes. I'm Elsa. And I know all about you. Mother said you—"

Charlie 'ook held up his hand. "Whoa-up. It looks like

we got plenty of disturbance as it is, without adding to it. What's this—a meeting?"

"Yes, that's right."

"What's the trouble?"

Hubert stepped forward, his fists clenched. "They won't give him up," he said. "They won't see—they just won't see. I told them what you said—about prison an' all, and I . . . and I . . ." His lips trembled.

"Cheer up," Charlie 'ook said, without lifting his eyes from the group at the table, "it can't be as bad as all that."

"Louis," said Dunstan with great emphasis, "is a member of the family. We all agree about that—except Hubert!"

"I do agree. I do!" Hubert shouted.

"You don't," Dunstan replied with calm distaste.

"Liar!"

"Hold on, hold on," Charlie 'ook raised his voice slightly. "Look," he said, directing his words at Dunstan, "you say Louis is a member of the family. Right?"

Dunstan nodded, frowning.

"How do you *know* he's a member of the family?"

"Because Mother said so," Willy answered.

Charlie 'ook stopped rubbing his lip. *"Mother* said so?"

"Shut up, Willy!" said Dunstan viciously.

"But she did!" The little boy was indignant. There was silence round the table. "Well, she did. Didn't she, Elsa— didn't she?"

Elsa lowered her head. "Yes," she murmured.

"See!" Willy was triumphant.

Charlie 'ook looked at each of the children in turn— Dunstan, standing now, dark and tight: Willy, smiling; Elsa, head turned away; Diana, withdrawn deep into herself; Jiminee, his whole body jiggling slightly; Hubert, angry and nonplussed; and Louis, looking from speaker to speaker, saying nothing, waiting.

At length he said, "When did Mother say that, Willy?"

Willy stopped smiling. He glanced at his brothers and sisters and none of them would look at him. "I . . . I forget . . ."

"He m-means," began Jiminee, "he m-means that we all p-p-prayed to M-M-M-M-Mother, and she answered our p-p-prayers."

"Prayers? I see." For the first time he smiled. Casually he glanced round the kitchen, taking in the high white Easiwork, the stove, the coloured mugs on the draining board, the neatness of it all. He took out his cigarettes and lit one, moving without haste. His hands were wide and flat with sturdy, smooth fingers, nails cut short and even. The faintest of nicotine stains discoloured his index finger. The children watched every movement.

"Well," he said at length, meditatively, his expression serious again. "Gerty was a member of the family, wasn't she?"

There was no answer. Charlie 'ook did not look directly at Dunstan. He continued slowly. "We lost her—didn't we?"

"She sinned," said Dunstan sharply.

Charlie 'ook raised his head a little. "And I suppose the wages of sin . . ."

"—is death. Yes."

Charlie 'ook didn't have to look at the children to know that imperceptibly the atmosphere had changed. They weren't as hostile to him—not quite.

"We're not talking about death, Dunstan," he said gently. "No one 'ere is going to die."

"I didn't say—"

"Arf a mo, will you? I want to finish, son." He paused. "You know what would have happened if it got out about Gerty—don't you? Elsa, you know, don't you?"

She nodded. She was looking at him now.

"You know too—don't you, Dunstan?"

"I—"

"Well, of course you do. There wouldn't *be* any family now, would there? It would be an orphanage for the lot of you—not together, neither. Separate. I wouldn't have been 'ere—I *wasn't* 'ere—to help you. It would have been good-bye to all this. You been lucky—very lucky. I'll not say you've not been clever. You 'ave. But you always need luck,

and you had it. The difference is now—the luck's run out."
He drew a deep breath of smoke. " 'cause they know now.
They've found out about Louis. They're going to take him
away. Whatever we do, they'll take him away. They don't
have no pity, you know. The law ain't like a human being.
It says 'do this'—and you do it. Or else. *Or else* is the
orphanage. An' if we don't look pretty sharp, that's what
it'll be. I'll go to jug most likely—but that don't matter.
What matters is that it'll be the orphanage for you lot. The
whole bleeding thing will come out. Not just Louis—the lot."

Dunstan started to speak.

"I haven't finished yet," Charlie 'ook said. "But we have
got a chance. Right now we got a chance. Miss Deke's willing to take Louis 'ome and keep mum about the whole
thing. That's our last chance. If we don't take that, then
they'll come and get Louis anyway. They'll take him back to
his mother and they'll take you away to the orphanage.
But if we let Miss Deke take Louis home now, we'll be all
right. An' it won't be the end of the world, you know. Louis
can come 'ere as much as he likes, he can come an' play—"

"Play!" Dunstan spoke in a fury of contempt. "Do you
think all we do is *play?* You don't understand an' you never
will. Louis is a member of the family—he's one of us. An'
we're going to keep him. Aren't we?" He challenged them.
For a moment they wavered and then they broke to him.

"He's ours."

"We love him and we're going to keep him."

"They can never take him away."

"We'll fight them."

"We won't let 'em in the front door."

Charlie 'ook listened. The hand in his trouser pocket
clenched tight. He'd played it too hard—he saw that through
the smoke that drifted from the cigarette in the corner of
his mouth. Maybe he'd even lost Hubert.

"All right," he said. They were victorious now. "All right.
So you keep him. If that's what you want." They were
calm and happy. Hubert had left his post by the door and

stood by the table. Charlie 'ook sighed. "If that's what you want."

He went to the back door and opened it. He stood, looking out at the black shapes of the garden. He tossed his cigarette and watched the stub hit the border and break into sparks and vanish. Slowly he turned round and came back into the kitchen.

They had waited for him.

"There's just one thing," he said. "I've heard you all say what you want. I've heard that. But . . . what about Louis? What's he say?"

They were quite silent.

Louis had said no word, and all the while they had been arguing the children had hardly noticed him. He had sat with his back pressed against the rungs of the chair, his head sunk on his shoulders so that the collar of his grey jacket brushed against his ears. His hands had been still in his lap—but his eyes had moved constantly from one to another.

He sat up and lifted his hands to the table. He held the pomegranate that Diana had given him. For a moment he rubbed it gently, then he placed it on the table. The skin of the fruit glistened.

He looked up. He was not shy. His gaze moved steadily round the table. Then he slipped from his chair and stood. "I think," he said softly, "that I better be going home now."

The electric clock on the kitchen wall buzzed with the assiduity of a summer fly. The only thing that moved was the red second hand, sweeping round and round, the perpetual mower.

"But Louis . . ."

The visible pain of the small boy's determination cut off protest.

"But Louis," Elsa's voice trembled, "don't you want to stay?"

"Yes, of course." He stood straight as a tulip. "But—but that's got nothing to do with it, you see."

"But Mother," said Elsa.

"Mother wouldn't," Louis struggled with words, "Mother wouldn't want me to stay if—if it meant the end of everything."

There was a long silence, as if Louis were waiting for each of the children to give him their inward permission. At last he said again, "I better be going now."

"You m-m-m-mustn't forget your p-p-presents, Louis," said Jiminee quickly.

Louis looked at the pomegranate and shook his head. "No," he said, "she'd never let me keep them."

"But Louis . . ."

He raised his head and smiled. "It doesn't matter," he said. "I've always got my ammonite."

Jiminee said, "We can b-b-bring your p-presents to school and you can p-p-play with them at school."

"Yes," Louis said. He moved round the table and came towards Charlie 'ook. "We better go up now, hadn't we?"

"Yes, that's right." Charlie 'ook pushed open the door to let the boy go first. Behind them as they mounted the stairs came the other children. Not a word was spoken.

Miss Deke rose from the black chair and came forward as Louis appeared in the doorway. Her hands seemed to move out from her body, but she caught them back quickly. "Hello, Louis."

"Hello, Miss Deke."

"Have you got your cap and coat?"

"They're in the hall."

Miss Deke followed him to the coat cupboard in the hall, the children making way for them. "Thank you, Mr. Hook," Miss Deke murmured.

"That's all right. Anything to obli——" He checked himself quickly. "I don't think there'll be any trouble now."

"I'm sure not. I'm sure." She put out her bony hand and he grasped it. "Thank you."

Louis had pulled on his overcoat. They watched him—the children, Miss Deke, Charlie 'ook—as he managed the buttons down the front. The light in the hall was dim, and the darkness seemed to rise out of the heavy black table and the panelled walls.

He finished at last. He put on his cap and brushed his dark hair under the peak. His hands fell to his sides.

"I'm ready."

"You didn't have anything else?"

"No."

She opened the front door and swung it wide. Louis followed her and then turned on the threshold.

"Goodbye," he said.

"Goodbye . . . goodbye . . . goodbye," the answering murmurs rose and were still, a wind touching a wheatfield.

"Good luck," said Charlie 'ook.

"Thank you, Mr. Hook."

For a moment Louis' dark eyes took in the scene in the hall. And then, arms raised to balance, he was going down the front steps. As they walked down the path, Miss Deke's hand strayed to Louis, but he did not seem to notice it. They reached the gate.

Suddenly the children were released. They ran out onto the porch. And they shouted, "Goodbye, Louis, goodbye, goodbye, goodbye . . ." Long after the gate had closed and Louis was out of sight and had turned from Ipswich Terrace, their shouts continued, dying, dwindling at last, until, like the last shot of the final defender of a fortress already overrun, only an echo struck back from the empty street.

"Come on," said Charlie 'ook, suddenly brisk, "let's get back inside, eh?"

The children did not resist him. They turned and followed slowly as he strode ahead of them through the melancholy of the hall.

28

The smell of stale dust from the old couch was strong. Once the front room had smelled of wax polish and comfort. Everything had been nice and looked after then. In the daytime its darkness had been warm and solacing. But now the lights were meagre against the outside night. The chairs and the table and the piano and the sideboard each stood ugly in isolation, as if whatever had drawn them together had dissolved.

The children waited, not meeting each other's eyes. Hubert tried to remember what it had been like when Gerty had gone. He remembered the burial . . . the mangled lilies . . . the service . . . Elsa weeping, not trying to hide it. There had been lots for them to do then. Now they had nothing to do but feel their grief. Nothing—except to watch Charlie 'ook.

He stood with his back to the fireplace, empty except for the cigarette stubs he had thrown there, gently bumping his shoulder blades against the high marble mantelpiece. He hummed an indistinguishable melody, all the while examining the children as they examined him.

Suddenly he slapped his hands together. "Well, it's a bit nippy in here, ain't it. What about a nice fire, eh?"

Hubert moved forward. "We—we haven't got any coal. We ran out."

"Logs?"

Hubert shook his head.

"Well, that settles that. 'spect the chimney smokes anyhow." He laughed. " 'ave to do a bit of P.T. to keep warm."

Hubert glanced sidelong at his brothers and sisters, standing in cold unease, and wished just one of them would try to help.

"Any suggestions?" Charlie 'ook was grinning, as if unaware of their lack of response.

"Er-er-er," began Jiminee, "there's a 'lectric f-f-fire in the s-s-spare room."

"Aha—all mod. cons. That'll take the chill off our livers."

"Shall I go an' get it?" asked Hubert.

"Let Jiminee get it—he had the bright idea. Okay, Jim?"

Jiminee nodded vigorously and turned and ran out of the room.

"Now let's see," Charlie 'ook felt in his pocket for cigarettes and drew out the empty packet. " 'ere, someone like to fetch me another packet from my coat in the hall? Dunstan—what about you?"

Dunstan hesitated visibly. He left the room with reluctance.

"What about a spot to drink?"

"Cocoa?" Hubert suggested.

Charlie 'ook laughed. "I wasn't thinking of cocoa exactly—something with a bit of alcoholic warmth is more in my line."

"We don't have anything like that here," Elsa said.

"What? Not even a little something for medicinal purposes?" He winked. The perfect closing of one eye, while the other remained completely open, made Willy give a little giggle. No one joined him and he shut up at once.

"Mother," said Elsa, "disapproved of drinking."

"Vi?" Charlie 'ook chuckled. "Come on—I don't mind betting there ain't a little something somewhere for when she was feeling a bit down in the mouth." He glanced at the sideboard. "What about that cupboard, eh? That's a likely spot."

"It's locked," said Elsa quickly as Charlie 'ook moved to the sideboard.

He looked at her speculatively. "I don't believe you want us to enjoy ourselves, do you? Who's got the key?"

Elsa stared at him and said no word. Nobody spoke.

"All right—we'll have to do without. The key, I mean." He smiled. " 'ere, Hubert, lend us your penknife."

He took the knife and opened the thinnest blade. He bent

down by the right-hand door of the sideboard and inserted
the blade between door and jamb. With a quick twist and
a pull he swung the door back. He fumbled inside for a moment and then pulled out two quart bottles and stood up.

"There we are," he said triumphantly, "brown ale. Just
the job, eh?" He clicked the blade of the knife shut and
lobbed it to Hubert. "Now who's going to get me a glass?"

"I will," said Diana suddenly. The children looked at her
with surprise and she blushed.

"That's my girl," Charlie 'ook called as Diana left the
room. "Now all we got to do is to sit down and wait."
He clinked the two bottles together and lifted them onto
the mantelpiece. "Safe from accidents there." There was
an easiness about all Charlie 'ook's movements that made
it difficult to stop watching him. He put the bottles on the
marble slab as though that were the only place for them.

When Dunstan came back and handed over the cigarettes,
holding the packet by the corner and stretching out his arm
to its full length, Charlie 'ook stripped off the cellophane
and pulled out a cigarette almost with one motion. " 'ere,"
he said, holding the cigarette on a level with his waist, "ever
seen this?" He flicked it twisting into the air, darted his
head forward, and caught the cigarette in his mouth.

There was an impressed pause, and Hubert noticed that
even Elsa looked interested for a moment. "D-d-do it again,"
said Jiminee, standing by the door with the electric fire in
his hand.

Charlie 'ook grinned. "Next time. Never do the same trick
too often—you might get caught. Let's plug it in and get a
bit of heat."

Gradually the grey coils of the fire began to redden, giving
up a scent of scorched dust that filled the room with the
indoor solace of winter.

"What I don't like about these things," he said, standing
with his back to the glowing wire worms, "is your kneecaps
freeze, while the backs of your legs are scarred for life with
third-degree burns."

Hubert struggled for something to say. "That's bad, isn't it?"

"I'll say!" Charlie 'ook stepped away from the fire and began to prowl about the room. He had a curious way of touching everything, as though for luck. "The piano work?" he asked.

"Yes," said Hubert. "Not as well as the one at school, though."

"School—blimey. We don't want to play no hymns on this one."

"On Sundays," Elsa said decisively, "Mother always used to play hymns to us on that piano."

Charlie 'ook sat down on the piano stool and swung round to face the children. "Put me foot in it that time good and proper, didn't I?" He laughed. "I don't object to a good rousing hymn myself on occasion—upliftin', definitely." He pushed up the lid of the piano and struck a couple of high notes. "See what I mean?" He broke into "Onward, Christian Soldiers," giving it a faintly waltz-time rhythm.

"Ah, the glass." He stopped playing and took the glass from Diana. He started to move towards the beer, then he turned back and patted Diana gently on the shoulder. "Thank you, love."

In silence the children watched him pour the brown ale into the carefully tilted glass. He filled it frothless to the top. "Well," he said, holding the glass up so that the liquid gleamed redly in the light, "and what shall we drink to, eh?" He looked enquiringly at each of the children, but none of them responded. "Got to be careful," he murmured. "Let's see—what about . . . 'a new start'?" It struck him suddenly as amusing, and he began to laugh so that his hand shook and drips of brown ran down the side of the glass. "That's it—a new start!" He lifted the glass, "God bless," and drank.

He had drunk most of the beer to the toast. He refilled the glass and put the bottle back on the mantelpiece. The room was a little warmer now from the fire, and the faint odour of cigarette smoke and beer seemed to disperse a little of the melancholy.

Charlie 'ook went back to the piano. He stood, playing scales with a couple of fingers and taking an occasional sip of beer. Now and again he looked at the children, hesitated and then continued the scales. At last he put his glass on the top of the piano and sat down. "Now," he said, "what about a song, eh?"

"That would be nice—"

"Yes, please . . ."

Diana and Hubert spoke at once and stopped, aware of the silence of the others.

"What shall we 'ave then? Elsa, what do you say?"

"I don't mind."

"A hymn, perhaps," Charlie 'ook grinned. "What about it, Dunstan?"

Dunstan frowned. "You can't sing hymns and drink at the same time."

"Ah, you see, but I won't do the singing. Now, which one of you's got the voice?"

"Jiminee's got the best voice," said Hubert.

"Okay, Jiminee, what d'you want to sing?"

Jiminee quivered—he tried to speak but the words got tangled before they reached his mouth, "I-I-I-I-I . . ."

Hubert moved close to him. "It's all right, Jiminee," he whispered. Then to Charlie 'ook he said, "I think he'd like to do 'There Is a Green Hill.' "

"My word, I 'aven't heard that in a hundred years. How's it go—something like this, eh?" He began to play. "Ah, that's it. Okay, Jiminee, ready?"

Jiminee nodded and took a deep breath.

"One, two, three . . ."

> There is a green hill far away
> Without a city wall

Without a trace of hesitation, Jiminee's voice cut cool and untroubled into the heavy, already smoky atmosphere

—moving the children into the memory of a Sunday world of lightness and clarity that had so long been absent. There had been no hymns in the tabernacle.

> Where our dear Lord was crucified
> Who died to save us all . . .

Hubert knew that he was crying. But this time it didn't matter. The others probably were weeping too. As the simplicity of the singing and the barrel-organ striving of the piano together penetrated from basement to attic of the house, Hubert felt that he was back again.

> O dearly, dearly has he loved
> And we must love him too,
> And trust in his redeeming blood
> And try his works to do.

As it ended, Hubert came slowly down from a great height. They were absolutely silent.

Charlie 'ook had taken his hands from the keys and was gently rubbing his upper lip. He reached up for his beer and took a long swallow. "Well," he said, swivelling the stool so he faced the children, "if you can all sing like that, we can start a blooming choir and make a mint."

Suddenly Jiminee was by his side, and Charlie 'ook lifted his arm and put it round the boy's shoulder. "We'll have to call you 'the lark.' " He smiled and looked up to the others. "Come on in close by the piano—we'll all have a go. What about—"

" 'The Teddy Bears' Picnic,' " said Willy.

"All right. Teddy Bear it shall be. All know the words? Right." He banged his fingers down on the keys and forced the old piano into a fortissimo it had long forgotten. "One, two, three . . ."

Charlie 'ook's head moved vigorously in time to the music, and, standing directly behind him, Hubert could see the thin strips of hair that stretched from one side of his head to the other gradually becoming dislodged. "Today's the day the teddy bears have their pic-NIC!" A long thread shook loose and flopped over to the other side of Charlie 'ook's head, where it wavered and danced to every beat of the tune. Hubert began to giggle, and one by one the others noticed it and began to giggle too. A second piece of hair joined the first one, and then, like a mass rout, a third and fourth and fifth. As the song ended, the dam of the singing was broken, and the children let go their laughter in a great burst—even Dunstan was shaken uncontrollably.

Charlie 'ook grinned at them, puzzled. Then he became aware of the threads of hair hanging over his left ear. For a moment he was serious and then, without attempting to put the hair back in place, he was seized with their laughter.

The main force had gone and their stomachs were weak, shaken with the pain of a renewed burst that gradually subsided.

"That was good, eh?" said Charlie 'ook. He drank some more beer. " 'ere, Else old girl, get us the bottle, will you? You know what that song reminds me of? The *army*. Bleeding Forces' Favourites—all the time we were in the desert, it was 'Teddy Bears' Picnic' and, what was the other one? Oh, yes, 'Land of Hope and Glory.' First one, then the other. Didn't seem to have no other records in the whole B.B.C."

"What d-d-did you d-do in the army?" Jiminee said.

"Me? Captain, R.A.S.C," he half laughed, half coughed. "Can't all be in the Guards."

"But on the letters it said lance-corporal," Hubert blurted.

Charlie 'ook glanced at him quickly. "Oh, yes—that was after my bit of trouble. Can't have it cushy forever." He filled his glass from the bottle Elsa brought him.

Jiminee said slowly, "Are—are you really g-g-going to st-uh st-uh st-stay?"

"Yes—I'm gonna stay." He drank a little from his glass.

"You haven't got any luggage," said Elsa.

"Like to travel light, see. Saves all that trouble—with porters and things."

"Are you," began Jiminee again, "are you r-r-r-r- . . ."

Hubert interrupted, "He means, are you really our dad, don't you, Jiminee?"

The boy nodded, his body trembling.

"Well," said Charlie 'ook, "in a manner of speaking—yes. Let's see, what they call it? Putative? Yes, that's it." He laughed. "Only don't you go calling me *Dad*." He looked momentarily fierce. "Charlie 'ook's my name. *Charlie* at a pinch."

"Charlie," said Jiminee.

"Charlie—that's a funny name for a dad," Willy said.

"Charlie . . . Charlie . . . Charlie . . ." The murmur spread in the room and died.

"That's right—Charlie. Come on—let's have another song."

They went through "The Minstrel Boy," "Old Black Joe," "The Bay of Biscay," "Tom Bowling," and then Charlie 'ook taught them the words of "The Quartermaster's Stores," "A Lovely Bunch of Coconuts," "My Old Man Said Follow the Van," and finally "The Spanish Onion."

Charlie 'ook sang the solo parts himself in a high strong tenor, keeping the children in tune in the choruses by his powerful lead, and thumping the tunes out into the neon-lit night of Ipswich Terrace that lay resting in mirthless and disdainful gentility.

> "He shall die, he shall die, he shall
> die-diddly-i-diddly-i-die-die-die-die-die-die
> -die-die-die,
> He shall die—he shall di————ie. . . ."

He stopped at last, the sweat glittering in white beads on his pink forehead and his hair dangling in abandon. He poured the last few drops of brown from the second bottle. "Well," he said, "that's it, eh?" He sighed.

The children stood close about the piano. They were tired but wanting desperately to continue.

"There's one thing," said Charlie 'ook seriously, "one

thing I don't understand. What'd you do with the old lady—I mean, Mother—when she died, that is?"

The children looked away from him and were silent.

"Come on, I'm not going to tell on you."

Hubert took a breath. "We buried—"

"Hubert!" Dunstan warned sharply.

"He's got to know—hasn't he?" Hubert turned directly to his older brother and challenged. "He's going to find out, isn't he?"

Dunstan stared. He opened his mouth, but said nothing.

Hubert relaxed. "We buried Mother in the garden—Gerty too. We did it at night, so's nobody would see us."

Charlie 'ook's hand tightened round the glass he held. Slowly he lifted the glass to his lips and swallowed the last of the brown. He put the glass down with extreme care.

When he turned to the children, he was thoughtful. "Well," he said, "you're a ripe bunch of little bastards, aren't you?"

And then he laughed.

WINTER

29

The sun shone east by southeast into the deserted garden. Its November warmth was not strong enough to melt the white coating of frost on the grass. In the sunlit stillness the sounds of Saturday morning came sharp but distant, barely touching the repose of Ipswich Terrace.

In Mother's room the yellow sunlight was fastened to the panelling above Charlie 'ook's unmade bed. Like an escutcheon it hung over the raised headboard, stained with the remnants of raindrops on the window. The runnelled sheets still gave up the odour of the nighttime sleeper to the empty room.

The room was changed since Mother's time. It lacked the permanence of the furniture that still stood, dampening to decay, in the tabernacle. It was bare. The window was hardly ever opened now—the curtains never closed. Anyone might have slept there for one night and then gone on without a single memory of the room. Only the desk remained as it had been, to lock in the past.

In the kitchen the sun struck through the windows of the back door and shot water gleams from the glassware in the open cupboard. All the heat and noise of the house was concentrated in the one room. The smell of breakfast was strong.

Charlie 'ook, shaved and hair immaculately combed, guarded two huge frying pans with his waving spatula. "Hubert—mind out for that toast."

Hubert whipped the tray from under the grill and expertly swivelled four slices of bread to expose the underdone areas to the heat.

"Right-ho!" Charlie 'ook laughed. "Bacon nearly done. Plates out, Di. Ready with the butter, Jiminee." He picked an egg from the bowl and cracked it against the edge of the frying pan, using only one hand. He dropped the empty shell into the tin pail under the sink and repeated the process.

"All right," he called, "bacon done. First plate up, Di. Ready to pass, Dunstan. Pour the tea."

Diana held out the first of the oven-warmed plates and Charlie 'ook forked three strips of bacon onto it and scooped up a clean white egg. "Next," he said. As Diana held out the second plate, Dunstan put the first one in Willy's place on the table. Hubert handed four pieces of toast to Jiminee, who began to butter them. Elsa carefully filled the mugs with tea.

"Why can't I do something?" asked Willy suddenly.

"You can put the sugar in," said Elsa.

"Three heaped for me," said Charlie 'ook over his shoulder.

For almost a minute there was silence except for the scrape of spatula against pan. Then it was all done and there was a plate at every place.

Charlie 'ook flicked the light out under the pans and dropped fork and spatula into the sink. He went to the head of the table. All the children stood at their places, waiting for him. "Well," he said, grinning broadly, "grub up, thank God!"

"Grub up . . . grub!" they echoed him, breaking into laughter. Already it was a ritual. "Grubup!"

"Fall to!" At the signal, they all sat down.

" 'ere, pass up that ketchup," said Charlie 'ook.

"You know what it is?" he asked, thrusting his knife into the neck of the ketchup bottle. "System. System—that's what gets things done." He spread the mound of ketchup over his eggs—he was the only one to have two ("bigger frame")—and began to eat. "I knew a bloke once who 'ad the perfect system. The horses. Blimey, absolutely perfect it was. It 'ad taken him years to work out. You used to see him at damn near every meeting in the country. 'How's the system, Joe?' we'd ask him. 'Oh, comin' along,' he'd say." He filled his mouth with tea. "He was testing it, you see. For years he was testing it. Then he started to bet. I remember the first time I saw him after he'd begun—at Redcar. 'Doing very nicely, thanks,' he said. And he was—even then you could see it. He had a new hat, I remember. Altogether he was more prosperous looking. Then after a bit we didn't use to see him anymore. I run in to him once or twice going into the members' enclosure. By that time he had a car with a chauffeur." Charlie 'ook sat back and sipped at his tea. A glint of butter from the toast shone on his chin. "He got fat too—I remember that." He stared meditatively out of the window. The children watched him. They had almost forgotten about their breakfast.

"Did he win a lot?" asked Hubert.

Charlie 'ook smiled. "I dare say."

"How m-m-much?" whispered Jiminee.

"Well," Charlie 'ook cocked his head to one side, "I don't suppose you could live like he did much under seven or eight thou a year. No taxes, of course."

"Eight thousand p-p-p-pounds?"

"Pounds—a year."

Dunstan banged his knife and fork against his plate. "Betting," he said, "that's sinful." The children glanced at him briefly, and then turned back to Charlie 'ook. *Poor Dun,* Hubert thought, *nobody listens to him anymore.* It was true —Dunstan's spurts of protest carried less force every day. He sat now, black, his clenched fist trembling slightly, glasses gleaming.

Apart from Elsa, only Charlie 'ook paid Dunstan any

attention now. "You're right," he said seriously, "absolutely right—unless you win, that is." He drank some more tea, then took out his cigarettes and lit one. He sat forward abruptly. "I bet none of you's ever been to the races, have you?"

They shook their heads.

"Tell you what—we'll all go. Have an outing. How'd that be, eh? In the spring, when the flat starts. It's no fun now—sticks are always chancy, and the wind on the course is enough to freeze your balls off." He winked and clapped his hands together. "What say, eh?"

Dunstan and Elsa were silent, but the others could hardly contain their excitement.

"Right, you're on. Well now, we got to sort out the Saturday morning jobs. Who wants to come shopping with me?"

"Me—me—me—me!"

Charlie 'ook laughed. "Drop more tea, Elsa. Last week it was—Diana and Elsa, right? Well, this week," he rubbed his chin gently, "it better be Dunstan and Hubert."

Dunstan frowned. "No, thank you very much. I never go shopping."

"Me, me—let me go instead," Willy cried out.

"Oh, come on, Dun," said Hubert, "it'll cheer you up."

Dunstan pushed his chair violently back and stood. "I don't want to be cheered up!"

"Hubert's right," Charlie 'ook said, looking curiously at Dunstan, "shopping on a Saturday can be a lot of fun."

"I want to stay here. You can't make me go."

"He's afraid," Diana said matter-of-factly, "he's afraid to leave Mother."

"I-I . . ." Dunstan's face turned deep red. His body quivered.

"You don't have to go if you don't want to," said Charlie 'ook.

Elsa leaned forward towards the standing boy. "Go on, Dun. Go with him." She was deadly serious.

The shock of her words made Dunstan let go his breath. "Elsa!"

"It's all right," she said urgently, "it's quite all right."

Amidst the silent children, Dunstan slowly sat down, staring at Elsa.

Suddenly Charlie 'ook put back his head and let out a gust of laughter. "Goddamit," he managed to get out, "goddamit—she wants you to keep an eye on me!"

Elsa flushed and turned on Charlie 'ook's laughter—but before she could speak, high above them was the sound of a hard knock on the front door.

Charlie 'ook stopped laughing at once. "We expectin' anyone?"

Hubert shook his head.

Charlie 'ook stubbed his cigarette out in his saucer. "I better go an' see who it is." He hesitated as if waiting for someone else to offer; then he got to his feet.

As soon as he was out of the room, Dunstan said to Elsa, "Why did you say that, Else—why?"

"Because," said Elsa quietly, "it's like he says—someone ought to keep an eye open." She glanced at Hubert.

"But couldn't you go?" said Dunstan almost pleadingly.

"I went last time."

"But why me?"

"I'd rather have you go than—than . . ." She didn't try to finish the sentence.

"You mean me—don't you?" said Hubert.

Elsa drew in her breath. "Yes," she said, "yes, I do mean you. You just don't care anymore, Hubert. You're a . . . a bad *influence*." She talked directly to him. "None of them care any more, and it's your fault!"

"It's not my fault. It's not me that doesn't care—it's you. You and Dun." Suddenly his own anger hit him like a blow. "You just sit there and blame somebody else—me. You don't do anything. You just blame. You've been like that ever since Gerty died—you don't see any good in anything. You just—just . . . *sneer*. That's all you do—what good is that? Sneering and blaming. Can't you see? Everything's all right now. But nothing's right to you two. Nothing's right except what you say's right—according to you. But you

don't do nothing. Can't you, can't you," he raised his hand
as if to tear understanding out of the air, "can't you see—
can't you let things *be*." He groped, "We're happy now—
aren't we? What's wrong with that?"

She did not answer him. She just sat there and it could
almost have been that she was going to cry. For a moment
Hubert saw her as the old Elsa—when they had been together against everyone, when he had looked up to her. That
he could attack her, that he could say such things to her,
shot a bolt of fear into his heart. For a second he wavered.
Then he looked away. "Come on," he said, "we got to do
the washing up."

The next instant Charlie 'ook came back into the kitchen.

"Well, well, well—what have you been nattering about?"
He slapped his hands together. "That was the coalman. Going to have lots of fires. I sent him round the back. He'll be
here in half a mo." He stood, half-aware of their tenseness,
but making his geniality ride over it. "Come on, what are
we waiting for? Let's go an' open the gate for 'im, eh?" He
flung open the kitchen door and stepped out into the bright
November sun. "Lovely day," he called, "come on." He
broke into a whistle.

They had not been in the garden for a long time. They
stood in a group with their backs turned to the tabernacle and
watched Charlie 'ook striding down to the garden door. He
shot back the bolt, flaking some of the black paint, and
opened the door to the street.

Hubert held his breath and then blew it out in a long
frosted plume. At the bottom of the garden, all the leaves
were down. They clustered at the roots of the three clumpy
box hedges. It was almost winter all right. Hubert let the
frosty air fill his mouth. It made him dizzy, like the cold
stuff the dentist gives you, he thought. Charlie 'ook's whistle
came faintly across the lawn. Hubert turned slightly to the
Halberts'. Old Halby's hedge was cut as precise as ever. He
looked up higher at the white-blue glittering sky. A million
miles away a silver silent plane flitted. He breathed in,
feeling the coldness filling his lungs until like balloons, at a

sudden release, they would carry him up, up out of the garden along the cord of his vision to the sky. He would mount and be lost forever in the blueness.

He caught at his breath, as if it were alive and would escape him. Then he looked down and the garden wavered. Coming across the lawn were Charlie 'ook and the coalman, a big sack bending him as if the sky had tumbled on his shoulders.

"In 'ere, mate." Charlie 'ook heaved the cellar door wide. The coalman put his shoulder against the boards that came halfway up the opening; for a moment he balanced, and then with a quick jerk started the cascade of coal. The black dust rose, sparkling into the sun.

"One," said Charlie 'ook loudly, rubbing his hands. "Cold, i'n' it?"

The coalman stood up. He nodded, folding the sack against his stomach, and slapping little spurts of dust into the air. "Warm in the sun, though."

He wiped his face with his hand, as if pondering. He settled his cap a little further back on his head. Even without the weight of the coal, he still stooped—his head, neck and shoulders forming a continuous sloping line. He walked back across the lawn, making another set of dark prints on the whitened grass. Behind him the dust still danced and the tarry smell of coal was sharp and satisfying.

They stood in silence, sucking at the smell.

"We're not going to be cold this winter," said Charlie 'ook at last.

"How much are you getting?" Elsa asked.

"A ton, my girl—one glorious imperial ton of black diamonds."

"We never had more'n six hundredweight before."

"Ah—an' I bet you all had chilblains."

"But we can't afford—" began Elsa.

"You leave that sort of thing to me, eh?" Charlie 'ook grinned at her and she did not protest anymore. She too felt the brightness of the day.

"Now," said Charlie 'ook, cocking his head to one side,

"what about a game? Get a little of the old circulation going."

"*He!*" said Willy.

"He? All right—who'll be it?"

"You!" came in a chorus. "You, Charlie."

"What, me?" He laughed.

"Charlie's it!" sang out Jiminee.

As Charlie 'ook took a step forward, the children scattered wildly. Charlie 'ook walked slowly, shaking his head and muttering, "Now who shall it be—who shall it be? A little tasty fat one or a big tall skinny one?"

The children formed a wide dancing circle around him.

"Charlie can't catch me!"

"I can't, can't I? I got eyes in the back of my head!" But he merely strolled. Then suddenly he turned and with python speed darted back on his tracks. Diana had followed behind him. She yelled with fear and laughter and ran. Her fair hair blowing out behind her, she sped across the lawn. She was the fastest of them all, but not faster than Charlie 'ook. He was almost up with her, when she stopped dead and turned smiling at his touch.

He couldn't halt himself in time and he crashed into her with a force that knocked her to the ground. Grabbing at his arm, she pulled him down on top of her. The children waited for tears. For a moment Charlie 'ook and Diana were still; then he hoisted himself on one elbow. "You're not hurt, are you?" he asked.

Diana lay on her back and looked up at him. Her hair spread out on the frosty grass. She closed her eyes and began to laugh. The children stood round watching the two of them. The girl's laugh was full and calm. It seemed to Hubert that he'd never heard her laugh like that before. She opened her eyes again and they caught the blue of the sky. Her gold hair spread, her blue eyes, her hands palm up, she laughed at her abandonment of flight.

Charlie 'ook grinned. He put his hand on the girl's side and moved it up under her armpit and began to tickle her. Her laugh changed to a higher pitch as she squirmed away.

She sat up abruptly. "I'm it, now." She looked smilingly around. Charlie 'ook heaved himself up and the children backed away. Then they were all running, filled with shrieks, with Diana after them.

Willy, scampering towards the house, tripped and fell. He lifted his head, his face formed to yell, but before he could utter a sound, Charlie 'ook caught him beneath the shoulders and lifted him high in the air. "She won't catch you now!" he said as he ran to the tabernacle and swung Willy onto the boards that served as a roof.

Willy stood amazed, not knowing whether to choose grief or laughter. Then, looking down at the running children, he stamped his foot in triumph. "I'm the king of the castle!" he called out.

Diana, almost up with Dunstan, glanced back and saw Willy prancing on the boards. She stopped and stared, the grin gone from her face. One by one the others turned too, until all of them stood in a scattered circle watching their youngest brother on his perch. And the little boy accepted their silence for admiration.

"I'm the king of the castle," he shouted in his glee, "get down you dirty rascals!"

"The tabernacle," murmured Diana, half-frowning.

Fist clenched, Dunstan stepped forward, then stopped.

The coalman had just emptied his second sack. He straightened his shoulders for a moment and saw Willy. " 'ere," he said, "you must 'ave wings to get up there."

"I have got wings," Willy shouted to his audience. "I'm an angel."

Charlie 'ook's laugh burst out into the morning air. The coalman was struck with a deep wheezing chuckle.

From coalman to Charlie 'ook the children looked in puzzlement. With timidity they began to smile.

"You can't catch me, Dinah! I'm the king of the castle!" Willy jumped up and down on the rattling boards.

Diana ran up to the tabernacle and put up her hand to grasp Willy's legs. He danced out of her reach. "Yah-boo! You can't catch me!" Standing on tiptoe and stretching her white arm to its fullest extent she could not quite touch the stamping feet in the centre of the roof.

"She l-l-looks like Alice in W-W-Wonderland!" said Jiminee.

Like a secret password, Jiminee's words released the children into sudden and consuming laughter. They ran forward—calling "Alice! Alice!"—and surrounded the tabernacle. They leapt up, trying to find a grip on the slippery smooth boards, and slithered back. They pounded with their fists, and their white breath shot up at Willy in soft darts.

Behind them, unnoticed, came the adult murmur of the male voices.

His voice sharp with delight, Willy lorded it over them. They could not reach him and did not try anymore. They beat their fists on the boards, drumming out the chant.

"I'm the king of the castle, get down you dirty rascals!"

On the roof of Mother's tomb Willy danced in time.

The drumming and the shouts carried clear in the Saturday still air. On the second floor of the Halberts' a curtain was moved aside and a face looked down into the Hooks' garden. For a while, the watching face remained. Then the curtain fell back.

High above, the silver plane had vanished at last.

30

Dunstan squatted on the hearth and watched Hubert scrumple the paper and push it down into the grate. The younger boy worked methodically. Each piece of paper was squashed to the same size. Then he laid the little sticks crosswise, leaving plenty of room for the flames to burst between them.

Dunstan stood up and took the matches from the mantelpiece and handed them to Hubert. Hubert glanced at him for a moment. "Thanks," he said. He struck a match and lit the newspaper.

"Don't you put any coal on?" asked Dunstan.

"Not yet," said Hubert. "It has to get hot first, so the coal will burn." He reached for the coal scuttle and selected a couple of small lumps of coal. He held them, waiting for the wood to catch. He was uneasy with Dunstan crouching like a frog beside him, and he looked into the fire as though his gaze were needed to keep it going.

Charlie 'ook wasn't up yet. He hadn't come back till long after the children had gone to bed last night. They'd had breakfast without him. Willy had wanted to rush in and wake him up, but Hubert had said no.

The front room was light and sunny and clean. It was like the old days. Diana and Hubert had washed the net curtains on Saturday afternoon, hanging them out to dry in the sun. This morning they had put them up again and now the windows shone in a brilliant mist of bridal white. It was the first time for ages that Diana had helped around the house.

Hubert reached forward and dropped a piece of coal into the nest of burning wood. "Do you think we ought to get him a Sunday paper?" he asked Dunstan.

Dunstan thought. "We don't know which one he reads," he said.

"No." Hubert dropped the other piece of coal into the fire. "Here, hand me the tongs, Dun."

"Of course," said Dunstan, "we could get a lot of them—could get them all."

Hubert looked at him in surprise. "But that'd be awfully expensive."

"Well, we've got the money, haven't we?—what was left over from shopping."

Digging into the scuttle for a large piece of coal, Hubert frowned. It was true that there had been nearly two pounds over from the ten Charlie 'ook had given them, but that was rainy-day money, like the post office savings. Hubert had six pounds, seven shillings and twopence in the nail box in his workshop drawer. How could he explain to Dun, who'd never handled more than ten bob at a time in his life, that this money wasn't for idle spending?

"We'll wait," he said finally, "we'll wait and ask Charlie."

Dunstan nodded. He didn't seem very interested—not in that.

Hubert settled the large piece of coal onto the fire and put down the tongs. He rubbed his hands on his trousers and stood up. "You don't like him much, do you?"

Dunstan glanced at him mildly. "Him? I don't mind him."

"We'd—we'd be in a pretty pickle if it wasn't for him."

Dunstan smiled. "We'd always have Mother, wouldn't we?"

Hubert sighed. He stepped back from the fireplace. It could be worse, he told himself, it could be—

"What did he want Jiminee for yesterday?"

"What?" Hubert jerked his head up.

"Yesterday afternoon—he and Jiminee were in here by themselves."

He temporized. "Were they?" he asked. He observed Dunstan cautiously—the elder boy still squatted, but he was interested now.

"Yes," said Dunstan, "they were. Was it about the cheque?"

"What do you know about the cheque?"

"Quite a lot."

"Who told you?" But he knew the answer already.

"Elsa." The reflection of the small flames glinted in Dunstan's glasses, obscuring his watching eyes. "It was about the cheque, wasn't it?"

"What's wrong with that?"

"Nothing's wrong. I didn't say anything was wrong. I just wanted to know, that's all."

Hubert picked up the poker and pierced the large piece of coal. It split in two and the flames ran up the smooth black walls the break had made and a sudden whirl of smoke blew into the room. Dunstan coughed and turned his head. He took off his glasses and rubbed his right eye with his fist.

"Got something in your eye?"

"It's all right," said Dunstan.

Hubert laid the poker down in the fender and moved closer to his brother. "Here, let's have a look."

Dunstan looked up. His eye was red and he kept blinking it.

"A bit of grit, I expect," Hubert said. "Here, put your head back."

"It's nothing," said Dunstan, but obediently he let Hubert lift the eyelid.

"Dunstan."

"Yes?"

Hubert hesitated. He thought again how much Dunstan with his glasses off resembled Louis. "Dun, you're not going to spoil anything, are you?"

Dunstan frowned. "What do you mean?"

"I mean about Charlie 'ook. You said you didn't mind him. You're not—you're not going to do anything, are you?"

Dunstan gazed at him steadily. "What could I do?" he said. Unguarded by glasses, his eyes had none of their usual menace. "What could I do?" he repeated. He turned his head and looked into the fire.

"I—I don't know."

"You know what he said?" Dunstan didn't look at his brother.

"What?"

"He said that he'd take me up the Charing Cross Road on my birthday and buy me some books."

"Why, that's super, Dun, that's—" he was puzzled at the detachment in his brother's voice— "wonderful."

"Do you believe he will?"

"Why—why, of course he will. If he says so." Hubert frowned. It wasn't his idea of a birthday treat, but for a bookworm . . . Yet he couldn't understand why Dun should doubt so. Couldn't he ever trust anyone?

Dunstan stood up abruptly and put on his glasses. "Well, we'll see, won't we?"

Hubert watched his brother walk to the door. "But," he began, "but—"

Dunstan looked back. "But what?"

"It's all right, isn't it? It is all right?"

Dunstan seemed to examine the fire for a long time. "Perhaps," he said, "perhaps it will be." He was gone.

Hubert went back to building the fire. It could be worse, he thought—worse for Dunstan. At least his brother wanted something.

He piled the coal on now, watching the brief crackle as the coal dust was consumed. The rise of the flames and their delicate tremble roused in Hubert a remembrance of the Sunday fires they used to have in the front room. There had been another smell then, besides the smoke and the polish and the warm dust—the scent of Mother's soap. He sniffed, thinking momentarily that the smell might come with the memory. In that moment, it was suddenly inconceivable that yesterday they had been pounding on the roof of the tabernacle. He glanced up.

Charlie 'ook stood in the centre of the room, regarding him.

"Morning, Hu." He looked tired still. "Nothing like a fire on a cold morning." He glanced round the room. "Posh. Like a blooming funeral parlour—only one thing missing. Flowers!" He laughed and then grimaced.

"Do you want some breakfast, Charlie?"

"I could do with a cup of tea. Unless . . ." He opened his jacket and took a fob watch out of his waistcoat pocket. He snapped it open. "A bleeding hour till opening." He groaned melodramatically.

"Charlie!"

"What?"

"That watch—can I have a look?" He sucked in a breath and held it tight.

Charlie 'ook grinned. "Recognize it, eh?" He held it out and Hubert took it gingerly from his outstretched hand.

"It is!" He turned it over and stared at the burnished inscription—C.R.H. "It works!"

"Of course—what's the good of a watch that don't work?"

It was alive in his hand, and warm from Charlie 'ook's pocket. He lifted it to his ear and listened to the tick. It had been months ago that it had stopped, but the tick was just the same as always.

"Had to put a new mainspring in. Must have had a hell of a bang."

"Yes." Hubert nodded. He looked at the face again, with its old-fashioned Roman numerals. There was no second hand to bother with. "It's yours, isn't it? I'm glad you've got it."

"The only thing the old lady ever give me—well, the only *proper* present."

"The old lady?"

"Your mother. Gave it me when we got married. Only secondhand, of course, but we weren't rich in those days—never could afford a chain."

Hubert passed it gently back to Charlie 'ook. "It needs a chain, doesn't it?" he said.

"I suppose it does really." He stared at the watch, rubbing the case with his thumb. "But she ain't here to give it me now, is she?"

"Well—well," unaccountably Hubert's voice trembled, "we could give you a chain—I mean all of us—for your birthday."

Charlie 'ook looked at him. "You wouldn't want to waste your—"

"It wouldn't be wasting."

They were silent for a moment, and then both smiled.

"Here," said Charlie 'ook, going back to the watch, "see the initials?"

"C.R.H."

"Ah, you're sharp. Coincidence, isn't it?"

"What you mean?"

"You think they're mine, don't you? Charles Ronald Hook?"

Hubert was puzzled. "Well . . ."

"They aren't, you know. They were on there when she bought it. That's *why* she bought it. Told you it was second-hand, didn't I?"

"You mean they're not yours at all?"

"Well—yes and no. They wasn't *meant* for me. This ticker's a good hundred years old, see."

"Whose are they then?" asked Hubert. Somehow his elation at the recovery of the watch had dwindled.

Charlie 'ook brushed his upper lip. "You're like your mother, you are. She used to spend hours puzzling over that. I remember she used to rather fancy *Cyril Rupert Haverford*. See me a Cyril! He laughed.

"But it's yours now."

"Yes. It's mine now." He slipped it into his waistcoat pocket and patted it. "Sounds like a bomb ticking away in there." He stretched his neck and yawned.

"I'll get you that cup of tea, if you like," Hubert said.

Charlie 'ook moved his head from side to side, easing the stiffness from his neck. "I got a better idea," he said. "A drop of Guinness." He went slowly to the black chair and sat down, sticking his legs straight out. "You can get it for me, if you like—in the cupboard. I brought in a new stock last night." He took out a cigarette and lit it, watching Hubert fetch the bottle and glass. "Here, pour it onto the side of the glass—otherwise all you get is half a pint of froth." He reached out and took the glass and drank.

Hubert sat on the hearth, the heat of the fire on his back. He pulled up his knees and rested his chin on them; his breath made small damp patches of warmth on his knee-caps. The blue smoke from Charlie 'ook's cigarette rose into the sunlight, wavered as it was touched by the draught, dipped, bobbed, and then was twisted tempestuously into oblivion.

"Where are the others?" asked Charlie 'ook lazily.

"Jiminee's drawing, I expect, and Dun's probably reading in the library an' Elsa'll be in her room, and Willy's playing, I expect."

"What about Di?"

"Di?"

"Diana."

"Well, I expect she's in . . . I expect she's playing too." He had been going to say she'd be in the tabernacle, but she didn't go there anymore, he realized suddenly. "Perhaps," he said tentatively, "she's swinging in the garden with Willy."

"Swinging," Charlie 'ook murmured. "That's nice." He drank more Guinness, then held out the glass to Hubert. "Here, like to try some?"

Hubert nodded and took the glass. He sniffed and looked up. "It smells burnt," he said. He tried a sip. "It's bitter!"

Charlie 'ook smiled and reached for the glass. "The more of that sort of bitterness, the better." He poured himself some more.

Hubert licked the traces of Guinness from his lips. "Charlie," he said, "what was Mother like—when you got married?"

Charlie 'ook flicked his cigarette into the fire with a snap of thumb and forefinger. "Learned that from a Yank in the army." He lit another. "She was pretty. Not just pretty. What's the word in the Bible? 'Comely,' that's it. Comely." He watched the smoke from his cigarette. "Good to look upon—that's from the Bible too." He laughed.

"Why are you laughing?"

"Oh, a thought—a passing thought. She was healthy—loved it. Loved all of it." He half closed his eyes. "You wouldn't have thought it, would you?—a vicar's daughter." He opened his eyes and looked at Hubert. "But you're a bit young to know about all that, aren't you?"

Hubert shifted away from the heat. "All what?" he asked.

"Women—men. Being married. Or not being married—'ere you'll have me spilling the beans if I'm not careful." He sat up a little and grinned.

"I don't . . ."

"Ah—forget it. She was a great girl, old Vi."

Hubert moved again. He touched the back of his sweater —it was almost scorching. "Why—why did you go away?"

Charlie 'ook blew smoke into the sunlight. "The war. Had to go an' fight."

"But afterwards," Hubert persisted, "couldn't you—"

"Afterwards?" Charlie 'ook spoke abruptly. All at once he was very still and thinking, and he didn't smile. He held his glass stiffly. "Afterwards." The smoke drew up to his eyes and he blinked. "I'd rather not talk about that." He waited for a moment and then took a long drink.

He looked round. "No Sunday papers?" His face relaxed again.

"We didn't know which one you wanted."

"*Sunday Pic, News of the World, The Dispatch*—the lot. Why don't you pop out an' get 'em for me?" He reached in his pocket and gave Hubert a half-crown. "Keep the change."

Hubert stood up—his legs were stiff and for a moment his head throbbed. "All right," he said, "it won't take me a mo." He walked to the door and looked back. "Charlie," he said, "you didn't mind me asking all those questions, did you?"

"Who me? Nah—that's all right, kid. It's only natural." He yawned. "What's for dinner?"

"Roast beef—Dinah's doing it today."

"Well, look, I've got to pop out for half an hour in a little while, but I'll be back before half-past one—so we can have it then, okay?"

"All right, I'll tell Dinah."

"You do that." He turned away and shifted his chair so it faced the fire more directly. Watching, Hubert saw him shiver. He closed the door gently.

31

He was gone only ten minutes. He ran all the way back—counting each of the mournful plane trees as a marking post for the record marathon. The sacred Olympic fire was hidden in the thick wad of folded papers. Triumphantly he leapt up the steps to the platform where the fire would burst into perpetual flame. Home and victorious.

Only half-aware that the front door was open, Hubert ran across the threshold and down the hall into the front room. "Here we are," he called, "I've got them. I've got the pap—"

He stopped dead.

Mrs. Stork turned her lips towards him. "Well, if it isn't Berty. Mother's little helper, I see—as always." She stretched her mouth into a smile and the heavy dewlaps obediently rose and flattened. "Or perhaps I should say *Father's* little helper?" She chuckled and glanced at Charlie 'ook. The dewlaps slumped.

Charlie 'ook was silent.

Mrs. Stork raised her voice a little. "I just got here myself. Look," she raised a paper-wrapped bunch of tired chrysanthemums, "I brought you some 'mums to brighten the place up."

All the children were there, but she had been talking only to Hubert. Now she turned to the others. "Well, I must say, you're a cheerful lot. What you staring at? Ain't you glad to see your Mrs. Stork again?"

Elsa spoke abruptly. "No."

"No? Well, well," said Mrs. Stork in a cheerful nothing-can-put-me-out tone of voice, "you was always such a polite little girl. Times change, eh? Times change. Don't they, Mr. Hook?"

Charlie 'ook cleared his throat. "Mrs. Stork—"

Hubert stepped forward, the papers poised as a weapon. He was conscious only of this old intruder in her threadbare, malice-black Sunday best. "What are you doing here?"

"Me? Old Mrs. Stork? I'm making a call." She coyly brandished floral evidence of her good intentions. "I come to ask after your mum. I do hope she ain't still poorly, Mr. Hook?"

"Yes, I'm afraid she is." Charlie 'ook came up to Hubert and took the papers. "Thanks," he said.

"I am sorry to hear that," murmured Mrs. Stork. "I don't see little Gert—is she ill too?"

Charlie 'ook laid the papers down on the table, turning his back on Mrs. Stork. When he faced her, he was smiling. "Yes —she's ill too. I sent them both off to Folkestone for a bit of sea air."

"Oh, that's ever so nice." She paused and shifted the flowers in her arms. "Expensive, though—ever so expensive them seaside resorts."

"Off-season rates this time of year." He rubbed his lip of invisible moisture. "But I don't have to worry about that. My sister Molly got a little place of her own down there."

"My, that's handy." Mrs. Stork moved the flowers to her other arm, but Charlie 'ook did not offer to take them from her. "Close to the sea, I hope."

"Stone's throw, as they say. Just a stone's throw." Suddenly he was confiding. "Molly runs a little fish and chip shop, see. Right off the esplanade. Two floors above, all her own. 'Tea room' she likes to call it—you get your cod and chips on a plate. None of this grease and old newspaper stuff. Half a dollar a time. Calls it 'plaice.' Tea, bread and butter, 'plaice and fried potatoes,' and a slab of Dundee cake. Nice little business—*verrry* nice little business." He screwed up his eyes to a seaside horizon filled with a silver rain of half-dollars.

"It sounds nice," said Mrs. Stork. Charlie 'ook ignored her. "Very nice. Some people are lucky." There was an edge of sharpness in her voice.

Charlie 'ook had lowered his eyes and was looking at the half-concealed headline of *The Dispatch*.

Mrs. Stork glanced behind her and started to sit down on the black leather chair.

"Have a chair, Mrs. Stork," said Charlie 'ook suddenly, loudly attentive. "Take the weight off your feet." He laughed. "'ere, Elsa, why don't you take Mrs. S.'s flowers down and put 'em in a vase, eh?"

White-faced, Elsa held out her hands for the flowers. She turned and left the room. They all watched her go, a sword of righteousness.

"Ah, that's better!" Mrs. Stork withdrew a blue silk handkerchief from her bag and dabbed at her forehead.

For a moment there was silence except for the faint stirring of the fire in the grate. The air in the room seemed to press down upon them, laden with things to come. A faint breath of cool outside air touched the back of Hubert's knees. The children stared and were quiet, waiting for Charlie 'ook to turn the old witch into a toad.

"The cost of living," murmured Mrs. Stork as if to herself, "the cost of living."

The spell was broken and she was not transformed.

Charlie 'ook sat down and reached for his glass of Guinness.

Mrs. Stork watched every movement. Her mouth pursed, she looked at the half-empty glass. She sighed, and then, as if following a previous train of thought, remarked, "Some have it good. That's the way the world is. Some have it good. Some don't."

"Like a drop, Mrs. Stork?"

Her eyes were at once alert. "What, me?" She hesitated, touching her lips lightly with her tongue, as if testing the flavour of her reply. Then, suddenly making up her mind, "Oh, no—not me," she said, "I never touch it—except for medical use, of course. My Tiger wouldn't like it." She attempted a titter of femininity.

Charlie 'ook remained looking at her with a thoughtful lack of smile.

Mrs. Stork sighed again and her glance flickered towards the children and then round the room and back to Charlie 'ook again. "It's ever so nice there's a man in this house at last," she said. "It was lucky you come when you did, Mr. Hook. Dear-oh-dearie me, what would they have done with no one to take care of 'em? What a pretty pass that would of been. Pretty pass." She smiled with melancholy. "Why, I expect they'd 'ave 'ad to call in old Mrs. Stork. I wouldn't be surprised. That is, *if* she'd been willing to come—after the way she'd been . . . well, I won't go on. What's done's done. That's what I say." She wiped the moisture from her palms with the blue handkerchief. "Mrs. Stork don't bear no grudges. You could never say that about old Mrs. S." She waited for Charlie 'ook to light his cigarette. "It's a lucky thing you come when you did," she continued, "very lucky. Of course it's not the same as a woman's touch. Every 'ouse needs a woman's touch." She glanced round the room, as if detecting beneath the superficial neatness a plethora of male grubbiness. She smiled indulgently. "All the years I spent in this house. Thursdays was my day. 'Happy' Thursday, my Tiger used to call it. Year in, year out all these years. An' we never met till now! Oh, o' course, I heard all about you. All about you, Mr. Hook," she said with the faintest emphasis on the *all*.

Charlie 'ook caressed his glass. "I heard a bit about you too," he said with a grin.

Mrs. Stork said benignly, "You don't have to be polite of pleasure. "Me? Well there's not much to tell about me!" She folded her hands in her lap. "Plenty I could tell, though. Plenty." She said it in a placid murmur, as if she knew that she could draw long comfort, if not perfect security, from the fact.

Charlie 'ook set his glass down carefully. He was almost grim.

Hand in hand with Diana, Willy moved restlessly. "Let's go in the garden and swing again, Dinah."

For a moment no one answered him, then Mrs. Stork cut in with sudden energy. "That's right, ducks, you go an'

have a nice swing. 'Nough to give anyone the fidgets standing there and listenin' to us talkin' away. I expect you'd all
like to run away and play, wouldn't you?"

"No," Hubert shook his head, "we'd prefer to stay, thank
you very much."

Mrs. Stork said benignly, "You don't have to be polite
with me. It's ever so nice in the sun. Why don't you all run
along, eh? and then me and your father can have a nice
little chat."

Charlie 'ook rose slowly. He looked from Mrs. Stork to
the children.

"We don't want to go," said Hubert firmly.

"But I think you better, dear. Don't you, Mr. Hook?"

Charlie 'ook rubbed his forefinger gently along his upper
lip. "Yes," he said at length, "yes, I think you better." He
paused, and then, suddenly jovial, he said, "You got to look
after that roast beef, haven't you, Di? Mustn't let the dinner
spoil."

The movement among the children was reluctant. "But,"
began Hubert, "but . . ." He could think of no adequate excuse to stay. Looking at Charlie 'ook, massive and smiling,
and Mrs. Stork, snug in her self-assurance, Hubert was filled
with a brief, fearful perception of something they understood
that he, reach out as he might, would never grasp. He
immediately obliterated the thought with an urgent obe-
dience to Charlie 'ook's command.

"All right," he said briskly, "come on, Jiminee." He
grabbed his brother's arm and half pulled him from the
room, the others trailing behind.

"And no listening at the keyhole, mind!" called Mrs.
Stork.

Hubert led the way downstairs.

In the kitchen, Elsa sat at the table, staring at the door
as they came in.

"Where are the flowers, Else?" asked Hubert.

"I threw them away." Her face was white and icy.

"You *what?*"

"I threw them in the dustbin." She looked at her brothers and sister with contempt, daring them to challenge her.

"What d-d-did you do that for?" said Jiminee.

"You wouldn't understand."

"Elsa!" It was Dunstan who spoke. There was an unbreakable principle among the children that no one should ever be vicious to Jiminee. Laugh at him, yes—but not hurt him. Momentarily Dunstan gained something of his old power as he rebuked his elder sister. "Don't talk like that to Jiminee."

"I don't care." She watched them almost imperceptibly draw together against her.

"Why did you chuck the flowers away, Elsa?" Hubert asked quietly.

"We're not accepting anything from *that* woman."

"But she can't do us any harm," said Hubert.

Elsa did not even look at him.

"Charlie will—"

"*Him!*" Elsa said violently.

Diana moved closer to the table. "What's wrong with him?"

Elsa moved her lips in the parody of a smile. "Wrong! He's a bad lot—that's what's wrong with him. Do you think he cares about us? No! All he cares about is himself."

"You didn't think that," said Dunstan, "when he first came."

"Yes, I did. And so did you!" she shot. "I just gave him the benefit of the doubt, that's all."

Hubert said, "But there isn't any doubt now."

"No, there isn't, is there? He's just a beastly good-for-nothing, that's all he is. Look at the way he drinks—getting drunk and smoking and spending money. Where's he get all that money from? And look at him now—hobnobbing with Mrs. Stork. He doesn't care about you, any of you. He's just a filthy, low-down—"

Diana, leaning over the table, brought her hand round hard and slapped Elsa across the face. "Don't you dare," she said in a low voice, "don't you dare speak like that about him. Ever. You're just jealous because he loves us, and because he doesn't love you most of all."

Elsa rose, the red hand-mark clear-cut on her cheek. "Loves us," she said expressionlessly. "All right, he loves us. But there was somebody else who loved us once—loved all of us. *Mother!* Remember, Diana? Remember that?"

She went to the back door and pulled it open. She walked into the garden without glancing back. No one needed to be told that she was going to the tabernacle.

Hubert turned and looked at Diana. Her cheeks were red and she gripped the edge of the table hard. Her hair gleamed like a helmet of brass. He was glad that she was his sister.

For the first time since they'd entered the kitchen he noticed the smell of roasting beef. He sniffed. It was a good smell.

32

The funfair was a great grey cavern. Like the inside of an enormous elephant, thought Hubert. The constant beehive bumbling of the pleasure-makers rose to the girdered roof high above—a comfortable blanket of indeterminate voices, with sudden undertones of menace as the switchback cars roared into descent, pierced by the riders' murderous screams of joy and the pell-mell shrieking of girls tumbling from the whirl-away cars. The brave tinkle-tinkle of the half-empty merry-go-rounds came through only now and again, in an unexpected hush, like a gentle reminder.

"What you want to see first?" asked Charlie 'ook, raising his voice to a shout.

"Tigers!" cried Willy.

"Tigers it'll be! Here," he bent down and swung Willy by the armpits up onto his shoulders, "now you can spit on the world!" He let out a burst of laughter. Willy gripped Charlie 'ook's brow determinedly. He looked down on the others staring up at him and put out his tongue. He turned his head away proudly as they laughed.

"Follow me, eh? And mind you keep together." Charlie 'ook began to push his way towards the low-roofed rectangular section where the animal cages and the side-shows were.

Hubert's trouser pockets were loaded down with pennies and shillings and sixpences. "A couple of quid's worth of mixed change please, miss," Charlie 'ook had said, slapping down two pound notes at the booth as they entered. *Mixed change*—it sounded rich and exciting. The coins clinked munificently every time he took a step.

"Look, look!" said Jiminee suddenly, grabbing at the tails of Charlie 'ook's jacket.

Hubert read the signs outside the side show—"The Tallest Man in the World," "Nature's Wondrous Marvels," "The Stick Lady," "The Fattest Man in the Universe."

"Only a bob a head," shouted the man at the entrance, and, catching sight of the children, "sixpence for the under-four-teens. I'll let the little fellow in for nothing."

"I'm not *little!*" said Willy loudly.

"Freaks!" murmured Jiminee as he gazed at the crude distortions of faces and limbs painted on the side of the booth.

"Want to go in?" asked Charlie 'ook.

"Oh, yes . . . yes . . . yes . . . yes, please."

As they entered, Hubert inhaled the smell of stale animals and straw and spilled beer and cheap sweets that was like the opening of the wide world.

French Philip, the fattest man in the universe, was over forty-two stone. His flesh, which almost completely concealed the tiny stool he sat on, was contained in short bright pink satin pants and a sleeveless salmon-coloured vest. He was a gigantic pink balloon from which a little air had seeped, so that the rubber flesh sagged and seemed almost to flow from him.

"He *is* fat," whispered Jiminee.

"Fatty Chance'll look like that if he's not careful," said

Dunstan unexpectedly, "when he grows up." The others
giggled.

Then French Philip, who with his buried eyes and complete
stolidity might not have been alive at all, began to move. His
bulk shifted sideways and a hand like a large pink fruit
reached slowly down and grasped the neck of a bottle of
lemonade at his feet. The bottle went up and up and
was plugged into the orifice of Philip's mouth. It tilted
gradually and stayed there for what seemed to the children
an age. At last it was withdrawn and lowered to rest on
Philip's immense thigh. But the fat man's mouth continued
to move with the gentleness of the kissing gourami. Suddenly the lips closed and were still. Then, with a huge brief
quiver of flesh, French Philip belched.

In a moment, the children were consumed in an explosion
of laughter. Up went their hands to their mouths, but nothing could contain their frantic mirth. Crippled with giggles,
they were bundled out by Charlie 'ook, " 'ere," he said, un-
able to conceal his own grin, "you mustn't laugh at the
poor bastard like that."

"But . . . but. . ." They couldn't speak. Hubert felt the
tears streaming from his eyes.

"He can't help being fat," said Charlie 'ook reasonably.

"But," Diana struggled, "but he was so rude!"

"Wouldn't, wouldn't it have b-b-been f-f-funny if his
stool had b-b-b-b-broke," said Jiminee.

"Cor blimey, you kids aren't 'alf macabre. Listen, he'd
only have to roll over once on you, and you'd never get up!"

Laughter struck them again in their stomachs. "Oh,
stop," said Hubert, "please stop, Charlie."

"Yes," said Willy from his height, "stop laughing." He began to drum on Charlie 'ook's head with his fists. "I want
to see my tigers."

" 'ere, Willy," said Charlie 'ook, glancing up and back,
"you sound just like Mrs. Stork."

"My T-T-Tiger," Jiminee managed to get out.

Charlie 'ook laughed outright too this time.

By the time they got to the tigers they were almost re-

covered. The shreds of Mrs. Stork had been blown to in-
visibility in the lofty cavern of the funfair. Charlie 'ook's
announcement, earlier in the afternoon, that Mrs. Stork
would be coming to do for them daily from now on, had
diffused a fear, more potent because vague, within the children that even Charlie 'ook's careful explanation had not
dismissed. But now, it seemed to Hubert, the fear was nothing; for, after all, Mrs. Stork was nothing—nothing to be
afraid of, not when Charlie 'ook was around.

Meagre in their ferocity, the tigers were a disappointment.

"Poke them," said Willy, annoyed.

"And get my hand chewed off? No thanks." Charlie 'ook
held up his wrist and flexed it lovingly. "I dunno about you,
but I'm fond of this hand—only got one other."

It is possible to circle the funfair indefinitely without
ever approaching the middle. For most people, the side
shows and the coconut shies and the shooting galleries and
the slot machines are merely a process of breaking in. There
are those who linger perpetually over the bingo or spend
their time forever rolling pennies down a chute to land on
a numbered square; there are the fat ones who merely come
to watch somebody else having a go; there are the bored ones
in crimson, gold-frogged uniforms, lounging in decayed
magnificence and smelling of the animals they guard. All
these never reach the centre. Most of them hardly ever even
raise their eyes to the big wheel or the switchback. They
watch somebody else having her features romanticised in
charcoal. They buy candy floss for the kids, and their duty
is done. They never know the fearful joy of the water chute
or the dignity of riding the horses with flared nostrils on
the merry-go-round.

By the time the Hooks reached the shooting gallery that
jutted out into the territory of the big rides, their fever had
mastered all timidity.

"Let's go on the switchback, Charlie."

"I want to slide down the tower with the chute."

"All right, all right," said Charlie 'ook in mock impatience. " 'ere, don't none of you want to have a go at the shooting?—you might win a rabbit."

"*You* go, Charlie."

"Nah—I had enough of that in the war." He grinned. "Besides, got my hands full here. Hu, you have a try—you ought to be pretty good."

"Yes—go on, Hu. Go on."

Charlie 'ook examined the guns. "This looks a good one, Hu." Hubert took it into his hand. The stock was cold and greasy with dirty oil. He hesitated. "Look, I'll show you." Charlie 'ook swung Willy from his shoulders and took the gun from Hubert. He demonstrated how to hold it. "Now you have a go. Ten shots he gets, doesn't he?" he called to the man.

"That's right. Ten shots for a bob." The attendant with the droopy moustache and the grubby white coat barely looked up from his examination of the caked grime in his nails. "If you knock down ten ducks while in motion you get the rabbit or any other of these magnificent toys—on the left 'ere—you may choose. Ten ducks—the toy of your choice." He sighed. "Or, 'aving achieved your perfect score, you are entitled to add to that score with another free round. Seven or more hits on your free round will make you eligible for the grand prize," he lifted his elbow to indicate a huge box with a teapot on top, "a beautiful genuine Wedgwood tea set as from the factory."

The ducks were on the top level and seemed to Hubert to be moving very fast. Below them a line of large mice went at a much slower pace. Hubert opened his mouth to speak.

"*Or*," said the man suddenly, "nine knockdowns entitles you to any object in that group, eight to any object in that group, seven to any object in that group. And—for five knockdowns you get one of these attractive cutie-pie dolls."

"What about six?" asked Hubert.

"Cutie-pie."

"What d'you get for knocking down the mice?"

"Mice don't count," snapped the man.

"We'll take a bob's worth," said Charlie 'ook. "Okay, Hu. Take a coupla' shots and see how you do. Most of these guns don't shoot true—you'll most likely have to aim off a bit to the right or a bit to the left. You'll soon get the knack of it."

Hubert tucked the stock against his shoulder and bent low. The ducks flashed past the sights. He pulled the trigger. Clang!

"You hit one!"

"Did I?" Hubert glanced up, smiling. It wasn't difficult after all. He bent low and pulled the trigger again. Unharmed, the ducks marched. Out of his ten shots, he hit three ducks and a couple of mice.

"Not bad for a first try," said Charlie 'ook. "Anyone else want a go?" He was half turning away already.

"I'd like a shot, please." Dunstan stretched out his hand to take the gun.

"Fancy yourself as a marksman, do you?" asked Charlie 'ook, and then, as if suddenly conscious of his sarcastic tone, he put his arm around Dunstan's shoulder. "I thought you was the studious one." He smiled.

Dunstan looked up at Charlie 'ook. "I've got a good eye," he said quietly. "I'm going to win a rabbit."

"Oh, ho!"

The man in the white coat sniffed briefly, loaded the gun and handed it to Dunstan.

The dark-haired boy was precise in his movements. He crouched over the gun for an age before he pulled the trigger. With his first shot he knocked down a duck. He didn't take his eyes from the sights. He hit another duck with his second shot.

"Go on, Dun, go on, you're going to do it," cried Hubert as Dunstan's eighth shot demolished a duck. "Eight out of eight!"

Dunstan looked up and smiled with restraint.

"Damn good," said Charlie 'ook, *"damn good!"*

Even the attendant stopped examining his nails and concentrated his attention on the ducks, as if his gaze would keep them up.

Dunstan fired again. Clang! A duck jerked, but remained steady.

"Nine!" shouted Hubert.

"Doesn't count," said the attendant.

"What do you mean *doesn't count?*" said Charlie 'ook loudly.

"Didn't score a knockdown."

"He hit it, didn't he? It went *clang,* didn't it?"

"Doesn't count."

"Of course it bloody well counts. Just 'cause you glue half your blasted ducks up—'ere," Charlie 'ook leaned far over the counter and showed his fist, "if I was to hit you with this —you'd count that as a knockdown, wouldn't you?"

The man in the white coat was quite still. He stared at Charlie 'ook without expression. Suddenly his eyes shifted to the small crowd that had drifted to the shooting gallery at the sound of raised voices.

"All right," he said, all at once brisk and loud, "fair's fair. I'll give 'im an extra shot. This one won't count, but he can have an extra shot for the same money—'ow's that?"

"Well . . ." began Charlie 'ook.

"That's all right, Charlie," said Dunstan. "Don't worry. I'll get the next two."

A couple of women in the crowd tittered.

"All right," said Charlie 'ook, "fair enough."

The attendant put an extra shot in Dunstan's gun. "This lad," he said loudly, "is trying for the big rabbit."

Dunstan raised the gun and fired almost immediately. Clang!

"Nine!" shouted Jiminee.

"One more to go," said the attendant.

Clang! The tenth duck flipped back.

"You done it, you done it!"

"Ten dead ducks!" Charlie 'ook laughed jovially.

"And the young gentleman has won himself one of these 'ere handsome rabbits." The man in the white coat took

down the huge tartan-clad rabbit. He held it high for a
moment and then presented it to Dunstan with a swoop-
ing flourish. "Why don't you have a try for a magnificent
rabbit, ladies and gentlemen?"

"Can't afford the lettuce," said someone from the crowd.
The attendant's face flicked into a twitch of a smile.

The children closed around Dunstan. They put out their
hands to touch the rabbit which the boy held fast in his
arms.

"It's a lovely rabbit."

"It looks like Mrs. S-S-St-Stork," said Jiminee and they
all laughed.

"We'll have to send you to Bisley," said Charlie 'ook,
rubbing his hand through the boy's hair. "Dead-eye Dunstan
the duck-shooting devil, eh?"

They moved away from the shooting gallery.

"What are you going to do with it, Dun?" asked Willy.

Dunstan stopped smiling. "I'm going to give it to Elsa," he
said gravely.

"That's a good idea," said Charlie 'ook quickly before the
children's surprise turned to disapproval. "We ought to take
her back some sweets, too. What about a nice stick of rock,
eh? Where's the rock man?" Charlie 'ook looked around.
"Saw 'im here a minute ago."

"*Rock!*" Diana's voice was hard and furious.

"What?" said Charlie 'ook.

"What you want to take her rock for?" Diana asked
fiercely.

"To cheer her up, of course. Sitting there at home all on
her lonely-own."

"She could have come if she wanted to, couldn't she?"

Hubert put his hand on his sister's arm, but she shook it
off.

"Well, yes," said Charlie 'ook, "but I expect she wasn't
feeling up to it."

"Huh!" said Diana contemptuously. "A lot you know."
For a moment her tone was pitying. Then she was hard
again. "She didn't come because she hates you."

"That's not true," Dunstan flashed out.

"No, it's not," said Hubert, half turning to Dunstan in surprise at their agreement.

" 'ere, 'ere, 'ere," Charlie 'ook's lower lip trembled momentarily as he took in a breath, "calm down there. We can't have this. Brothers and sisters squabbling. We all love each other, don't we?" None of the children answered his smile. "Look," he said, trying again, "perhaps she don't like me as much—as much as you do. But we're not all made the same —not by a long chalk." He paused to rub his upper lip. "If Elsa's a bit stand-offish, we got to make allowances. Haven't we now?" He directed his question at Diana.

"Giving her presents isn't making allowances."

"Oh, yes it is. Definitely. If she don't like us, we've got to like her." He surveyed the children with regained aplomb. "Do unto others as you would be done by. Right, Dun?"

Dunstan nodded. But it wasn't right, thought Hubert. It wasn't her brothers and sisters that she didn't like—it was Charlie 'ook.

"But," began Diana without confidence, "but—"

"Let's drop it, shall we?" said Charlie 'ook briskly.

For a moment they stood in silence. Hubert didn't know what to do with his hands. He felt the deadweight of change in his pocket. He glanced up at the switchback, but somehow the excitement had been stolen away. The sea roar of the funfair swooped and then receded so that they heard the fierce swinging drone of the death riders' motorbikes rising to a sudden menace.

"What about a go on the big wheel?" said Charlie 'ook, putting his arm around Diana. Abruptly she turned to him and burst into sobs.

"That's all right, that's all right." He touched her hair. Tightly she hugged him. He crouched down and took out his handkerchief. "There's nothing to cry about, Di," he said gently, drying her cheeks.

"You love us. You do love us, don't you, Charlie?"

"Of course I love you." He put his cheek next to hers.

Her golden hair and his thinning locks intermingled. Then he drew back.

"Cheer up, ducks." He smiled. "Feel better now?"

She nodded. Taking hold of her hand, he stood up. They returned from their momentary privacy to the others.

They rode the big wheel. They went on the switchback and plunged down the water chute. They watched the riders of death. And yet despite the excitement, Hubert was somehow uneasy.

At one moment a small fox-faced man, pulling two little girls by the hand, had stopped dead as he was about to pass them. "Hello, Charlie 'ook," the man had called with a grin of yellow teeth. Charlie 'ook had hesitated and then just nodded and turned the other way. When Hubert looked back, the man was still grinning. He paid no attention to one of the little girls who had started to cry.

Hubert wished they hadn't met the man. As he paid out sixpences and shillings, he wanted more and more for his trouser pocket to be empty and for them to be on their way home. He remembered a day when Elsa had been with them on an expedition—the day in the park with old Halby. He had not wanted to go home then. But now . . . now he wanted to see Elsa's face when she got the rabbit.

And when at last they were home, he and Dunstan—with the rabbit tucked under his arm—raced up the stairs as quick as the wind.

The door of Elsa's room was shut. They pushed it open.

"Here we are," said Hubert.

She sat on the bed with her hands in her lap.

"Hello," said Dunstan.

"Hello," she answered, almost inaudibly.

"I've—I've brought you a present." He stepped forward and held out the huge fur animal. For a moment Elsa didn't move; then she stretched out her hands and took it.

"It's a rabbit," said Dunstan.

She let the rabbit rest in her lap. "Yes," she said.

"I won it."

She raised her head. "Did you?" She looked down again

and touched the floppy pink-lined ears. "It's nice," she murmured.

"You do like it, don't you?" Dunstan asked anxiously.

"Yes. Yes, I do." Suddenly Elsa smiled.

They were silent. Hubert looked from Elsa to Dunstan and back again. They weren't noticing him. "You should have come, Else," he said, and immediately wished he hadn't as Elsa's smile vanished.

"Why didn't you come?" he persisted in spite of himself. He didn't want to give way to the feeling that somehow he was being left out.

"She didn't come because she didn't want to come," said Dunstan reasonably.

"But—"

"No—that's wrong," said Elsa. "I didn't come 'cause I didn't want to be anywhere near *him*."

"What's wrong with him?" Hubert asked loudly.

"He isn't as bad as all that," said Dunstan.

"Isn't he? Isn't he?" Elsa's hand rested on the furry head of the rabbit. "He took the savings book," she announced calmly.

Dunstan frowned. "Well, I don't see . . ."

"Don't you? Hubert does, though—don't you, Hu?—although I expect you won't admit it."

"Admit what? See what?" Hubert was angry. "I don't know what you're talking about."

Elsa said carefully, "Mrs. Stork told him about the savings book. That's why she came back. That's why she's going to stay. Do you think she'd come back for nothing? She's going to get her share. Her share of *our* money. And he'll draw out the rest and spend it."

"What'd he want to do that for?" asked Hubert, but Elsa just turned her head away.

After a while she began to stroke the rabbit. Watching her, Dunstan smiled. Then he went across the room and drew the curtains. He came back and sat on the floor and watched Elsa.

"She'll betray us," murmured Elsa.

"What?"

"Mrs. Stork—she'll betray us."

Hubert took a deep breath. "But Charlie explained all that—why she's got to come back. She won't tell if she comes back. She'd only split if she *didn't* come back. She won't find anything out."

Elsa sighed. "She'll betray us when the money runs out. And he will too—that's when he'll betray us."

Dunstan frowned. "You can't say that, Else. You don't know. How can you know?"

"Besides," said Hubert, "there'll always be the cheque."

She shrugged impatiently at Hubert's interruption. "The cheque won't be enough. Not with his—style of life. You wait and see."

"You're wrong," Hubert said angrily. "He'd never do that. You're just making it up. It's just because you hate him. Diana was right—you—"

"Hubert!" Dunstan's glasses flashed. "Be quiet."

"It's all right, Hu," said Elsa coldly, without looking at him. "You needn't worry. I'm not going to make a fuss."

He could think of no answer. He shut his lips tight. Somewhere far down within him something jerked—a cord, a flutter of distant wings.

"Tea-eee! Tea-eee!" The cry from the hall reached them faintly.

"You coming, Else?" Dunstan asked.

"I don't mind." She put the rabbit on the pillow and stood up. "Thank you for the rabbit, Dun."

Dunstan blushed. "Perhaps," he said, "there'll be hymns after tea. You'll join in, won't you, Else?" He got to his feet.

Elsa reached up and switched off the light. "I expect so," she said.

Dunstan and Elsa went ahead down the stairs. Hubert followed slowly.

Elsa was wrong. She was dead wrong.

33

Weak with winter, the nine-o'clock daylight filtered dimly through the dusty panes of the transome above the front door. Hubert placed the cup of tea carefully on the hall table and picked up the letters from the mat. He held the envelopes close to his eyes. The first was addressed *Captain Charles Hook*. Hubert turned it over curiously. On the back was the printed inscription, *C. Bodger & Co., Turf Accountants*. *Turf*—he smiled suddenly; it could be a surprise. Perhaps Charlie 'ook was going to have the back lawn done over with new grass—he thought of the slabs of rich green grass backed with chocolate-brown earth that he'd seen last year stacked outside the Halberts', waiting to be put down. He slipped the letter beneath the other two before he had time for doubts.

The next one was familiar—*Mrs. Violet Edna Hook,* neatly typed—it was the monthly cheque. He was glad he didn't have to bother with that anymore.

The third letter was addressed to *Samuel Halbert, Esq., 40 Ipswich Terrace*. Hubert started to reach up to open the front door and call back the postman. The letter felt heavy and important. But the postman would be gone by now. I'll deliver it myself, thought Hubert. There was plenty of time on Saturdays now. That was one good thing about the return of Mrs. Stork—the only good thing, thought Hubert.

He sighed and pushed the letters into his trouser pocket. Gingerly he picked up the cup of tea. For a moment he balanced it, making sure the cup was firm in the saucer. He dipped his finger quickly into the milky tea—it was tepid, but that was the way Charlie 'ook liked it. Shoulders hunched and eyes fixed, he started forward.

"Hello, Berty. Brought a cup of tea for your old Mrs.

Stork—well, isn't that nice." Mrs. Stork stretched out a skinny hand.

Hubert put his foot on the last step. "It isn't for you," he said, without looking up. "It's for him." He moved his head in the direction of Mother's room.

The hand dropped away. "My," she said in a voice of eggshell tenderness, "aren't *you* the thoughtful one!"

He gained the landing. Her distinctive odour of dust and dripping and furniture polish and old starch wafted over him. "It's his morning tea. I always fetch it on Saturdays and Sundays."

Mrs. Stork unexpectedly cracked a finger. Her face lifted to a smile. "Well, ducks, you don't have to bother. Mrs. Stork can take care of all that. A woman's touch. A woman's touch." She reached out again for the cup. "I'll take it in to 'im."

"No, thank you very much." Hubert pulled the cup away and the tea slopped into the saucer. "Now look what you've done!"

"Oh, I'm ever so sorry." But, looking at the wrinkle of her smile, Hubert knew that she wasn't sorry at all.

"Silly old Talk-Stork," he muttered under his breath.

"What did you say, dearie?"

"Nothing." Grasping the banister in one hand, he brushed by her and knocked on the door of Mother's room.

"Manners maketh man. Manners maketh man." Behind him he heard her short twittering cackle.

He pushed open the door and went in.

Charlie 'ook was half awake. He rolled over, eyeing Hubert. "What's that noise?" he asked.

"It's Mrs. Stork," said Hubert, loudly enough, he hoped, for her to hear. "She's laughing."

"Silly old bag," murmured Charlie 'ook.

Hubert grinned and sat down on the bed. He liked to watch Charlie 'ook drink his tea. It was the best part of Saturdays and Sundays almost. There was a smell of man and warm bedclothes, and he liked the way Charlie 'ook would rub at his itching beard.

"Ah, nice and tepid—just right. Never could see this steaming 'ot stuff."

Hubert smiled at him happily—he always said that about "steaming hot stuff."

"You got some post, Charlie." He pulled the letters out of his pocket and handed them over.

"Christ!" said Charlie 'ook, dropping the letter from the turf accountants as though it were hot. "Ah," he held the second letter up to the light, "this'll be the cheque, eh?"

"That's right."

"Well, we'll have to get Jiminee on to this." He clattered the cup onto the floor, pushed back the blankets and swung his legs out of bed. "Here, Jiminee," he yelled.

He glanced briefly at the third letter. "What's this?"

"Oh, it was delivered wrong," said Hubert, "it's meant to be next door."

"*Samuel* Halbert. Samuel—I should think so, almost as bad as Cyril, eh?" He stood up and stretched, his unbuttoned pyjamas revealing a smooth, strangely feminine chest.

"Charlie?"

"What?" He yawned.

"You know what day it is today, don't you?"

"Pay day, old pal—pay day!" He chuckled. "Reminds me of when I was in the army. There was this Tynesider in the next bed to me, see. He had a mate called Dai. Every Friday, he used to wake up and then shout out at the top of his bleeding lungs to his mate, 'Wake oop, it's pie die t'die, die!' It was the accent, see. What he meant was 'It's pay day, today, Dai.' Only he couldn't say it like that." He rubbed the bristles on his upper lip and smiled. "Lot of uneducated bastards, up north."

"No, but I mean there's something else," said Hubert anxiously.

"There is? Let's have it!"

"It's Dun's birthday."

"Dun's birthday!" Charlie 'ook opened his eyes in exaggerated surprise. "Blimey, I almost forgot."

"You haven't forgotten, have you?"

"No, no—not now you reminded me. Eleven he's going to be, isn't it?"

"Yes. But you haven't forgotten what you *promised?*"

"Promised?" Charlie 'ook frowned.

"To take him up to Charing Cross Road—as his birthday treat. To buy books."

"Faith an' b'Jasus, and so I did," said Charlie 'ook, mock-Irish. "Well, and so I will—'ere, wait a minute," he was serious, "no, I can't."

Hubert stood up. He was suddenly cold. "Why not?"

"I got to go to Hurst Park today. Promised I would."

"But—but you promised Dun!" cried Hubert.

Charlie 'ook looked at him carefully. "Yes, I know I did. But that was a long time ago, see. And—" He stopped. "He'd be upset, wouldn't he?"

Hubert nodded. "Can't you put off the Park?"

"Nope. Can't be done. There's a sure thing—a *dead* sure thing in the two o'clock. And I've got to be there. Can't get any more credit, see, but I got a bundle now with the cheque. Hey, Jiminee," he yelled almost absently. He thought for a moment, rubbing delicately at his upper lip. "Tell you what I might do, though. I could take him with me, eh? That'd be a treat, wouldn't it?"

Hubert was doubtful.

"I mean, if he's going to buy books, he's got to have some cash, ain't he? Well, if he comes with me, he can win a few quid. He *will* win a few quid, I'll make sure of that. Then he'll have a whole pile to blue on the bleeding books—and I'll take him up next week. How's that?"

"Well," said Hubert, "it's betting, isn't it?"

"Betting, my boy—it certainly is! The Races—the Sticks—the Glorious Turf—the Sport of Kings the Universal World Over! What's wrong with that?"

"Well, Dunstan doesn't approve of betting."

"Doesn't approve?" said Charlie 'ook incredulously.

"Well, he didn't used to," Hubert apologised.

"I'll soon talk him out of that. Nobody ever turned down a sure thing. Don't you worry," he was suddenly buoyant again, "everything's gonna be all right." He bent down and picked Hubert up and pushed him high in the air. "Have you ever known Charles Ronald Hook to go back on his given word?" he asked sternly.

Hubert laughed despite himself. "No," he said.

"Well then," Charlie 'ook let him go and then caught him again before his feet touched the floor. "Well, then," he grinned down at Hubert. And Hubert grinned back.

"What are we going to do about this letter to old Samuel Halbert Esquire, eh?"

"Oh, I'll take it," said Hubert.

"All right then. Off with you. I gotta get dressed." He clapped the boy on the buttocks.

As Hubert went to the door, Jiminee appeared. "D-d-did you c-c-c——"

"Aha! Yes, I did. 'ere," Charlie 'ook reached onto the bed for the letter with the cheque in it and tossed it to Jiminee, "do you want to do your stuff on that, eh?"

Jiminee held the envelope up to the light. "It's the cheque, isn't it?" he asked.

"That's correct, absolutely correct. I got to have it in half an hour. Can you manage it?"

Jiminee nodded professionally. "I think s-so."

Charlie 'ook rubbed his hands briskly. "Cold as a bleeding graveyard in here."

"Graveyard? My, we are morbid this morning, aren't we?" Mrs. Stork chuckled from the doorway.

Charlie 'ook made a face. " 'ow long have you been there, Nosey Parker?"

"Long enough, long enough," said Mrs. Stork, displaying her wrinkled grin. She turned to the boys. "Now why don't you run off an' play, dears, eh? Like good little boys. And let your *father* get himself dressed. He's got to be on his toes today—going to make all our fortunes at the races, so I 'ear."

Charlie 'ook laughed. "Blimey, you must 'ave ears in your little fingers."

Mrs. Stork nodded knowingly. "I got my spies. My spies.

An' what will the master have for his breakfast this grave-yard morning?"

Charlie 'ook glowered melodramatically. "A plate of juicy fat toadstools!"

For a moment all four were caught in the same burst of laughter.

Then Mrs. Stork began to bustle. "Come on, come on," she said, beckoning them from the room, "I 'aven't got all day. Got to make *his* breakfast, the lazy thing, and do the shopping and, oh, ever so many things. Your Mrs. Stork is not a one for taking things easy. No, she isn't." She let the boys precede her, then shut the door, leaving Charlie 'ook alone. "No, she isn't."

Hubert and Jiminee stood on the landing and watched Mrs. Stork hurrying down the stairs to the kitchen.

"Hu—d-d-do you think he really l-l-likes her?"

Hubert shook his head emphatically. "Course not. He's got to keep in her good books, that's all."

Jiminee thought for a moment. Then he said, "We've all g-got to b-b-be in her g-g-g-good b-books, haven't we?"

"Yes."

Far below a door slammed. Hubert tapped the letter in his hand against the rail of the banister. "Where's Dun?"

"I think he's sw-swinging with Willy," said Jiminee. "I g-got to go an' d-do this." He opened the envelope with his forefinger and drew out the pink cheque.

"Okay." Hubert started down the stairs. "I'm going to find Dun," he called over his shoulder.

Mr. Halbert's letter would have to wait.

34

Hubert and Jiminee climbed the front steps and turned to look at the thin glitter of snow in the neon-lit brightness of Ipswich Terrace. Pulling off his school cap, Hubert felt the icy crust of the fallen flakes on the brim turn to water under the heat of his thumb.

"D-do you think it'll l-lie?" Jiminee asked anxiously.

Hubert shook his head. It was almost rain even now, and his shoes were wet with the slush they had walked through on their way home from school. And in the momentary hush of the main road traffic you could even hear the gentle mouse feet of the flakes. It would have to get a lot colder before the true snow silence came.

"P'raps it'll t-turn to ice then?"

"It might," said Hubert.

They watched quietly.

"I think it's more icy n-now," said Jiminee after a while.

Hubert smiled, without looking at his brother. "It won't happen in a twinkling of an eye," he answered.

"Well," Jiminee began doubtfully, then suddenly he brightened. "Look, old Halby's car."

The black Daimler drew up slowly in front of number 40, the windscreen wipers moving with opulent lethargy and the tyres sucking at the slush-filled gutters.

"Old Halby's b-back home from the office."

"He's early," said Hubert. From the window of his workroom he had often seen the Daimler return as late as seven and even eight in the evening.

"I expect it's because of her," said Jiminee.

"What's wrong with her?" asked Hubert. The car had stopped now and the windscreen wipers were at rest. Inside the car there was the glow of a match and then the smaller glow of a cigarette.

"She's w-w-wa-wasting away!" said Jiminee.

"Who says?"

"Joan says—*that's* who. I heard her t-talking to the p-p-post-man."

"Joan's only the maid—what would she know about it?"

"She d-does. I heard her. She says Mrs. Halb-bert spends all d-day in b-bed and then—and then she screams at n-night. Something t-terrible, that's what Joan says."

"I never heard her," said Hubert.

Jiminee hesitated. "P'raps she screams soft—p'raps she don't want n-n-no one to hear."

"Doesn't," corrected Hubert.

"Doesn't."

"Stuff and nonsense," said Hubert halfheartedly. Mr. Halbert had opened the door of the car and was getting out. He wasn't wearing a coat. He reached into the front seat for his briefcase and umbrella. Then he shut the door and locked it and turned towards the house. He stood for a moment, smoking his cigarette and looking up at the light snow. They could see his white face clearly, the eyes blinking against the falling moisture which glistened like tears on his cheek.

Instinctively the boys moved a little deeper into the shadow of their own front porch. A moment later there was a loud burst of laughter from the front room. Abruptly Mr. Halbert lowered his head. He dropped his cigarette on the pavement, pushed open the gate of number 40 and walked up to the house. They heard the key in the lock and a few seconds later the slam of the door.

Hubert looked at Jiminee. "Who's in the front room?"

Jiminee shrugged. "I dunno."

They entered the house. In the hall they took off their satchels and hung their damp coats and caps in the cupboard. "The others are home," said Hubert. Above each peg was a label with the names of the children written in Mother's neat and curling hand. All the pegs were full, even the one marked *Gertrude*. The labels were faded and peeling now, and long ago the children had ceased to hang their coats on their own name pegs. I'll make new ones tomorrow, thought Hubert, then we can all hang our things in the proper place.

"I expect they're making tea," said Jiminee.

"Yes."

They walked down the hall. Hubert stopped beside the door to the front room. It was closed. The voices from inside were indistinct.

"I 'spect Charlie's got some of his friends in," murmured Hubert.

In the last few weeks there had been a lot of them—of the friends. They hardly ever seemed to be the same ones. Some were fat and smelled of whiskey and others were thin and bony and always came without coats. Sometimes they came back with Charlie 'ook from the races. Sometimes they just knocked on the door and always looked surprised when one of the children opened the door. "Must 'ave come to the wrong 'ouse," one or two of them had muttered. But Hubert knew they hadn't—there was no tingle of excitement or fear now when he went to open the front door. Once or twice there had been women—ladies? When they went away, the front room smelled for a long time of their scent.

There was more laughter. Hubert listened anxiously.

"Sounds like old T-Talk-Stork," said Jiminee.

It did. Hubert wanted to push open the door and walk in but—

"Shall I knock?" asked Jiminee.

—but somehow he didn't think Charlie 'ook liked to be interrupted when he was with his friends. Yet, if it was only old Mrs. Stork . . .

"Perhaps we b-better go an' have t-tea first?"

"Yes." Hubert made up his mind. "Yes. All right."

As they went down the stairs to the kitchen, Hubert wished he'd had enough courage just to barge in on them upstairs. After all, they couldn't bite your head off.

He pushed open the kitchen door.

"We been waiting for you." It was Elsa who spoke. They

were all standing. Hubert saw that the tea things were not laid, and there was no kettle on the stove.

"What's the matter?" he asked cautiously.

"You tell him, Dun," said Elsa.

Dunstan looked around uneasily and Hubert knew at once that he didn't want to speak up. Hubert drew an inward sigh of relief—his constant fear was that Elsa would persuade Dunstan to side with her completely and then try to destroy everything.

"What's up?" repeated Hubert.

"The tabernacle's gone," said Dunstan, getting rid of the words quickly, as if they didn't really belong to him.

"The tabernacle's gone?" It was half question, half statement. He felt hardly any sense of shock; somewhere at the back of his mind he had been expecting this, or rather he thought of it as already having happened. But, watching the faces of his brothers and sisters, he realised that such a thing had not entered their heads. Even Diana seemed somehow dazed—waiting for a word from him to clear it all up.

"Have a look for yourself," said Elsa.

Hubert nodded. He opened the back door and went outside. To his left the light from the kitchen windows shone on the wet leaves of the lilies of the valley that looked like dark exhausted tongues. On the right, the hump of blackness where the tabernacle should have been was missing. There was no light from the Halberts' beyond. He thought of Mrs. Halbert hidden behind the curtains in one of the rooms, and he remembered suddenly the face that had looked out at him when he'd been playing in the garden weeks ago. He touched his hair, damp with snow, and shivered. It was cold. He should go in. He turned and went back slowly.

"Well," Elsa said, "are you any the wiser?"

"It's not there," Hubert said simply. He felt languid—what did it matter if it was gone?

"It must've b-been t-took away," suggested Jiminee.

"*They* took it away," said Elsa.

"Who's *they?*" Hubert asked it automatically. He knew.

"Charlie 'ook—and the Storks. They're upstairs now. *Celebrating.*"

Hubert smiled.

"What are you grinning at?" Elsa made it sound like murder.

Hubert rubbed his finger under his nose. "You're not afraid of the *Storks,* are you?"

"Afraid?" Elsa was astonished.

"I don't see what all the fuss is about," he said, before she had time to assert her indignation. There wasn't going to be a row if he could help it. He didn't look away from Elsa, but he sensed that both Dunstan and Diana were relieved.

"Fuss?" She was unsure of herself. "They've *destroyed* the tabernacle. Don't you understand what that means?" She glanced at the others, but there was no response. "It means—it means we can't have Mothertime!"

"Well," said Hubert, "we haven't had Mothertime for ages anyway. Not since Charlie 'ook came."

"Dunstan!" She was pleading. "Dunstan, you understand what they've done, don't you? You mind, don't you, Dun?"

Dunstan frowned. He moved his hands awkwardly. "They should have asked us," he said.

"Perhaps," said Jiminee, "they're going to b-build us a sunk g-garden, like Mother p-promised."

"Super!" said Willy delightedly.

Elsa looked around at their suddenly grinning faces. She opened her mouth as if to speak, but said nothing. And then Hubert was sorry for her—more sorry than he had ever been. Once her authority had been second only to Mother's, and now . . . now he saw the glitter of tears in her eyes and the false firmness of her lip. "Look, Else," he said, "we'll ask Charlie why he did it. He must have had a good reason. We'll ask him to explain—how's that?"

It sounded silly, futile to him as he said it, but the children murmured their approval. Elsa nodded without a word, but he knew it wasn't that she agreed—she just wanted them to look away, not to notice her.

"Let's have tea then. We'll go up after. Let's have tea first."

"Let's g-get tea in a record!" said Jiminee.

They were all caught in the activity of excited relief. They banged the plates down on the table, noisily scaring away the vestigial ghost that hovered somewhere in each of them. The water was poured at the first tentative scream of the kettle and the bread was buttered rough with hasty lumps.

Throughout tea, Hubert tried to put away the thought of going upstairs. *Always let well alone,* Mother had said. It was funny how he remembered that. But he'd promised Elsa, he'd promised and he didn't really know why he didn't want to do it.

The door of the front room had been opened a crack. Standing before it, Hubert plucked at his determination. Behind him the children formed in line, and he was at once struck with the remembrance of a night long ago, when again they had all waited in front of a door, but it was not he, but Elsa who had entered first.

Snatches of talk from inside came to them as they waited.

". . . full of rot from top to bottom—they all are . . ."

"Bleeding white elephant . . ." That was Tiger Stork's voice.

"White elephant with athlete's foot." There was a cackle of laughter.

Hubert gave the door a quick push. It swung open slowly. The room was filled with smoke of cigarettes and stuffy with the heat of the huge orange-bright fire around which the three of them sat.

Charlie 'ook turned as the draught from the open door touched him.

"Well, if it ain't the kids," he smiled and Hubert drew a breath of instant relief.

Hubert stepped into the room and the others followed him.

" 'ave you had a nice tea?" enquired Mrs. Stork with smiling tenderness.

"Yes, thank you."

Tiger Stork said nothing. He still wore his working clothes, thick with earth, and his flat cap. He held his whiskey glass directly below his chin in both hands. His small tongue whipped like a sun lizard's, and the head twisted one way, then the other—alert for invisible prey.

"Well, come on, shut the door—Mrs. Stork's old blood is thin as cheesecloth these days."

Somebody closed the door. The children were ill at ease. The adults were still, waiting for something perhaps. Hubert tried to meet Charlie 'ook's eyes, but Charlie 'ook turned his head, as if afraid of giving something away.

"Well, I told you. That's five bob you owe me, Mr. Charlie 'ook." Mrs. Stork was triumphant. "I *told* you they wouldn't notice. I know kids—wrapped up in their own world, that's what they are. Wrapped. No eyes for nothink else." She chuckled.

Charlie 'ook grimaced and passed two half-crowns across to her waiting hand. He stared at the children. "I'm disappointed—I really am. To think that any kids of my wife—" a giggle from Tiger Stork broke his words—"shouldn't see what's before their very eyes. Don't none of you notice anything new?" He raised his whiskey glass and drank, looking at the children across the top of his glass.

"That!" Jiminee moved forward and pointed.

"A telephone," breathed Diana.

"I saw it! I saw it!" cried Willy. He ran over to the table and put his hand protectively on the black instrument. He grinned at the laughter of the adults.

"Does it ring?" said Willy.

"Of course it rings," said Charlie 'ook with mock indignation. "Ah, sweet music to the ears." He intoned solemnly, "Mr. Hook? We are happy to inform you that you are the lucky winner of two hundred nicker on the four o'clock!"

"What do we need a telephone for?" asked Dunstan.

"What do we *need* a *telephone* for?" Charlie 'ook took a

deep breath as if calming himself. He glanced down at his empty glass and made to get up, then changed his mind. " 'ere, Hubert, give us a refill all round, eh?" There was silence as Hubert expertly took the bottle and filled the glasses.

Charlie 'ook sipped. "This 'ere telephone," he began slowly, "is the greatest blooming invention there ever was—with the possible exception of the French letter," he cleared his throat. "With this telephone I can talk to anyone in the whole world. Kings and emperors and presidents and prime ministers—and the off-licence. Why, I can have a cosy chat with Ava Gardner right from this chair!" He put down his glass and lifted the instrument into his lap. "I can ring up the Seceshay-Gen—— the Secretary-General of the United Nations!"

"G-go on!" said Jiminee disbelievingly.

"Go on? Right, I will. I'll do just that." He picked the receiver from its cradle and dialled once with a dramatic flourish. " 'ere, operator? Operator—get me the United Nations. UNO. The United Nations! *U* for—*up*, as in 'up yours,' *n* for—*nipple*. No, no, no, no—not *cripple*, that's a *c* ain't it? *Nipple*, them things you—that's right." He took the phone away from his ear. "They ain't half dumb. United Nations, that's right." He held the base of the phone firmly with his free hand. "UNO? I want to speak to the big man— the Secretary-General." He winked at the children and the snickers of the Storks went up a note. "No, it don't matter who I am. Yes. Hullo, that you—I mean, him? Well, listen, cock, what you going to do about it? What do you mean *about what?* The whole bleeding mess, of course! The problem of unmarried fathers!"

Mrs. Stork's shrewd cackle rose high, while Charlie 'ook's big body palpitated with laughter. He leaned back, closing his eyes and letting his hand fall away from the base of the phone. The hook sprang up, released from the pressure of his finger, and the children clearly heard the urgent tone from the receiver.

"B-but you weren't t-talking at all!" said Jiminee.

"That's right—I wasn't t-t-t-t-talking at all," mimicked Charlie 'ook. He dropped the receiver into its cradle and reached for his glass.

"Mr. 'ook," said Tiger Stork, nodding quickly, "you're a real comic. That's what you are—a comic."

Jiminee looked away. The hand by his side had begun to clutch convulsively.

"I don't see what's funny," said Elsa.

"You don't, eh?" He leaned forward and the drops of sweat gleamed on his upper lip. "Ah, but then," he said winningly, "you wouldn't. You ain't got no sense of humour. Just like your sainted mum, you are. But it don't do to take life too serious. Ain't that so? Dunstan will tell you. A bit of fun at the races is a lot better than all them books and things, ain't it, Dun?"

Dunstan kept his face turned away from Elsa. "Yes," he murmured almost inaudibly, blushing as though he had uttered a blasphemy.

"But life ain't all a bed of roses," sighed Mrs. Stork. "Ain't that so, Tiger?"

Tiger Stork nodded delightedly. "The wages of sin is death," he said and at once began to giggle.

Charlie 'ook started to laugh and was caught in a fit of choking. Immediately Diana was at his side, bending over the chair and patting his back.

Calmed, Charlie 'ook put his arm around the girl's waist. "Well," he said, "and how's the love of my life?" He grinned at the Storks. "Takes care of her old man, don't she?" Abruptly he seemed to notice the other children standing watching him. " 'ere," he said with a frown, "why don't you sit down? You look like a bleeding deputation of undertakers."

Hubert was conscious of the others moving to sit, but he remained where he was. "Charlie," he said, "Charlie—what's happened to the tabernacle?"

"Tabernacle?"

"He means that old shed in the garden." Mrs. Stork's laugh rose shrill, but not as shrill as Tiger's.

"It's not an *old shed*," Hubert shot at her.

Charlie 'ook held up his hand. "Mustn't be rude to Mrs. Stork," he said solemnly, "our jewel." His glass was empty again. "Hubert—another round."

Hubert did not move. "The tabernacle," he repeated.

"Oh, that." Charlie 'ook waved impatiently. "Me and Tiger took it down this af'ernoon—didn't we, Tiger?"

"Why?"

"Why—why? What d'you mean *why*? 'Cause it was a bleeding eyesore, that's why." He reached for the bottle and poured whiskey sloppily into his glass. "My house is a respectable house, that's what it is!"

Mrs. Stork started on a cackle.

"Shut up," Charlie 'ook shouted. He stood up, pushing aside Diana's arm. "You kids better get that into your heads. What d'you think this is—a bloody circus or something?" He stared at Mrs. Stork, but she kept her eyes low. "What I say goes—goes. See? An' there's one thing 'as gone and that's that mucking taber—— shed. Good riddance."

He waited for a challenge, but none came. "Besides," he said, relapsing into geniality, "we'll be able to grow more of them lilies now, eh?"

He sat down in the silence broken only by his own pleased laughter.

Hubert was cold and white. If he tried to speak, he knew the muscles in his cheeks would be stiff. To himself he murmured, "It's not the end." Only the fierceness of that thought prevented tears. *It's not the end.*

He turned and left the room slowly—he was not running away. As he reached the door he heard the voice of Charlie 'ook, mellow as it ever was: "Don't pay no attention to me, kid—I'm pissed."

He crossed the hall and started down the stairs to the basement.

In the kitchen he stared out of the window, deliberately allowing his eyes to lose focus, so that all he saw was the

blurred white and yellow reflection of the kitchen. There
need be no outside in such dark.

He was not surprised at Jiminee's voice behind him.

"What's wrong w-w-with Charlie?"

It's not the end, he told himself harshly. Aloud he said,
"It'll be all right in the morning."

"Well . . ." Jiminee began.

"It'll be all right in the morning," he repeated patiently,
"you'll see."

He screwed up his eyes and the white and yellow reflection
shimmered and danced. In the quiet he was distantly aware
of the hum of the electric clock.

"Is it still sn-snowing?" asked Jiminee.

"No," answered Hubert. "No. It's stopped now."

35

The white glare woke him early.

He lay for a while wondering at the strange brightness of
the ceiling. And then abruptly he knew. He kicked his legs
out of the bedclothes and darted to the window.

It had lain. After all, it had lain. The joy leapt to his
throat at the sight of the snow, deep and smooth and soot-
less. The branches of the trees were moulded with snow,
as neat as the icing on a slice of cake. The garden was
white, and the Halberts' garden and, beyond that, the Fin-
negans' garden. Where the sun touched, the snow shone
and the sky was blue.

Hubert turned to wake Dunstan, and then, at a thought,
turned back. With care for the broken sashcord, he opened
the window and leaned out. Below, the lilies were invisible
and the snow covered the wound of the uprooted tabernacle.
Hubert gathered a handful of snow from the windowsill.

"Dun, Dun," he shook his brother hard. "Look!" he held
the ball of snow in his hand. "It snowed, Dun, it snowed."

Dunstan blinked and reached out to touch the snow. He smiled and sat up and started to say something, but Hubert was rushing to tell the others.

"Snow, snow, snow!"

"Come on, get dressed."

"It doesn't matter about washing your face!"

Dressed and half-dressed, one after the other they pushed down the stairs, thumping their feet, obsessed with laughter.

They flung open the back door and ran out into the snow. The thin crust broke and their feet sank to the ankles. They paused, dazzled for a moment, turning their happy faces upwards, watching the mist of their breaths, taking in the changed forms of familiar things.

"Coo, it's d-deep," murmured Jiminee. He squatted down and picked up a handful of snow. He pressed it into a snowball and stood up slowly. Then suddenly he flung it into the air with a shout.

In a moment snowballs were flying into the air all over the garden. Gurgling with laugher, Willy scooped up the snow and threw it in a white shower over his head.

"Look at Willy!"

"Look at Willy!"

The little boy's hair was white and matted. He accepted their laughter with beaming triumph. "Watch," he cried, "watch me!" He closed his eyes and, stiff as a pole, allowed himself to fall face down in the snow. He wriggled quickly onto all fours. "I'm a polar bear," he growled, and, to his indignation, Hubert tossed a snowball at him.

The fight began. The snow was light and feathery and powdered at once when it hit. In the circle of the children there was a wild rain of whiteness and shrieks. Hubert ran quickly to an untouched patch and made half a dozen snowballs. Gathering them in his arms, he charged back into the circle, tossing them fiercely. Caught in momentary surprise, the other children turned on him together.

"All on Hu, all on Hu," they cried, and he stood in the centre as the snow hurtled at him from all sides. Smiling, not attempting to retaliate, he tasted the brittle wetness on his lips. He shut his eyes and lifted his head and the snow poured onto him like a blessing.

"Hu's a snowman!"

He looked down at his whitened jacket. His wrists were sore with damp where the sleeves rubbed and he could feel the moistness of his shirt sticking to his skin. He grinned.

"Let's b-b-build a snowman!" Jiminee shouted.

"What about a snow woman," said Diana and they burst into giggles that shook them and twisted them and flung them down into the snow.

"After breakfast," said Hubert, still standing. "Let's build a snow woman after breakfast." He glanced up at the windows of Mother's room and was surprised to see the curtains drawn back. That meant Charlie 'ook would be down any minute. The memory of last night had been temporarily washed away by the snow, but now it returned and his mirth stiffened inside him. "Come on," he said. "Breakfast."

Nobody argued and they trooped back into the kitchen. Hubert pulled out the damper of the stove and filled its mouth with coke.

Upstairs the front door slammed. The children stopped what they were doing and looked up questioningly. Fear swept into Hubert. *He's gone,* he thought, *he's left and he'll never come back.* And at that moment he knew beyond all doubt that it didn't matter what Charlie 'ook said or did or was, he was the most important thing in the world to them all. The only disaster was that he should leave them. "Charlie!" he cried.

As if in answer, they heard the quick footsteps coming down the kitchen stairs.

Charlie 'ook pushed open the swing door and stood looking at them.

"Oh, you haven't gone after all," said Hubert.

Charlie 'ook smiled with one side of his mouth. "No—I come back." He was wearing his feathered hat and his camel's-hair coat. His shoes were crusty with snow. The children watched him silently as he unbuckled his coat and took out a packet of cigarettes. His fingers shook a little as he lit the cigarette. He took a deep breath of smoke and stepped aside so that the door swung back, shivered for a moment, and was still.

"I been an early bird this morning." He took off his coat and tossed it over the back of a kitchen chair. Looking at the children, his grin kept coming and going, as if he had some secret smiling knowledge that could not be kept down.

"We were just going to make breakfast," said Hubert stolidly, but inside he was consumed with an unthought incantation: *thank you God, thank you God, thank you God.*

"Oh, Charlie," cried Diana suddenly, running forward and embracing him round the neck, "we thought you'd gone." She stood on tiptoe and raised her head.

He put his arm lightly round her. "Ah, come on, kid." He said it gently, so that it was an endearment, not a dismissal.

"Breakfast," said Hubert.

"Hold on a minute, Hu." Charlie 'ook frowned and cleared his throat. He lowered his eyes as he addressed them. "I want to say something. I want to—well, I want to explain something. That tabernacle, see, well—"

"We don't care about the tabernacle," Diana interrupted, "we don't care, Charlie!"

Charlie 'ook shook his head. "I want to explain, all the same. See, why we took it down was 'cause we wanted them bricks—we want the bricks to build a sunken garden, like you was promised." He looked up quickly, then down again.

There was a long silence, broken at last by Dunstan. "Thank you for telling us, Charlie," he said. "A sunken garden will be very nice. We've always wanted one, haven't we?" He stared hard at the other children.

"Yes," they murmured. "Thank you." "Thank you very much."

"Well, that's all right then, eh?" He was cheerful. "Now I got a surprise for you." He beamed at their sudden excitement. "But after breakfast."

"Why not now?"

"What is it? Tell us!"

"Now, now."

Charlie 'ook laughed. "Come on, you can wait ten minutes. Gotta have a cuppa to prepare yourselves for the shock!"

Breakfast became a race, so that by the time Charlie 'ook was only half finished, the other dishes were washed and stacked. "All right, all right." Charlie 'ook took a final sip of tea and stood up. "Follow me!" he commanded.

He pushed open the front gate and let the children run out onto the pavement. "There, what d'you think of it?"

They halted, not knowing at first where to look.

"The car," called Charlie 'ook, "the blooming car!"

In their awe, there was nothing they could say. It was huge and grey, like an immense lean greyhound. The doors were high up and tiny, like a racing car, thought Hubert, and the bonnet was the longest he had ever seen.

"Is it a B-B-B-Bentley?" whispered Jiminee.

"No, lad," said Charlie 'ook complacently, "it's a Lagonda —the finest car on the road."

"How fast can it go?"

"Hundred easy," Charlie 'ook chuckled.

Diana reached out and touched the polished paintwork. "Is it *really* ours?"

"Yes."

Reassured, the others moved closer and stretched out their hands to feel the reality. Willy stood on the running board and looked through the cracked windows. "It's red inside," he said.

Dunstan looked up doubtfully at Charlie 'ook. "Can we— can we have a—"

"Of course you can, that's the whole idea." Charlie 'ook clapped his hands briskly. "But none of you's had a look at the back."

They rushed to look. Strapped to the iron grill at the back was a large wooden sledge, with red metal runners. The wood shone with fresh varnish and the paint gleamed.

"A sledge!" shouted Jiminee.

"Takes three at a time," said Charlie 'ook's voice behind them.

"Three!"

"It steers, see, with this here rope."

Hubert took a deep cold breath. If there was one thing the children had never even hoped for in their brightest dreams, it was a sledge. In the park, in other winters, they'd watched the fur-mittened children, of the private schools and the moneyed parents, skidding down the little hills on oners and two-ers, and they'd laughed at the flying snow and gone home to talk excitedly about the sledges and the speed, but no more hoped to have one themselves than to ride the lions at the circus.

"A sledge!" said Hubert softly.

"Don't you like it?" Charlie 'ook's voice was touched with anxiety at their absorbed silence.

"Like it?" Diana turned to him. "Oh, Charlie, it's better than anything, anything in the whole world."

Charlie 'ook regarded her; he rubbed his upper lip gently and a faint blush touched his face. "Yes—well," he cleared his throat, "well, I thought it might make a sorta nice change, eh?"

And then they were all laughing together—even Elsa grinned. Charlie 'ook dusted some of the snow off the canvas top of the car onto Jiminee's head. Jiminee brushed it off onto his hand. He put some in his mouth and smiled. "It t-tastes n-nice," he said.

"Can we have a go on the sledge soon?" asked Dunstan seriously.

"You're going to have a go this morning," Charlie 'ook answered, the grin of secret knowledge blossoming on his face. "We're going to drive out to the park—not this tiddly one 'ere," he waved his hand at the park that began at the end of the road, "the Big Park."

"The Big Park!" They'd never been there—even Mr. Halbert hadn't taken them that far. The Big Park was just like country, they'd heard, and you could go anywhere you

wanted, and climb the trees, and there were no notices saying
KEEP OFF THE GRASS, DO NOT PICK THE FLOWERS.

"Will there be a band?" asked Hubert impulsively.

"A band?" said Charlie 'ook, puzzled.

"On a bandstand."

It was Elsa who answered, smiling indulgently, "Not in
winter, Hu. The band only plays in the summer."

"Oh." Hubert looked down at his feet.

"'ere," said Charlie 'ook, concerned, "we don't need a
band, not with the sledge. We wouldn't have time for a
band." He rubbed Hubert's hair. "Tell you what, we'll go
an' hear the band in the summer—how's that?"

"Will we really?"

"Of course we will, of course. . . . Well, who's ready
for the park?"

"You mean we can go now?"

"As soon as you get your 'ats and coats on, we can."

With one accord, they dashed for the house, jostling and
slipping on the snowy path, and stampeding into the hall.
Hubert was last and he turned to glance at Charlie 'ook
standing by the car. Within himself there was a gentle
quietude that was not the same as the joy of the others. He
loved Charlie 'ook.

As he watched, the man raised his hand to his forehead
and for a moment massaged slowly with his fingertips. His
hand dropped and he stared down the road to the spot where
on more clement days the prostitutes would wander. When
he turned his head and saw Hubert watching him, he
smiled, but it was a smile of effort.

Soberly Hubert fetched his coat. Suddenly he grasped
what the others were talking about. "What?" he said in
amazement.

"We thought it would b-be n-n-nice to have Louis with
us," said Jiminee.

"Louis?" repeated Hubert.

"Why not?" said Elsa. "Why shouldn't Louis have a treat
too?"

"Well," said Hubert, "his mother would never—"

"Why not?" said Charlie 'ook from the doorway. "We can but try."

"But how can we ask him?" Hubert saw ten thousand difficulties.

"The blower, remember?" He smiled at the children's puzzlement. "The telephone. We'll ring him up." He strode into the front room, the children crowding behind him.

"Grossiter," he flipped rapidly through the pages. "Ah, this'll be it." He began to dial.

"Mrs. Grossiter. Ah, well, this is Mr. Hook. Yes, Hook. That's right. And how are you? In the pink I do sincerely 'ope. Well, Mrs. Grossiter, I really feel I never apologised properly to you for that, er, nasty little business we was involved in. Oh, I agree. Quite. Of course it wouldn't have happened if I'd been here. Most unfortunate. Nothing like a man about the house, eh? And how's Mr. Grossiter? Oh, he is? He has? Well, well, well, I wish I could say the same for myself. Yes, still on the road, but we live in hopes. You must be very happy to have him 'ome. Ah, yes, well I was wondering—you see, Mrs. Grossiter, to tell you the truth, I feel I ought to make up for that little trouble—in however small a way. I was wondering if I could, er, take Louis off of your hands for the day. I know how it is on a Saturday— nice to have a bit of peace and quiet about the house, eh?" He winked at the children. "Slip off for a quick one or spend the afternoon at the flicks. Don't have to worry about the nipper. The park—yes. I got a sledge for the kids. They are —excited, oh, my word yes. Give 'im tea. Bring him back about six, all right? He would? Well, that's settled then. Oh, don't you bother about that, Mrs. G., we'll pop round right away and pick him up. Yes. Yes. And, oh, give my congratulations to Mr. Grossiter. And to you?" Charlie 'ook opened his eyes wide in mock astonishment. "My word—my blooming word. That *is* good news. Wonderful. New life— nothing like it. You're a very lucky woman, Mrs. G. Who, me?" He assumed a tone of brave melancholy. "Ah, well, that's water under the bridge. Never again." He sighed. "Water under the bridge—she wouldn't be up to it. No.

We're getting on, see, both getting on. Here, what am I moaning for, eh? I got six, that's—seven? Ah, yes, seven. You're right—just shows 'ow you lose count, don't it?" He laughed genially. "Okey-dokey then, we'll be round in two ticks."

Charlie 'ook put down the phone. He stared thoughtfully at the children.

"Is he c-c-coming?" asked Jiminee.

Charlie 'ook turned on his swift grin. "Of course he is." He stood up, rubbing his hands. "Where's my coat, eh? Then we'll be off!"

36

The keeper signalled them to slow down as they entered the park. He came over and Charlie 'ook pushed open the side window.

"Morning, sir," said the keeper, brushing the peak of his cap. The dog by his side barked abruptly. "Where was you going, sir?"

"We thought we'd go up the Big Hill," said Charlie 'ook.

"The Big Hill." The keeper's ruddy face moved a little closer. "Well, that's all right, but you want to watch the road, sir, up the hill. Slippery, sir, very slippery." He paused, visibly wondering whether his admonition was strong enough. "Could 'ave a nasty accident, you wasn't careful." The dog started to bark again. "Quiet, Friend," said the keeper.

"Is that his n-n-name?" said Jiminee from the back seat.

"That's right, son. Friend—a dog's a man's best friend. Get it?" He paused, unsmiling, and then spoke to Charlie 'ook again. "So you'll be careful, sir, won't you?"

"Right," Charlie 'ook nodded, "I'll drive as careful as an old lady."

The faintest of disapproving frowns wrinkled the keeper's forehead. "I wouldn't worry about old ladies, if I was you,

sir. Just keep your eyes on the road and your 'and steady."
He nodded and stood away from the car.

"Silly old dot," said Charlie 'ook jovially, shutting the
window and putting his foot on the accelerator, "he'd be
scared to death in a pram."

The keeper stood in the middle of the road, watching the
big Lagonda draw away. "Wants to watch out with all
them kids," he muttered, stooping to pat the head of his
black mongrel. "I know that type. Smart aleck—smart
aleck, that's what he is, Friend."

"Louis," called Charlie 'ook over his shoulder, "I hear
you're going to have a little brother."

Wedged between Elsa and Jiminee in the back seat,
Louis looked up. "It's going to be a sister," he said confidently.

"Your mother going to have a baby?" asked Elsa, her
face suddenly alive.

"Yes," Louis nodded, smiling. "It's going to be in July."

"*My* birthday's in July," said Willy proudly. "It's the
best month." The children laughed.

Louis is different, thought Hubert; he isn't nearly so shy
and he doesn't mind laughing anymore. It occurred to
him suddenly that they didn't have to be sorry for Louis now.

As they reached Big Hill and jumped down from the high-
sided car and dragged the sledge to where the slope really
began, Hubert watched the infection of excitement blossoming in Louis.

"Bags I first," Louis shouted.

"And m-m-me!" added Jiminee.

"All right," said Charlie 'ook. "You two go first. And Di
can go too—can't have all the men together."

They climbed on the sledge, Diana in front to steer. "Now
hold tight," said Charlie 'ook. He bent down behind the
sledge and gave it a hard shove. It moved reluctantly and at
first they thought it would stop, but, as it reached a
sudden dip, it gathered momentum.

"There they go!" Willy danced. "Swish!"

The red runners were a continuous streak of scarlet as

the sledge sped down the broad bosom of the hill. A fine spray of snow shot up from either side and suddenly the sledge seemed miles away.

"Shall we go an' help them?" asked Dunstan.

Charlie 'ook shook his head. "No—they'll bring it back. Your turn next."

Far below the sledge had stopped and its riders were so small it was hard to tell them apart, except for Diana's golden hair. To the right of them, on the more accessible side of Big Hill, they saw the figures of other sledders. Their shouts reached the children thinly and faraway.

Charlie 'ook reached in his hip pocket and took out a leather-covered flask. He unscrewed the cap and put the flask to his lips.

"What's that?" asked Willy.

"I know what it is," said Dunstan, "it's what you take to the races, isn't it?"

"That's better," Charlie 'ook murmured, wiping his lips on the back of his hand. "Yes, that's right, Dun. Saves you having to pop in the bar all the time."

"Aren't there any races today?" Hubert asked.

"Nah—cancelled, 'cause of the snow. Can't 'ave the fillies getting their tootsies wet." Charlie 'ook chuckled at some private thought. "But it don't matter to me," he said, "I've got a bleeding lucky streak going as I've never had in me life." He hesitated a moment and then went on, "Got a hundred nicker on at Cheltenham this afternoon. A sure thing— can't miss, not with my luck this season." He considered for a moment. "You know what? I bet I know what done it. It's you kids—you brought me luck, that's what you done. Ever since I come home, I haven't been able to go wrong. Of course, I had a bad moment or two—who doesn't?—but on the whole, on the whole, I never had it near so good. Not near." He took another drink. "It's a miracle." He seemed to be talking mainly to himself, and as he focussed on the children they had the guilty feeling of eavesdroppers.

Charlie 'ook waved his flask. "So what ho! Not to worry." He glanced down the hill. "They're nearly back—who's next?"

As Hubert climbed onto the sledge and felt Dunstan grip him firmly round the waist, he wondered for an instant whether Charlie 'ook would have brought them if the racing had not been cancelled. But all thoughts were whisked from his mind as the sledge jolted and then began to slide into a great smooth long run and the icy wind flashed in his face.

"Hu, do you think there's wolves in there?" Willy pointed at the woods that stretched behind them at the top of the hill.

"I don't think so," Hubert answered. He was trying to hear what Louis was saying to Jiminee—the two of them stood off a little. "Perhaps at night. But not in daytime."

"They'd be asleep in daytime?" Willy persisted.

"I expect so." Hubert made a decision. He let go of Willy's hand and walked over to where Jiminee and Louis were standing.

"Hello," he said.

Louis smiled back. "Hello, Hubert—look at my knife." He extended his hand to show the penknife. "It's got *everything*," he said, "even a thing to take stones out of horses' hoofs."

"May I hold it?"

"Yes."

Hubert took off his glove and held the penknife in his hand. It was smooth and white and heavy. It *had* everything.

"His m-mother gave it him," said Jiminee.

Hubert was surprised. "But I thought your mother didn't like you having presents."

Louis nodded. "She didn't used to. But it's different now Dad's back. She gives me presents all the time. I'm going to get a watch next week."

Hubert handed back the knife. "Have you still got your ammite?"

"Ammonite," Louis corrected. "Oh, yes, I got it. I got lots of things now. I got a fort." There was a pause, and Louis blushed, as if aware that he'd been boasting. "Can I take my presents you gave me back with me after tea?"

he asked. "I'm sure Mum wouldn't mind me having them now
—they're *much* the best presents I ever had."

"All right," said Hubert, pleased. "Louis," he didn't quite
know how to put what was in his mind, "Louis—is your
mother pregnant?"

Louis nodded with vigour. "Oh, yes. She's really big. Much
bigger than when she had me—that's what Dad says." He
waited, sensing that Hubert had more to say.

"Did—did she want to have another baby?"

"Of course," said Louis, "Mum and Dad wanted to have
one before it was too late."

"Your Dad wants it too?"

"He must do—mustn't he?"

Hubert was nonplussed. "Why must he want it?" He
looked at Jiminee, but Jiminee just smiled encouragingly.

"Well," said Louis, "she couldn't have it without him,
could she? I mean, that's why my Dad come back—so's we
could have a baby sister."

"Why—does he have to be there the whole time?"

"Oh, no—he goes to the office an' things like that. But
he's got to be there at the beginning, hasn't he?"

"Of course." Hubert spoke abruptly. He was irritated with
himself for asking so many questions.

Louis hesitated and then said, "Don't you understand about
all that, Hubert?"

"Of course," he repeated shortly. "Of course I understand.
I was just asking, that's all."

"What's the matter, Hu?" asked Jiminee.

"Nothing's the matter." He turned away. He was angry,
and he didn't know why. He looked across at Charlie 'ook
standing on the very edge of the steep slope. He watched
him intensely as the man raised the flask and drank, as he
puffed at his cigarette and then let it fall in the snow, as he
pushed his hands into the deep pockets of his camel
coat and stared down at the shouting children below. Charlie
'ook had always been there really. Always. He'd written to
Mother, hadn't he? That proved it. He'd just gone away now
and again, but really he'd always been there.

Hubert looked back at Louis and Jiminee. "I can *ask,* can't I?" he said fiercely.

They stared at him in bewilderment, but he didn't see. He ran to Charlie 'ook, calling his name.

"Hello, what's up?"

"Can I stand by you and watch, Charlie?"

Charlie 'ook laughed and made a sweeping gesture with his arms. "Take your fill, lad. It's yours, all yours—as far as the bleeding horizon."

37

It was hot in the back of the car. But the words of the hymn that Jiminee was singing—about the rock—made him think how cold it was outside, how very cold. Yet when they stepped out of the car into the garden, by the pool, it wasn't cold at all.

He looked down at his legs and they were brown and he was wearing summer sandals. One by one, he was handing Louis his presents. And there seemed so many of them, watches and penknives and toy soldiers and a huge rabbit and a book and a penny. But, after all, the pomegranate was missing and he was suddenly stabbed with despair. And then he glanced up, and there on the tree were the rich golden pomegranates, just as they'd always been. He reached and gently pulled down the branch and plucked a pomegranate. Its skin was as smooth as wax.

And he handed the last of the presents to Louis, who said simply, "I must go home now."

Hubert kicked off his sandals and pulled his shirt over his head and undid his belt so that his trousers fell down to his ankles. And he felt the breeze blowing on his body. It was like water, so smooth and milky warm. He swam a few strokes in the pool and watched the great green lilies. He was happy because he remembered it all, exactly as it was.

He could close his eyes and remember every detail, and when he looked again, he was right. It was just so.

He swam to the edge of the pool. He smiled, for there was the black dog with curling hair on his neck. He wasn't barking now.

"Hello, Blackie," said Hubert. And then he frowned. This wasn't Blackie—Blackie had moved away ages ago. This was—he tried to remember. "Friend! I mean Friend." He smiled up at the dog. He put his hands on the side of the bank and pulled his shoulders out of the water. Soon it would be teatime.

But the dog gently put its paw on his head and, with the faintest of growls, pushed him back into the pool. Hubert went in over his head and, when he came up again for a little while he couldn't see for the water in his eyes.

He grinned to himself and swam to the other bank and started to get out. But Friend had followed him and pushed him back once again, this time more roughly.

"Good old Friend, good dog," coaxed Hubert, as he gripped tight at the bank. This time Friend put both his paws on Hubert's shoulders and forced him down. He uttered a single bark.

"Don't bark, please," said Hubert, spitting the water from his mouth, "you'll wake the others." He swam cautiously away and then darted back and heaved quickly.

He was almost out, and would have been if his foot had not slipped as Friend charged him with loud barks.

"Hush," said Hubert anxiously. His arms were weak and he could only just keep his head above the water. It was growing cold too.

"Please let me out, Friend," he said, but he knew that the dog could not be won by persuasion.

Again and again he tried, each time more feeble. And now Friend had set up a continual howl and was prancing wildly on the bank.

"Please, please," cried Hubert, trying desperately not to weep—for his tears would only make more water for him to drown in.

He could try no more. It was too late. He felt the water on his face and in his nostrils and his eyes. Only his ears were clear and in them was the wicked triumphal bark of Friend, louder and louder and filled with ever more frantic rage.

He sat up, his eyes staring in the darkness, noting the familiar chink of lighter night outside the curtains, but he heard it still—the barking, barking. Or was it laughter? And now it seemed to rise and scream.

Then it stopped. There was suddenly such silence that he could hear Dunstan breathing in the bed against the wall.

He lay down at last. There was no more noise. But it was a long time before he shut his eyes.

SPRING

38

Hubert stood at the door and sniffed at the ebb-tide smell of beer and dead cigarette stubs. The front room was dark, lit only by the strips of daylight round the closed curtains.

He moved into the room and sniffed again. There was another smell, a sweet cheap perfume that could come from scented tobacco or . . . Hubert frowned. He walked slowly over to the windows and pulled back the curtains. He un-latched the window and heaved it open as wide as it would go. He bent down and looked out.

The streets were quiet. A grey spring rain was falling gent-ly. Hubert stared over the hedge at the spot where the Lagonda should have been. It hadn't been there for weeks. Perhaps at the back of his mind he had hoped it would miraculously appear this morning—ready and waiting only a word from Him to carry them off to a day in the park, or the country, or down to the sea. But it wasn't there.

He looked in front of the Halberts'. The road was empty there too. Mr. Halbert wouldn't keep his Daimler out in the rain.

He thrust out his arm and felt the rain on the back of his hand. It was cool, and the street was so silent, you could hear the drops on the leaves. It was too early for the

postman, or even for the milkman. Somewhere a policeman would be sheltering in a doorway—but all the rest of
them were asleep.

Hubert drew in his head and turned to look at the room.

There was the usual group of empty beer bottles on the
mantelpiece, their labels stained with slopped beer. The marble mantel was ringed beyond cleaning. Matches meant for
the fireplace landed there and burned themselves black on the
stone. Most of the furniture was scarred now with grooves
from cigarettes or matches left to burn their way through
wax and varnish. A deep wrinkle cut the carpet and almost
in the center was a new stain—beer, whiskey, coffee even.
It would never come properly clean.

Hubert sighed at the crammed ashtrays and the half-empty
glasses—witness to Charlie 'ook's habit of taking a new one
before he'd finished the old—and the coffee cup lying
crooked in its saucer. He moved away from the window,
shutting the lid of the piano automatically and bending to
pick up a scrunched cigarette packet.

"I better clean up, I suppose," he murmured aloud. If he
didn't do it, no one else would. Mrs. Stork was no more than
an irregular visitor these days, dropping in at any time of
the day for a cup of tea in the kitchen or a bottle of
brown in the front room. Sometimes she put on her apron
and took up a duster, but they were merely the badges of
her right to open every door and ask any question. She didn't
lift a finger to the dusty corners or the unmade beds. Sometimes she'd pick up the phone and order Spicers' to send
round a couple of dozen eggs and some tins of salmon and
baked beans. But that was about all.

Salmon and baked beans. His mouth went dry with distaste. A year ago, three months ago even, he'd never have
believed he'd be tired of salmon or of baked beans. But now
it made him sick to think of them, dinner after dinner, tea
after tea. He longed for meat suddenly, for roast potatoes
and cabbage, big thick leaves of cabbage with "plenty of
chew." That was Mother's phrase—"plenty of chew."

He stood in the centre of the room and looked round slowly, taking in everything. *Mother's phrase. Mother's time.* He recalled without effort how it had been in those days—the black leather chair had gleamed and the net curtains shone white and there had been that always present smell of dust mingled with the faintest scent of soap, of Mother's soap, and, in the springtime, lilies of the valley.

Why don't I cry? thought Hubert. He remembered it all so clearly. He remembered those days and Gerty's laughter —he'd not thought of Gert for a long time—and the great Sunday dinners and the bustle and the clap-clap of Mother's hands when a rule was close to being broken. And the rule was that you must eat your greens. And the rule was that you must wash your hands before dinner and put on your galoshes when it rained and remember Jesus and make your bed directly after breakfast. The rule was "enough is enough."

He did not think of baked beans or salmon, but his mouth was still dry. He reached out his arms, and he thought of the hymn-singing on Sunday evening and of the piano thumping and Jiminee's voice rising above all the others and the wisp of hair bobbing on Charlie 'ook's head— and suddenly the memories were all mixed. He closed his eyes. *Why don't I cry?* he demanded fiercely, and he clenched his fists tight.

"Mother." He tried the word on the empty room—but the word too was empty. He sighed and opened his eyes. The dead cigarettes and the empty glasses—this was the way it really was. The heaviness was still there, pushing him down, waiting even in the early-morning stillness for something to happen. He did not try to think about that *something* —you could not lay your finger on it or look at it. No, *it* was looking at you, pointing *its* finger at you. And the only thing you could do was to clean up the front room, to wash the glasses and lay the fire. And if you didn't and if you looked round too fast, you'd see the whole world was—

There was a noise from upstairs and Hubert ducked quickly. He held his breath, but he heard nothing but the blood in his ears. Perhaps that's all it had been—the blood in his ears. He straightened up slowly. He took another deep breath and smelled the cool morning air from the window. And far away he heard the milkman call. He pushed away the terror and began to stack the glasses. It would soon be time to take His tea up.

As he mounted the stairs carrying the cup of tea, he met Elsa coming down. They both stopped.

"Hello," said Elsa.

Hubert kept his eyes on the tea. "Hello," he answered.

"Taking the tea up?"

He nodded and then glanced quickly at his sister. Her hair was braided carefully and her face had a very washed look and her dress was ironed. He tried to think of something to say—and for an instant he realised that she was too.

"Well," she said. Then the moment was gone and she went on down. Hubert waited until he heard the hall door open and close, then he continued.

Charlie 'ook was asleep. Hubert put the cup down on the bedside table and looked around. Charlie 'ook's trousers and jacket lay tumbled on the floor, a shoe with laces still tied on top of them. The other shoe was on the chest of drawers. Hubert went across the room and picked it up and put it softly on the floor.

He fingered the chest of drawers. It had suffered badly in the damp of the tabernacle; the whole of the top was peeling and parched. He ran his hand across the roughness. Then he stopped. Just visible under Charlie 'ook's old handkerchief was the tip of the savings book. Slowly Hubert withdrew it. He held it for a moment while he glanced back at the sleeper, then he turned the pages. There were a lot of entries and even more withdrawals. He looked at the balance on the last page: 15-0*d*. Fifteen shillings—a measly fifteen bob. Hubert tried the next page, but it was blank. It was unbelievable—and yet, somehow it did not shock him as much as it should have done. He knew Charlie 'ook had hit a streak of bad luck, the Lagonda sold, Mrs. Stork not paid, the lack of treats—but *fifteen shillings*.

He slipped the book back under the handkerchief. As he touched the linen and looked closer, he saw that it wasn't Charlie 'ook's handkerchief after all. He raised it slowly. It was lacy and small. He lifted it to his nose. *That* was the smell downstairs. He sniffed—it was the same, only more sickly, stronger than . . . He looked down and there, until now concealed by the handkerchief, was a lipstick case and a powder compact. He knew at once what they were. Elsa had pointed out just such the same as these in Woolworth's window—oh, ages ago.

He turned to see Charlie 'ook sitting up in bed, staring at him.

"Blimey," said Charlie 'ook hoarsely, "you don't half make a shindy. Want to wake the dead or something?" Then he saw what it was that Hubert was holding and he laughed. "Always leaving her bleeding paraphernalia about, she is." He yawned. " 'ere, why don't you run off, eh? I need a bit more kip." He lay back and shut his eyes, wincing as he did so.

Hubert returned to the front room. It was passable now. The fresh air filled the room. The net curtains trailed and swam in the breeze. He closed the window.

The glasses and empties were gone and the mat straightened and ashtrays emptied. Tomorrow it would be just the same. And tomorrow and tomorrow.

Fifteen bob, only fifteen bob! And Mother's cheque wasn't due for nearly three weeks yet. Hubert thought of the money in the drawer in his workshop and was glad that some instinct had warned him against telling anyone about it. He'd saved it for a rainy day, and now here was the rainy day. Of course, perhaps Charlie 'ook had some other money somewhere, perhaps—but he was quite aware that it was a false hope. If Charlie 'ook had any money, they always knew about it.

The abrupt sound of the doorbell jerked Hubert as if he were a marionette. He went to the doorway of the front room and looked down the hall. The ringing came again.

Since Charlie 'ook had installed the doorbell, every caller sounded petulant.

Hubert wondered whether he ought to answer it. He didn't want to. Most likely it would be one of Charlie 'ook's friends—the well-worn overcoat, the small hole in a finger of one glove, the eyes that always seemed to be looking for the bar and the breezy, "Charlie 'ook up and about yet? No, ah, well—think I'll come in and make meself at home, okay?"

He walked slowly to the front door and laid his hand on the latch. As he swung the door open, there was a burst of activity from upstairs. He stared at the caller, aware of hurrying footsteps on the stairs behind him.

It was Mr. Halbert.

"Hello," said Hubert.

"Good morning—er—Hubert, isn't it?" He was wearing a blue-tinted tweed suit with plus fours. He was bareheaded and his bald scalp was without its usual gloss. Hubert remembered that Mrs. Halbert was ill; perhaps she was too ill to polish it.

"I'd like a word with your father, if he's up."

Hubert was aware of a mild disappointment. He would have liked to have talked with Mr. Halbert. He imagined for a moment sitting on the front seat beside Mr. Halbert in the big Daimler and driving slowly through the park. But Mr. Halbert made no offer.

"I'll tell him you're here," he said. "Won't—won't you come in?"

"No thanks—ah."

Hubert glanced round to see Charlie 'ook standing behind him.

"Ah," repeated Mr. Halbert. "Mr. Hook?"

"That's right. Who are you?"

Hubert moved surreptitiously to one side. Charlie 'ook was in a bad mood.

"I'm Halbert. I'm next door—number forty."

"Number forty, eh?" Charlie 'ook interrupted smoothly.

"Well, number forty, do you usually go about ringing door-bells at the crack of dawn?"

Mr. Halbert's face showed no reaction. "It's after nine, Hook," he said steadily. "I wanted to have a word with you about the rather considerable noise coming from this house last night."

"You did, did you?"

"You may recall I telephoned you last night several times."

Charlie 'ook grinned. "There was some silly bastard that kept ringing up."

There was an edge of hardness about Mr. Halbert's com-posure. "It's not the first time the noise from this house has disturbed a number of people, Hook."

Charlie 'ook leaned forward. "*Mr.* Hook to you. And while you're about it why don't you run off home and mind your own bloody business?"

"Very well." Mr. Halbert nodded. "I warned you last night that I should be forced to make a complaint."

"You can do what you bloody well like."

Mr. Halbert, hesitating, glanced at Hubert. "There's just one thing, Hook. My wife is a very sick woman—every mo-ment of sleep is precious to her. I'm afraid you woke her up several times last night."

"Get 'er a couple of ear plugs then," said Charlie 'ook, "they're cheap."

Mr. Halbert regarded him for a moment. "You really are a nasty piece of work, aren't you, Hook?" His tone was conversational.

Charlie 'ook jerked back as if he'd been hit. For a second, Hubert was sure he was going to strike Mr. Hal-bert. But he didn't. He gripped the edge of the front door to steady himself. "Why you . . . why you . . ."

But Mr. Halbert was already down the front steps and walking towards the gate. Charlie 'ook watched him go. Abruptly he stepped inside and slammed the front door with all his force. "Cocky bastard!"

Then he noticed Hubert. "Well, and what are you staring at?"

"Nothing," said Hubert—he was surprised he had a voice.

Charlie 'ook turned his head this way and that, as if he were searching for something to fix his rage on. Suddenly he looked hard at Hubert. "Shocked at me having a tart in, is that it?"

Hubert shook his head.

"No?" He twisted his body restlessly. Then he smiled and was still. "I expect you got used to Vi 'aving her men in, eh?"

The hall clock ticked loud in the morning silence.

"Well, she did, didn't she?" Charlie 'ook pushed his face close to the boy's. "I knew old Vi—never could do without it for long." He waited and Hubert felt his breath upon his cheek.

Slowly Charlie 'ook straightened up. "Lucky for you that, eh? Otherwise you wouldn't be 'ere. None of you would." He laughed, then touched his hand to his forehead. "Christ, I need a hair of the dog."

He hitched at his trousers and moved off into the front room.

Hubert stayed quite still where Charlie 'ook had left him. He stared down at the patch of polished board by the threshhold. It was fainter now, but the boot mark was still there. It was funny how he hadn't noticed it for so long.

Hubert blinked, concentrating on the boot marks, trying to remember something, something important.

From the front room Charlie 'ook called, his voice remote and faraway, "Where the hell are the mucking glasses?"

39

"Morning, son."

"Hello."

"Your dad in?"

"No—he's out."

The policeman was immobile. His cape glistened with the morning rain. "Be back soon though, I expect?"

Hubert stared up at him. The eyes were concealed by the shadow of the helmet's brim and the mouth moved only to speak.

"I don't know when he'll be back."

The policeman was patient. He would look like this if he were helping an old lady across a street or if he were arresting a murderer.

Something took a plunge within Hubert. "What . . ." he started to say; he glanced at the street—but there was no Black Maria waiting, no police car.

"Just wanted a word with your dad." The policeman reached up and lifted the helmet from his head. He took out a handkerchief, folded it into a neat pad and wiped his forehead. He suddenly looked ordinary—with brown hair receding at the temples. "Quite sure you don't know when he'll be back, eh?"

Hubert shook his head. He hesitated. "He's gone round to the pub," he brought out.

"Ah." The policeman replaced his helmet and put away his handkerchief. "I don't suppose your mother would be in, would she?"

"No—no." Hubert's voice wavered for a second. He'd been in the garden this morning for the first time for—for weeks. Still tired with winter it had been. The grass was overdue for its first mowing—but Tiger Stork didn't come these days. The jumble of bricks, once Mother's tabernacle, lay beside the half-dug hole that was to be the sunken garden. The lilies of the valley had almost entirely covered the raw scar of earth where Mother was buried, but they were late this year and had not yet begun to bloom.

"What?" said Hubert quickly.

"All alone, eh?"

"Oh, no—there's my brothers and sisters." *Why doesn't he go?* thought Hubert. But he found the presence of the policeman somehow comforting.

"You been crying, haven't you, sonny?"

Hubert's lips tightened. "Of course not." Now he wished the policeman would go—go, go, go.

But he didn't. "What's up, son? You can tell me."

And suddenly Hubert recognized that tone of voice—the gentle assurance that there was nothing, nothing at all, that couldn't be quietly and decently solved. He'd heard it before —in another place, at some other time. Then he remembered—he remembered—he remembered running down Hatton Alley pursued by the whispers of the leaves. He remembered the sudden collision with the policeman under the light, and the strong hands and the voice, the same voice—"What's after you, son?"

"Nothing," he said violently, "nothing!"

The policeman paused. "All right," he said. "You can tell your dad that I was round. I'll come—" he turned as he heard the voices at the gate.

There were three of them. A small, plump man—not a loose, jolly plumpness, but as if tightly wedged under the skin was all the food he'd ever eaten—with a black hat and a fussy manner, and a youngish man and woman, both blond, white-faced and with an air of forever combatting colds in the nose.

The small man hurried up the path and climbed the steps rapidly.

"Morning, Mr. Moley," said the policeman.

"Oh, oh—good morning, officer, good morning, officer." He glanced quickly from the policeman to Hubert and back again. "Nothing amiss, I hope?"

"No, sir—except we could do with a bit of sun."

"Yes, yes." Mr. Moley directed his attention at Hubert. "Tell Mr. Hook Mr. Moley's here, please, with some clients."

"I'm afraid you'll find he's not in, sir," said the policeman.

Mr. Moley turned impatiently. "Not in? They never are, they never are. Most irritating." He puffed his cheeks. "Well, we'll just have to have a look round without him. I don't suppose it matters much," he inclined his head to his clients, "I pride myself I know all these houses inside out." He took a step forward.

Hubert didn't move. He kept his hand firmly on the front door. "I'm afraid you can't come in," he said. "My father will be back soon—you can come round then if you want to see him."

Mr. Moley opened his small eyes to their fullest extent. "No—absolutely not. Don't be ridiculous, boy, of course we're coming in." He pushed against the front door.

"Excuse me, Mr. Moley, I take it you have an order to view?"

Mr. Moley pursed his lips. "Of course I have, of course, of course." He felt in his overcoat pocket and produced a slip of paper. He held it out to the policeman, who glanced at it and nodded. Mr. Moley thrust it at Hubert. "I hope that satisfies you too, young man."

Hubert didn't look at it. "You can't come in," he repeated.

"Can't I, can't I just—you see." He stepped across the threshold—at the same moment Hubert tried to slam the door. But Mr. Moley had wedged his foot firmly between jamb and door.

"I don't think—" began the white-faced wife.

"Open up, open up," cried Mr. Moley angrily.

"Excuse me, sir," intervened the policeman, "don't you think it might be wiser to come back at some time Mr. Hook is available?"

Mr. Moley lost his temper. "I do not, I certainly do not. My clients have come up from the country especially to view this house—especially. And I'm a very busy man, officer, exceedingly busy—"

"It would really be quite convenient for us to come some other time," said the wife with a sniff.

"Nonsense," Mr. Moley almost shouted, "absolute nonsense." With an effort he controlled himself. "I haven't been an estate agent for thirty years for nothing," he said. "We have a perfectly good right to view this house, and we're not going to be stopped by the whim of some child." He gave a strong push and forced the door open. "There now, step in please."

"What do you want?" asked Hubert desperately.

Mollified by effecting his entrance at last, Mr. Moley spoke calmly. "We are just going to have a look at the house. You want to have nice people to live here after you've gone, don't you?" He even tried a smile.

"We're not leaving!"

"Well, you're not staying—not after I dispose of the lease for your father. *When* that'll be," he said, glancing round the hall with a disapproving air, "I don't know."

"You mean sell the house?" The bird within Hubert was doing terrible things.

"In a manner of speaking, yes—the lease, you know, only the lease. Mr. Hook wants to make a fast deal. I'm willing." Moley rubbed his fat hands together.

"But he *can't* sell the house!" cried Hubert.

"What, what? Why can't he? Of course he can."

"It doesn't belong to him!"

"Eh, what?" Mr. Moley was suddenly alert. "Who does it belong to then?"

"It belongs to *us!*"

"Us? Who's us?"

"All of us—the family. My brothers and sisters and me."

Mr. Moley relaxed. "That's a good one." He turned to his unsmiling clients. "Well," he said, businesslike at once, "let's look it over."

"But it does!" cried Hubert. "It does, it does—Mother left . . ." He could have bitten his tongue out. But nobody seemed to have grasped what he was saying.

"Oh, Jim," murmured the white-faced girl to the man, "the poor little boy—they didn't tell him they were selling the house."

The man coughed. "Yes, well," he raised his hand vaguely at Hubert, "jolly bad luck, old boy." He coughed again.

"Come on, come on," said Mr. Moley impatiently.

"Here, son," said the policeman, "why don't you stay here with me, while they have a look round—they won't be long."

But Hubert was gone.

He ran frantically up the stairs. The shape of the banisters, the colour of the wallpaper, the pattern on the worn piece of landing carpet flashed upon him with lightning familiarity, and was past. He was conscious of his knees bobbing up and up, and up and up, white and white, but in his mind was only the thought of Elsa.

"Elsa!" He stood, panting, the backs of his legs pounding with ache. She looked up from her book.

"Elsa, he's selling the house—they're here, the people what's going to buy it. They're downstairs."

Elsa laid the book down on the bed and stood up. She looked at him calmly. "Get the others," she said.

"But," said Hubert, his hand shaking, as he brushed the hair from his eyes, "but . . ."

"Pull yourself together. And get the others. Hurry."

She stood like a poker, unyielding, strong as iron. His hand stopped trembling. He turned and ran back down the stairs.

The six of them stood by the banisters on the first landing. They could just see the face of the clock in the hall. Below them came the occasional sound of a shutting door.

Mr. Moley and his clients were down in the kitchen. Soon the children heard their feet on the kitchen steps and as the hall door opened, a snatch of words. ". . . lovely workroom, or a nursery for the kids. That's what a lot of people have done with these houses. Easy access to the garden, see. Don't have to worry."

They were coming up the stairs now.

Elsa spoke softly. "Be absolutely still, children. I don't want anyone to say a word."

"Why—" began Willy.

"Shh—shut up!"

They reached the little landing by the library. They glanced up and saw the children. Mr. Moley frowned and turned to the library.

"In here," he said, twisting the handle, "is a nice little spare bedroom. Do for a maid—if you had one."

But the couple was not listening to him. The woman was whispering into her husband's ear. He nodded and coughed.

"Mr. Moley," his voice was almost inaudible, "seen enough . . . very nice . . . not necessary . . . fair idea . . ."

"But that's not the half of it," Mr. Moley answered loudly. "Why, you haven't seen the master bedroom yet, and—"

The white-faced man murmured again.

"Well, I don't see much sense in coming all the way from Haslemere and then not making a proper inspection." He shrugged his shoulders. "But it's up to you."

More murmuring and then the little party turned and began to descend. As they reached the bottom, the woman looked up at the children. Her face was blurred in the dim light of the hall, but she might have been smiling.

Their footsteps echoed in the hall and then the door slammed and they were gone.

Hubert broke the silence. "I wonder if the policeman's still there."

"What policeman?" asked Elsa.

"He came to see Charlie—he's going to come back again," he said.

"It doesn't matter about the policeman," Elsa said after a moment's thought. "Tell the others what you told me."

Slowly, trying to get it in order, Hubert told them what he had heard, what Charlie 'ook was going to do.

"But there must be some mistake," said Diana.

"No, there isn't," Elsa answered decisively.

"Perhaps," said Jiminee, "perhaps Charlie is b-b-buying us a house in the c-c-country."

"Why wouldn't he tell us?" said Elsa.

Jiminee's face twitched and he began to quiver.

"It's all right," said Hubert quickly and he took his brother's hand and held it tight.

"We'll all go down to the front room," Elsa announced.

"What for?" asked Willy.

"To wait for him," Elsa replied.

The front room was chilly, but none of them thought of lighting the fire that was carefully laid and waiting.

"Elsa," said Hubert, "he can't sell the house. It's ours. The will says so."

"There isn't a will," said Elsa.

"But—"

"He tore it up. I found the bits in the wastepaper basket."

"But why didn't you tell us?" asked Hubert, aghast.

She didn't answer immediately. When she did, she lifted her head and spoke with great calm. "Because, Hubert—because what could you have done about it if I had told you? And if you'd *believed* me? You're blind—all of you's blind. You haven't seen what's under your noses. You've never seen that Charlie—*Charlie 'ook,*" there was a sudden fierceness of contempt in her voice, "doesn't care about anything but himself. He lies, he's always lying. He says he loves you—but he doesn't. He doesn't love no one. He's nice enough on the outside, but inside he's vile, he's—"

"Shut up!" It was Diana, her voice queerly high.

And Elsa nodded. "All right. I will. You just see. Wait and see."

Dunstan spoke. "I agree. I think we should wait and see what Charlie has to say too."

Elsa smiled faintly.

"What's funny?" asked Dunstan, frowning.

"You," said Elsa. "You're funny—that's what. You didn't wait and see with Gerty, did you? You weren't so keen on Charlie neither till he bribed you with books and things."

Dunstan's face flushed red. "That's not fair—that's not . . ."

He looked around at the others, but none of them looked

at him. "Mother would have . . ." he let the sentence trail into nothing.

"I love Charlie," said Willy suddenly.

There was a tiny murmur of frightened agreement from the children.

"I never said you didn't," said Elsa. "It's just that he doesn't love us."

"He does, he does." Diana rose from the chair she'd been sitting on. Her golden hair shook as she said it again and again. "He does, he does, he does!" She burst into tears. She sank to the floor and bowed down, holding her hands in front of her face. Her words became sobs that went on and on. It seemed a long while before she quietened.

The children were silent, watching her, looking round the room, but not at each other.

At length Jiminee spoke. "What's g-going t-t-t-to—"

Elsa shook her head. "Wait and see. It won't be long. He'll be back soon." She folded her hands in her lap.

40

Closing time came and went. The clock in the hall chimed three, four. The rainy daylight slowly changed into darkness.

Elsa moved once to switch on a single lamp. Once Hubert got up and drew the curtains across the windows.

Otherwise, they sat, hardly shifting, not speaking—waiting.

The light reflected from the leather surface of the black chair. It was empty, waiting for Charlie 'ook. The rest of the room was dim, the faces of the children a white circle looking into the pool of light.

He came at last, just as the clock struck five.

They heard the key in the lock—Hubert's heart moved to that sound of homecoming and then tightened, overridden by the terrified wings of the bird within. The front door clicked half-shut and then was pulled back and slammed hard.

They heard him grunt. There was silence and then the scratch of a match. And then his feet came towards the front room.

He just walked in and sat in the black chair and rubbed his hand over his face several times.

He lay back and closed his eyes. The smoke from the cigarette between his fingers wavered slightly, then continued straight up to the invisible realms beyond the reach of the lamp.

Charlie 'ook opened his eyes and for a moment stared intensely at the children. He shut them again.

"What's this—a bloody reception committee?" He mumbled. His voice was without vitality.

"Get me a Guinness, Hu." He sighed. He lifted the cigarette to his lips and took a long drag. The smoke drifted reluctantly from his mouth, his nose.

The children did not move.

"I said get me a Guinness, Hu."

He stretched out his legs and put the toe of one shoe under the heel of the other and pushed. The shoes loosened, he shook them off and kicked them aside. For a few moments he flexed his toes rhythmically.

He sat up abruptly. "Didn't you hear what I said?" His face was red and violent.

Hubert didn't move. He couldn't move.

"We want to talk to you, Charlie." Elsa's cold voice.

Charlie 'ook grimaced. "Natter, natter, natter—bunch of bloody old women," he said with contemptuous mildness. He stood up. "Get it myself—said the little red hen." He let out a single chuckle.

The bottles clinked as he fumbled in the sideboard. He came back and rested against the mantelpiece. He tilted the glass and let the dark brown liquid trickle gently to the bottom. When it was full, he put the bottle on the mantelpiece and took a drink.

"Bloody Arctic in 'ere," he murmured. He shivered. "Light the fire." He knelt down gingerly and bent over the fire. He found a matchbox in his trouser pocket and shook it and opened it and struck a match. The draught from the chimney blew it out. He tried another and it caught. His hand trembled as he offered the flame to the ends of newspaper under the kindling.

"Bugger!" The match had burned his thumb. He reached for the mantelpiece and pulled himself up. He was breathing hard when he sat down. "There." He lit another cigarette and shut his eyes again.

"We want to talk to you, Charlie."

"Talk away," he answered in a distant voice.

"Why are you selling the house?"

"Who said I'm selling the house?" His eyes were still closed, but he was a little alert.

"Mr. Moley, the estate agent."

He was listening now all right. His head came down and he watched the children carefully. "Lots of balls," he said. "Moley's got it all mixed up."

"It isn't true, is it, Charlie?" said Diana urgently.

"Of course not, love," Charlie 'ook answered, giving her a quick smiling glance and turning back to Elsa.

Elsa spoke slowly, as if to a child. "Some people came today—with Mr. Moley. They want to buy the house."

"They do, eh? Well, I tell you, Moley's got it mixed up, like I said."

"*What* has he got mixed up?" Elsa asked quickly.

Charlie 'ook hesitated for a half-second. "It's like this, see. We're broke, see. I'll admit that—we're broke. So what am I going to do, eh? Get a mortgage, that's what I'm going to do—on this house." He winked at them. "That's like a loan, see—with the house as security. That's where old Moley comes in. He gets a good offer from some bloke who wants to buy it—and that price, see, that's the valuation. The higher it is, the more money we get. Easy as winking." He smiled round at them.

"I don't believe it," Elsa said coolly.

"Hark at 'er! What are you, a financial genius or something?"

She waited for a moment, then she said slowly, thinking

it out, "Even if what you said was true, you've got no right
to do anything with this house. It's *our* house, not yours."

" 'ow d'you make that out?" He still grinned.

"Mother left it to us—in her will, she left it to us."

Charlie 'ook chuckled. He took a swig of Guinness. He
brought the glass away from his lips too quickly and the dark
liquid splashed down onto his waistcoat. He looked down,
hesitating, then wiped his hand on the wet patch on his dark
green waistcoat. He spread his fingers and stared at his wet
hand. "Bugger," he murmured. He rubbed his hand on his
trousers and looked up again at Elsa. "What makes you
think the old girl made a will?"

"Because," said Elsa quietly, "I saw it. And so did Hubert.
And so did you."

"You lost your bleeding marbles—there never was no will."

"Yes there was. You tore it up. I found the bits in the
wastepaper basket."

Charlie 'ook began to laugh. "That's rich," he said. "Very.
You got a bleeding good imagination—just like your mum."

"I thought you might say that, so I took a precaution. I
stuck all the little bits together. They're all there—not one
missing." She drew a folded sheet of note paper from the
pocket of her dress and held it up. "You can read every word,
if you like." She bent her head and flattened the paper so it
caught the light. She read: "I, Violet Edna Hook, of 38 Ipswich Terrace, being of sound mind, hereby bequeath: the
lease on 38 Ipswich Terrace; all the furniture and contents
of the house; the money in my post office savings bank; and
all my personal effects to my dear children, Elsa Rosemary,
Diana Amelia, Dunstan Charles, Hubert George, James Mc-
Fee, Gertrude Harriet, and William John Winston, to be
divided equally among them as they shall decide. . . ."

Elsa folded the will in her lap and raised her eyes. "So you
see?"

Charlie 'ook sat absolutely rigid, staring at her, his hand
clasped tight round the glass. "That won't get you very far,"
he said at last, his voice strained. "That don't mean a bloody
thing."

"It means what it says: the house is ours—Diana's and Dunstan's and Hubert's and Jiminee's and Willy's and mine."

"It doesn't mean a bloody—"

"Charlie," cried Diana, "Charlie—"

"Shut up!" he said viciously. "I'll tell you why it doesn't mean anything. You're minors—the bleeding lot of you. Minors—know what that means? It means you can't own anything. Nothing at all, not till you're twenty-one. *See?* Not a sausage. The house is mine. I own it and I can do what I bloody well like with it. Get it? This damn great white elephant is mine, every bit of it—and it's about all I bloody well have got."

"You g-g-got us," said Jiminee tremulously.

"*Got* you?" Charlie 'ook seemed to spit the words. "I've bloody well *had* you!"

He rose to his feet. He staggered and clutched at the mantelpiece to steady himself. At the same second Diana ran to him and tried to put her arms around him. He put a hand on her chest and gave her a shove. "Leave me alone!" he shouted furiously.

Diana stumbled back and half fell, half let herself fall to the floor. She stayed there, crouched, staring up at him.

Charlie 'ook poured himself another glass of Guinness. He replaced the bottle on the mantelpiece and turned to survey the children. He raised a finger and gently massaged his upper lip. His face was red and a long piece of hair dangled over his left ear. But it wasn't funny.

The nightmare stirred deep in Hubert. "Charlie," he said, hearing his own voice as though it came from another, "you've been joking, haven't you?"

"Joking?" He took a long drink of stout. "Yeah—I been joking. Joking about a hell of a damn sight too long." He put his elbow on the mantelpiece and leaned back. Already there was a faint smell of scorching flannel from the backs of his trousers that were too close to the gleaming fire. The children watched him now, none of them capable of movement.

"I'm going to tell you kids something," he started, confidentially. "Some home truths. The facts of life." He chuckled.

"That's a giggle—the 'facts of life.' You know what? I been bum-sucking to you kids too damn long. You're getting on my wick. Now you're going to listen, see? Listen to *me*. Your prig of an oldest sister is right for once in a way—I *am* going to sell this house. This mucking motheaten old mausoleum." His voice was strong and hard and he seemed to delight in every word. "I'm getting out. Quick. I've had it—up to here," he lifted his hand to his throat and sliced. "Chocker. So I'm getting out—and so are you. Out—that's where you're going. *Out!* Into the bleeding orphanage—and we'll see how you square up to that! You won't be pampered there —not on your bleeding whining little lives, you won't.

"And me? Me? I'm going to be free. Free, like a blooming bird. You know what—I'm sick of the bloody sight of you. 'Charlie this and Charlie that'—I'm sick to death of it. Snooping around, prying—making bloody prune faces every time I take a drink. Christ, I dunno how I stuck it. *Christ*. Just like your mucking mother—the whole lot of you. Your mother—that—"

"Leave Mother alone!" Dunstan had risen. His face was absolutely white and his black eyes reflected the red firelight. "Leave her alone!" he cried.

"Leave her alone, you bloody little bookworm? I left her alone for fifteen years." He began to laugh. "Leave 'er alone!" The laughter gripped him and he shook, spilling the beer from the glass.

Hubert was on his feet too. He was hot, terribly hot, and he tasted the blood from his bitten lip. He bit it again, harder, and for a moment he was able to speak above the noise of the sea-pulling blood in his ears. "You were here, though. You were, you must 'ave been—you must have!"

"Must 'ave—bollocks! I didn't go near the fat old tart for fifteen years!" He frowned at Hubert and then his face broke into a smile. "I get it! Blimey, I get it!" he said in a tone of wonder. "Christ—you ignorant bloody kids. You still don't know, do you?" He looked at them one by one, smiling at the puzzle and terror that he saw. "Well," he said, "let me straighten you out about your sainted mother. *You* can't

remember me being 'ere ever, can you now? None of you. That's because I wasn't. I wasn't 'ere since before any of you was born. You know what she used to call me? 'Charles!' Imagine. 'Charles!' I couldn't stick it. Let 'er 'ave my kids? And 'ave them brought up to talk like you lot—la-di-mucking-da? Not bloody likely . . ."

The room was entirely black to Hubert—except for the scarlet of the firecoals and the orange flames and the huge shadowed figure that rose up above it and from whose lips the jumbled words were smashing down like stones. The stones fell and then there was a sudden pause.

"Jiminee, take Willy out of the room." Elsa's voice cut across the thick vicious tones of Charlie 'ook.

"Stay where you are!" he roared. "No one's leaving this mucking room till you've heard what I've got to say. You asked, didn't you? Well, you're bleeding well going to listen." He turned and spat into the fire. The spittle hissed fiercely for a moment.

"She was an 'ore—a tart, a bleeding tart! She wasn't even choosy—she'd pick 'em up from anywhere—sailors, God knows what else. Wouldn't be surprised if one of you didn't have a bit of nigger blood in you. She didn't care. She just closed her eyes and opened her legs and—Jake's your father!" He chuckled. " 'ow do I know? 'cause I took the trouble to find out, that's 'ow. I probably got more of an idea of who your father is than she did. She didn't care. Why should she? She was just 'ot for it. Precautions? Not on your nelly. It would be against religion, wouldn't it?" He pulled a crumpled cigarette from his pocket and stuck it in his mouth. He stared at the silent children angrily. "She was an 'ore—d'you understand! A *prostitute*." He was shouting. "You're all a bloody lot of little bastards. Bastards! You're not 'ooks—you're Smiths and Browns an'—an' *Millards!*" He was triumphant. "Millards!" He shook the matchbox. It was empty. He let it drop into the fire and looked around. "Got to get bleeding light," he mumbled, patting his pocket. He pulled out a piece of paper. "Ah!"

Now Hubert was frozen—a cage of ice for the birds that

had gone quite mad inside him. He saw the huge figure turn and kneel down in front of the fire—and the heat was cut off and he was colder still. He was surprised he could move, move to the side and close so he could see the orange coals. And the paper flared and the smoke clouded up from the cigarette. And now Hubert was hot again, burning in the fiery furnace.

" 'ere, reach us the poker, Hu." The hand stretched out towards him, open. The fingers snapped. "The poker."

The brass knob was cool as a golden pomegranate, and the sceptre was heavy. He looked down, way down and beheld the face turned up to him. It was a blood-red face and flickered as the blood of the fire trembled, and the eyes were blue, light blue like Cambridge, and a fine network of red lines covered the whites. And the lips were stained with brownish froth. They moved—and Hubert bent closer to hear the words that were so far away. "Come on, come on—give it me . . ."

The lips were like worms writhing. He raised the poker slowly. He had all the time in the world. It was alive in his hands. And it was then he saw the face change: the teeth showed suddenly, brown and cracked, and the nostrils collapsed inwards all at once, and the eyes—they were bigger and, yes, bluer and they—they were afraid. Afraid. He saw this quite clearly before the poker struck and there was a noise like the slap of a hand on a deal table and the figure swayed gently backwards and sideways and fell.

So long he took to fall.

41

"He's d-dead!"

The little flames of the fire curled and licked at the coals, and Jiminee's whisper hissed as the fire hissed when a bubble of coal gas suddenly flared.

The body lay twisted, as if in the abandonment of exhausted slumber—the right shoulder propped in a final shrug high against the stone corners of the fireplace, the left arm outstretched still to grasp the poker. In the fingers of the right hand the freshly lit cigarette was held upright and the smoke drifted towards the grate, lingered, then slipped smoothly up the chimney.

Diana rose from her place on the floor. She knelt by Charlie 'ook and took his head into her hands. She lowered her face until her hair quite covered his open blue eyes, and she rested her cheek against his, as if to listen to a message which only she could hear. She stayed for a long while thus, in the motionless attitude of prayer.

At last she looked up. She stared steadily at Hubert, the tears filming her eyes with light and wetting her face so that it shone. She withdrew her hand carefully from the lolling head and held it out to Hubert. There was blood on her fingers.

"Is he d-dead *really?*" Jiminee whispered.

"Yes, he's dead," said Diana.

A sigh of indrawn breath rose from the children at her words.

"He's dead," she repeated quietly. She lowered her hand and looked down once more at the dead face.

Hubert rubbed his upper lip. It was cool and smooth with sweat. But the hot and the cold had left his body now. He reached back and slipped the poker into the rack of fire tools. Then he too knelt.

The green of Charlie 'ook's waistcoat was stained dark with Guinness. When he had fallen, the gold fob watch had slipped from the lower pocket. Hubert took the watch gently in his hands. It was quite warm, and it was sticky with the spilled beer. He wiped it dry on his sweater and turned it over and read once more the great curling initials—*C.R.H.* He frowned at the inscription, trying to remember the name of the real owner. *Cyril Rupert Haverford*—that was it. It didn't really sound a fancy name at all. It sounded like an old man with a bald head and whiskers and pink cheeks and a long black coat like they used to wear in the old days. He put the watch to his ear and listened.

He turned, the watch in his outstretched palm. The children stood behind him. Their gaze shifted from the body to the watch.

"It still works," said Hubert.

As he stood up, Dunstan quickly stepped back. After a moment's hesitation, Jiminee and Willy did too.

"What's wrong?" Hubert asked in bewilderment.

They didn't answer him.

"What's wrong?" he repeated. He tightened his grip on the watch.

"He's dead," said Dunstan. There was a pause, then, "You killed him."

"But," Hubert began, "but . . ." It might have been an accusation. He didn't know. He looked at each one of them in turn and suddenly he was alone again. All at once the heat of the fire on his back was unbearably intense. The room started to sag to the left, to the right, and he saw everything as if through an underwater shimmer.

"You killed him." And this time it was surely an accusation.

His knees trembled and in a moment he knew he would fall. Then Elsa was beside him and her arm was round his shoulder.

"It's all right, Hu," she said. She turned to the others. "I killed him, just as much as Hu did. And so did you, Dun."

"Hu had the poker," said Dunstan sharply. "I didn't, *he*—"

Elsa overrode him fiercely. "You'd have done it though, wouldn't you? If you'd had the poker, you'd have done it?"

Dunstan wavered. "Well, I . . ."

"Of course you would. We all would. He deserved it."

"P-p-perhaps it was an accid-d-dent," Jiminee said earnestly.

"No." Elsa shook her head. "He didn't care for us. He didn't love us—not one little bit. Didn't you hear? Didn't you listen? He betrayed us."

There was a pause.

"He was a traitor," Dunstan said, and his voice had lost its uncertainty.

Diana looked up. Her cheeks were channelled with the dirt of her dried tears. Carefully she removed her hands, which cupped Charlie 'ook's head. She rose to her feet. "It wasn't his fault," she said quietly.

"But he was a traitor," repeated Dunstan.

"It wasn't really his fault. He didn't mean any harm—not, not in his heart of hearts." Diana looked down at the body. She rubbed the tearstains from her cheek with a swift backward movement of her hand. "He was just weak, that's all."

Each of them regarded the body. Hubert stooped down and picked the still smouldering cigarette from the dead fingers and dropped it into the fire. For some time nobody spoke.

"We haven't g-g-got anyone n-now," said Jiminee, "we haven't g-got anyone at all."

"We got Mother," said Dunstan quickly. "We've always had Mother. It's just—just that we forgot," he ended lamely.

Elsa shook her head.

"We have," Dunstan insisted. "I can feel her—here in this room. Can't you feel her?" he challenged Elsa.

"No," said Elsa, "I can't feel Mother."

"Well I can," he said, but it was unconvincing. Already the reality of Mother was as distant as the thought of snow in spring.

"When did Mother die?" said Willy.

Elsa answered him. "A year ago. Almost a year ago."

Willy put his head on one side to consider. "That's a long time," he said, "a very very very long time."

"No, it's not," said Dunstan. "It just *seems* long, that's all. Mother's here just as she always was. We'll rebuild the tabernacle and we'll have Mothertime again and Diana will read us the book again and it'll be just like it was before." He turned pleadingly to the sister he loved most of all. "Won't it, Dinah?"

"No," she answered gently, "I don't think it'll be the same anymore."

And Hubert felt a great opening within himself as he heard her words—it was as if the bird had been freed at last, freed to soar beautifully into the sun.

"B-b-but," began Jiminee again tremulously, "we haven't got anyone—"

"Yes, we have," said Hubert. He lifted Elsa's arm from his shoulder and went over and touched Jiminee's hand. "We've got each other. That's enough, isn't it?"

"Well," said Jiminee doubtfully; and then he brightened. "Perhaps we c-c-could get Louis b-back?"

Elsa answered him: "No, Jiminee, Louis's happy now—he wouldn't want to live with us."

"B-but we'll be happy t-too, won't we?" insisted Jiminee.

One by one, as if by some unspoken agreement, the children turned to Diana.

Diana looked down at her hands. She held them before her and they were touched with the drying crimson-brown of Charlie 'ook's blood.

She raised her head. "Yes," she said gravely, "yes, we'll be happy. Not just yet. But we will be."

It was then that Dunstan began to cry. He didn't cry with the angry sobs of defeat and he didn't turn away. He just took off his glasses and let the tears run freely down his cheeks. And, without his glasses, Dunstan's face was all at once gentle and helpless. Hubert smiled.

And, though he wept, Dunstan managed to smile back.

42

The small Sunday crowd in front of 38 Ipswich Terrace waited unblinking in the weak sunshine. Sometimes a ruffle of murmurs would disturb the impassivity of the watchers. A head would turn, a hand flutter, a finger point. Then gradually they would settle back into their silent staring.

Newcomers would ask a question and, nodding sagely at the reply, be absorbed into the group. Occasionally somebody would detach himself and drift away.

Soon after the arrival of the two dark police cars, which now rested at the curb, the little crowd had begun to gather. In the first hour of waiting it had been stirred with excitement several times as various people had passed the constable at the front door and been admitted to the house. Long negative hours followed.

At about two o'clock a small grey Austin drove up and parked behind the police cars. The driver, a worried-looking man in a blue blazer with a nameless crest, got out and slammed the door hurriedly. He hesitated at the sight of the crowd and then pushed his way through to the gate, murmuring, "Excuse me please, excuse me," and giving automatic smiles. He ran jerkily up the steps and spoke to the constable on the porch. As the front door was opened and he stepped inside, the crowd pressed forward to catch a glimpse of the dark hall.

Upstairs in the workshop, Hubert stepped away from the window and turned round. "Somebody just came," he said.

All the children were there. Jiminee was doodling at the table; Dunstan was reading. The others just sat.

"Who?" asked Elsa, dully.

"A man." He waited for someone to ask him what sort of man, but no one spoke. "Like a schoolmaster," he said.

"He walked like this." Hubert thrust his head forward and turned out his feet in imitation of the urgent nervousness of the man who had just come.

The children eyed him.

"I 'spect," Jiminee said, "I 'spect he's the orphanage m-man."

Hubert let his hands fall slowly to his sides. "Yes," he said miserably. He sighed—if only he could get one of them to smile.

He went over to Jiminee and looked down at the random patterns of the pencil. "What are you drawing?" he asked.

Jiminee glanced up at him. "Nothing," he said.

"Why don't you use some of your crayons?"

"They're packed," he answered. "This is all I g-got left." He waited for a moment, looking at Hubert as though his brother could suddenly miraculously produce a fistful of coloured crayons.

Hubert turned away. He thought of the piled and strapped suitcases in the hall. "You can take anything you like," Miss Deke had said as she'd helped them with their packing. *Anything you like.*

He went to his worktable. There were still a few tools that he had not put in the case. He lifted his sharpest chisel and felt the edge with his thumb. All at once he remembered Louis—Louis sitting at the table, painting his box light blue. The tears rose in Hubert's eyes. He fought them down. With great care he began to fit the tools into the case.

Anything you like, she'd said. But what use would tools be to him at the orphanage? He didn't want them. He didn't want to take anything. All he wanted was to stay here—in this room with Jiminee and Elsa and Dunstan and Willy and Diana.

"Hu?"

"Yes," he turned round abruptly.

It was Dunstan, holding his book poised on his knees. "How much longer have we got?"

Hubert felt the weakness in his knees. If it could be forever. "I expect," he said, trying to beat down the tremor in

his voice, "I expect we'll have tea before we go. It's . . .
it's . . ."

"I don't want any tea," said Willy.

Hubert nodded. He didn't want any himself. None of them
had been able to eat the lunch that Miss Deke and the policeman had brought up on trays. None of them had touched
a mouthful. They'd had nothing to eat all day. Even breakfast . . . that seemed like years ago. Hubert frowned. Mrs.
Stork had come before they'd even started breakfast. And
when she'd gone, it was as if they were paralyzed, sitting,
waiting for the inevitable ring of the doorbell. And then,
politely but inevitably, the grave plainclothes policemen had
stepped inside.

All day their house had been filled with strangers.

"I d-don't want any tea either," said Jiminee.

"Well," said Hubert, "I don't expect they'll make us eat
it if we don't want to." The grownups now were all quiet-
voiced and kind, and you didn't have to do anything you
didn't want to—except to go away.

"Will we—will we be able to see each other?" Dunstan
whispered.

"Of course we will." Hubert turned to Elsa. "Won't we,
Else?"

He saw her take a deep breath. "Yes," she said, "yes,
of course."

"How often?"

"Well, I expect—I expect . . ." He faltered. He had no
idea, none. They hadn't even dared ask Miss Deke.

Willy stood up. "I don't want to go," he said firmly.
"My black wife doesn't want to go too. We want to stay here
forever an' ever."

No one said a word. There was such utter silence that they
could hear the faint movements of people downstairs in the
front room.

Hubert bit his lip. He crossed the room and looked out of
the window so that no one could see his face. He let the
tears come.

43

In the front room Mr. Halbert also stood by the windows. Invisible behind the lace curtains, he stared out into the front garden. Once or twice he glanced back briefly at the room. He smoked incessantly.

The inspector sat behind the small table, which had somehow gained the formality of a desk. To his right was a sergeant with a notebook. On the sofa, which had been moved back against the wall by the door, Miss Deke sat still as a waxwork. Beside her, fidgeting continually, was the man in the blue blazer who had just come in. The chair in front of the table, directly facing the inspector, was occupied by Mrs. Stork.

"Just once more, Mrs. Stork. When did you first begin to suspect something was wrong?"

"Oh, right off. First thing—as soon as I come in this mornin' I knew at once. *Smelled it,* you might say. They was quiet, see. Unnatural for kids to be quiet on a nice bright sunny morning, I said to myself. And then when I asked 'ow Mr. 'ook was," she hushed her voice, "God forgive the poor man—well, when I asked that, you should 'ave seen their faces! I knew then, right off. Something fishy 'ere, I thought. Definitely." She paused to touch her forehead delicately with her fingertips. She went on solemnly, "My suspicions began to increase when I saw 'is bed had not been slept in. Then when I took a look out of the winder—then I knew. Wot they been digging up the garden for? I asked myself. Before I even asked myself the question, I felt the chills up my spine. Then I 'eard that voice behind me—'Wot are you doing 'ere, Mrs. Stork?' I can tell you, I jumped clean out of me skin. It was Berty—he said it. But they was all there, just looking at me—like I was, like I was a—"

"Yes, yes, Mrs. Stork," the inspector interrupted, "we've

287

heard all that. My question didn't refer to what happened this morning. I want to know when you first began to notice something wrong in the Hook household."

Mrs. Stork leaned forward, clutching her handbag. "Wrong?" she said somberly. "There was nothing ever *right* in this 'ousehold—and that's the truth."

The inspector sighed. "When did you last see Mrs. Hook?"

She ignored the question. "I could tell you a thing or two about this 'ouse, I could. It's cursed, that's what it is. Whenever I come in the door, I get the shivers. An' it's not just me. My Tiger, he feels just the same. He'd always dread coming to work 'ere. *Dread* it. He's sensitive, my Tiger is. He's that—"

"Mrs. Stork, when do you recall last seeing Mrs. Hook?"

"When do I recall last seeing Mrs. 'ook? Ah—that's a long story, that is. Depends what you mean by 'see', don't it?"

The inspector said nothing.

"Well," said Mrs. Stork, sitting upright again, "I suppose—a year ago, maybe?"

"And why didn't you do anything at that time, Mrs. Stork?"

"Why didn't I do anything? Why? Well, I couldn't be *sure*, could I? It might 'ave all been in my head?" she said in a tone of evident disbelief. "Mightn't it? And besides, it's not my place to go poking my nose in where—"

"Thank you, Mrs. Stork, that will be all." The inspector stood up.

"*All?*" cried Mrs. Stork, aghast. "But I ain't 'ardly begun yet!"

"Perhaps we'll want to ask you some questions later on, but that's all for now. Thank you, Mrs. Stork."

"No it jolly well ain't." Mrs. Stork's mouth grew stubborn.

"I think if you go out through the garden, it would be preferable," the inspector was saying.

"I said it ain't all!"

The inspector looked down at her. "You have a question you wish to ask?" he enquired.

"What about me wages?"

For the first time the inspector's face moved in human surprise. "Your *wages?*"

"I'm a working woman, ain't I? I'm owed me wages. Who's going to pay? That's what I'd like to know."

The inspector stared at this plump, thin-faced woman sitting angrily rigid on the hard chair. "I think—" he began, but he was forestalled.

"How much are you owed, Mrs. Stork?" Mr. Halbert had moved from the window and stood over her, wallet in hand.

"Well . . ." said Mrs. Stork uncertainly.

"This enough?" Mr. Halbert slipped a five-pound note from the wallet.

"Let me see now," said Mrs. Stork, all at once amiable, "there's three weeks due, or is it four?"

Mr. Halbert added another fiver and held out the notes to her.

"That'll be quite satisfactory. Quite satisfactory. Much obliged, I'm sure." She took the notes and tucked them leisurely into her handbag. She snapped the fastener shut. "There!" She dusted her skirt and rose to her feet. "Thank you, gentlemen."

"There's a constable in the kitchen who'll show you through the garden," said the inspector.

Mrs. Stork turned at the door and surveyed the room. "I'm a workin' woman, I am, but I got my feelings too—you mustn't think Mrs. Stork don't have feelings. I love those kids like they was my own, I do." She opened the door. "I been like a mother to them all these years. Just like a mother."

There were several moments of silence after she'd left. Mr. Halbert took out his silver cigarette case and lit a cigarette.

The man in the blue blazer cleared his throat. "I say," he began.

"Yes?"

He got up and came across to the table. "I say, you know.

I can't manage all of them in my little car. Six of them, aren't there?"

"We've taken care of that. Mr. Halbert's kindly volunteered to take them along in his car." The inspector raised his voice a little and looked towards Miss Deke. "But I expect you can give Miss Deke a lift. She ought to see them safely installed."

"Oh, quite. Delighted." The man smiled back at Miss Deke. He turned to the inspector. "You know, uh—where are the children now?"

"Upstairs. In what they call the workshop."

"Well, I was thinking. You know, I really ought to see them first—give them the once-over, if you know what I mean." He smiled nervously.

The inspector regarded him. "I'm not quite sure I do know what you mean, Mr. Bolton."

"Well, ah—I'm thinking of the other kids, you know. The ones we've got already. Ah—these children, well, I mean—quite an experience. Just what sort of children are they?"

"They're quite ordinary children, Mr. Bolton," said Miss Deke suddenly.

Mr. Bolton flashed a smile. "Ah, but are they? We've got an awfully jolly little bunch, you know. Don't want to rock the boat or anything, but, I mean, well—disruptive influence, shocking experience, criminal tendencies, all that—"

"As Miss Deke said," cut in the inspector, "I'm sure you'll find they're quite ordinary children, Mr. Bolton. I don't think it's necessary to disturb them in their last hour in this house."

"An hour?" Mr. Halbert glanced at his watch.

"Yes," said the inspector briskly, "we ought to have the garden all cleared up by then."

"Well," persisted Mr. Bolton, "I expect you're right. But, ah, I mean what about this chap Herbert—he's the ringleader, isn't he?"

"Hubert," said Mr. Halbert. He took a puff of his cigarette. "Sensible little fellow, I thought."

"Don't worry, Mr. Bolton," said the inspector, "you'll see them before you go."

"Yes," began Mr. Bolton, but he was cut off by the knock at the door of the room.

"Come in," called the inspector.

"Excuse me, sir," said the constable who opened the door. "It's the children." He was trying to hold back the thrusting bodies behind him. "They want to go outside and—"

Jiminee slipped under the constable's arm and pushed into the room.

"It's L-Louis," he said. He looked round for a familiar face and settled on Miss Deke. "Louis's outside. C-c-can we go and s-see him?"

The inspector rose and glanced questioningly at Miss Deke.

"Louis is a friend of theirs," said Miss Deke gently.

"Well," said the inspector to Jiminee, "I'm sorry, sonny, but we can't let you go out there."

"Please, oh, p-please." Jiminee began to quiver. "We promise to c-come back. We promise."

The inspector shook his head apologetically.

"Wouldn't it be all right, inspector," said Mr. Halbert, "to ask the little boy into the house?"

The inspector looked at Miss Deke.

Miss Deke smiled. "I really don't see that it could possibly do any harm, inspector. Just for a few moments, to say goodbye."

"Well," the inspector considered. "All right. Just for a minute or two."

"I will go and fetch Louis," said Miss Deke. "You are to wait in the hall, Jiminee, with the others." She got up. "Thank you, inspector."

The constable closed the door behind her.

44

"Hello, Louis."

He looked at them gravely. "Hello," he answered.

Miss Deke had left them alone in the hall.

They gathered slowly around Louis.

He watched them. Then he noticed the suitcases and the big trunk by the clock. "You're going away," he said.

"Yes," said Jiminee.

"Will you be gone for a long time?"

The children looked at each other. "Yes," Elsa answered, "I think so."

In the silence the hall clock ticked loudly.

"My mum's going to have the baby next month," said Louis.

"What sort will it be?" Hubert asked.

"A little girl. We're going to call her Hilda."

"Hilda's a jolly n-nice name," Jiminee said.

"Do you really like it?"

"Yes." The children murmured their approval.

Louis was silent for a moment. "My dad says it's an unspoiled name," he offered.

"It's a nice name."

"It's a *very* nice name," said Willy emphatically.

Louis blushed a little. "I still got your pomegranate, Dinah."

Diana smiled.

"My dad's varnished it. It doesn't half shine now," he said earnestly, "and it'll last forever."

"Have you got my penny?" Willy demanded.

"Oh, yes. I got it. I got all your presents. I got the hanky and the little blue box and the pomegranate and the *History of Manchester and Its En-en-*"

"*Environs*," said Dunstan.

"Environs," Louis smiled. "And I got your picture," he said to Jiminee, "hanging up in my room."

"You have really?" said Jiminee softly.

"Yes, really. I got all your presents. They're the nicest presents I ever had in my whole life."

"What about your penknife?" Hubert asked.

"Oh, that's just an old penknife. Everybody's got a penknife."

Somewhere downstairs in the basement a door slammed and there was the sound of movement.

"You got a lot of policemen here, haven't you?" Louis enquired.

Hubert nodded. "An' there are two police cars outside as well," he said.

"Yes. I saw them."

Hubert thought it didn't seem so bad somehow—saying it to Louis like this.

"Louis, I want to whisper you something." Willy came to Louis and pulled his head down.

Louis listened. "All right," he said, nodding. "All right, I will."

He straightened up and took the hand Willy held out.

"You will what?" asked Jiminee.

Louis looked doubtfully down at Willy. "Can I tell?"

Willy nodded his head vigorously.

"He wants me to take care of his black wife while you're away."

"Oh, Willy," said Elsa, with a grin.

"Well, why not?" said Willy. *"They* won't allow wives, I'll bet."

Suddenly all the children were grinning too.

"Well they won't, will they?" Willy challenged.

"No," said Louis seriously, "I don't think they will. Anyhow, I'll take good care of her, don't you worry." He tightened his grip on the little boy's hand.

Willy smiled. "She likes crumpets," he said.

"I won't forget." He looked around the dim hall. "I've

got to go now," he said. "I promised Mum I wouldn't be long."

"Oh, don't go yet."

"Not yet."

"Please not yet."

Louis hesitated. He let go Willy's hand and fished in his pocket.

"I got something for you," he said.

He held out his hand. Resting on Louis's palm, it looked just like a piece of stone at first. Then Jiminee picked it up.

"It's your fossil," he said.

"Ammonite," corrected Louis. "It's yours now. I brought it for you."

The children crowded round and touched the amber coils that ran around the stone.

"It's beautiful," murmured Diana.

"Is it really very old?" Hubert asked.

"It's millions of years old. Millions and millions and millions."

"A million million?" whispered Willy.

"More," said Louis. "It's older than anything."

"And it's still h-h-here," said Jiminee.

"Can we really have it?" said Willy.

Louis nodded. "Yes. I brought it for you."

"But," said Elsa, "it's your most precious possession—you told us."

"That's why I want you to have it," answered Louis.

"Oh, Louis!"

"Can you really spare it?" Hubert asked.

Louis nodded.

"It's the loveliest present of all," said Diana.

"Thank you, Louis."

"Thank you."

"Thank you very much *indeed*," said Willy.

Louis blushed. "I'm glad you like it," he said.

"We do." "We do." They looked round at each other and smiled.

Louis blinked his large brown eyes. "I must go now—Mum will be ever so cross if I don't."

He hesitated. "I expect it'll be all right, you know—where you're going."

The children stood mutely around him.

"Well, goodbye, then," he said.

"Goodbye, Louis." "Goodbye."

He went to the front door, but Hubert was there before him and twisted the latch and pulled the door wide. The uniformed constable guarding the door stepped aside, and the yellow spring sunshine filled the old hall.

"Goodbye," said Louis from the doorway. He turned and ran down the steps.

Suddenly the children pushed forward, out of the door, onto the front porch.

As he shut the gate behind him, Louis turned and waved. Then the little crowd moved aside for him and he was gone.

The children burst out with their farewells.

"Goodbye . . ." "Goodbye, Louis . . ." "Goodbye!" "Goodbye!"

Their clear shouts rang out into the sunlight of Ipswich Terrace, over the heads of the group at the gate.

At last the children fell silent. They turned back slowly to the hall.

Miss Deke was waiting for them, putting on her gloves, by the hall table.

"Come along, children," she said. "Get your hats and coats on. It's time to go now."